Brought up in London and Wales, Babs Horton now lives in Plymouth where she teaches at a school for children with special needs. Her debut, *A Jarful of Angels*, won the Pendleton May Award for the Best First Novel of 2003, and was shortlisted for the Authors' Club Best First Novel Award.

WILDCAT MOON

The Skallies was a row of tumbledown houses built on the windlashed coast. Ten-year-old Archie Grimble, with his crippled leg and one good eye, lived a miserable existence there. Then a chance encounter with an unhappy little girl and the discovery of a locked diary set him on a mission to unravel the mystery of a boy who drowned off Skilly Point in August, 1900. But Archie's investigation was to have unexpected consequences. A shocking murder and an unexplained abduction were to shatter his world forever. Only years later, on his return to the ruined Skallies, does Archie stumble on the answer to a puzzle that has haunted him since childhood — and the extraordinary truth about the fate of Thomas Greswode is at last revealed.

Books by Babs Horton
Published by The House of Ulverscroft:

A JARFUL OF ANGELS
DANDELION SOUP
RECIPES FOR CHERUBS

BABS HORTON

WILDCAT MOON

Complete and Unabridged

CHARNWOOD
Leicester

First published in Great Britain in 2006 by
Pocket Books, an imprint of
Simon & Schuster UK, London

First Charnwood Edition
published 2009
by arrangement with
Simon & Schuster UK, London

British Library CIP Data

Horton, Babs
    Wildcat moon.—Large print ed.—
Charnwood library series
    1. Children with disabilities—Fiction 2. Boys—Diaries
—Fiction 3. Murder—Fiction 4. Suspense fiction
    5. Large type books
    I. Title
    823.9'2 [F]

    ISBN 978–1–84782–536–0

Published by
F. A. Thorpe (Publishing)
Anstey, Leicestershire
Set by Words & Graphics Ltd.
Anstey, Leicestershire
Printed and bound in Great Britain by
T. J. International Ltd., Padstow, Cornwall

This book is printed on acid-free paper

For Pat and Terry Cowan

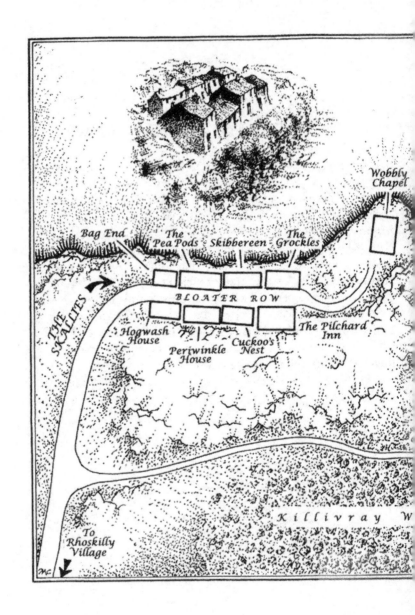

Wobbly
Chapel

Bag End

The
Pea Pods

Skibbereen

The
Grockles

THE SCALLIES

BLOATER ROW

Hogwash
House

Periwinkle
House

Cuckoo's
Nest

The Pilchard
Inn

To
Rhoskilly
Village

Killivray W

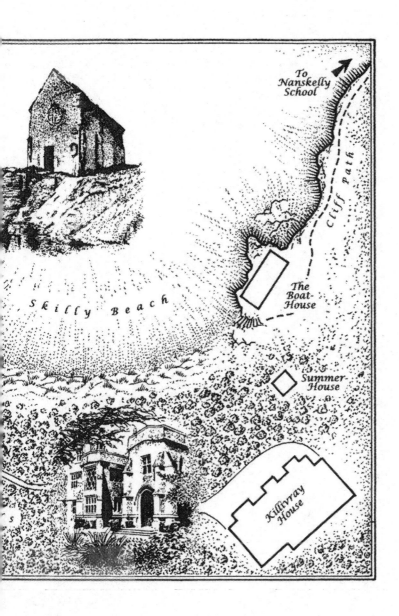

To
Nanskelly
School

Cliff Path

The
Boat-
House

Skilly Beach

Summer-
House

Killivray
House

Acknowledgements

My thanks for everything to my husband John. To my children Laura and Jack and my family and friends for all that you do. As always to Clare Alexander, Kate Lyall Grant, Kate Shaw, Nigel Stoneman, Tara Wigley and Nina Leino. For Brigid Foley of Tavistock. A very warm thank you to Val Duffy-Cross and the staff and students of Langley School, Solihull, who made my debut into public speaking an absolute delight. To the many teachers in English departments in Plymouth that I have visited for keeping the love of literature alive against all the odds. To the staff and students of the Young People's Centre and the Hospital School; I will miss you. My very grateful thanks to all the people who have taken the time to write to me about my books.

To those on the islands of Ischia and Gozo who made my stay so special.

Part One

Part One

December 1959

Clementine Fernaud arrived at Paddington Station, bought her ticket and asked a porter which platform she needed for the train to St Werburgh's. He pointed her in the right direction with barely a glance at the matronly woman before him.

She stood alone, not seeking to make conversation with other waiting passengers, keeping a watchful eye out; she didn't want anyone spotting her and ruining her plans, though she was sure that no one from her past life would recognize her dressed as she was.

Soon she would be safely out of London and on her way to her new post as a governess. She smiled wryly and stamped her feet to keep warm. Imagine! Clementine Fernaud a governess!

At least no one would think of looking for her in an isolated country house. How her old friends and acquaintances would laugh if they knew what she was up to. The idea to apply for such a job had been a stroke of genius. She had been shown the advertisement placed in *The Times* on the same day as her own photograph had appeared on the front page. Both started with the word WANTED!

3

Wanted. Governess to teach ten-year-old girl, French speaker preferred. Large country house close to the coast. Immediate start. Good references required.

The wages offered were excellent and accommodation and food were provided. But she was hardly governess material, was she? She was well educated and trilingual, but she was not, by any stretch of the imagination, the serious studious type! She could think of nothing worse than being cooped up in a schoolroom with a bore of a girl.

Still, it would only be for a few months and when the fuss had died down she'd be able to go back to France, or Italy perhaps, and make a new life for herself somewhere she was not known.

She looked down at her clothes and grimaced. These sensible lace-up shoes were just too terrible. And the thick brown stockings quite disgusting! The dull grey costume she'd bought was drab to the point of being mannish. And her hair! Mother of God! It was changed beyond all recognition. Gone were the stylish golden curls, replaced by a neat grey bun coiled on the back of her head. The round spectacles gave her an air of bookishness, making her look very prim indeed. Why, if she had a best friend who was to pass by now she would not recognize the vivacious and fun-loving girl of her past.

She'd been amazed at how easily she had fooled the woman from the agency. Miss Vera Truscott had seemed perfectly happy with her and not glanced twice at the forged documents. She had telephoned straight away to a Mr Greswode and on Miss Truscott's recommendation he had offered Clementine the job there and then.

Tonight she would break her journey in a small hotel near Reading and tomorrow take the train to her destination. She was to arrive at St Werburgh's Station in the early afternoon and a car was being sent to pick her up and take her to Killivray House near the village of Rhoskilly.

She smoked a cigarette with enjoyment then picked up her valise and boarded the train.

★ ★ ★

No one could remember how the Skallies got its name, or the name of the lunatic who built Hogwash House on the shelf of rock above the beach at East Skilly.

Legend had it that it was a ragged-arsed Spaniard washed up from the sinking Armada who didn't have the strength to make it as far as Rhoskilly village. Yet this first house was followed by another and another until there were seven ramshackle houses huddled together in what became known as Bloater Row.

It was an inhospitable, unsheltered spot and the winds that blew in from the worrisome sea whipped sand into every widening crack and crevice of the Skallies.

Bag End, the Peapods, Skibbereen and the Grockles faced the sea and took the worst battering and in winter, when the storms came, the waves hit the base of the rock and the spray

5

went up over the roofs trapping all but the foolish inside.

On the right of Bloater Row, backed up against the crumbling rock face, were Hogwash House, Periwinkle House and Cuckoo's Nest.

There was a small inn called the Pilchard with porthole windows and a cellar where old bones were buried. And at the furthest point towards Skilly Beach there was a windblown wobbly chapel with a round window fashioned from fragments of glass washed up from the sea.

It was a wild, curious place inhabited by misfits and cripples, foul-mouthed women, talking parrots and wildcats. There were halfwits and Irish tinkers, and an army of bright-eyed kids and toddlers with nits and sharp teeth. A place where, when a house was suddenly deserted, someone miraculously drifted in from somewhere else to take their place.

★ ★ ★

The sun died and darkness came down swiftly over the Skallies. A frosty-lipped wind blew in from the sea sucking wisps of smoke from the chimneys of the houses in Bloater Row and making the wildcats yowl in the backyard of the Pilchard Inn.

Up in his low-beamed bedroom in Bag End Archie Grimble lit a greasy candle stub and placed it on the battered chest of drawers near the door.

He watched as the darkness weakened around the edges of the room. A whisper of light flickered across the curled-up picture of the Virgin Mary that was hung above the wash-stand and her eyes blinked as though she was waking from a long, deep sleep.

The growing light showed a small iron bed with blurred edges, a frayed rug on the bare boards and Archie's own stooped shadow looming on the far wall.

Archie stood in front of the ancient wardrobe mirror and looked at his wobbling reflection in the mottled glass. His pale, bespectacled face stared forlornly back at him, and from behind his round, pink-rimmed National Health spectacles, his lazy eye flickered nervously. The other eye was hidden behind a lens covered with sticking plaster.

One-eyed Willy the other kids called him.

Cripple.

Stickman.

He pulled up his faded grey shirt, tried to puff out his belly and failed miserably.

He had a chest like a collapsed washing board. Tin ribs you could play a tune on.

He turned away from the mirror and glanced over his shoulder.

Jesus! Look at the state of him. The rag-and-bone man wouldn't give a balloon for him.

He had shoulder bones like angel wings. Legs thin as a chicken's poking out of his frayed shorts. His even skinnier left leg caged in an ugly metal calliper.

No wonder the other kids took the mickey.

Peg leg!

Peg leg!

He looked like one of the sad-faced collecting boxes that stood outside chemist shops, chalk-faced statue boys with a box at their feet in which to collect pennies and halfpennies.

He clenched his small fists in anger. He hated his bad eyes and his gammy leg, hated the bloody limp and the way it made him walk like an old codger.

One day, though; one day he was going to be rich, rich enough to buy one of those Charles Atlas kits he'd seen in the newspapers and he'd grow muscles as big as old potatoes.

Then he'd teach them all a lesson. All the ones that picked on him had better watch out then.

He'd be Archie Grimble, strong man of the Skallies.

He'd kick sand in their faces all right. And he wouldn't be afraid of anything or anyone. Not even Donald Kelly.

He put up his fists. Boxed his reflection. Side-stepped. Right. Left. Duck and feint. Leading with the left. Jab with the right.

SMACK! WHACK! SPLAT!

'Take that, you lanky streak of piss!'

BASH.

'And that, pea brain Kelly.'

He paused, wiped the imaginary blood from his fists, blew on them and set to again.

'Call me names would you, you big, bloody fat arse!'

8

BIFF! WALLOP! THUMP!

'What the hell's going on up there, Arch? You'll have the ceiling down in a minute.'

His mammy's voice brought him up short.

He put down his fists, opened the door and called sheepishly down the stairs, 'Sorry, Mammy.'

Archie sighed. He hated being such a weedy specimen and he hated having to hate so many people.

He hated his own father for a start and it was against the rules to hate your own father. But he did.

He hated him so much it made his belly fizz and his ears burn.

His father was a pig. Worse than a pig. A big, fat, stinking, hairy porker.

The way he spoke to Mammy was terrible.

Do this! Do that! Boil water for the bath. Fill the bath. Bank the fire. Where's my tea, woman?

Oh, and when he ate it was sick making, stuffing the food in his slobbery chops, gravy running down his sandpaper chin. And the way he stubbed his cigarette butt out in the ruins of his food and then burped without even putting his hand over his mouth.

Archie pulled a face at himself in the mirror then walked nervously across to the sash window, opened it carefully and listened to the sounds of the windblown night.

He heard the rattling of glass in ill-fitting windows and the pounding of the sea on the rocks below the Skallies.

The words of the Donkey Song drifted up from the Boathouse on Skilly Beach where mad Gwennie lived all alone,

There's a song in the air
But the fair señorita
Doesn't seem to care for the song in the
air . . .

He was terrified of mad Gwennie. Everyone was, even the Kelly boys. Mad Gwennie was a wizened-up old thing, with skin as dark and hairy as a coconut and eyes crafty as a monkey. She was bent-backed and almost toothless and prone to violence when riled his mother had said many a time.

Once she'd taken a shotgun to a tramp that had knocked on her door in search of a glass of water.

When she was hungry she went on the hunt for hens like a fox, bit off their heads, squeezed out their blood and drank it down in one gurgling gulp.

The Boathouse was supposed to be stuffed to the rafters with things that she found on the beach. Glass bottles with messages from foreigners. Giant crab claws and whale bones. Sailors' ribs coughed up from the deep. From Davy Jones's locker. Broken lobster pots and sharks' teeth. Rope thick with tar. Shrivelled-up mermaids.

Unexploded bombs and grenades that could go off at any minute. Blow you to Buggery. And back again.

Señorita donkeysita, not so fleet as a mosquito,
But so sweet like my Chiquita,
You're the one for me.
Olé!

Archie braced himself. He had to do it some time. He didn't want to though. He hadn't so much as looked across at Hogwash House in weeks. He just couldn't face it.

Ready steady go.

He glanced nervously across Bloater Row.

Hogwash House was all in darkness and a lone gull was perched on the chimney as though keeping watch.

Archie swallowed hard. There was no point being afraid. You had to face facts. Hogwash House was empty. No one lived there any more. Benjamin Tregantle had gone down with a crab pot and drowned not two weeks since.

And he wasn't coming back. Ever.

Thinking of Benjamin made Archie shiver and he struggled to hold back his tears. Along with Cissie Abelson who lived in the Pilchard Inn, Benjamin had been his best friend even though he was a grumpy old bugger.

Ever since Archie had arrived in the Skallies Benjamin had always called out goodnight to him from his window opposite.

He wouldn't any more though. Never, ever again.

Archie stifled a sob. Every night since the old man had been gone Archie had cried himself to sleep.

Moonlight shone now on the dusty windows of Hogwash House and turned the hanging cobwebs to silver drapes. Benjamin had never got rid of cobwebs like other people did. He used to say what right did anyone have to destroy other creatures' homes that they'd worked so hard to build. Benjamin wasn't . . . hadn't been like other grown-up people at all. He was kind and funny and he swore an awful lot even in front of kids.

Archie willed himself to keep his eyes fixed upon the window and wondered if he stared long and hard would he be able to conjure up the old man's face. Benjamin had a face like the man on the sardine tin only uglier.

Wouldn't it just be the tops if it was all a mistake and Benjamin had come back from the dead and was there in Hogwash House? Any minute now a candle would be lit and the window would be thrown open.

He'd see the wrinkled old face and the bright blue eyes and hear his voice, a voice that sounded like a piece of coke trapped under the coal house door.

' 'Night, Arch! To sleep, perchance to dream; aye there's the rub.'

Archie had never really known what the last bit meant but he liked the sound of the words.

The window in Hogwash House stayed firmly shut even though Archie stared at it until his eyes ached and his face was frozen by the bitter wind that was blowing in off the rough sea.

Away over in Killivray House where the lah di dahs lived the clock on the stables tinkled the hour and was followed, seconds later, by the echoing dong of the church clock in Rhoskilly village.

Archie continued to stare at the window.

Mammy had cried when Benjamin died and said that she'd miss him something terrible about the place, but at least he'd reached a good age and now he would be up in heaven with the angels and happy as a sandboy.

That was rubbish, though, and even if it was true, Benjamin would hate being stuck up on a fluffy cloud with a bunch of half-baked angels playing the harp and singing hymns. Benjamin hadn't believed in all that stuff and he had never set foot in Rhoskilly Church until he had no choice.

He'd said that religion was mostly all bloody mumbo jumbo and that it was just to keep poor people in their place, keep tugging their forelocks and saying yes sir, no sir, three bloody bags full sir . . .

Archie jumped in alarm then as the seagull lifted off the chimney of Hogwash House and flew screaming over the rooftops of the Skallies.

He turned his eyes angrily away from the window and wiped his tears on the frayed cuffs of his shirt.

He was a big boy now, ten and a bit, too old to believe in daft stuff like magic. Or miracles. Or God. God never listened to anything you said to him. However much you prayed he took no notice. Like he had an earache from all that listening and had stuffed his ears with olive oil and cotton wool.

The dead didn't come back to life. And that was a fact.

Benjamin Tregantle was dead and buried in Rhoskilly graveyard amongst the chipped cherubs and blackened headstones. He was buried in the grave next to Old Mr Greswode who used to live in Killivray House. Everyone said that they'd both turn in their graves because Benjamin and Old Greswode had been sworn enemies and used to cross the road to avoid each other.

Archie closed the window quietly. He opened the cup-board where he kept his few toys and lifted down the box that contained his Detective Kit. He lay belly down on the bed and opened the box. He'd been so excited when he'd found it in his Christmas sack last year. It was like lots of things, though, the outside of the box promised buckets full of excitement but when you opened the box it wasn't quite like they'd promised it would be. It was a rubbish toy really. He tipped the contents out onto the bed.

There was a magnifying glass, a pair of broken handcuffs that Benjamin had had to saw off Archie's wrists because he'd put them on and locked them and dropped the keys down a crack in the floorboards.

It was so embarrassing, a detective being locked in his own handcuffs.

There was a wallet, a fountain pen and a recipe for making invisible ink. You had to follow the recipe and then fill the pen up with it and write secret letters. That experiment had been a disaster too. He'd written a letter to Cissie Abelson and told her to warm the letter and see

14

the writing appear like magic, just like it said in the instructions. He should have realized you don't tell someone who's not right in the head to play with fire. She'd held the letter over a candle flame, set light to the bedroom curtains and singed half her hair off.

Cissie was real nice but wasn't much cop as a detective's deputy, not the sort of Dr Watson he'd have chosen.

He hadn't been able to solve one single mystery, he hadn't even found one to solve in nearly a whole year!

Nothing exciting ever happened in the Skallies.

It was dead boring.

He turned over onto his back and stared miserably up at the ceiling for a long time until he drifted off into a fitful sleep.

He woke later at the sound of the wireless being turned off downstairs and he heard the click of his mammy's ruined knees as she climbed the steep stairs.

She paused on the landing, called out as she always did, ''Night, Arch, sleep tight, love.'

''Night, Mammy.'

'Be sure to say your prayers and keep the window closed, mind, or you'll have your death of cold. There's mention of bad storms tonight on the wireless.'

'I've closed the window and I won't forget my prayers.'

'There's a beautiful full moon tonight, Arch. Take a look and make a wish before you go to sleep.'

'I will.'

He sat up suddenly at her words.

There's a beautiful full moon tonight . . .

The first full moon since old Benjamin Tregantle had died.

Bloody hell!

With a jolt he recalled old Benjamin's strange words to him, the very last time they had been together. Benjamin had been away for a few weeks and just got back and they'd been down on the beach collecting driftwood.

'When I'm dead and gone, Arch,' he'd said, 'I want you to do something for me, boy.'

'Don't talk about dying, Benjamin,' Archie had replied.

'Death's nothing to be afraid of, Archie . . . You been dead before, haven't you?'

'No.'

' 'Course you have. You're alive now and before you were born you must have been dead, stands to reason. And that wasn't so bad, was it?'

'But I can't remember before I was born.'

'You'd remember, though, if it were bad, wouldn't you, you silly young bugger!'

That was the thing Archie had loved about Benjamin, he made you think about things in a different way. He wasn't like the other grown-ups. Most of them had their minds made up about what they believed but not Benjamin.

'When the first full moon comes after I'm gone, take yourself down to the wobbly chapel, Arch, you might be lucky, find yourself a proper mystery to solve there, a real piece of detective work.'

'I don't understand.'

'Most of us don't understand what's really important but you've a good head on you, Archie Grimble. You're a scholar and a gentleman, the type of boy who could find out things like a proper detective if you put your mind to it and stopped being so afraid of every bloody thing.'

'But no one's allowed to go in the wobbly chapel, it isn't safe, and anyhow, it's locked.'

'There are no secrets locked away in this world that the curious can't find a key to open up.'

He listened to the sound of the shutters being closed in his mammy's room, the soft rustle and the breathless puffing as she pulled on her voluminous winceyette nightdress.

He heard the scrape of her rough heels on starched sheets as she climbed into bed, the slither of the threadbare eiderdown as she pulled it up over her enormous bosom. The sound of her false teeth clinking, sinking like a holed boat down to the bottom of the glass that stood on the bedside table. Once she'd had beautiful teeth but the porker had knocked them out over the years.

Mammy settling down in the big, high bed where they'd once slept together on winter nights. That was in the good old days when the hairy porker had been away sewing mail-bags up London way.

He imagined Mammy closing her eyes. Her red raw hands clasped tightly together. Lisping prayers.

Prayers for Archie's gammy leg and his wonky eye.

Prayers that his father, Walter the Pig, wouldn't come back from the Pilchard Inn dead drunk again tonight and start his antics.

Then the hushed secret prayers for her long-dead sister whose name was never mentioned out loud.

Her name was just a lisp of a name, like wind blowing through the long grass of the sand dunes.

Lissia.

Archie opened the bedroom door and stepped out on to the landing. Through the arched window that faced out to sea he could see the full moon. A huge moon bursting at the seams, hovering in the peat-black sky.

It was so beautiful it made the tears prick again.

There was no point in wishing, though. Wishing was daft; it was kids' stuff.

Oh God, there was no way that he could keep his promise to Benjamin and go down to the wobbly chapel in the pitch dark. It was too terrifying.

There were ghosts that roamed the Skallies at night. Loads of them. Donald Kelly had seen one down by the Pilchard Inn. It was naked and it had no head and chains around its ankles.

There was a Spanish pirate too with one eye and hooks where his hands should have been.

But the worst one of all was the Killivray ghost. A great big black fellow who came wandering down through the grounds of Killivray House, moaning and sobbing and wringing his hands.

18

It made Archie feel sick with fright to even think about it.

He'd promised Benjamin, though.

Why had he when there wasn't a hope in hell of him keeping a promise like that?

And why had Benjamin asked him? He should have asked one of the Kelly boys, they were all daredevils. They weren't afraid of anything or anyone, except mad Gwennie.

Everyone knew Archie Grimble was a coward. He was famous for it.

Archie Grimble is a bloody big babby.
Archie Grimble wears nappies and sucks on a titty bottle.

He'd promised, though, with his hand on his heart.

'You'll find a bunch of keys in the porch of my house, on the third hook along from the door; take them and keep them safe. After I'm gone they'll belong to you. And anything they open, Arch, will be yours.'

The wobbly chapel had been closed up for years because it was dangerous, about to tumble into the sea at any moment. And why had Benjamin got the keys to the chapel? He'd had no time for churches and stuff like that.

It was no good. He couldn't do it.

But a promise was a promise. You must honour the wishes of the dead.

Archie waited until it was quiet in Mammy's room. When he was sure that she was asleep he sat down on the side of his bed and put on an extra jersey. It was cold enough inside the house tonight but out in the Skallies it would be perishing.

He pulled a pair of old, darned fisherman's socks over his boots and up over his calliper so as not to make too much noise.

He took off his spectacles, breathed on them, wiped them on his jersey and put them back on. Then he took the tiny silver capsule that contained the battered saint from beneath his mattress and pushed it down into the pocket of his shorts. For good luck.

Finally he made his way awkwardly down the stairs and let himself quietly out of the front door and into the wild windy night.

★　★　★

Up in the nursery in Killivray House Romilly Greswode lay in bed, ears pricked for any noises.

Downstairs in the drawing room a decanter clinked. Crystal on crystal. Whisky on ice. Muffled voices.

A stray dog barked nervously over in the disused stables.

Romilly sniffed the air warily, just the usual nursery smells: mothballs and starch; cold cocoa; goose fat and liniment to ward off chills.

There was just a faint whiff of something different tonight, though.

Midnight in Paris.

Mama's perfume still lingering after a hurried goodnight kiss. Perfume and held-back tears.

More ice clinking downstairs. More whisky.

20

Papa has been home for two whole nights and he is angry again.

Papa is always angry.

Tomorrow Mama is going away again for the sake of her nerves. And a new governess is coming.

Boo!

Miss Naylor, the old governess, has left. Hooray!

Miss Naylor was a bossy britches and smelled of cold cream and damp woollen vests. Once Nanny Bea whispered to Miss Naylor that Mama was a blousy trollop.

Romilly rolled the words around on her tongue.

Trollop. Trollop. Trollop.

Blousy. Blousy. Blousy.

Mama is a blousy trollop.

Nanny Bea smells of cough drops and dying roses. She wears a hairnet at night and has varicose veins that look like swollen rivers beneath her skin.

Nanny Bea was Papa's Nanny when he was a little boy and she does not like Mama although she pretends to.

Romilly sniffed again and then drew in her breath sharply.

There it was, the peculiar smell growing stronger, a strong musty whiff of a smell. The smell she dreaded most of all.

The smell of tigers on the prowl.

Nanny Bea said that on a damp day the house still stinks of tiger's piss that no amount of scrubbing can remove.

21

Romilly shivered.

Once, when Great Grandpa Greswode was alive, Killivray House had been full of wild animals that he had brought back from foreign places.

There were servants with black faces at Killivray then and there were parrots in the drawing room and peacocks on the lawn. Monkeys with red fez hats climbed the shelves in the library and fat snakes coiled in wicker laundry baskets frightened the scullery maids.

And once a baby elephant ran amok, crashing through the rhododendrons and flattening the pergola.

Amok is one of Romilly's favourite words. She would like to run amok.

She would like to turn cartwheels down the smooth striped lawns, swing through the branches of the horse chestnut trees, kick cow pats and roll over and over in the mud at the end of the far field.

She would like to take off her clothes and run into the cool sea on a hot summer's day.

All of Great Grandpa Greswode's animals were dead now; some of them had been stuffed and given awful eyes made of glass.

But sometimes in the night, the animals come alive again and stalk the corridors of Killivray House.

Mama once said they should have had Great Grandpa Greswode stuffed and mounted in the study.

Romilly is glad that they hadn't. If they had then he may have walked at night too, like the animals did. Great Grandpa Greswode is buried in the overgrown graveyard beneath a giant stone angel with feathered wings. She was put there to keep a lid on him, making sure that he can't get out.

Charles Lewis Lloyd Greswode.

Romilly stiffened.

From across the room the black and white rocking horse eyed Romilly fearfully, the whites of his eyes bright in the moonlit room.

He could smell tigers a mile off. They spooked him.

The one-eared teddy bear perched on the window seat stared ahead unfazed.

The tiny light inside the dolls' house illuminated the lattice window panes.

All was safe inside there.

Romilly wished that she could magic herself so tiny that she could go in through the little front door, climb the stairs, and get beneath the pretty pink gingham counterpane in the spare bedroom.

Inside the house the doll people would be sleeping soundly. The mother and father dolls were cuddled up snugly beneath their pink and blue patchwork quilt.

In the nursery two identical girl children slept in single beds. Sisters. A black and white collie dog was curled up in a basket in the corner of the room.

Up in the attic the two maids were asleep, lying top to tail, their wooden feet and mob caps peeping out from beneath the grey blankets.

The rocking horse creaked fearfully.

The dying embers of the nursery fire glowed behind the fireguard and a stray spark drifted away up the chimney.

The tigers were on the move now. She felt the hairs on the back of her neck standing to attention and her heart thumped noisily against her flannelette nightgown.

She heard them climbing up the steps from the dark, cobwebby cellars, then the jingle of ladles and spoons as they squeezed through the kitchen . . . Now the pad of their velvet paws on the worn hallway carpet.

Moving past the drawing room where tempers are frayed.

Where Papa is shouting at Mama.

'The child needs to be here with her mother.'

'She needs to go to school and have friends of her own age.' Mama now, pleading.

'School! Don't talk to me of school! No child of mine will ever set foot in a damned school.'

'I've written to the headmistress of Nanskelly School, an excellent girls' school. She could go each day in the car.'

'You had no business to make plans for her without consulting me. She will *never ever* go to school, so get that into your thick head. I will not have her mixing with God knows who and being corrupted.'

'It's a school, for goodness sake, not a house of correction.'

'She's doing perfectly well here and here she stays. She has everything that a child needs.'

'She needs more freedom, more company, more time to be a child. I need more freedom

24

too. We can't be kept shut up here for ever . . . '

'Oh, my sweet darling, I think you can.'

'You can't know what it's like for us cooped up in this mausoleum of a house. You're never here.'

'I have business to attend to as well you know.'

'And we all know what sort of business that is!'

'I won't listen to another word of your ranting. I have already engaged another governess. She will arrive tomorrow. I have arranged for a car to fetch her from the station.'

'I sometimes think that these governesses of yours are really here to keep an eye on me rather than Romilly.'

'Nanny Bea does a good enough job on that score.'

'One day, I swear to God that I'll leave here.'

'And if you do you know the consequences. You will lose the child and never see her again and you will be, amongst other things, penniless.'

Romilly pulled the bedclothes up over her head and covered her ears with her hands.

The tigers were getting nearer now. They always came when people got angry.

Closer and closer they came. Eyes bright with hunger. Whiskers twitching. Coming stealthily up the stairs.

At the top of the stairs.

They were outside the nursery door now. Their agitated breath rasping, breath thick with the smell of stale blood.

If they pushed against the door it would open with a soft click. She imagined their sharp claws, ripping through the blankets. The feel of their huge teeth as they sank into her goose-pimpled skin. The spurt of red blood splattering the white, starched sheets.

She held her breath until the blood pumped noisily inside her ears and her lungs felt like balloons that might pop at any moment.

The tigers were moving away now.

Restless. Hungry.

Pawing at Nanny Bea's door in the room next to the nursery.

Nanny Bea was too old and tough to eat.

Silence again.

In Nanny Bea's room milk bubbled over onto the hotplate ring and hissed. She heard Nanny Bea shuffling across the room in her tartan slippers, cursing softly so as not to wake Romilly.

Romilly heard the cap of the bottle removed and the sound of liquid pouring. Nanny Bea's nightcap. A full mug of brandy laced with hot milk.

Away in Rhoskilly village the church clock chimed mournfully.

She heard the click of the tiger claws on the bare boards in the attic rooms above her head.

Prowling. Growling. Pacing.

Downstairs a glass is smashed.

Footsteps cross the hallway. The front door is opened and wind rushes into the house and rattles the loose antlers of the stag's head that hangs on the wall.

The front door bangs shut. Angry heels grinding into the gravel. A car door opens and slams. Roars away down the drive.

She can hear the low rumble of the tigers' empty bellies echoing through the house.

The grinding of gears as the car moves on.

Then silence.

Out on the landing the stuffed brown bear at the top of the stairs yawns and closes its glazed eyes. She heard the click of his yellow teeth as they knocked together.

Down in the smoky drawing room Mama winds up the gramophone. Now that Papa has gone the elephant's foot pouffe begins to tap out a tune:

To Bombay a travelling circus came,
They brought an intelligent elephant
And Nelly was her name.
One dark night she slipped her iron chain
And off she ran to Hindustan
And was never seen again!

Perhaps one dark night she and Mama will slip their iron chains, run away to Hindustan and never be seen again.

She lay listening to the moaning of the wind in the chimneys, the far-off crash of the sea on the rocks and the wildcats howling over in the filthy place they called the Skallies. Papa said the Skallies was a blot on the landscape and if he had dynamite he'd like to blow it to Kingdom Come. It was a place not fit for man or beast. It was dirty and dangerous and full of mad people who didn't wash behind their ears and didn't know their place.

Romilly and Mama had never been allowed

anywhere near there.

She closed her eyes, heard the soft purring of the tigers, sleeping now like giant pussycats curled up among the junk in the attics. Resting their enormous heads on piles of mouldy theatre programmes, old diaries and journals with pages the colour of saffron cakes.

Downstairs the music continued and Mama laughed loudly then sang along:

The head of the herd was calling far far
  away;
They met one night in the silver light
On the road to Mandalay . . .

In the tiny bar of the Pilchard Inn Nan Abelson threw a log on to the fire and watched as a flurry of sparks escaped up the chimney.

She pulled her old grey cardigan closer around her shoulders and stood looking into the heart of the fire.

The flames danced wildly and the embers glowed with a fierce intensity.

She thought of how she'd loved to sit and stare into the fire for hours when she was a child. She used to watch the pictures in the embers, to breathe in the smells of the different woods: olive and pine; apple and oak.

For a moment she allowed a chink of long-buried memory to bubble to the surface.

She pictured the little house in Bizier . . . herself as a child carrying armfuls of kindling along the path from the woodshed. Mama standing at the stove in the kitchen, turning to look at her and smiling that sweet lopsided smile. The sound of Papa humming cheerfully in his workshop for the last time.

She closed her eyes, willed herself to stop the memory. It did no good resurrecting the past. The past was done and dusted. Ashes to ashes, dust to dust.

Only the pain remained.

She stirred herself, tried to shrug off the feeling of uneasiness that was growing in the pit of her stomach.

'Another pint of your best when you're ready, Nan. A man could die of thirst while you're staring into that fire.'

Walter Grimble's voice dragged her back from her unsettling thoughts. She went back behind the bar and expertly pulled a pint without looking once at Walter Grimble. She knew, though, that his bloodshot eyes were on her, looking her up and down as though she were a piece of tripe on the butcher's block.

Nan Abelson despised Walter Grimble. He had a leery eye and a nasty temper and he treated his wife and little Archie something rotten.

'It's blowing up real rough out there, Nan. You could do with a good man to keep you warm tonight,' Walter said, leaning further over the counter to get a look at her legs.

Nan ignored him, plonked a glass pot down on the worn counter and turned away quickly.

Walter Grimble slurped the froth off his pint greedily and belched loudly. He thought that it was unusual for Nan not to give a sharp retort; perhaps she was sickening for something. He caught sight of her reflection in an old mirror on the back of the bar and for a moment he was sure that he saw a tear wind its way down her flushed cheek. It wasn't like Nan to show any emotion. She was a handsome woman but as hard as bloody nails where men were concerned. Something must have got into her tonight, though, to bring a tear to her eye; maybe she did have a heart beneath that shabby cardigan after all.

Nan Abelson was feeling rattled. She'd felt that way ever since old Benjamin Tregantle had passed away, as if the balance had somehow gone out of the Skallies and the world wasn't such a safe place any more. Maybe she'd got too complacent over the years since she'd come here, stopped being afraid. She needed to keep her ears and eyes open now, be on her guard, especially with old Benjamin gone. She swallowed hard, tried to stem the tears that were never far away. She was missing Benjamin something terrible. She could hardly bear to look at the Grandfather chair where he'd always sat close to the fire.

No one sat there now.

Walter Grimble had plonked his fat behind there the same night as they'd heard the news of Benjamin's drowning, but she wasn't having any of that.

'You can move your arse right now. No one sits there. That seat's reserved,' she'd said, surprised at the intensity of her own anger.

And he had seen the look in her eye and moved without a word.

She glanced briefly across at Walter Grimble, barely able to keep the look of scorn off her face.

Cocky bugger that he was. He'd never be a quarter of the man old Benjamin had been, not as long as he had a hole in his fat arse. However cold she got in the nights it wouldn't be him she'd like to cuddle up to. God knows why Martha had ever married him. Martha Grimble would be a good-looking woman if she wasn't so worn out all the time fetching and carrying for that lazy lump. She must have been drunk or out of her mind when she'd agreed to marry that old fartpot.

'I'll not be hanging about long, Nan,' Charlie Payne called out from his seat over near the window. 'I'll have one more and then be off; going to be a rough old night tonight and a fair bit of damage done, I'll wager.'

'We've had some bad storms here in the Skallies but one of the worst I ever remember was the night they buried Charles Greswode, from Killivray House,' Freddie Payne said.

Nan smiled across at the two Payne brothers. They were identical twins who had lived in the Skallies all their lives and made their living by fishing, as their ancestors had done before them. Folk said there'd been Paynes living in the Peapods as far back as anyone could remember.

'That were a few years back,' Nan said. 'Before my time.'

'Bloody old lunatic that Charles Greswode's father was,' Freddie Payne remarked, putting down his glass.

'He were a horrible man. Went off to foreign parts, came back here to live while his brother were abroad. Asked the locals in one Christmas Eve for mince pies and punch . . . ' Charlie added.

'That was nice of him,' Nan said. 'No one gets invited in there these days. Like bloody hermits they are. Never see them out and about like normal folk.'

Charlie Payne began to laugh, blowing foam from his pint all over his whiskers.

'What's tickled your fancy, Charlie?'

'I were just thinking, it weren't that nice for that young kid from up Rhoskilly.'

'Why's that then?' said Nan with a broad grin.

'Well, while they was in Killivray this kid slipped away from everyone else and went snooping about upstairs.'

'And?'

'He come face to face with a live tiger on the landing!'

'Never!'

'In a terrible state he was. Cacked his pants on the spot, had to be taken home to change and his mother give him a right pasting.'

'Don't tell your bloody lies, Charlie Payne.'

'No, honest to God, Nan. Greswode kept all sorts of creatures in there. Me and Freddie weren't born then but they reckon it was like a bloody menagerie.'

'He had pythons as well,' Freddie Payne added with enthusiasm.

'Thirty foot long some of 'em was,' Charlie said.

'You can remember hearing about when that kid seen the tiger, can't you, Billy?' Charlie called out across the bar.

'I can. The nosy little bugger could have been killed. I heard that a servant got between him and the beast and saved his bacon. Some black fellow that Greswode brought back with him from his travels. Couldn't get hardly anyone local to work for him, not after that scullery maid got bit by a monkey.'

'Now, what the hell was that black fellow called? Funny-sounding name he had, Rory Obory or something like that.'

'I can't remember his name after all this time. They reckon those tigers were beautiful though,' Billy mused shaking his head.

'There was lions as well,' Freddie said.

'No, there weren't no bloody lions, you add yards on, you do. There was monkeys, though, and a bear.'

'Whatever happened to them all?' asked Nan.

Charlie Payne took a long draught of beer then continued, 'Well, out of the blue Greswode married some big piece of goods from up the line and they had a son, Charles. She wouldn't let him keep his pets so he had to get rid of them all.'

'What did he do with them?'

'Had some of them shot and then stuffed. They reckon that's why that black fellow did what he did.'

'What did he do?' Nan was fascinated.

'Topped himself,' Charlie said.

'That's terrible.'

'Grew up with them tigers and they was like family to him, I suppose. Blew his brains out in the wobbly chapel years later.'

'Our old mother always reckoned he was having a bit of a thing with Gwennie and when he done himself in that's when she went all peculiar.'

'Do you think that's what happened to her?' Nan asked.

'No, they say she were always a bit unusual, high-spirited, even as a kid. A bit of a wild thing she was,' Freddie chipped in.

'Did Gwennie grow up in the Boathouse then?' asked Nan.

'No. She were a Skallies girl, lived over in the Grockles where that queer fellow Fleep is now. Gwennie used to work in Killivray, only local who dared to.'

'Beautiful-looking girl she were, apparently, and good with animals and kids, she weren't afraid of nothing. Then one day, not long after the black fellow died, she upped and buggered off without a word and was gone for years and years,' Freddie added.

'A lot of folks said there was talk of her and Greswode carrying on,' Charlie muttered.

'That were only rumour,' Freddie said. 'Our mother said she wouldn't have looked twice at that ugly bugger.'

'So when did she come back?'

'Good few years back now, Nan. About the same time as Benjamin came back and that were a year or so before Charles Greswode died. Altered beyond belief she was, gone all peculiar.

34

Old Greswode let her live in the Boathouse rent free which were a bit odd 'cos he were a tight old sod.'

'Now I come to think of it, I fancy Greswode gave most of the monkeys, parrots and stuff to that circus that used to come here donkey's years ago.'

'Cranky's Circus,' Freddie said.

'What the hell is Cranky's when it's out of bed?' asked Billy Nettles.

'The circus, you soppy sod. Remember when we was kids we used to go and see it. They use to set up camp over in Arnold's Hole every other year.'

'I do remember now you've said, Charlie. There was clowns, bearded ladies and a mermaid in a tank. And trapeze artistes, weren't there?'

'That's right, Billy; the Flying Fernandez the trapeze artistes was called. Wonderful they were. I used to have my bloody heart in my mouth watching them.'

'Nan, you would have loved it here when the circus folk used to come down. They used to stick their posters up all round Rhoskilly then come down here to make merry. They drunk this place dry many a time,' Freddie said wistfully.

'We could do with a bit of trade like that now,' Nan sighed.

'It's Charles Greswode's son that's got Killivray House now,' Billy Nettles said.

'That's right. That side of the Greswodes shouldn't have inherited Killivray, by rights it should have gone to his cousin, young master

35

Thomas, but he disappeared.'

'How do you mean disappeared, Charlie?'

'Queer old affair that was, Nan. He took a boat out, Benjamin Tregantle's boat it were. They found it further round the coast, drifting. He were drowned. A strong swimmer he was too. They reckon he must have fallen overboard, got the cramp, or maybe he had a weak heart. Tragic it was, he was only a young lad. It were three weeks afore he were washed up.'

'That Jonathan Greswode at Killivray now is hardly ever there, lives most of the time up London. Bit of a nancy boy, I've heard. All dickie bows and hair oil,' Walter Grimble chipped in.

'He can't be a nancy boy, he's married, got a child with a funny name,' Billy Nettles answered.

'Romilly, I think she's called,' said Nan.

'I've never even seen her,' Freddie piped up.

'Hardly anyone has. They keep her inside mostly, like a bloody hot-house plant. There's talk that she ain't the full shilling,' said Billy Nettles.

'There's a lot of that in them aristocracy types . . . too much inbreeding and eating fancy food . . . cousins marrying and all that, ain't never right if you ask me.' Charlie shook his head knowingly.

'There was some talk about the mother years back. She was an actress, make-up artist or some bloody thing,' Billy said. 'But they reckon she's gone all religious since she married, always going off to some nunnery for months on end.'

'Who looks after the kid then?' Nan asked.

'They got an old nanny lives there, been there

36

for ever. And that governess woman you see up at the Post Office once in a blue moon,' Charlie Payne added.

'I heard she's gone. She were a frosty-faced old bag, looked like she got something wedged up her arse.'

'Language, man!' interjected Billy Nettles with a sniff, glaring at Walter Grimble.

A fierce gust of wind rattled the windows and smoke blew out of the fire and into the bar.

'Spirits on the move tonight,' said Charlie, nodding towards the fireplace.

Nan eyed him sceptically. 'Don't talk daft; it's just the wind, that's all.'

'The dead like to make their mark every now and again, show us they're still around in some shape or form. That'll be Benjamin Tregantle, I'll bet.'

Freddie looked at the fire warily.

'It's a full moon tonight. He's making his last visit to the Skallies before his soul flies off wherever the souls of awkward old buggers go to.'

'That's fanciful talk, Charlie. Anyway I liked him.'

'We all liked him, Nan, he were a good old stick, don't mean he weren't a cantankerous old sod.'

More smoke blew out of the fire and Nan hurried out from behind the bar and flapped her apron to try and clear it then went across and opened the door.

The wind was getting up rough and twigs and leaves skittered along Bloater Row, and somewhere a loose shutter banged noisily. She looked

37

left down Bloater Row. At the far end past Hogwash House old Benjamin's upturned boat was rocking from side to side in the wind as though something were trapped underneath. She shivered.

Then a movement to her right caught her eye. She peered warily into the darkness. She couldn't see anyone but if she wasn't mistaken someone or something was lurking about in the shadows over near the wobbly chapel. It was high time that place was pulled down. It was a bloody good job it was locked up and none of the kids could get inside, it was a death trap.

For God's sake, Nan, she chided herself, you're letting your imagination get the better of you. It was all that talk of the dead that had made her jumpy . . .

The trouble was these days you didn't know who was hanging about. Take that poor little girl up in London . . . disappeared on her way home from school in a snowstorm and the body still not found weeks later. Poor little dab was there one minute and gone the next.

Nan stepped back into the warmth of the bar and closed the door quickly. 'The forecast was right, boys, there's a hell of a storm on its way. So last orders, gentlemen, please.'

★ ★ ★

Fleep stood at the window and looked out into the night. Occasionally a wave hit the rocks below the Skallies and spray hit the windows making him jump. He turned and looked across at the bed longingly. If only he could get some sleep . . .

It was a long time now since he had had a good sleep. He had learned to live with a few alcohol-fuelled hours of fitful rest here and there over the past years.

He had become accustomed to perpetual tiredness, but he was a burnt-out crock of a man without desire or purpose left in him; an aimless drifter, who had somehow been washed up into this curious little backwater.

He couldn't even remember how the hell he had come to be in the Skallies. His memory was shot to pieces.

He remembered vaguely the time he had spent in a convent with nuns fussing around him, ministering to him, spoon-feeding him with broth and milk puddings. The next memory was of being holed up in the attic room in Paris out of his head on booze and later being thrown out . . . then just some dreamlike remembrance of falling asleep and waking up with the key to the Grockles in his hand. And then he'd somehow made his way back to England and down here to the Skallies, a godforsaken place full of people as odd as himself. But nonetheless the people here seemed aware of his need to be alone. Ever since he had arrived no one had bothered him or tried to make his acquaintance.

He had sought no company for he had nothing left to say to the world. He had no reason to get up in the morning or go out other than to simply exist. Existing was easier than not existing. He looked across at the parrot in its cage and it stared back with those knowing eyes that looked a thousand years old.

The parrot was a mystery to him too. How had he come to be in possession of a foul-mouthed bloody parrot? Had he bought it? Stolen it?

'I bet you could tell a few tales, old fellow?' he said sadly.

'*Mange la merde et morte!*' yelled the parrot.

Fleep shook his head. He'd stay here in the Skallies just a little while longer until he summoned up the energy to put himself out of his misery.

★　★　★

Down below the Skallies the waves were racing up the beach, the wind whistling through the eyeholes of dead crabs, rattling winkle and cockle shells, whisking fish bones into whispering piles around the upturned boats.

The wildcats wailed in the backyard of the Pilchard Inn and somewhere a scullery door slammed shut and tin mugs and battered spoons that hung on rusty nails rapped out a tatta tat tat.

Archie Grimble inched his way slowly over towards Hogwash House, his head bent against the icy wind that was howling along Bloater Row. He lifted the latch on the outside door and stepped quickly inside the porch.

It was dead spooky standing in there all alone. Hogwash House still smelled of Benjamin. The whiff of Camp coffee and Everton mints, of rum and snuff, of stored apples and liniment.

He stood on tiptoes and yanked the bunch of keys off the hook.

Benjamin's old tweed jacket was still hanging on a hook as though he had just come in and taken it off. Archie stepped towards it nervously.

Then he buried his face in it, sniffed up the familiar woolly smell. He put his hand nervously into the right-hand pocket. The paper bag was there unopened. Archie's Saturday sweets.

Chocolate chewing nuts.

Benjamin had always bought them on a Friday up in Rhoskilly and on Saturdays he'd say, 'Put your hand in that there pocket, Arch, and see if there's anything there for you.'

Sometimes he used to tease him and put them in the other pocket.

He stood there sobbing softly, the coat rough against his damp face, the smell of the old man strong in his nostrils. After a while he let go of the coat, took off his spectacles and wiped his eyes. When he put his spectacles back on he noticed the envelope sticking out of the left side pocket. He took it out and turned it over.

To MASTER ARCHIE GRIMBLE. PRIVATE.

Archie wiped his nose on his sleeve and sniffed. He'd never received a letter in his life.

It was too dark in the porch to read it and he dare not switch on his torch.

He slipped the letter into the pocket of his trousers and then beat a hasty retreat.

He moved slowly along Bloater Row, keeping a look out with his one good eye. The cobbles were wet and slippery beneath his feet and the icy wind made his teeth chatter uncontrollably.

As he passed Periwinkle House he heard the tinkle of ancient bone china as the spinster Misses Noni and Agnes Arbuthnot sipped cocoa and listened to posh music.

A black cat crossed his path. That meant good luck. He watched it creep silkily in through a gap in the kitchen window of Periwinkle House.

Archie felt for the saint in his pocket. As he passed the door of Skibbereen he could smell herrings dipped in flour hissing and spitting in a pan as big-bellied Mrs Galvini cooked supper and sang softly in a sweet but mournful voice that brought a lump to Archie's throat.

Mrs Galvini had no children of her own but in the spare bedroom she had a wicker crib all ready and a pile of knitted baby clothes in pink and blue and yellow. Sometimes he'd seen her in her garden kneeling in the cabbages, looking to see if the stork had managed to leave her a baby but he never had. It wasn't fair because he gave Mrs Kelly loads and she didn't even know how to look after them.

Archie stopped outside Cuckoo's Nest and held his breath.

The Kelly family lived in Cuckoo's Nest, next to the Pilchard Inn.

He could hear them in there now, squabbling and arguing. He could smell the Kelly smell and it made him gag. Shite from the nappy bucket that festered near the front door and the stink of unwashed bodies: ear wax, sweat and rancid chip fat.

Archie was terrified of the seven Kelly boys.

There were four red-faced tiny ones who

bawled and bit and spat and licked their own snot off their faces.

Three big ones.

Donald was the oldest. Then Kevin and Peter.

Peter was nice, not like the rest of them. He'd have liked to be friends with Peter.

Mammy said it was like he wasn't out of the same litter.

The other Kelly boys were rough as guts.

Donald and Kevin waited for Archie behind hedges when he came home from school and bashed him up nearly every day. They gave him dead legs and Chinese burns.

Wrenched his arm up behind his back and took his Saturday sweet money. They kneed him up the bum and brought tears to his eyes. The worst, though, were the rabbit punches that they gave.

They could kill people like that but they didn't care.

And Mrs Kelly never even told them off if she caught them at it. All she ever said was, 'Boys will be boys, Archie, you should toughen yourself up a bit and not be such a fanny.'

They never laid a finger on him when Benjamin was around, though. They were afeared of Benjamin. Now he was gone the Kellys would be tormenting him all the time.

Mr Kelly spent half his life hiding in the outside lav and the other half far out at sea, fishing. He never spoke, only grunted, but his wife never stopped; she was a sour-faced old bissom and dirty about herself. Mammy said that in the Kelly house you needed to wash the soap before you used it.

Archie ducked down and scuttled as quickly as he could past their greasy window.

From the Pilchard Inn voices drifted out through the porthole windows along with the clink of dominoes and the thud of darts on a well-soaked board.

He peeped warily inside, careful not to be spotted.

It looked cosy in the small bar with the fire roaring up the chimney, candlelight glinting off the blue and green glass pots that Nan served the beer in.

Nan Abelson was behind the tiny bar lifting a glass pot up to the candlelight. She was big and beefy and very beautiful and smiled a lot. She had arms the colour of corned beef and a coiled black plait that swung between her shoulder blades like a hangman's noose.

Beneath her fringe she had a scar on her forehead but you only got to see it when she got hot and brushed her hair to one side.

Nan Abelson could swear like a man.

She used all the four-letter words when she got mad.

Fart and Damn; Shit and Piss.

Nan was tough as old boots and could throw a punch like a kangaroo when her dander was up. No one messed with her.

Once she pasted Donald Kelly when he stole Cissie's toy monkey and piddled all over it accidentally on purpose.

There were four people besides Nan squashed into the bar of the Pilchard. Charlie and Freddie

Payne were playing dominoes together at a table not far from where Archie stood.

His own father was sitting up at the bar, thankfully with his back to Archie. Billy Nettles was playing darts. Archie moved on. He stopped again when he reached the house where the new man called Fleep lived alone with his parrot. Fleep's parrot was green and red and could speak three languages. A foreign one, English. And filth.

He'd read somewhere that parrots could live to be a hundred.

Fleep's house was called the Grockles and it was the only single-storeyed house in Bloater Row. It had been empty as long as Archie could remember. Fleep had turned up a few weeks back but hadn't bothered to get to know anyone yet. He was an odd sort of fellow and mostly he stayed shut up in the house but sometimes Archie had seen him walking alone on the cliff path towards Nanskelly. He kept himself to himself and hardly anyone had heard him speak. As Archie got close to the window Fleep's parrot shrieked, '*Mange la Merde!*'

Archie's heart was already galloping and his breath escaped in wreaths of steam on the cold night air.

He tried to slow his breathing down.

A fierce gust of wind roared along Bloater Row and a tile blew off the roof of the Peapods and exploded onto the cobbles. A tin bucket hurtled past him and clattered away down Bloater Row towards the hole in the rocks that led down to Skilly Beach.

The parrot squawked again.

'The King Lives . . . Long live the King.'

Inside the house Fleep laughed loudly and made Archie jump. It was the only sound Archie had heard him make and it echoed eerily inside the house.

From inside the Grockles a wireless stuttered out the shipping news and a cork escaped from a bottle with an echoing pop.

Archie moved on, made it safely to the end of Bloater Row, turned to his left and looked nervously at the wobbly chapel.

The night was bitterly cold, the wind getting ever wilder, whistling round the chimneys of Bloater Row and making the old timbers of the chapel roof creak ominously.

Archie was shivering violently and his legs had a life of their own; he was dancing up and down with nerves, like a puppet worked by a madman. Already his gammy leg was weakening and the chilblains on his toes were beginning to throb.

He took the keys from his pocket and looked down at them. There was one large key and two smaller ones.

He took a deep breath and stepped up to the door of the old chapel. He put the largest of the keys into the rusty lock hoping that it wouldn't fit, and then he could say that at least he'd tried to keep his promise.

He groaned inwardly as the key turned slowly and the door opened with a juddering sigh.

He removed the key and stepped breathlessly into the musty, dusty darkness of the chapel and locked the door behind him.

Nan Abelson locked and bolted the door of the Pilchard Inn and raked the fire. She washed and dried up the pint pots and placed them on the shelf behind the bar. Then she made her way through to the kitchen. The wildcats growled and spat as Nan opened the back door. Then they grew quiet, their eyes glowed eerily in the moonlit yard. They were better than any guard dogs. Nan threw them a handful of scraps, then bolted the back door and climbed wearily up the steep stairs.

In the large upstairs bedroom Cissie was asleep. She lay curled up in the big bed, her thumb stuck between her damp lips, snoring softly, a ragged monkey clasped tightly to her chest.

Nan stood looking down at the child, safe and cosy beneath the dusky pink eiderdown. She hoped that she could always keep Cissie that way, hoped that she lived long enough to see the child grown and settled. The only thing about having a child like Cissie was the worry that when Nan was dead and gone there would be no one left to love her. As long as she had breath in her body Nan would fight tooth and nail to keep her safe, make sure no one did her harm but after that . . .

Nan walked across to the tallboy, picked up the elephant bookend and sat down on the window seat. She ran her fingers deftly over the smooth wood of the carved elephant remembering her fascination years ago when she had first been shown the elephant's secret. It was

47

originally one of a pair but the other had gone missing years before. The elephant was joined to a wooden book and looked like a simple bookend. But if you knew how, you slid down the spine of the book revealing a tight-fitting wooden panel that slid open. Inside was a space to hide valuables.

One day she'd show Cissie how it worked, when the time was right.

She slid down the wooden spine of the book and at her touch the panel slid out easily. She pulled out the photograph and a sea shell and stared down at them. The photograph had been taken during the war. The camera had captured two small girls standing at the edge of the sea. Two dark-haired little girls giggling and holding hands. One of them saved and one of them lost.

Nan closed her eyes and put the shell to her ear . . . She remembered the lapping of the waves and the laughter of children playing. A baby crying and gulls screeching overhead. Together they had hunted for shells and picked up the most beautiful and put them in their pockets . . .

Then Papa calling to them both to smile for the camera . . .

She opened her eyes and wiped her tears.

This tiny photograph and shell kept safe inside the elephant were the only mementoes of Nan's past life, the only thing that she had been able to bring with her from a dark, tormented past.

She replaced the photograph and shell, put the bookend back together and put it back on the tallboy.

Nan looked out into the stormy night. Far in the distance around the coast she could see the lights glittering in the isolated school that stood alone on the headland.

In the Boathouse on Skilly Beach a candle flickered in the arched window. Mad Gwennie, like a hermit all alone in there with the music she played over and over. Nan had rarely seen her, just caught the occasional glimpse of her every now and then down on the beach at dawn or at nightfall when no one else was around. As she watched now the door of the Boathouse opened and a small hunched figure was silhouetted against the light.

Nan stared intently as the figure climbed carefully down the steps on to the beach and then hurried towards the dunes, head bent against the fierce wind. Then she was lost to sight as she headed through the dunes towards the high wall that bordered Killivray House.

Only a lunatic would venture out on a night like this.

Nan looked down into Bloater Row and from where she stood she could see into the living room of the Grockles. She wondered if the house had been empty ever since mad Gwennie had run away? Most of the windows were cracked and the gap under the front door was wide enough for a fat rat to run under.

The large room was sparsely furnished with ancient furniture and dimly lit by a hurricane lamp. It looked cold and uninviting with no fire lit in the hearth. The newcomer Fleep must be freezing his cobs off in there.

49

He was an interesting fellow, this Fleep. A handsome man, she'd wager, if he had a shave, put a bit more meat on his bones and an occasional smile on his chops. Rumour had it that he was on the run from gangsters in London but rumours always abounded in the Skallies where newcomers were concerned.

Catching sight of Fleep sitting at the back window looking out into the night, she snuffed out the candle so that if he turned and looked up he would not see her spying on him.

She watched him for a long time, watched as he raised a bottle to his lips, drank thirstily and carried on staring out into the night like a man in a trance. He was sitting so still that for a while Nan was not sure if he had fallen asleep.

Then suddenly he turned around as if startled by something.

Nan shrank back away from the window. Fleep put down the bottle and crossed the room on tiptoe. He disappeared from sight and then she saw the front door opening just a crack. He stepped outside into Bloater Row, looked to the right and the left. The wind blew his long hair around his face. He glanced up at the window and Nan thought for a moment that he'd seen her. She wouldn't forget the terrible look of fear on his face in a long time. Then he hurriedly closed the door and the light was extinguished.

Nan pulled the curtains across and hastily undressed, climbed quickly into the warm bed and put an arm around Cissie. Cissie groaned softly and pushed her small body closer to Nan. The wind whined around the old building and the ancient floorboards creaked as though bare feet were crossing them.

She closed her eyes, hugged Cissie even closer to her and fell asleep listening to the wind buffeting Bloater Row and the angry sea pounding onto the rocks below the Skallies.

★ ★ ★

It was dark inside the wobbly chapel and it stank. There was the funny holy smell that all churches had but it smelled of other things besides. Mouse droppings, mouldy flock, damp hymn books and woodworm.

And the faint but definite whiff of Benjamin's pipe tobacco. Old Shag.

Archie took his cheap torch out from his pocket. It was part of his Detective Kit, the only bit that worked properly. He found the switch and turned it on. There were no windows in the chapel that could be seen from Bloater Row, the only window was the one above the altar that faced out to sea. No one would know that he was inside the chapel snooping around.

The beam of light from the torch was weak but he could just make out the outline of the pews on either side of a narrow aisle.

The chapel was tiny and would only have fitted twenty people in it at the most. He shuffled down the aisle until he came to the altar.

The altar was made of rough uneven wood and was covered in a thick coat of dust. The base was made from the front part of a boat. He got closer and screwed up his eyes. There was a name engraved on the side of the altar cum boat, but he couldn't make out what it said.

A curious-looking crucifix stood on the altar between two ancient candlesticks that were crusted with candle wax.

Archie put his head on one side and studied the crucifix with interest. All the crucifixes he'd ever seen were made from gold or wood but this one looked as though it was made of two large animal bones tied together with twine. Suddenly light flooded into the chapel through the window above the altar. Archie stood stock-still. There must be someone down on the beach with a spotlight, someone who'd seen the light of his torch, someone who knew that he was inside the chapel.

Then he relaxed. It was only the beam from the lighthouse out beyond Skilly Head that was lit on very stormy nights. He counted fifteen between each beam of light . . .

Each time the beam came the round window above the altar glowed for a brief moment and lit up a glorious kaleidoscope of coloured glass.

He swung the torch around the chapel. There were some ancient plaques on the wall with peculiar writing on them.

Beneath his feet the floor was damp and sticky with mould and mountains of mouse droppings. There were a few scattered books and some rotten hassocks strewn around. He stooped to pick up a prayer book and opened it gingerly.

The beam of the torch picked out a name on the fly leaf.

He screwed up his good eye and read,

This book was given to Thomas Gasparini Greswode on the day of his first Holy Communion . . .

The date written beside the name was so faded that he couldn't read it . . .

This couldn't be what Benjamin had meant him to find, a mouldy old prayer book with the name of someone he'd never heard of in the front.

He walked gingerly around the chapel. Dust and cobwebs lay thick over everything he touched and when he shone his torch up towards the roof, the eyes of a startled bird stared back at him from a nest in the rafters.

There was an ancient-looking font at the back of the chapel and Archie edged slowly around it. It was elaborately engraved all around the sides but it was so old and filthy that it was hard to make out what the writing said. The words weren't in English either, Latin maybe, or French?

He shrugged his shoulders and looked around him. What had Benjamin been thinking about, sending him here? There was no mystery about this place, it was just old and dirty and tumbling down.

He made his way carefully back towards the door. As he turned for one last glance around the crumbling chapel he noticed a small door to the left of the altar. He walked nervously across to it, lifted the latch and stepped into a large cupboard.

He swung his torch around. There were just a few bare shelves and a mouldy old black cloak hanging on a peg. He swept the cloak to one side and had to hold his nose to keep out the shower of dust that engulfed him.

Just then a blast of wind hit the chapel and the rafters groaned above his head. He looked up, and through the gaps in the broken tiles he could see the stars glittering fiercely. Then he squealed with fright as part of the wooden panelling fell towards him with a clatter.

Awkwardly Archie knelt down. The wooden panel looked just like the rest of the wall except that there were hinges on the bottom and a clip that slotted into a groove. Archie got to his feet and gazed at the gap in the panelling before him. He moved forward hesitantly and pointed the torch into the darkness.

A blast of icy air hit him in the face, making him gasp. He peered warily into the hole. He could hear the sea somewhere beneath him, crashing mercilessly onto the rocks.

He stared with fascination as the torch picked out a step, and then another, a twisting narrow stone staircase leading downwards into the damp and freezing darkness.

It must lead down to Skilly Beach, somewhere opposite the old Boathouse where mad Gwennie lived . . .

He'd read about secret passages and stuff in history books; they were usually used by smugglers or priests hidden away in the olden days.

A gust of wind rattled the chapel again. The floorboards moved beneath his feet.

This was real interesting but he needed to get out of here quick before the whole bloody chapel blew away with him in it.

He stepped out of the cupboard and closed the door.

It was lighter in the chapel now. The moon was directly in line with the glass window above the altar and it was lit as if by a spotlight. The colours of the glass in the window were astonishingly beautiful and Archie was bathed in a rainbow light. He looked like Joseph in his coat of many colours.

He must have stood there five minutes or more when a cloud blotted out the moon and the chapel was thrust into darkness.

That was it. He'd been brave enough. All he wanted to do now was to get out of the spooky place, hurry home and snuggle down in his bed.

He unlocked the chapel door, opened it just a crack and peeped out into Bloater Row.

It was dark, the wind as wild as hell and he saw with dismay that the lights were out in the Pilchard Inn.

Damn and blast.

Nan must have closed up early and that meant that his father would already be at home.

Hell's bells! He would have pulled across the bolts on the front door. Archie was locked out.

He tried to think fast but panic was dulling his thoughts. He couldn't stay outside all night in this weather; he'd freeze to death by the morning. But where could he go? He'd have to go back into Hogwash House and stay the night in there.

Then he stared in absolute terror. There was a shadowy figure outside Hogwash House, someone looking to the left and right as though they shouldn't be there. They were trying the door of the porch. Burglars.

Ghosts on the loose.

Benjamin got up out of his grave.

Suffering starfish!

He could see the figure moving around inside the porch.

He could hear the rattle of keys or, more likely, the clanking of chains.

He must be imagining it.

He blinked, shook his head. When he looked again there was no sign of anyone. It was just his nerves making him jumpy, he was all to pieces.

He stayed very still, sure that he could hear another noise, someone or something breathing heavily nearby. There was someone hiding in the shadows not far from where he stood.

The place was alive with ghosts and ghouls and God knows what else.

A spasm of fear rattled up his backbone.

He ducked back into the chapel, locked the door with a shaking hand and then backed away.

Moments later he thought that he heard the sound of someone trying the door . . .

Holy Jesus and all the saints of heaven protect me.

A rat ran across the floor, brushing against his foot.

Frantic with fear he crossed to the cupboard, slipped his good leg over the wooden panelling and felt for the first step on the narrow staircase. If he could climb down the steps to the beach at least he could hide. He climbed cautiously down, one foot in front of the other . . .

He slipped, clutched out wildly at the slimy walls and saved himself.

He took another step downwards into the dank, salty darkness. And another.

Then he fell.

His calliper clattered against rock and for a moment he felt as if he were flying, hurling downwards into the darkness.

For a fleeting moment he was surrounded by stars and then he felt the water sucking him under.

Deep, deep icy water.

Too deep for a boy who couldn't swim to save his life.

★ ★ ★

It was almost pitch black in the woods but old Gwennie didn't need a light to find her way through. She could navigate her way by the feel of the trees, the gnarled oak and the horse chestnut, the outline of the tiny gravestones in the animal graveyard.

She moved slowly, surely, until she came to the edge of the woods and then she stepped out onto the moonlit lower lawns.

57

Killivray House loomed up eerily before her. A light was on downstairs in the drawing room and another upstairs in the nursery.

She crossed the lawn as quietly as a cat, climbed the steps that led to the rose garden and hurried through. She crept across the top lawn, taking pigeon steps along the terrace as she made her way towards the drawing room window.

She stood in the shadows of the old house, watching the huge moon, listening to the roaring of the wind in the trees; the swirling of the leaves across the gravel drive; and the creaking of the ancient eaves in Killivray House.

Then she peeped through the window.

Margot Greswode was sitting hunched in a high-backed chair, an empty glass in her hands and her eyes closed, although Gwennie could tell that she was not sleeping.

It was the first time she'd seen Margot Greswode up close and in the flesh. She looked the worse for wear, her lovely face was flushed and streaked from crying and her pretty hair bedraggled. By the looks of her she'd had a good skinful and please God she'd sleep tonight.

Gwennie stood there for some time looking intently at the woman and then she made her way back across the terrace and on down to the summerhouse from where she could keep a watch on the house.

The summerhouse was unlocked and the door rattled noisily as she stepped inside. She shivered now for it seemed even colder inside than out. She breathed in the damp and decay that was all around her; the place hadn't been used for years. The gingham curtains were gone from the windows, scraps of rotten material hung there now and cobwebs covered every surface. The broken door on the cast-iron stove hung on one hinge and creaked in the draught. Cracked picnic crockery lay under layers of grime on a lopsided shelf.

She clasped her hands tightly together and recalled a summer's evening here a long, long time ago.

The air was soft, heavy with the heady scent of honeysuckle and herbs. Beyond the windows the sky was streaked with crimson weals. Wood burned in the stove and steam rose from the kettle. The cracked leather couch in the corner was bathed in the last of the sunlight and dust motes fizzed in the air. There were yellow poppies drooping in a chipped blue vase and a wasp was busy in a box of windfall apples.

She had watched him approach, making his way across from the house. She could still hear the sound of his feet on the gravel, the profile of his face as he passed the window and the sound of the door opening like an intake of breath.

He had stood for a second, framed in the doorway, the pale moon rising like a halo behind his head.

Then the feel of his arms around her, the smell of his warm skin and the first ever touch of his soft lips on her neck.

She remembered the call of the haughty peacock from the lower lawn and then suddenly a squirrel chattering angrily at them through the window.

The sound of their laughter ringing out.

Standing there together in the gathering darkness, waiting for the soft fall of night . . .

What a fool she'd been for thinking that anything could come of it or that it could ever have worked out between them. It was the arrogance and innocence of youth, she supposed, those headstrong days when everything seemed possible if only you wanted it badly enough. They'd loved each other with a passion, but they were poles apart, a huge void of class and culture between them.

It was doomed from the start and they should have known better, should have put an end to it, but they hadn't and as a result lives had been blighted.

The light went out in the drawing room of the house and a few minutes later a light was switched on in an upstairs bedroom.

Gwennie watched, waiting impatiently for the light to go out when suddenly Margot Greswode appeared at the window. She stood with her nose pressed against the pane, the palms of her hands pressed against the glass like a woman in despair, a woman desperate to escape.

If she was that unhappy all she had to do was come down the stairs and walk out into the night. But perhaps it wasn't that simple for her?

Gwennie watched the woman, tried to feel some sympathy for her but she couldn't, she didn't have it in her to feel anything other than hate and scorn for the Greswode family.

Margot Greswode remained at the window for some time and then suddenly she stirred herself, closed the curtains and soon the light went out. There was only the faint glimmer of a night light in the nursery now; the rest of Killivray House was in darkness.

Gwennie waited until she was sure that everyone was asleep, then she made her way round to the back of the house. She tried the kitchen door but it was locked. Taking a sheet of newspaper out from her pocket, she worked it underneath the door. Then she took out her penknife and stuck the blade into the lock and wiggled it around.

After a few moments the key slipped from the lock and fell onto the paper. She bent down and carefully pulled the paper towards her. The gap at the bottom of the door was just wide enough to allow the key through.

She picked up the key and let herself into the house and crept through the once familiar rooms to the hallway.

If she hadn't caught sight of her reflection in the mirror of the hallstand she could have fooled herself into thinking that time had not moved on, that she was young again and full of hope. She glanced with disdain at her reflection, at the stoop-backed woman who looked back at her, a wizened old crone, eyes bright with a hint of madness.

The house had barely changed in all the years since she'd last been here, except for the absence of the animals of course. What a madhouse it had been!

The carpets were worn now and the furniture jaded but still the silver clock tinked in the drawing room and the old stag stared patiently from his place on the wall.

She climbed the staircase one step at a time. The fifth step still creaked as it always had. The stuffed bear at the top of the stairs looked down at her enquiringly, as if to say, you've taken your time coming back.

The nursery door opened with the tiniest of clicks. She stepped inside the room and looked around her. The rocking horse still creaked in the draught and the dying embers in the fire glowed brightly. A one-eared teddy bear sat on the window seat eyeing her balefully. A dolls' house had replaced the wooden fortress of the old days and on the clothes-horse there were girls' clothes now.

How she had loved this room once. She'd always thought it would be a wonderful room for a child to have as its own. She'd hoped that one day her own child would wake in such a room as this.

She bit her knuckle to batten down the sob that was rising. Then she made her way on tiptoe towards the bed where the child lay sleeping.

The girl lay half in and half out of the covers as though she had slept restlessly. Her eyelids flickered and her mouth twitched into a fleeting smile.

So this was Charles Greswode's granddaughter!

The child whimpered and Gwennie backed away from the bedside. If she awoke now she would be terrified to see an ugly old crone staring down at her like something from a nightmare.

The girl snuggled further under the covers.

Gwennie moved closer.

She wouldn't harm a hair of the child's head of course, even though she was a Greswode. She just wanted to see her out of curiosity. She'd never clapped eyes on the girl in all the time she'd been living in the Boathouse. Poor little maid was kept like a prisoner.

She drew closer to the sleeping girl and smiled with delight. This child wasn't anything like Charles Greswode or his son Jonathan to look at. Thank God! She didn't take after her mother much either. Apart from the long hair she was the very spit of Thomas Greswode when he was a boy. She even had the small star-shaped birthmark on her neck. Gwennie ached to reach out and touch the silky hair, trace the outline of that determined little chin and stroke the soft downy skin on her cheeks. No matter that her father was determined to keep her away from the world, this child had spirit and he wouldn't be able to keep her down for ever.

★　★　★

In Nanskelly School Miss Eloise Fanthorpe stood in the upstairs study looking out as dawn broke. The storm had blown itself out during the night and now the sea was calm beneath a sky streaked with a pink and golden wash.

She turned away from the window and smiled

to herself as her eyes rested on the large, framed photograph that hung above the fireplace.

It was of a group of men standing outside an ancient house deep in the French countryside. Her father was in the photograph and on his left was a small fellow not much bigger than a dwarf but with a gigantic moustache that curled up almost to his eyes. He was holding a baby in the crook of his arm, a baby looking straight into the camera, eyes enormous with surprise. On her father's right stood a nun, smiling brightly.

She looked closely at her father's face, the sweet whimsical smile that belied such a brave heart, particularly where children were concerned. He was standing there, a frail old man although looking so vibrant, so alive and yet, a few weeks after this photograph was taken, he was dead.

She stirred herself suddenly. All this reminiscing wouldn't get her jobs done. She crossed the room and settled down at her desk to write the letters she'd meant to finish last evening.

She picked up her pen, dipped the nib into the inkpot and began to write,

Nanskelly School,
Linketty Lane
Near Freathy

Dear Mrs Greswode,
Thank you for your enquiry regarding a place for your daughter Romilly at Nanskelly School. The entrance examination takes place in May of each year and if successful your

daughter would be able to join us in September 1960. There are several scholarships of full fees available for those girls gaining a distinction in the examination . . .

When she had completed the letter she put it into an envelope, sealed it and added it to a pile that she had written earlier. Later she would ask William Dally the gardener to walk down to the village and post them.

She smiled to herself then. She was very much looking forward to meeting young Romilly Greswode. She was quite intrigued to know why the Greswodes had thought of choosing Nanskelly for their daughter considering the bad blood between Nanskelly and Killivray House in the past. Still, the past was the past and maybe it was time to bury old enmities.

She wondered if Romilly's mother was the actress Margot Lee Greswode. She and Hermione had seen her once in a play in a London theatre; a most talented and charismatic young woman and quite exquisitely beautiful too. And yet she'd played the part of a very old woman and very convincing she'd been too. Hermione had thought that she would achieve great heights on the stage, and then suddenly she had disappeared from public life.

Miss Fanthorpe stood up and stretched, then made her way down the stairs and out of the front door. It was her habit each morning to take a stroll while the girls of Nanskelly still slept.

She made her way across the lawns, past the hockey pitch and the peeling sports pavilion and on down the steep steps carved from the rock that led down to the beach.

She walked slowly along the sand, stooped to pick up a shell, turned it over in her hands and marvelled at its beauty. Further round the coast she could see the small houses in that peculiar little place that was built on the rocks; it really was quite amazing it hadn't been blown away years ago.

She could see wisps of smoke rising from the chimneys and washing already pegged out on washing lines down on the beach.

Then she noticed half a dozen cigarette butts wedged into a crack between the rocks along with an empty bottle of whisky.

That really was most odd. This was a private beach and the main access to it was from the path down which she had come. It *was* possible to get down to the beach if one walked from the opposite direction but it was one hell of a climb down and whoever had managed it must be very fit indeed. And who would make such a journey to drink and smoke themselves silly?

She walked back along the beach then climbed slowly up the steps, pausing halfway up on the viewing platform to catch her breath.

When she arrived back at the school the rising bell had gone and the girls were up, the building filled with the sounds of frantic scurrying between washrooms and dormitories.

Hermione Thomas greeted her from the doorway of the library.

'Eloise, dear, I've been to call Miss Moses and it seems she's unwell this morning and won't be able to take the girls on their morning run.' She edged closer to Eloise and whispered, 'Personally, I think she takes a little too much strong liquor before retiring and hence finds the mornings difficult.'

Eloise Fanthorpe smiled. Hermione Thomas, despite her diminutive form, could knock back several very stiff gin and vermouths most evenings!

'I'm sure she's just got a chill or an upset stomach and she'll be back on her feet in no time at all. Why don't we take the girls down onto the beach for a walk, it's a wonderful morning.'

Fifteen minutes later the fifty girls of Nanskelly School, resplendent in their scarlet uniforms, set off down towards the beach. Miss Thomas was leading the crocodile line and Miss Fanthorpe bringing up the rear. Halfway down Miss Thomas stopped on the viewing platform and gathered the girls around her. She was about to wax lyrical on the beauty of the morning when one of the smaller girls standing close to her gasped and slapped her hand over her mouth, eyes wide with surprise.

'What is it, Eveline?'

This first gasp was followed swiftly by a ripple of stifled giggling from the gathered girls.

'Silence, girls, please. This behaviour is most unbecoming.'

The girls of Nanskelly bit their lips and covered their mouths with their hands but their shoulders shook with the effort of not laughing.

Miss Thomas turned and looked down towards the beach.

She drew back aghast, threw her hands into the air and shrieked, 'Dear God in heaven, what is the world coming to?'

A man stood quite still at the edge of the sea, with his back to them. A young man as brazen as you like, standing there as naked as the day he was born. His pale flesh was goose-pimpled and his buttocks were clenched tightly against the cool wind.

Suddenly the man turned around and looked up in astonishment.

Miss Thomas screeched. 'Everyone back up the steps now! This instant! Miss Fanthorpe! We must ring for the police!'

Miss Fanthorpe was still staring at the agitated young man and wishing that they might borrow him for a life-drawing class. A very fine specimen of the male form he was too.

The girls of Nanskelly clattered noisily up the steps, past Miss Fanthorpe turning to get a last glimpse of the bewildered man who was scrabbling to pull on his trousers and make his escape. Miss Fanthorpe watched him steadfastly. If she judged that look on his face correctly it had not been merely an early morning skinny dip he was intent upon. Oh, no, here was a young man very at odds with the world, a very interesting young man indeed. She turned and, deep in thought, followed the hysterical girls back towards the school.

★　★　★

In the nursery in Killivray House Romilly Greswode ate her breakfast reluctantly. The egg was over boiled and the toast soldiers already limp and cold.

She had woken several times in the night and had a headache that was making her eyes ache.

Nanny Bea shuffled about the room, banked the fire, tidied away dirty laundry and then poured herself a cup of tea and sat down opposite Romilly at the small table near the window.

She thought that the child looked even paler than usual this morning and the dark circles beneath her eyes made her look quite ill.

She hadn't slept well herself what with the terrible storm and then worrying about Master Jonathan driving off like that after the argument he'd had with the mistress. Presently she'd ring the house in London and check that he'd arrived safely. It was quite absurd really, the way she worried about him and still called him Master Jonathan. Lord, he was a grown man yet she still thought of him as the sensitive little fellow he'd been as a child.

That first day when he'd been sent off to school had been one of the worst days of her life. He'd been little more than a baby really, just seven years of age and he'd clung to her skirts and sobbed enough to break his poor heart.

In the end Old Master Greswode had threatened him with a whipping and dragged him into the car.

He was a cruel old thing, the old master, and

that stuck-up wife of his was of no comfort to the boy at all.

'Eat up, Romilly. When I've finished my jobs we'll go downstairs and you can say your goodbyes to your mama.'

Romilly put down her spoon and looked up at Nanny Bea. 'How long will Mama be away this time?'

'About six weeks your papa said.'

'But that's ages and I don't want her to go.'

'She has to go and, you'll see, when she gets back she will be well again.'

'But I don't think she is ill now, so why does she have to go?'

'All these questions, Romilly, are really very tiresome. Your mama needs a change of air and the Anglican nuns at St Mary's will see to it that she gets the treatment she so badly needs.'

'Why is she going to St Mary's?'

'It's a new place your papa has found, rather more, er, secure than the others, where they will guarantee her a good rest.'

'But why can't she rest here? There's nothing to do here at all, she could lie down all day if she wanted to.'

'Your papa thinks a change of scenery will do her a power of good.'

'Can we go to the railway station and wave her goodbye?'

'No, dear, it's far too cold. And besides, we must prepare for this afternoon. It will be exciting to meet your new governess, won't it?' Nanny Bea said, changing the subject.

Romilly stared sullenly up at her. 'Will it really?' she said.

There was a note of sarcasm in her voice that took the old woman by surprise.

There had been a change in Romilly of late, a growing insolence about her and a tendency to sulks and flounces.

She'd started to be quite secretive about things and had been behaving in a peculiar fashion. Several times she had overheard her talking to herself. It had given her quite a turn the first time; she'd been walking past the library and for a moment she'd have sworn that Romilly really was talking to someone in there. She fervently hoped that she wasn't going to turn out anything like that damned mother of hers, all theatrical and highly strung. God alone knew that one like that in a family was enough!

'When Madame Fernaud has arrived we shall have tea in the drawing room with scones and your favourite raspberry jam.'

Romilly sighed and did not answer.

She looked out through the window and watched the smoke from the chimney on the Boathouse, where the mad woman lived, rise into a clear blue sky.

Then she said quite sweetly, 'May I leave the table, Nanny Bea, and go and play?'

'Eat up that last soldier and then you may.'

Romilly did as she was bid, then left the nursery, hurried along the corridor and climbed the narrow, uncarpeted stairs that led up to the attics.

She paused outside the attic door and listened.

Mama was still in the bathroom and Nanny Bea was humming to herself as she cleared away the nursery table. She took off her shoes and slipped inside the attic.

There was no electric light but the skylight windows let in enough daylight for her to find her way around the piles of old junk.

She tiptoed carefully across the bare boards, squeezed between an ancient gramophone, a bird cage and a broken card table and then settled herself down on the floor next to a wooden trunk. Carefully, tongue poking out in an effort of concentration, she eased the heavy lid open and looked inside.

There was a name written on the inside of the lid.

'Thomas Gasparini Greswode'. This was her secret treasure trove. She loved the smell of the trunk when it was first opened, the heady whiff of camphor and mystery.

She pulled out the scrap book first and laid it in her lap. It was old and fragile now and the dust got up her nostrils and she had to squeeze her nose to stop herself sneezing because if Nanny Bea caught her up here she'd have a telling off and the door would be locked again.

She opened the scrap book and looked in fascination at the first page.

There was a photograph of a man hanging upside down on a trapeze and a woman flying through the air towards him.

The photograph always made her gasp because there was no knowing whether the man had ever caught her.

How awful if he hadn't! She imagined the woman's face as she realized that it had gone wrong. The sweet smile turning to a terrified gasp. Then falling and falling and knowing she would die like a broken doll.

She turned the page with a shudder.

On the following page there was a photograph of a man and a woman getting married. They were standing outside a tiny church and looking at each other with soppy eyes.

Ugh. Romilly was never ever going to get married.

When you got married your husband bossed you around all the time and wouldn't let you do what you wanted. Nanny Bea would probably know who the people were in the photograph if she asked but she couldn't ask because then she'd know that Romilly had been snooping, and snooping was forbidden.

On another page a circus programme had been carefully glued in. 'Fun for everyone!' There was a picture of a smiling elephant and a monkey dressed in human clothes.

Some of the other pages were covered in boring things. Newspaper cuttings and postcards from faraway places with peculiar names.

Carcassone. Viana de Castello. Paris. Napoli. San Donato. Sienna.

On the last page of the scrap book was another photograph. It was of a boy standing outside the summerhouse in the garden at Killivray. There were pretty curtains at the windows and the door was open; she could just make out someone inside in the shadows.

The boy was dressed in a sailor suit and was holding some sort of bat; his hair was sticking out as though he had just been swimming. He was smiling at somebody or something not shown in the photograph. He had the kind of smile that made Romilly want to smile too. He looked so happy, like he was having the very best day of his life.

Sometimes, when she was allowed outside, she walked down to the gloomy summerhouse in the hope that she might find him there but she never had.

She closed the scrap book and replaced it in the trunk. Next she took out a bundle of dreary-looking letters that she couldn't be bothered to read.

There was a mouldy old atlas, a half-filled stamp album and the diary she'd found beneath a broken floorboard in the summerhouse; a diary with a lock on the front but no key.

Lastly she lifted out a small metal box and opened it carefully. Inside were the most wonderful treasures of all.

A small silver capsule that pulled apart revealing a tiny replica of a holy saint. She turned it over in her hands and marvelled at the detail on such a tiny thing. She put the saint back into the capsule and put it back into the box.

Saints were not allowed in Killivray House. Or holy pictures. They were Papist paraphernalia and once Papa found Mama's secret rosary and broke it in half and the beads fell onto the wooden floor of the dining room and made a sound like hailstones on the nursery window-panes.

Finally, she took out her most favourite possession of all.

She had found it in the nursery, wedged down behind the skirting board. She'd been afraid that Nanny Bea would take it off her so she kept it here in the secret trunk. It was a silver bird through which a tangled silver chain was threaded.

'Romilly! Romilly!'

Heck! Nanny Bea was calling loudly from the nursery.

Romilly piled the treasure hastily back into the trunk, closed the lid and tiptoed back across the attic. She put on her shoes and went quietly down the stairs.

'I'm coming, Nanny Bea,' she called when she was safely back down on the landing. 'I was just in the long room looking at a picture book,' she lied cheerfully.

Down in the hallway Mama stood beneath the huge stag's head, dabbing her nose with a handkerchief.

She had been crying and the skin around her eyes was as puffy as pink marshmallows.

She held out her arms and Romilly ran to her eagerly.

Mama hugged her tightly and Romilly breathed in her lovely smell, rose-perfumed soap that she bathed in each morning, *Midnight in Paris* perfume and an overlay of menthol cigarettes that she smoked when she had a headache.

Mama whispered in Romilly's ear, 'Be good, my darling, while I am away.'

'I will.'

'I promise you that whatever it takes this is the last time we shall ever be separated.'

Romilly whispered back, 'Oh, Mama! I hope so. Can we go with the elephant on the road to Mandalay?'

'Perhaps.' She kissed Romilly gently on the forehead.

'Mama, may I play the gramophone records while you are gone to remind me of you?'

'Of course.'

Outside a car parped its horn impatiently and Mama let Romilly go reluctantly.

'Make sure that she gets plenty of fresh air and is not kept cooped up all day in the house.'

Nanny Bea nodded curtly.

Romilly ran behind Mama to the door but Nanny Bea caught hold of her arm and pulled her back.

Instead Romilly watched from the window as an old man got out of a grey car, lifted Mama's suitcase into the boot then held the back door open for her.

Mama looked out through the window and waved, trying to keep a smile on her face.

Romilly smiled back and blew a kiss.

Nanny Bea turned away from the window with a sly smile. From what Master Jonathan had told her, Margot Greswode would be away for a great deal longer than six weeks and good riddance. Maybe, just maybe, Master Jonathan would come home more often and things could be like they used to be.

'Romilly, come away from the window please.'

But Romilly hadn't heard a word she was saying. She was staring at the small boy who was standing in the doorway of the summerhouse, a small boy standing quite extraordinarily still, looking steadfastly back at her.

'Romilly, do you hear me?' Nanny Bea's voice was sharp with impatience.

'Why is there a boy in the summerhouse?'

Nanny Bea rounded on her, 'Don't be so ridiculous.'

Romilly didn't reply, she was too busy watching the boy.

'I think, Romilly, you are having one of your sillier moments.'

'I think his name is Thomas Greswode.'

Nanny Bea stared hard at the child. 'Thomas Greswode died before you were born, before even your papa was born.'

'Who was he?'

'He was your grandfather's cousin, I believe, and not a nice boy, not a nice boy at all.'

'But he only looks about the same age as me.'

Nanny Bea stepped up to the window and looked fearfully down towards the dilapidated summerhouse.

There was no sign of a boy. How could there possibly be?

She looked at the child with concern. Romilly was transfixed as if she could really see someone.

'He's smiling at me,' she said in a faraway voice. 'I think he'd like to be my friend.'

'Well, I won't be smiling at you if you don't come away from that window this instant and put an end to this nonsense.'

Romilly turned away from the window and followed Nanny Bea obediently across the hallway without a murmur.

Nanny Bea needed a drop of medicinal brandy. Hearing Thomas Greswode's name mentioned after all this time had made her feel quite out of sorts.

★　★　★

Archie Grimble woke with a start. He was stiff and sore and his brain felt as though it was wrapped tightly in muslin, like a boiled pudding.

He sat up and touched the back of his head gingerly; there was a bump there the size of a gooseberry. He scrabbled around for his spectacles, found them and put them on.

One lens was cracked and it took some moments for his eyes to get used to the dim light. He looked around him and gasped.

He'd expected to see the familiar surroundings of his bedroom but he realized with a shudder that he had spent the night on the floor of the wobbly chapel.

He wriggled out from a black cloak that was wrapped tightly around him and tried to stand but his legs were too weak. He slumped back down onto the floor and cradled his head in his hands. His thoughts were all jumbled up as though he were half in the real world and half in a dream.

78

He could vaguely remember putting the key in the lock and coming inside the chapel but after that his thoughts were all blurred up.

He remembered being afraid because someone had tried to get into the chapel. He'd gone down some steep steps, then stumbled over something in the dark and fell.

That must have been when he'd banged his head.

He winced now as he remembered falling, then hitting the water and going down and down.

His feet touching the sea bed, cheeks puffed out with air, eyes bulging, fighting desperately to get to the top. Then the waters parted and he was gasping and coughing. The starlit sky was quivering above him and somehow he'd managed to heave himself up out of the water and onto the rocks.

He could have drowned. He hadn't though. He must have swum. Eejit! He couldn't swim . . .

He looked down at his skinny legs; they were criss-crossed with scratches, his pale skin streaked with dried blood.

Somehow he had dragged his bad leg up over the rocks, miraculously finding his way back up through the hole he had earlier fallen through. Then, trembling, his body racked with cold, sobbing with fear and relief he had found the first of the steep slippery steps that led him back up to the cupboard into the chapel.

His brain was slowly warming up, his memory returning.

He remembered that he hadn't been able to go

home because Nan had shut the Pilchard early.

He stood up again, leaning against a pew to gather his strength. His clothes were filthy and damp and he stank of mould and salt and mouse shit. He'd never been so dirty or so cold in all his life.

Mammy would have a blue fit if she saw him like this, especially if she knew he'd been out all night like a bloody tom cat and nearly drowned himself to boot. Oh, my God, by now she would have realized that he hadn't slept in his bed . . .

She'd be hysterical and the fat porker would be angry and all the men from the Skallies were probably already scouring the countryside.

Then he remembered with relief that today was market day in St Werburgh's and Mammy would have left early to catch the bus from Rhoskilly. On market days during the school holidays she always left him sleeping.

He watched as a mouse scurried down the aisle and came to rest on top of an old hymn book, whiskers twitching, eyes bright in the gloomy dawn light. It looked up at Archie curiously for a moment and then hurried off.

He could hardly believe that all this had happened to him and all because he'd made a daft promise to old Benjamin. He had been brave enough to come out in the pitch black and get into the chapel!

It was the first time in his life he'd been brave!

He didn't have much to show for it though. A bump on the head and his clothes ruined. His spectacles were cracked, his detective torch at the bottom of the sea and his legs skinned almost to the bone.

He'd done it, though, just like he'd promised and Benjamin would have been really proud of him. But he hadn't discovered any mysteries to solve.

In the distance the church clock in Rhoskilly Village chimed eight.

He'd just have to pray that he would be able to creep back into Bag End without being seen, get himself cleaned up and have a sleep, and try to get his strength back.

He made his way towards the door and just as he was about to turn the key, sunlight flooded in through the chapel window and he was bathed in a myriad of dancing colours. It was as though he had been dropped inside a kaleidoscope. He watched as the colours played across the floor and the walls.

He looked down and realized with a shudder that he was standing on a flagstone with someone's name on it. He stepped quickly to the side and peered down at the inscription.

THOMAS GASPARINI GRESWODE
BORN DECEMBER 17TH 1888
IN SANTA CATERINA ITALY
TRAGICALLY DROWNED OFF SKILLY POINT
AUGUST 21ST 1900.

Archie reckoned up in his head.

The poor thing had been only about twelve years of age when he had died.

He shivered. Poor bugger to have died of drowning.

And he was only two years older than Archie was now.

December 17th. That was today.

Happy birthday, Thomas Greswode, whoever you were.

If he'd lived he'd have been an old man by now.

Archie looked around him and thought that the chapel looked even more ghostly in the daylight than it did at night.

It was as if one day it had suddenly been abandoned; the people had left in a hurry; the door was locked and the place left just as it was.

The hymn numbers were still up on the board.

15
176
33

He knelt down and picked up the prayer book he had seen last night. There on the front page was the same boy's name. Thomas Gasparini Greswode. He flicked through the yellowing pages then slipped the prayer book into his pocket.

Then he remembered the letter addressed to him that he'd found in Benjamin's jacket.

Damn and double damn. He must have dropped it last night.

He made his way back to the cupboard and let out a delighted squeal when he saw the letter on the floor. It must have fallen out of his pocket when he'd climbed into the hole. He picked it up eagerly, put it into his pocket, hurried back through the chapel and let himself out.

The sun was rising above Bloater Row and the world was filling up with the colours of day. The sky was awash with pink and yellow streaks like a painting done with too much water on the brush. The dark roofs of the houses in Bloater Row were lightening from black to grey and the bright green moss that grew in the guttering glistened with dew. The worn-down cobbles were dappled with a syrupy light and the porthole windows of the Pilchard Inn glowed like eyes.

Outside the Galvinis' house the Virgin in her little case set into the wall peered out through the misted glass, the candle at her feet spluttering with the last of its life.

A bad-tempered crow called out from the roof of Cuckoo's Nest where the Kellys still slept behind newspaper curtains. A cockerel crowed and silver-winged gulls keened and swooped through the wisps of smoke that drifted up from the chimney of the old Boathouse.

Archie hurried along Bloater Row, the door to Bag End was unlocked and with relief he crept inside. He stood in the hallway and listened out for any sounds. The fat porker was snoring away upstairs in the bedroom. He was safe! Archie climbed quietly up the steep staircase, tiptoed across the landing and made it thankfully into his own room. He slipped out of his filthy clothes, crawled beneath the thick eiderdown and slept.

Fleep hurried back along the coastal path. He was breathing heavily and the muscles in his legs ached from running. He climbed down the path that ran behind the old Boathouse leading down to Skilly Beach. He stopped for a moment and bent double to ease his stitch.

Then he made his way across the beach and up through the hole in the rocks. Hurriedly he opened the front door to the Grockles and let himself in.

'Filthy bastards!'

Fleep spun around in fear. From his perch the parrot eyed him balefully.

'You bloody thing, you're enough to stop a man's heart!'

'Fetch the tea!' the parrot squawked.

Fleep threw himself down onto the bed. What a time he'd had. Dear God, he'd almost died of embarrassment. If only he had! Hell, that moment when he'd looked up and seen a whole army of schoolgirls grinning down at him from the cliff top. And then that old woman screaming like a raving lunatic!

Christ! He was mortified.

He lay very still for a while, hands covering his flushed face.

He couldn't get anything right, could he? If he'd managed to walk out into the sea as he'd planned then a bloody sailing ship would have come to his rescue! But to have your last swim in this world witnessed by an audience of hysterical schoolgirls and two middle-aged school mistresses. How was he to know that there was a bloody girls' school perched up on the cliffs? God almighty! He began to laugh then, quietly at first and then louder. The parrot echoed him.

Haaaaaa! HAAAA!

Fleep laughed until the sparsely furnished room echoed and somebody next door banged loudly on the wall. Then, exhausted, he closed his eyes and drifted off, for the first time in many months, into an exhausted but welcome sleep.

★ ★ ★

Walter Grimble woke, sat up and stretched out a hand for his cigarettes. He tipped up the packet and grimaced when he found it empty. He checked his watch, it was just gone eleven and Martha wouldn't be back from the market until late in the afternoon. He couldn't wait that long for a smoke. Nan Abelson, God bless the frosty bint, kept a glass jar full of fags behind the bar in the Pilchard and sold them separately. If he could get his hands on Archie's money tin he'd help himself to a couple of bob, maybe enough even for a couple of pints. A man was entitled to a few pleasures in life after all.

He sat up and listened. It was quiet in Bag End, just the tick of the clock down in the parlour and the drip of the scullery tap.

He pulled on his clothes, crossed the landing and opened the door to Archie's room. He was put out to see the boy lying asleep in his bed.

Archie woke with a start, looked up and saw

his father standing in the doorway. He flinched; he hadn't heard him get up, if he had he'd have been out of the house like a shot.

Walter stepped into the room and spotted the pile of filthy clothes in the corner where Archie had left them. He lurched over to them, lifted them up with his big toe.

'Look at the bloody state on these!'

Archie sighed.

'And good God, boy, look at your face! You look like you've been licking a cow's arse.'

'I'm sorry for getting dirty and ruining my clothes.'

'Sorry! So you bloody well should be. Where the hell have you been to get in such a state?'

Archie fell silent, bit his lip. He wasn't going to tell about the chapel.

Not even if he got belted.

'What have you been up to?'

'I . . . I d . . . don't . . . '

'Don't stammer, Archie, you know I can't abide stammering!'

'I . . . I . . . I f . . . f . . . fell in the sea.'

'Fell in the sea! Don't make me laugh! You never get close enough to the sea to fall in it!'

Archie stared down at the floor miserably.

Walter Grimble smiled, a cruel, thin-lipped smile.

'You've been up to your old tricks again, ain't you, Arch? You been sleepwalking again. Tell the truth and shame the devil.'

There was no way out. Archie nodded slowly, averted his gaze.

'It ain't natural, Archie. Normal people don't

get up in the middle of the night with their eyes shut and wander about the place like bloody ghosts.'

'Sorry.'

'Sorry my arse. Think I don't know what goes on in my own house? Think I don't know that the last few weeks your mother's been washing the sheets out every morning and the stupid clot thinks I don't realize! Always covering up for you, Archie, she is.'

Archie blushed.

His wetting the bed was a secret between him and Mammy.

Mammy said not to go worrying his head about it. It was probably to do with the shock of Benjamin dying. Worrying only made it worse. She said he'd grow out of it and that thousands of kids had the same problem.

'You piss the bed regular and you're ten years of age. Bloody disgusting that is, Arch. She should rub your bloody nose in it!'

Archie flinched and brushed away a tear.

'I blame her, mind, always treating you like a bloody baby, mollycoddling you. She wants to let you harden up a bit, make a proper boy out of you.'

'I am a proper boy,' Archie mumbled.

Walter Grimble threw back his head, opened his mouth and laughed loudly, spraying spit all over the place.

'You're an apology for a boy, Archie Grimble! A bleeding embarrassment as a son, that's what you are. And let me tell you this, keep up the sleepwalking and pissing the bed and you'll end up in a place where they take boys like you.'

Archie swallowed hard and said nothing.

'There's homes, institutions for cripples and halfwits where they shut them up, keep them out of the way so normal folk can get on with their lives.'

Archie felt the tears stinging his eyes and his throat tightening until he could barely swallow.

'Tell you what, though, maybe I'll let you off, Arch, this time. Don't suppose you've a few bob saved up?'

Archie nodded and went slowly across to the cupboard and took down his savings tin. He took out a half-crown and held it out with a trembling hand.

Walter Grimble took the half-crown but kept his hand held out, waggling his filthy fingers.

Archie went back to the cupboard and took out his last half-crown and handed it over.

Walter Grimble winked at Archie and left the room, whistling cheerfully as he went down the stairs.

Archie threw himself down on the bed and punched the pillows with his clenched fists. He hated that bloody man. He was not going to let the bloody porker put him away, locked up in an asylum.

Eventually he calmed down. He went downstairs, washed his face and helped himself to a handful of biscuits from the tin in the scullery. Then he went back to his bedroom to read the letter from Benjamin. He opened the envelope carefully, lifted the pages up to his nose. He could almost smell the old man's skin.

He'd never seen Benjamin's handwriting until now.

Dear Archie, by the time you get this letter I will be long gone. I wanted to say goodbye to you in person but that wasn't possible. I wonder if you ever will get into the wobbly chapel? Don't worry, old son, if you can't face it, I was a daft old bugger to ask you in the first place. It's a queer old place — quite ancient — and built by the first settlers in the Skallies going back to the 1600s. The same fellow who built Killivray House built the chapel and the houses here in the Skallies.

Well, my son, I've lived a colourful old life, not proud of all of it but no man is perfect, that's a fact. I've learned a lot as I've gone on and the biggest lesson I ever learned was to change, to keep on changing and never stand still in your thinking. People aren't always what they seem — usually they're a lot better, but not always. Trust your instincts, Archie, and you'll be all right.

Life brings its share of knocks and losses but we have to get by and make the most.

I've had a feeling in my water these last weeks that things may start moving and changing in the Skallies. There's a restlessness in the air and things don't stay the same for ever. I've been real fond of the Skallies, Arch, it's a quaint old place and I'll be sorry to leave it all behind — it was a sanctuary to me for many years — kept me in touch with normal

89

folk, folk down on their luck. A lot of people look down on the Skallies people but that's just ignorance and fear. It's a Halfway House of a place — but people need to move on. The tide washes over some secrets and covers them up but it throws up others, like flotsam and jetsam.

The truth is always the best option, I believe, however painful. So be sure to *search* for it and know what it is when you find it. Nan is a good old stick — tetchy but truthful. Someone you can trust.

You've hopefully got the keys by now — anything they open will be yours, remember that. Whether you find the right locks to open, well only fate will decide. Mayhap you'll find out the secrets of the past and mayhap you won't. Perhaps you don't need to and I'm just being a silly old bugger!

Trust in yourself, though, Arch, and don't let people put you down. Be sure to look after and respect that brave mother of yours, God knows she hasn't had it easy. As for the porker, well who knows — maybe his ship will come in one of these days. I've put a few shillings away over the years and there's a few bob for you when you're twenty-one. Nan knows about this and if you move on you need to let her know where you're going — best not for your mammy to know just yet. If you get in any difficulties, Arch, there's a couple of old biddies over at Nanskelly School who would do you a good turn if you were in need: Miss Thomas and Miss Fanthorpe. And of course the Galvinis can be trusted. Watch out for them Kellys, though I don't need to tell you that.

With love, old son, Benjamin

Archie folded the letter and hid it under the mattress. He'd read it again later when his eyes weren't so watery. Now he needed to get out of the house. He had to get some air into his lungs and blow away the stench of his father.

Archie stepped out into Bloater Row and looked across at Hogwash House. It would never be the same to him now. Someday someone would turn up and move in and wipe all traces of Benjamin away. They couldn't wipe Archie's memories away; he'd got them to keep. He'd treasure the letter from Benjamin and keep it for ever.

★ ★ ★

In the Boathouse Gwennie filled the battered kettle from the tap and put it on the stove to make a brew. She was all of a quiver this morning. She'd been unable to get to sleep when she'd got back from Killivray House and when she had finally drifted off she'd been plagued by terrible dreams.

It had been daft of her to go back, silly bugger that she was. She'd sworn years ago that she'd never set a foot back inside that house ever again. Yet last night she'd felt drawn to the place, felt she had to step inside one more time.

It was just an old woman's daftness, an old

91

woman still mithering about revenge. Revenge for what? For her own stupidity?

There was no one left to blame except herself and fate. It did no good going back over what might have been. If, if . . . If only. What was it her mother used to say? 'If stands stiff in a poor man's pocket.'

She filled a tin mug with tea and wandered to the window.

She opened the curtains and looked across the beach to where the window of the wobbly chapel glinted in the sunlight.

She could have sworn that there'd been someone in there with a torch last night.

Why, though? Why the hell would someone want to get in there in the dead of night?

She wouldn't go in there, not even if she was paid a King's ransom. The sooner the wind took that place away the better.

The sea was calm now after the storm and yet she knew that something wasn't right. She'd felt it ever since Benjamin had been buried. There was a peculiar tension in the air all around, a wild spirit blowing in off the sea. And that always meant trouble in the Skallies.

She knew it from the way the smoke rose from the chimneys of the houses in Bloater Row, from the strange ripples in the sand that the sea left behind and the desperate keening of the gulls out past Skilly Point. Things were out of kilter, that was for sure.

She closed the curtains, moved around the cramped room, running her hand along the rusted anchor, sidestepping the figurehead from an old ship, a sly-eyed monster of a woman with enormous breasts carved from wood. She opened the warped drawer of an old chest, took out a small metal box and lifted out a pair of tiny mittens. She held them in her gnarled hand, clenched them between her fingers, then she lifted them up to her face.

There was no smell to them that mattered any more. Just ageing wool and mildew but once they had smelled of him.

She closed her eyes and remembered the small fingers grasping her own, oh so tightly. She'd thought that he would cling on to her for ever and nobody would be able to part them.

She recalled the flicker of his eyelashes as he opened his milky blue eyes. The smell of his brow and the pulse of first mother's milk filling her breasts . . .

Then the tiny fingers being forcefully peeled away from her own and the sound of crying, sharp as glass on the freezing air. There was nothing left of him now, just this box of mementoes slowly turning to dust.

★ ★ ★

Outside the wind was fresh after the storm and the sky lightening. Archie made his way thoughtfully along Bloater Row and as he stepped through the hole in the rock he came face to face with the two eldest Kelly boys.

Donald and Kevin.

Archie stepped backwards in alarm.

They'd be bound to notice he'd been crying

93

and poke fun at him.

Donald Kelly punched him playfully on the arm. 'All right, Archie?'

He smiled a horrible, filthy-toothed smile.

Kevin smiled too; smiling didn't suit the Kelly brothers one little bit.

'Can't stop, Archie, got to go, haven't we, Kevin? We're going fishing with the old man.'

Archie stiffened, any minute now and they'd whack him.

But to his amazement they didn't, they edged carefully past him. Donald winked at him and then they raced down Bloater Row and in through the door of Cuckoo's Nest.

Archie shook his head in disbelief; someone must have cast a spell on them both.

Archie climbed carefully down to the beach.

He stood looking out to sea, the cold wind ruffling his fine hair and adding a brushstroke of colour to his pale cheeks.

He looked up at the round window of the wobbly chapel. From outside the window was nothing special but the colours when the light shone through it were wonderful.

He could hardly believe now that he'd been inside the chapel. He'd have to be brave again and go back in there, he was sure there was more that Benjamin had meant him to find, something that he had missed in the terror of last night.

He glanced warily across at the Boathouse perched on the rocks at the opposite side of the beach. The door was shut and the curtains closed, a thin wreath of smoke like a question mark rising from the lopsided chimney.

He limped down towards the water's edge, knelt down and dipped his fingers in the water. It was icy. It was a miracle to him that he had, only last night, been in the sea, touched the bottom and lived to tell the tale. It was a miracle! For a moment he thought he heard stifled laughter. He stood up and turned around quickly. The beach was empty, just the wind rustling through the reedy grass of the sand dunes.

Then he saw it.

A bottle lying half buried in the sand.

Archie gasped. He'd always hoped that this would happen one day, that he'd find a message in a bottle that would add some excitement to his dull life.

He took off his spectacles, rubbed his eyes, put them on and looked again.

It was an old green bottle, frosted with age, a rough cork stuffed into the top. Through the misted glass he could see that there was something inside the bottle. He knelt down awkwardly; his legs were stiff and sore from his battering last night. He stretched out his trembling hand . . .

The cork eased out with a gentle pop. He tilted the bottle and shook it but the piece of paper would not come out. He scrabbled around in the sand until he found a thin twig. Then he sat down, jiggled the twig around in the bottle, gently easing the piece of dirty paper towards the neck of the bottle.

Easy, easy. Damn and blast.

This time, this time. Slowly, slowly, catchee monkey.

He pinched the protruding end of grubby paper between finger and thumb and drew it out from the bottle. He unfolded it carefully, his breath scratchy with excitement.

With astonishment he saw his own name written at the top of the scrap of paper. He adjusted his spectacles and read on excitedly.

TO ARCHIE GRIMBLE
Archie Grimble has a spotty arse.

He threw down the paper, screwed up his eyes, turned around and with utter dismay saw the Kelly brothers racing down the beach towards him, whooping and shrieking like Red Indians after scalps.

He barely had a chance to get to his feet before they were upon him. He was trapped: the Kellys in front of him and the sea at his back. There was no escape.

Donald Kelly spoke first. 'What's up, peg leg, did you think someone had sent you a message?'

Archie felt the blood rush to his face. What a silly fool he was. The Kellys had always teased him and Cissie for searching the beach for bottles with messages in. He should have known that they'd had something to do with this. He'd been tricked all right. Fell for it hook, line and sinker.

Laughter cracked around him like shot glass.

'Who'd send you a message, Archie Grimble? Who'd ask you for help, eh? You couldn't punch your way out of a paper bag.'

'Why would I be in a paper bag in the first place?' Archie stammered.

Donald grew red in the face.

'Think you're funny, Archie Grimble?'

'No.'

'Shut your gob then.'

'Okay.'

'I said shut your gob.'

'I just did.'

'Go on, Donald, make him shut his big gob,' Kevin urged.

Kevin was second in command. Donald was the leader, the eldest and the one with the biggest trap.

Archie flinched as Donald grabbed hold of the front of his jersey and pulled him up close. Face to face.

There was green slime wedged between Donald's pointy teeth and his breath smelled of fried spam and onions.

A stye on his eye oozed puss. Archie could see the lice eggs in his hair, tiny orbs clinging to the strands. The frayed collar of his shirt was sticky with grease.

'Go on, Donald, whop him quick before somebody comes.'

Just then Peter Kelly came running down the beach and reached them, breathing heavily.

'Why don't you just leave him alone?' Peter said. He was the youngest of the three eldest Kelly boys.

'Why will I leave him alone?'

'Because he's littler than you, that's why.'

'So? You're littler than me and I'll belt you any day of the week.'

'He hasn't done anything to you though.'

Donald ignored him.

'What did the message in the bottle say, Archie?'

'You should know, Donald Kelly, you wrote it.'

'He couldn't have. He can't write,' Peter said with a grin.

'I can so. Just shut your mouth, Peter.'

'Don't lie, you can't even write your own name.'

'What did it say?' Donald twisted Archie's jersey into a knot bringing their faces even closer together.

Archie bit his lips and swallowed hard. There was no way he was going to repeat the words on the paper.

Not even if they tortured him.

'Say the words or I'll stick you in the guts with my penknife.'

'Say what it said, peg leg.' Kevin spat the words at him.

Archie willed the tears to wait.

'Go on, one-eyed Willy, tell us.'

'Remember, Donald, to make him take his spectacles off before you hit him or else there'll be trouble,' Kevin said.

'Take your spectacles off.'

Archie took them off and put them into his pocket.

Donald's face swam before his eyes.

'SAY IT!'

'Archie Grimble has a spotty arse.'

'Show us then.'

Archie gasped, kicked out suddenly and caught Donald on the shin with his calliper.

'You bastard cripple you. Look, he's made me bleed. Grab him, Kevin.'

Kevin got behind him now, yanked his arms up behind his back.

'Pull his trousers down,' Kevin yelled.

Archie bucked, struggled with all his might to get free. His shoulders burned beneath Kevin's grip.

Hands grabbed for his shorts, wrestled with the cricket belt, yanked them downwards. The air was cold on his skin and goose bumps erupted like molehills on his belly.

The wind whistled up the baggy legs of his underpants.

He began to sob.

'Get them down.'

'Don't, Donald!' Peter Kelly again now.

'Shut up, gobshite.'

'Bloody leave him be. Can't you see he's upset?'

'He's upset,' mimicked Donald in a squeaky voice. 'Archie Grimble is upset and crying like the big babby he is.'

Archie closed his eyes, felt the tears squeeze out between his lashes. He just couldn't bear it.

Donald yanked at the loose elastic, gave a tug.

'You'll be sorry if you don't stop.' Peter's voice now, wobbly with fear.

Gunshot rang through the air.

Echoed for ever.

Seagulls shrieked and far-off dogs barked.

Kevin let go of Archie and he fell onto the wet sand, grabbing for his underpants and shorts . . . He pulled them up over his trembling legs.

They were sopping wet and cold and the salty water stung his scratched legs. He fumbled in his pocket for his spectacles and put them on.

The world around him shifted from thick cloud to daylight.

The Kelly boys were standing before him as still as stone as if they were playing a game of statues. Their faces were as white as chip fat, eyes bulging with shock. Archie turned his head to the left.

Mad Gwennie was out on the steps of the Boathouse.

A pall of smoke twisting upwards from the gun she was pointing in their direction.

There's a song in the air but the fair señorita doesn't seem to care . . .

The Kellys were suddenly restored to life and were gone like the wind, leaping and skittering for cover.

Mad Gwennie with a gun.

Mad when riled his mammy had said.

Archie Grimble limped behind them up the beach expecting a bullet between his shoulder blades at any moment.

Oh, sweet Jesus, please make her miss . . . I'm only ten. Too young to die.

The sound of mad Gwennie's voice was echoing inside his head: 'Get off home, you little bastards, before I pepper your arses for you!'

He was crawling up the dunes, too afraid to

look behind him, sobbing and spitting out sand. He paid no heed to the barbed wire or the PRIVATE signs, he was over the fence and off into the tangled undergrowth.

★ ★ ★

By the time she reached the summerhouse Romilly Greswode was breathing heavily and her usually pale skin was flushed with colour, her eyes shining with exhilaration and fear.

She leant against a tree to catch her breath and looked anxiously back towards Killivray House. She only had a few minutes because she was supposed to be in the library reading quietly while Nanny Bea was busy making scones in the kitchen.

The summerhouse was in a sorry state. The wood was rotting and weeds and moss grew between the cracks.

The door was ajar and Romilly took a hesitant step closer but was too afraid to go inside.

In the photograph in the scrapbook the summerhouse looked such an inviting place, an exciting place for a child to enter into. The boy, Thomas Greswode, had looked so very happy standing outside there, smiling that lovely smile of his.

She tried to find the exact place where he had been standing when the photograph was taken. Just about where she was now. She turned her back to the door, took up the boy's pose, her arm raised as though she too were holding a bat and looking out at an imaginary photographer.

She smiled awkwardly; she wasn't used to smiling.

Behind her the summerhouse door creaked ominously.

Romilly turned around quickly.

The door blew gently inwards with a groaning noise.

Romilly stepped closer, pushed the door and took a deep breath as she stepped nervously inside.

It was damp and cold and the smell of decay was strong in the fetid air, cobwebs shivered in the breeze. She looked down at the ground and saw the footprints in the dust.

So someone *had* been in the summerhouse recently. Yet no one ever came to Killivray except for Papa and the delivery men from St Werburgh's. It must have been the boy Thomas, so maybe she hadn't imagined him after all.

She lifted down a cracked cup from a dusty shelf. As she tipped it towards her a woodlouse fell out of it, landed on the dusty floor and scuttled away.

She replaced the cup hurriedly and wiped her hands on her pinafore. To her right there was a large disintegrating leather sofa, riddled with holes through which tufts of horse-hair poked out. Behind the sofa there was a glass-fronted bookcase. She inched towards it, her breath loud in the silence. The glass was thick with grime, the lock rusted. She could see the shadowy outline of old books and ornaments behind the glass, a line of lead soldiers collapsed onto their sides.

She tiptoed slowly around the summerhouse.

In one dark corner there was a tea chest of old toys shrouded in cobwebs. There was an old horse carved from wood with a cart attached to it, a deflated leather ball, cracked with age and nibbled by mice and a cricket bat green with mould.

She moved back towards the door and noticed the notches cut into the door frame. Someone had made marks there as though measuring a child's height. On the left side there were marks and initials. CG 3'11". TG 3'9".

TG had grown to a height of five feet two and a half and after that there were no more measurements. TG hadn't grown very tall at all, not much bigger than Romilly was now.

CG had been the tallest by far and standing on tiptoe Romilly read six feet and one inch.

CG. Charles Greswode — that could be her grandfather.

TG. Maybe that was Thomas Greswode!

Perhaps Thomas Greswode had never grown up like other people did. Perhaps he had remained a child for ever, a child who was still around Killivray, a ghost child.

Suddenly gunshot rent the air.

Rooks exploded out of the trees in the wood with a terrible squawking. The cracked crockery on the shelf jiggled and Romilly stood rooted to the spot with fear.

A gust of wind blew the door to the summerhouse shut and the glass in the windows rattled.

She clenched her small fists and giggled

103

nervously; it was only someone out in the woods poaching.

Rough people from the Skallies looking for their dinner.

Silence now.

She walked across to the window and peeped out at Killivray House. She shivered with pleasure; how good it felt to be outside looking in instead of being shut up inside for hours on end.

She could see the shadowy movements of Nanny Bea in the kitchen. She backed away from the window and perched on the edge of the sofa, sitting on her hands to keep her clothes clean.

She thought how lovely it must have been in here in the olden days. She imagined the room cleaned up, the dust swept and the cobwebs cleared away. She imagined bright new curtains hung at the windows, wood crackling in the little iron stove and a hurricane lamp lit to chase away the gloom. Maybe you could even make a pot of tea and fill a tin with biscuits.

If only it could be like it must have been once, she could have a little hidey hole of her own!

She closed her eyes and pictured Thomas Greswode curled up on the sofa, eating a windfall apple and reading his favourite adventure book. Maybe he even slept out here in the summer?

The creak of the summerhouse door opening startled her. She opened her eyes and stared in trepidation as the door opened further.

Then it stopped. She could hear laboured breathing. A madman on the loose with a gun? A lunatic escaped from the asylum? Why hadn't she listened to Papa? He had always warned her and Mama about straying too far from the house.

You didn't know who was hanging about these days, the world was full of ne'er-do-wells and felons. She slipped silently off the sofa and ducked down behind it.

She bit her lip and made the sign of the cross the way she'd seen Mama do. Beneath her Viyella blouse her heart flailed wildly and her throat tightened with terror.

Whoever had opened the door was now inside the summerhouse and she heard the door close with a rasping noise. Stealthy footsteps crossed the dusty floor.

She must hold her breath, stay absolutely still, and keep her head down. The minutes ticked on. She was terrified of being found but even more terrified not to know what it was that she had to be afraid of. She peered warily around the side of the sofa.

A man stood with his back to her, looking out of the largest window towards Killivray House. He was humming softly to himself, a tune that her mama had in her record collection:

'*Ol' Man River, That Ol' Man River*
He must know sumpin',
But don't say nuthin',
He just keeps rollin' . . .
He jus' keeps rollin',
He keeps on rollin' along . . .'

He stopped humming and stiffened as if he had seen something unexpected. Then he turned around very, very slowly. Romilly ducked back down behind the sofa.

She'd only had the briefest glimpse of him. He wore a beige belted mackintosh and a hat that was tilted down over his eyes so that his face was completely in shadow.

For a moment she was sure that he had seen her, then she breathed out with relief as he crossed swiftly to the door and let himself out.

Romilly waited a while and then got awkwardly to her feet and made her way to the door. She peeped outside. All was quiet, just a light breeze stirring through the fir trees and the sound of the distant sea.

She stepped outside and stared into a face as startled as her own.

★ ★ ★

Clementine Fernaud checked her appearance in the mirror in the lavatory at St Werburgh's station, applied a smidgeon of powder to her nose, adjusted her hair and her spectacles and then went outside to look for the car that was to take her to Killivray House. The train had been two hours late arriving and she hoped that there would still be a car waiting for her.

She was quite exhausted and utterly frozen having spent an hour in the waiting room at Reading Station waiting for the connecting train to St Werburgh's.

She smiled with relief when she saw the car on

the station forecourt.

An elderly man got out of the car and shuffled towards her.

'You'll be the new governess for Killivray, I reckon,' he said, looking her up and down with interest.

'I am so sorry to be late,' she said politely.

'Don't worry about that. Trains never arrive here on time.'

The old man struggled to lift her valise into the car and Clementine resisted the urge to giggle as he handed her clumsily into the back of the vehicle.

'You planning on staying at Killivray long?' the man asked, glancing at her in the mirror.

Clementine kept her head turned away; she didn't want to look into his eyes.

'A few years, I dare say.'

'Suppose it won't be so bad for someone middle-aged like yourself. I reckon it would drive a youngster mad shut up there away from the world.'

Clementine smirked. Middle-aged indeed! Well, the wig and glasses had certainly worked their magic!

'Why do you say shut up away from the world?'

'Because, Ma'am, the Greswodes don't come out much. Funny lot of buggers they are. No visitors ever. I only get called out to drive about three times a year. Couple of trips to St Werburgh's and the rest of the time they stay cooped up in the house.'

'I see,' said Clementine.

'Still you're a foreigner, aren't you? Mayhap

you won't find them strange at all.'

Clementine put her hand to her mouth to cover her smile. Soon he grew tired of talking and she stared out of the window as the car bumped along the narrow country lanes.

The closer they got to Killivray House the more excited she became. This was going to be one of the best acting roles of her life and when this unexpected episode was over she would be free and life would never be as bad again. She got out of the car, thanked the driver and gave him a half-crown.

'First tip I ever had doing this run. Tight as a camel's arse that lot are, as well as peculiar,' he said, nodding towards the house.

Clementine Fernaud took a deep breath and walked up to the front door, tugged the bell pull and waited expectantly.

★　★　★

Archie Grimble gawped at the open-mouthed girl standing before him. This must be the little girl from Killivray House, the one the Skallies folk said wasn't quite right in the head.

The girl stared back at Archie, her nostrils quivering with fear, eyebrows arched. She looked Archie up and down curiously, walked around him slowly, put out a trembling hand to touch him and then seemed to think better of it. Then she said, 'Are you Thomas Greswode?'

Archie stared at her in astonishment. He shook his head and tried to find his voice.

'No,' he squeaked.

'Are you quite sure?'

People were right about her, she was nuts all right.

'I'm sure I'm not.'

'You're absolutely positive? You look a little like him.'

'Do I? Well, I'm not him because Thomas Greswode is dead.'

The girl cocked her head on one side and narrowed her eyes. 'I'm afraid you are mistaken. He, Thomas Greswode, is not dead because I saw him just this morning.'

Archie felt the hairs on the nape of his neck bristle and a tremor of fear rattled up his backbone. He took a small step backwards away from this peculiar girl; he'd met enough bloody lunatics for one day.

He knew that you were supposed to humour mad people until you had the chance to run away. You mustn't startle them or they were apt to do dangerous things.

'W . . . where did you see him?' he asked.

'He was standing inside the summerhouse,' she said defiantly. 'He was looking out of the window and he smiled at me.'

'Oh.' Archie looked uncomfortably down at his feet.

'You don't believe me, do you?' There was a tremor and the hint of a challenge in her voice.

'I, the thing is, there's a kind of gravestone thing in the w . . . wobbly chapel with his name on and it does say that he's dead.'

'When was he supposed to have died?'

'August the, er, 21st 1900.'

'But that was ages ago.'

'He drowned off Skilly Point. He was only twelve.'

The girl stuck out her chin and said haughtily, 'He couldn't possibly have drowned anyway because he's a very good swimmer.'

'How do you know that?'

'I've seen swimming certificates from his school — he can swim a mile,' she said, stepping closer to Archie.

Archie gulped.

'There are loads of his things in a secret trunk up in the attic.'

The girl smelled of roses, of cinnamon and freshly washed cotton.

'Did he used to live here then?'

'Of course he did, he was a Greswode. Greswodes have always lived here.'

'It says on the gravestone thing that he was born in a place called Santa Caterina in Italy.'

Romilly looked closely at the boy.

Archie looked away and glanced across at Killivray House.

'It's a nice house,' he said, trying to change the subject.

'No it's not. It's horrid and haunted and I hate it.'

'H . . . how do you mean it's haunted?'

She moved closer to Archie and dropped her voice to almost a whisper, 'At night the creatures come alive.'

Archie swallowed hard and crossed his fingers behind his back for luck.

'What sort of creatures?' he asked anxiously.

The girl eyed him steadily. 'Tigers mostly and sometimes bears.'

She was crackers. Loop the loop.

He couldn't think of anything to say and looked down at his feet.

'Why did you come here?'

'S . . . someone w . . . was chasing me and I escaped into the woods.'

'Was it a madman after you with a hatchet?'

'Ah, no, just some kids who don't like me. I think I'd best be going now.'

'Where do you live?'

'In Bag End.'

She wrinkled her nose and then smiled.

She had a nice smile.

'That's a funny name. Where is your house?'

'Over there in the Skallies.' He pointed towards the woods.

She opened her mouth in surprise and said breathlessly, 'Is it true that all the people who live there are mad?'

'No. Well, some of them are. Have you never been there?'

She shook her head.

'I could take you there one day if you wanted,' he said, and then wished that he hadn't.

'I'm not allowed.'

'Why?'

'Papa thinks the world isn't a good place for a child to roam in.'

'It sounds funny you saying 'Papa' like that.'

'Why?'

'Kind of old-fashioned and posh.'

'What do you call your papa?'

'Father, mostly,' Archie said, 'and something else besides.'

'What?'

Archie lowered his voice, 'The big, fat, stinking, hairy porker.'

Romilly slapped her hand over her mouth to stifle her laughter. She'd never heard anything so rude or so funny.

'Say it again.'

'The big, fat, stinking, hairy porker.'

'Quick, come into the summerhouse. If Nanny Bea hears me out here then she'll kill me. I'm not supposed to be out in the garden alone.'

Blimey, this girl was more of a prisoner than he was.

He followed her obediently but reluctantly into the summerhouse.

'Tell me, did you see a man coming out of here?'

'Where?' Archie looked round fearfully.

'From the summerhouse? I mean he's gone now, but he came in here and I hid behind that smelly sofa over there. It's very peculiar because no one ever comes to Killivray, ever.'

'I didn't see anyone at all.'

Archie looked around the summerhouse in wonder. It was a dump of a place all right but a very interesting dump.

'This is a great place,' he said. 'Imagine if you could make it into a den, you could play here for hours.'

Romilly stared at Archie. 'That's what I was

just thinking before you came but I wouldn't be allowed.'

'Why? Wouldn't your mammy and daddy be glad for you to be out from under their feet?'

'I'm not allowed out on my own. I shouldn't be here now.'

'What do you do all day?'

'I read. Have boring lessons with my governess. Play with my toys.'

'Do you have many toys?'

'Hundreds,' she said quite simply.

It was Archie's turn to stare now. She must be very rich.

'I'll have to go in a minute,' Romilly said, 'but would you promise to come back here again one day?'

Her voice was eager, her eyes very bright in the dusty gloom of the summerhouse.

'I don't know,' he said uncertainly.

'Maybe I could find out more about Thomas Greswode, prove to you that he's alive,' she said hopefully.

'Okay then. Would I just knock on the front door?'

'No! Nanny Bea would shout and send you packing. I have an idea though. Why don't you leave me a letter inside the stove over there and if I can escape again I'll write back.'

Archie grinned. 'I have some invisible ink at home, I could use that.'

Romilly's eyes lit up. 'Oh would you? That would be fun!'

'All you need to do is warm the paper up, but be careful, you don't want to burn your hair off!'

'I'll be careful, I promise.'

'Is it safe for me to come into the grounds, there aren't any dogs or anything?'

'No. Just a ghost dog who lives in the stables. But don't get seen by anyone in the house whatever you do. Now I have to go or else.'

'I don't even know your name.'

'Romilly Greswode.'

'I'm Archie Grimble.'

'Goodbye, Archie Grimble.'

And with that she was out of the door and he was left alone in the spooky summerhouse where the smells of mould and decay mingled with the sweet scent of cinnamon and roses.

He hoped that the man Romilly had seen didn't decide to come back now and catch him in here. He wondered if she really had seen a man or whether she'd just imagined it. After all she'd said she'd seen Thomas Greswode and that was impossible. Perhaps she saw things all the time, ghosts and dead creatures; things that weren't really there.

Weak sunlight streamed in through the window and dust motes swirled in the air and for a moment he felt as though he was not alone; his skin tingled and the hairs on his arms prickled with fear. Then he saw the writing on the window. On the dusty pane someone had written two words, *Murder Scene*.

Archie shivered.

Had Romilly Greswode written it herself?

He looked out anxiously through the summerhouse window towards Killivray House.

It was an ancient house with walls the colour

114

of pencil lead, and enormous windows made up of hundreds of tiny diamond panes. Above the giant front door there was a faded coat of arms and the date 1640.

A light burned behind one of the downstairs windows and a stooped figure moved slowly behind it.

It was a very beautiful house but there was an air of grim melancholy about it that seemed to seep into Archie's bones as he stood looking at it.

He felt curiously drawn to the house, aching to get closer and peep in through those intriguing windows.

He thought of Thomas Greswode who'd lived there all those years ago and ended up drowning off Skilly Point when he was only twelve years old.

It was odd that Thomas Greswode's name seemed to keep popping up everywhere he went.

Maybe the funny little girl really *had* seen the ghost of Thomas Greswode, maybe he roamed the grounds because his soul couldn't rest; he'd heard that the dead did that sometimes. Perhaps Thomas Greswode hadn't drowned at all. Maybe he'd been murdered!

At last, he really might have a real mystery to solve.

★ ★ ★

In the drawing room Romilly sat beside Nanny Bea on the sofa opposite Madame Fernaud who sat sedately in a wingbacked chair. Romilly ate a scone daintily and sipped her tea politely but she did not once take her eyes off the face of the new governess.

Romilly thought that she was a very dull-looking woman, a charcoal sketch of a woman, all shadows and harsh lines.

She had horrid thick grey hair the colour of wire wool and a funny way of wrinkling up her nose when she drank her tea. She was constantly patting her mouth with a napkin and adjusting her spectacles. She smiled at Romilly uneasily and the girl stared back with steadfast politeness but without returning her smile.

Romilly didn't like the look of Madame Fernaud one little bit and it irked her that Nanny Bea seemed so friendly towards her. Romilly definitely was not going to be friendly with her; she already knew that she was going to hate her as much as she had hated Miss Naylor. Even more. There was something rather peculiar about the new governess. She was quite plain and dowdy yet behind the exterior there lurked something very powerful, something dangerous. Romilly could feel it.

After a while Romilly closed her eyes and listened half-heartedly as the two women discussed Romilly's school timetable. There was tedious talk of Mental Arithmetic and mathematical problems; of history and geography; drawing and needlework; French and Latin lessons.

Romilly stifled a yawn and Nanny Bea, noticing, said, 'Romilly, you poor child, you look absolutely exhausted. Why don't you take a rest in the nursery while Madame Fernaud and I become acquainted with one another?'

Romilly stood up, flicked a weak smile at Madame Fernaud and then left the room, closing the door quietly behind her.

Instead of going upstairs she doubled back through the dining room and hid herself under a table behind the far door of the drawing room from where she could eavesdrop on the conversation. If Nanny Bea left the room she would have time to race up the servants' stairs and get into the nursery before she was discovered.

Nanny Bea poured more tea for Madame and herself and settled back on the sofa. She was quite enjoying her conversation with the new governess. She spoke English quite beautifully though with a very faint French accent. She seemed such a very sensible type of woman and well educated for a French person. She smelled quite pleasant too; there was no whiff of that awful garlic and oil that the French were wont to drown their food in. She looked as though she had her wits about her and would be able to keep a very sharp eye on Romilly. She didn't look the sort of woman who would brook any nonsense at all, thank goodness.

'I'm so very glad that you're here, Madame Fernaud, it's so good to have some adult company again. And since Miss Naylor left us it really has been far too much for me looking after a young child at my age.'

Clementine Fernaud smiled and put down her tea cup. 'I shall endeavour to keep Romilly fully occupied. I think maybe her education has been a little, er, spasmodic of late?'

Nanny Bea beamed, how intuitive this woman seemed to be, a trustworthy type of woman, one you would be able to confide in.

'The last governess left rather suddenly, she was a very nervous woman, very fretful and dreadfully poor company.'

'Does the child have no mother?' Madame Fernaud asked hesitantly.

Nanny Bea coughed then said, 'Oh, yes, she does *have* a mother, but it's rather a delicate issue, you understand. Her mother is greatly troubled by nerves, always was since she was a young girl.'

'Ah, the nerves are a very troublesome thing, *n'est ce pas?*'

Nanny Bea leant towards Madame Fernaud and lowered her voice, 'Just between ourselves, of course, the master has had a very hard time with her. She is quite unstable at times, although thankfully not dangerous either to herself or others.'

'I see.' Madame said thoughtfully.

'It wasn't a suitable marriage for the master if you understand my meaning.'

'I see.' Madame Fernaud smiled sympathetically and lowered her eyes.

'The mistress was from a moneyed family but a family devoid of good breeding.'

'Where is Romilly's mother at the moment?' Madame Fernaud asked.

'She is with the nuns at St Mary's. It's a private nursing home for those of a delicate nature.'

Madame nodded and sipped her tea.

'I understand a little about these things, I had a distant cousin much the same. It was a tragedy of course, such a handsome man and yet unable to live a normal life. Indeed his papa had to have him watched constantly and it was such a strain for all the family.'

'What happened to him?'

'Ah, so sad, he swallowed poison and died, a terrible ending for him but some peace at last for the family.'

Nanny Bea leant closer to Madame Fernaud. 'You understand so well, my dear, the master has had the same terrible worry, it's why we live here so quietly. Indeed much of my time was spent keeping an eye on Mrs Greswode. I'm afraid it's all been such a strain on me, why I haven't had a holiday in three years.'

Madame Fernaud threw up her hands and quite startled Nanny Bea. 'Mon dieu! That is most terrible, so bad for the health to be so long without a rest!'

Nanny Bea sighed. 'Yes, I used to spend a few weeks each year with my sister in Dorset and I have to admit I miss it sorely.'

'Maybe, maybe in time, when Romilly and I are used to each other, you might be able to take a little holiday if Mr Greswode approves.'

Nanny Bea smiled and patted the governess's hand fondly. She was going to get on famously with Clementine Fernaud and she was sure that Master Jonathan would be very pleased with this new governess and her sensible ways. She was really quite the sort of woman he should have married, if she hadn't been quite so plain and foreign of course.

Just then the telephone rang and Nanny Bea stood up stiffly and made her way into the hallway. She returned a few moments later and sat back down heavily.

She looked quite flushed, her eyes very bright.

'Is everything all right?'

'That was the master checking that you had arrived safely, such a very thoughtful gentleman. Some troubling news, though, I'm afraid.'

'What has happened?'

'The nuns have just telephoned Mr Greswode. It is as we expected. The mistress has arrived in the most terrible state, quite deranged it seems! She will, I fear, be a very long time away this time.'

'How very sad,' said Madame Fernaud simply.

'Yes, very sad indeed, but not entirely unexpected.'

★　★　★

Romilly splashed her face with cold water and stared at herself in the mirror above the washstand. Her face was very pale, her eyes red-rimmed and ugly from crying and there were smoky smudges beneath her bottom lashes. Her hair was tied as it always was in two tidy plaits with blue gingham ribbons at the ends. How she would like to take up a pair of sharp scissors and cut them off!

She studied her face carefully; she had none of

Mama's pretty features. Romilly's nose was more like an afterthought, blobbed carelessly in between her large eyes. Unlike Mama she had a wide mouth and fuller lips. Her eyes were larger than Mama's, but the same inky blue with thick eyelashes.

She breathed in and out slowly and tried to calm herself. Nanny Bea was a liar, a hateful, hateful liar. There was nothing wrong with Mama; it was just being shut up here all the time that made her restless. Killivray House was enough to make anyone go mad!

Nanny Bea had said Mama would be away for a very long time. How long was a very long time? Every time she went away it seemed like an age before she came back again and each time she did she seemed a little thinner and paler. Romilly worried that one day she would be sent away and disappear altogether. And then what would become of Romilly?

If only she were brave enough she would chop off her silly hair, borrow some clothes from Archie Grimble, find a suitcase, pack her things and run away. Maybe she could find out where Mama was and she could take one of Papa's guns and frighten the nuns, make them give Mama back. Romilly would rescue her and they could hide up in the mountains and live in a cave where no one could ever find them.

She turned away angrily from the mirror, wandered across to the window and stood looking down towards the sea.

To the left of the beach she could see the hole in the rock that led through to the place they called the Skallies. The houses were hidden but she could see the smoke rising from the higgledy-piggledy chimneys. She wondered what the boy Archie Grimble was doing right now? Was he in the funny house called Bag End having afternoon tea with the big, fat, stinking, hairy porker? She giggled at the thought. Maybe at this very moment he was writing her a letter with his invisible ink. She hoped that Archie Grimble would come back soon and leave her a note in the little stove. How exciting it would be to have a secret friend! Tonight when she knelt down to say her prayers she'd say a prayer for Archie Grimble.

And two for Mama of course.

But tonight she wouldn't pray for horrid Nanny Bea or bad-tempered Papa. And never for Madame Fernaud whose silly cousin drank poison and died.

She walked across to the door that led into the schoolroom, turned on the light and went in.

The light was dim and the room was cast in gloomy shadow. There were four ancient desks in the schoolroom and a larger table with a globe on top of it.

She turned the globe round slowly, found the boot shape of Italy and traced her finger dreamily around it. She screwed up her eyes and looked to see if she could find a place called Santa Caterina.

There was no sign of such a place. That's

because Thomas Greswode hadn't been born there at all.

She sat down at her desk, opened the lid and took out her dog-eared atlas. She turned to the index at the back and looked up Santa Caterina.

No sign of it.

She looked down at the atlas and found Naples without too much trouble. Then she noticed that further along the coast someone had ringed a spot on the map with a pen. Alongside it they had written, Santa Caterina!

Romilly sucked in her lips and thought hard.

Perhaps, just perhaps, Thomas Greswode *had* been born in this faraway place. Perhaps he had really died off Skilly Point just like Archie Grimble had said. Maybe she'd just imagined seeing him because she'd been so desperate for company.

She wished now that she'd paid more attention to Miss Naylor's geography lessons. She did remember a little about Italy though; it was warm and they ate loads of tomatoes, had good singing voices and ice creams as big as your head. Why had Thomas Greswode come all the way from sunny Italy to gloomy old Killivray?

Maybe he had sat right here in the schoolroom at one of these desks, looking out through the windows at the grey skies and dreaming of Italy.

It was so sad if he really had died like the boy Archie Grimble had said, drowned when he was only twelve years old.

When she could escape again she was going to go back to the attic and find out as much as she could about Thomas Greswode. Maybe she'd get an exercise book and write down anything she found out about him and when she met up with Archie Grimble again, if she ever did, she would tell him everything she had learned.

What was it that Nanny Bea had said about Thomas? He was your grandfather's cousin and he wasn't a nice boy, not a nice boy at all!

Romilly didn't care what Nanny Bea said! In the photograph he looked like a nice boy, in fact he looked like a very nice boy indeed. Anyway, if he wasn't the sort of boy that Nanny Bea would like then Romilly was bound to like him.

Archie Grimble wouldn't be the sort of boy that Nanny Bea or Papa would like one little bit. A grubby-faced boy with scruffy clothes and hair that looked as if it had been cut with a bread knife. A real, live, rough boy from the Skallies! Romilly hugged herself with excitement.

She had found a friend. Her first ever friend was a funny little boy with round spectacles, enormous blue eyes and a skinny leg in a cage.

Romilly replaced the atlas, closed the desk and looked up in alarm to see Madame Fernaud standing in the doorway watching her.

Romilly blushed and looked down at the desk.

'You are very keen, Romilly,' Madame Fernaud said smiling.

'Not really, I was just looking something up in the atlas.'

'Anything that I may be able to help you with?'

'No, thank you.'

'Tomorrow we shall begin our work together,

Romilly, won't that be good, eh?'

Madame Fernaud suppressed the desire to laugh for she could see from Romilly's carefully controlled face that she could barely disguise her dislike of her new governess. Madame Fernaud smiled her sweetest smile and thought that she would soon have Romilly Greswode eating out of the palm of her hand and then the fun would start.

Part Two

It began to snow in the Skallies; large, feathery flakes drifted down from a sky the colour of navy chiffon.

Archie Grimble stood alone looking up in wonder at the moon that glittered above the ragged rooftops while all around him a strange white silence fell.

In the candlelit windows of the houses in Bloater Row the tinsel on makeshift Christmas trees glistened. Christmas was almost here and there was a hint of the smell of tangerines and sticky dates in the icy air.

He heard the howl of the wildcats in the yard of the Pilchard Inn and the tinkle of wistful piano notes from Periwinkle House.

In the distance the stable clock of Killivray chimed the hour and an owl called out timidly from the woods. He wondered if the ghost animals were on the move in Killivray House. He imagined Romilly Greswode caged in behind the frosted windows of the old house while the ghost child Thomas Greswode peered in from outside or padded about up in the attics.

He waved up at Cissie Abelson who was looking down from her bedroom window above the Pilchard Inn. She grinned down at him, her face a pale moon; waved a podgy hand and then blew him a puckered kiss.

He'd called for Cissie earlier but Nan said she

had found a hidden selection box and stuffed herself stupid. She'd been sick twice and put to bed early.

Archie lingered outside the door of Skibbereen where Mr and Mrs Galvini lived. He closed his eyes, sniffed up the host of glorious smells that drifted out from the house and licked his cracked lips.

The Galvinis' house breathed out the smells of food.

Ham and sausage; cheese and pastry; marzipan and almonds; oranges and lemons.

It was such a happy house, full of chuckling and laughter, nothing like Bag End where he lived.

A sound startled him and Archie opened his eyes. Mrs Galvini stood wedged in the doorway of Skibbereen, hands clasped across her ample bosom, looking down at Archie.

'I didn't see you standing there,' Archie muttered.

'I think for a minute you sleeping standing on your feets,' said Mrs Galvini, a wide smile jerking her eyes into twinkling stars.

'I was just thinking.'

'You stops thinking now. Too much thinking boils your brains. Come in, come a in. *Mama Mia* you must be freezed to death, Archie! It's enough to freeze them kernackers off the china monkeys. Come see, I have made much food tonight. You must eat some and be full up and warm your bones.'

Archie stamped the snow off his boots and followed Mrs Galvini eagerly into Skibbereen, along the draughty hallway and past the door on the left that led into the front parlour.

Archie was fascinated by the Galvinis' parlour; it was more like a grotto than a room. In a glass-fronted cabinet there were delicate flowers and tiny animals made from glass of every imaginable colour. On a polished sideboard there were intricate music boxes and fancy ornaments. On the walls there were framed Madonnas of every shape and form. There were fat ones and thin ones, miserable ones, and brazen ones with eye shadow and ruby lipstick.

The parlour in Bag End was brown and dowdy. Two mean-faced greyhounds with rabbits in their mouths guarded the window sill. An ugly king glowered from the front of a mug on a worm-eaten shelf. On one wall there was a picture of a faded pope and a china angel with a busted wing sulked on the mantelpiece. The parlour in Bag End smelled of polish and flypapers. And damp, rising fast.

The Galvinis' parlour smelled of lemons and lilac and freshly starched antimacassars.

Reluctantly he drew his eyes away from the treasures of the Galvinis' parlour and followed Mrs Galvini into the warm fragrance of the kitchen.

'Sit down and I gets you something to eat. Feed you up a bit, eh? Not enough of the fat on you to grease a blooming kipper.'

Archie smiled, rubbed the steam from his spectacles and sat down at the big scrubbed table.

'See this house I lives in is called a Skibbereen,

eh? From this funny name of place there are starving people who come across the sea many years ago?'

'Ah yes, Skibbereen was in Ireland where they had the potato famine. Ireland is where my mammy was born, but just after the potato famine I think.'

'I says to my Alfredo, our house called after starving-people place but no one ever starve at the Galvinis' now, eh?'

Archie giggled and looked around him. A kitchen dresser groaned beneath the weight of glass jars stuffed with all kinds of lovely things to eat. Fat, red tomatoes and pears the colour of gold. Goooseberries and grapes. Peaches and plums.

Out in the pantry he could see the dark shapes of the smoked hams that hung from hooks and sausages dangling from the ceiling like meaty stalactites.

Mammy said even the woodlice in the Galvinis' garden were giant-sized and the mice were as big as cats and too fat to get back through the holes in the skirting boards.

'Nearly a Christmas now, little Archie?'

'Only a few days away.'

'What you a want for Christmas?'

He wanted to say that he'd like a policeman to come and cart the porker away to gaol, but he didn't.

'A book on Sherlock Holmes and a penknife with a tortoiseshell handle.'

'You don't want much. I ask that Kelly boy, the ugly one, and he tell me a list as long as a sausage.'

132

Archie giggled.

'Mrs Galvini, have you ever heard of a place in Italy called Santa Caterina?' he asked innocently.

Mrs Galvini wrinkled up her nose. 'Santa Caterina? How you spell this place, Archie?'

He spelled it out from memory.

Mrs Galvini spun around. 'Ah! Not like you say Santa Kate-rina. Iss Santa Caterina!'

There was a trace of tears in her eyes as she spoke. 'Santa Caterina. Oh, so beautiful a little place, I been there many times. How you know this word, Archie?'

'I . . . I looked it up in the dictionary,' he lied and blushed. He tried to keep the excitement out of his voice as he spoke. 'Did you live there, Mrs Galvini?'

'No, me I come from Napoli.'

Archie tried to hide his disappointment. 'Is Alfredo from Napoli too?'

'No, no, my Alfredo he is from island called Ischia but he has an aunt in Santa Caterina — she's a, how do you say here, a nun, yes a nun. A holy sister. Now she very old but still got all her own teeth.'

Archie wondered if Alfredo's aunt would be about the same age as Thomas Greswode would have been if he'd lived.

'I have snapshot of Sister Isabella. Let me find for you while you eating. *Una momento.*'

Mrs Galvini opened the door of the oven and lifted out a large plate-sized pastry in the shape of a big yellow sun. Archie stared at it in fascination as Mrs Galvini began to slice it expertly.

'Here for you some Napoli pizza. Eat and make you strong.'

Mrs Galvini left the room and he heard her rummaging about in the parlour and muttering to herself.

Archie ate hungrily, wondering as he did if this Isabella person might have known Thomas Greswode when he was little, in the days before he came to Killivray House.

Mrs Galvini bustled back into the room blowing and beaming, put down an old chocolate box on the table, pulled up a chair and sat down heavily next to Archie.

'Let me find for you. Ah, here we are. See, this is Sister Isabella.'

Archie looked down at a faded brown and white photograph of a young girl smiling cheekily at the camera. She was wearing a long, white party dress and her hair was tied in untidy pigtails.

He looked up at Mrs Galvini with a confused expression on his face.

'This is Isabella when she a little girl. Alfredo's mama say she very beautiful and always very full of the mischief. One day she wants to join the circus and then one minute she in love and then, boom! All of a sudden she goes off to be a nun. God is calling her, you see. And when the good God calls you must answer him.'

His mammy always said the same, that when God called you must answer him but Archie had made up his mind that he wasn't going to. If he heard God calling him he was going to hide under the stairs and cover his ears.

'See here is another one, outside the convent where she been many, many years a nun.'

Archie looked down at a photograph of an elderly woman dressed in a nun's habit standing outside an ancient building with barred windows like a prison.

'How did you meet Alfredo?' Archie asked, changing the subject.

'Me and Alfredo we meet on ferry boat and he making big eyes at me like this.'

She demonstrated a lovesick Alfredo and Archie laughed and blushed at the same time.

'What's it like, this Santa Caterina?'

'Iss very beautiful.'

'Is it a big place?'

'No, is very small.'

'So would Alfredo know everyone who lived there?'

'*Si, si*. Alfredo go there for the holidays when he a little boy. Know nearly everybody there then but now it's a long time since he been there. Sister Isabella, though, she got a mind like the elephanto, she know everything go on in Santa Caterina even though she shut up in the convent.'

Archie sighed, how he'd love to go and talk to this old woman. Try and find out a bit more about Thomas Gasparini Greswode.

'You enjoy my cooking, Archie?'

'Oh, yes, it's lovely.'

He eyed the pizza hungrily and Mrs Galvini ruffled his hair affectionately then cut him another large slice and pushed it towards him.

'One day, I say to my Alfredo, one day we

135

open a shop or maybe a *ristorante* like we had in Napoli and we sell lots of Napoli pizza but he says, Lena, it will never catch on, eh. So we still living here in these Skallies,' Mrs Galvini said sadly.

'Don't you like the Skallies, Mrs Galvini?'

'Ah, *si*, for me this is home for now; one day when it's safe maybe I go back to Napoli though. Maybe even go to Santa Caterina again for holiday,' she said in a dreamy voice.

'Isn't it safe in Napoli?'

'Not for my Alfredo, some bad men there, very bad.'

She motioned someone slitting a throat and Archie watched her with wide eyes.

He wondered how Mr and Mrs Galvini had found their way from Napoli to the Skallies.

He was about to ask her when the front door opened and Alfredo Galvini came hurrying into the house bringing with him a flurry of snow.

'Ah, Lena, I am freezed to the bloody bones. Hey, Archie boy, it's good to see you.'

'I just telling Archie that in Napoli we have a little *ristorante* but bad men make trouble and we have to go.'

Alfredo pulled off his overcoat and muffler then sat down at the table.

'Don't be telling him all the bad things, Lena, he only a little boy.'

'Little boy maybe but very clever boy, he just asking me all about Santa Caterina. He seen it in a what you call it, dishionary.'

Alfredo Galvini scratched his head and looked long and hard at Archie.

'Not a dictionary exactly, Mr Galvini, an atlas, we have them in school.'

Alfredo leant across and stroked Archie's cheek. 'It's a good place Santa Caterina, very warm in the summer; you can swim all day if you want. So many fish too, you can pull out a fish fresh for your supper from the sea. You would like it there, Archie. Maybe one day you go and see for yourself, eh?'

'I'd like to but I don't expect I ever will. I don't suppose I'll ever even leave the Skallies.'

'When I was little boy, I never think I leave Italia and come all way here,' he said, but there was a wistfulness in his voice that made Archie feel sorry for him.

The Galvinis hadn't chosen to come to the Skallies, they'd come to escape from the bad men of Napoli. He wondered for the first time ever why his mother had left Ireland behind. His father was English so they must have met after she left and then come to the Skallies together. He knew from some old photographs he'd found in a tin under his mammy's bed that the house where she had grown up had been big and she'd had her very own pony. And her sister, the one with the whisper of a name, once had a dog called Pickles, who chased chickens and buried his bones in the rose bed. Why would his mammy have left all that behind to come to the Skallies? Was she running away from bad men too? She didn't need to, he thought sadly, she'd brought one along with her.

'Mr Galvini, do you think that everyone who lives in the Skallies is here because they're running away from something?'

Mr Galvini sighed and helped himself to a slice of Mrs Galvini's Napoli pizza. He chewed thoughtfully for a few seconds and then said, 'Maybe, Archie, maybe we all running away from something. Some of us knows it and some of us don't. Somehow we finds this little place up here on the rocks. And for a while we all safe, eh? Then one day maybe we go away as quickly as we come. No one knows what the future is holding for us.'

'Do you think that Benjamin Tregantle was running away from something?' Archie asked.

Mrs Galvini laughed, 'No, he was very brave, very brave man. Nothing ever frighten him! If he catch the bad men from Naples he tell them take a jump. Then he go Poof, poof and knock them down flying.'

Archie smiled at the thought of Benjamin fighting off the bad men from Naples.

'Did Benjamin live all his life here in the Skallies?'

'No, I don't think so,' Mr Galvini said. 'I think he live with his papa and mamma in 'Ogwash 'Ouse but then he away a long time then come back here to place where he born when he much older.'

Archie was puzzled. Something was bothering him. Benjamin had left the letter for him in his jacket pocket so did that mean that he knew he was going to die? He couldn't have, though, because everyone had said it was an accident, hadn't they? Maybe it wasn't an accident, maybe Benjamin had been murdered? Maybe Benjamin

and Thomas Greswode had both been murdered.

And if that was true then the Skallies wasn't a
safe place to be at all.

'Well, I best be going, Mrs Galvini, Mr
Galvini. Thanks a bundle for the food.'

'You welcome here any time, Archie. You come
Christmas morning, eh, and I have little surprise
for you,' Mrs Galvini said.

He took his leave and closed the kitchen
door, pausing outside the parlour for another
glimpse at the gaudy treasures inside. He
heard Mr Galvini say quietly, 'He asking many
questions, Lena, be careful what you tells him.'

'He's just a curious that's all.'

'It's not for us to interfere, Lena. We don't
know why his family comes to the Skallies, eh?
Mrs Grimble keep herself very private. Never
saying anything 'bout where she come from.
Maybe she got something secret she don't want
no one to know, like the rest of us.'

Archie stepped out into the icy night and
closed the door to Skibbereen quietly.

The parrot in the Grockles squawked, 'Shoot
the bloody bastards!'

He wondered if everyone in the Skallies had
something to hide. Did Nan? And the quiet
Misses Arbuthnot? Even his own mother!

Maybe the porker wasn't his real father.
Maybe his real father was a prince or a rich man.
Just a nice one would be okay.

That would be a great secret.

Archie walked towards the hole in the rock
and stood looking down on to Skilly Beach. In

139

the window of the Boathouse a candle burned fitfully. He wondered what mad Gwennie was doing in there all alone? She wasn't a safe person to be around, that was for sure.

He looked up at the enormous moon that sailed above and drew in his breath. It was the sort of moon old Benjamin used to call a Wildcat Moon.

He remembered Benjamin once saying, 'Look up there, Archie, don't see the moon like that often. Look close and you'll see the imprint of a cat's paw. That's a Wildcat Moon tonight.'

And while Archie had strained his one good eye to look for the paw in the moon the wildcats in the yard of the Pilchard had started to wail.

'Listen to them, Archie, it's like an invisible conductor in an orchestra has waved his baton. A Wildcat Moon always means change, Archie, whether we want it or not.'

Archie hurried along Bloater Row and let himself into Bag End just as the wildcats began to wail.

* * *

Clementine Fernaud hurried away down the drive of Killivray House, head bent against the icy wind, snowflakes settling on the brim of her felt hat and twinkling in the gloaming.

It was a long walk to the village but she had to get to a telephone box and put through an urgent call. She couldn't have risked telephoning from the house; Nanny Bea wasn't a problem, but Romilly had ears like a bat and always seemed to be watching her, scrutinizing her suspiciously as if wanting to find fault.

She couldn't afford to let the child know who she was and give the game away, too much depended on keeping her identity a secret.

When she reached the village she looked around at the twenty or so houses that made up the main street of Rhoskilly. The curtains were all drawn against the cold night and the smell of wood smoke was strong in the air.

She found the telephone box and was dismayed to find it occupied by a large man with his back towards her. She stepped into the shadows and waited.

She heard scraps of the conversation from inside the box: 'I tell you there could be money in it for you. I've been in there and there's a fair few antiques. I've helped myself to a few already. All we need is transport . . . wait for the right moment . . .

'Of course it's safe. I've had about as much as I can take here. I've been enquiring about a school, an institution for the cripple . . . and then I'm out of here. Of course Martha'll come, she'll have no bloody choice . . .

'You think on it. I can't take much more of this godforsaken hole. Easy pickings, man. I'll ring you after Christmas.'

With that the man slammed down the receiver.

Clementine moved further into the shadows and watched as a fat, unshaven man came out of the telephone box. He cleared his throat, spat into the snow, took a cigarette from behind his ear and struck a match.

For a second the man's face was illuminated.

He had pockmarked skin and a large, bulbous nose. One of his front teeth was missing. He was an ugly-looking brute if ever she'd seen one.

Clementine drew in her breath as he passed close by her, the smell of tobacco and stale sweat strong in the clean night air. She waited until he reached the end of the road and then she saw another figure emerge from a house further down the road. He kept to the shadows as if he was following the first man and didn't want to be seen. She slipped silently into the telephone box, took out a scrap of paper from her coat pocket and made a call.

It seemed like an age before the call was answered. When she at last heard the woman's voice she spoke rapidly for several minutes, then bade her farewell.

When she had replaced the receiver she leant her head against the side of the box and breathed a sigh of relief. She was safe for now. Thank God! All she had to do was keep her composure when Jonathan Greswode arrived for Christmas and all should go well.

If she were discovered, though, God knows what would happen!

The sky was darkening and the snow falling faster. She hurried along, careful not to lose her footing on the slippery ground, pausing after a while to relieve the stitch in her side. She looked around her and realized with annoyance that she'd taken the wrong road.

In the distance to her right she could see the

chimneys of Killivray looming up against the night sky. She must have gone straight ahead at the crossroads instead of going right. She was on her way down towards the place called the Skallies.

She walked on for a while, turned a bend in the road and stopped.

The tumbledown houses built on the platform of rock looked almost picturesque beneath the covering of snow. She made her way down the narrow cobbled street along which the houses were huddled together.

There was no one about and she glanced inquisitively in through the lighted windows. Through one she saw a couple of old dears taking tea together, through another what seemed like a horde of children scrabbling around a table.

When she reached the Pilchard Inn she paused for a moment to catch her breath. She peeped in through the small round window. It looked so cosy inside. There was a roaring fire in the hearth and candles burned in niches set into the walls. Behind the bar a handsome woman was reading a newspaper.

Just as Clementine was about to move on the woman looked up suddenly, saw her and smiled. Before she had a chance to hurry away the door opened and the woman looked out.

'Are you looking for someone?'

'No, no, I was on my way home but I took a wrong turning.'

Clementine made to hurry away but the woman caught at her sleeve and said, 'Well, come in and have a drink, warm the cockles of your heart before you go.'

'No, no, I really must be on my way.'

'Maybe you're thinking that around these parts it doesn't do for a woman to be seen in a public house? Well, have no worries on that score, believe me, the Skallies doesn't have the same rules as the rest of the world. And besides it's just me and my daughter who's in bed upstairs. Come in, you must be frozen to the bone.'

Overcome by the cold and full of curiosity Clementine stepped hurriedly inside the Pilchard Inn. The warmth was wonderful after the rawness of the night and she walked gladly towards the roaring fire.

'Thank you, I'll stay for just a while. You are really most kind.'

Nan Abelson poured a glass of brandy and took it across to the woman with a smile.

Clementine sipped from the glass, sighed and thought how much she would like to make herself comfortable by this glorious fire and spend a whole evening away from the gloomy chill of Killivray House. Just this one drink, though, and then she must hurry back. It was far too risky to mix with outsiders, she couldn't afford to be discovered and already this landlady was looking at her too inquisitively for her liking.

'I haven't seen you round before,' Nan said nonchalantly. She knew everyone in the surrounding area and few strangers ever drifted into the Skallies by accident.

'I am, er, the new governess from Killivray House.'

Nan Abelson pricked up her ears. This woman had a faint French accent, from near Paris if she wasn't mistaken.

For a moment Nan hesitated. What if this woman had been sent here, what if someone had tracked Nan down even after all this time?

She chided herself for her suspicions. She'd been far too on edge since Benjamin had died.

'Quite a lonely old place to work, I should imagine?'

'Oh, really, it's not so bad.'

'You teach the little girl?'

Clementine nodded and sipped her brandy.

'It's a little lonely to be sure but it has its compensations.'

'And they are?'

Clementine stiffened, on her guard. 'I enjoy working with children, the sea air is very beneficial too for the health.'

Curiosity had brought her over the threshold but now she felt that she was being quizzed she was wishing herself gone.

'Where did you work before you came to Killivray?'

'I, er, I was engaged by a London family with three children.'

'Whereabouts in London?' Nan said busying herself with washing glasses whilst taking surreptitious glances at the woman. She noticed that her eyes belied the rest of her appearance; she had a plain face and yet inquisitive eyes, with a trace of cunning.

Clementine felt the panic rising and willed herself to keep calm.

'Great Cumberland Place,' she said, remembering an advertisement she'd once seen for a small hotel there.

Nan's breathing quickened and she struggled to stay composed. Great Cumberland Place! Such memories that name brought back to her. She had spent her first months in London staying hidden in a grand old house there until the fuss had died down.

'How lovely,' Nan said at last. 'I don't know much about London but this street I've been to once or twice.'

Clementine nodded but did not reply.

Nan went on, 'Such a wonderful view of the Tower of London from there.'

'Yes, a wonderful view,' said Clementine.

'Well, any time you want a little relief from the peace of Killivray you're welcome to come here. I am discreet by nature; maybe we could take a little drink together one evening? On Thursdays I don't open to the public.'

'I should like that very much but my employer is a very private man and I don't know that he would like me to frequent a public house.'

Nan smiled encouragingly, 'I could let you in the back way and we could drink a glass or two of wine, maybe get to know each other a little?'

The woman turned then and looked across at Nan. Nan thought that there was something a little familiar about her. She was quite sure that they hadn't met before and yet there was something that tugged at Nan's memory.

Clementine finished her brandy and took her leave.

Nan waved to her from the door and watched her walk through the gap in the rock and down towards the beach. As she closed the door she smiled to herself. A great view of the Tower from Great Cumberland Place! Ha! Not a chance. One thing she knew about the new governess from Killivray was that she had not lived in Great Cumberland Place! But why on earth should she choose to lie? If she had been sent to spy then Nan would call her bluff. If she dared to cause trouble then she would have no compunction in silencing her. Nan closed the door and went thoughtfully back behind the bar.

★　★　★

The Christmas Bazaar at Nanskelly School had been Eloise Fanthorpe's brainwave to keep the girls busy in the feverish run-up towards Christmas.

The majority of the girls had returned to their homes for the Christmas holidays and those remaining were those with no homes to go to.

The assembly hall was a hive of activity. The girls were busy setting out stalls in preparation for the following day. Eloise Fanthorpe was perched precariously on top of a stepladder trying to put a battered angel on the top of the Christmas tree. Hermione Thomas was trying unsuccessfully to untangle last year's paper chains and worrying whether anyone would make it to Nanskelly the following day.

147

Miss Fanthorpe had driven out in the ancient Ford and put up posters in the shops in St Werburgh's and Rhoskilly but if the snow kept coming down at this rate it would be impossible for anyone to get out to Nanskelly.

Two dark-skinned girls who looked like sisters were arranging chipped vases, bookends, paper knives and toast racks on the White Elephant stall, all unearthed by Miss Fanthorpe from the cellar. At another table a blonde girl was stacking books and crumpled comics, and at another a ginger-haired girl with a face full of freckles was laying out handmade calendars and hastily knitted dishcloths.

Tomorrow the jams and preserves would be lined up on the tables along with butterfly cakes and Victoria sponges. Sweets and trinkets had been carefully wrapped in tissue paper and stuffed down into the Bran Tub.

There was a garish booth covered in crepe paper and a poster announced that Madame Zsa Zsa would be telling fortunes at tuppence a go.

The money they hoped to make from the bazaar would enable Miss Fanthorpe to go into St Werburgh's and buy small presents for the girls' Christmas stockings.

Money was very tight at Nanskelly and if things didn't improve soon, then the school would have to close. If that were to happen the girls with free places would be left to the mercy of the state and would no doubt end up in orphanages or going into service.

There were fewer paying pupils coming to Nanskelly each year and without the fee payers they would be unable to take in the scholarship girls who came from far and wide.

Miss Fanthorpe hoped that their efforts would not be in vain and that a fair-sized crowd would brave the long walk up Linketty Lane and then down the rutted drive to the school. She knew that most of those making the journey would probably be more interested in getting a glimpse of the two eccentric spinsters who ran Nanskelly School than in buying any of the assorted bric-a-brac for sale.

With a deft manoeuvre Miss Fanthorpe managed to hook the angel on top of the tree. She climbed down the ladder slowly, sighing. Next term she would have to consider selling some of her father's paintings in order to make ends meet.

★ ★ ★

Romilly had spent a good hour after breakfast hanging about on the landing trying to slip unseen up the stairs to the attic. She was desperate to rummage through Thomas Greswode's trunk and examine everything in there again to see what she could find out.

Every time she got anywhere near the attic stairs either Nanny Bea or Madame Fernaud appeared as if by magic, putting an end to her adventures. She was quite sure that Madame was spying on her. She always seemed to be popping up at unexpected moments. Sometimes she stared at Romilly with a very curious expression on her face as though she was about to say something but thought better of it at the last moment. Once Romilly had seen her going through Papa's desk in the library and another time staring fixedly at his gun cabinet.

She'd had to abandon her plan to get up to the attic in the end because Madame had called her for the start of morning lessons at half past nine.

For the past hour and a half she had been writing a composition called, 'The Place I Would Most Like to Visit'.

She'd wanted to write that she'd most like to go to visit her mama or else the Skallies where her secret friend lived in a house called Bag End, but she couldn't of course. Instead she'd written about leaving Killivray in the dark of night and going on a train to Italy to a place called Santa Caterina where there were enormous ice creams and the sun shone every day and Romilly was allowed to swim in the sea and stay up late.

At her desk Madame was reading her composition while Romilly copied out her spellings for the weekly test that Madame was going to have on Fridays.

Romilly closed her spelling book quietly and looked up at Madame Fernaud. She had put down Romilly's exercise book and was sitting slumped at her desk staring out through the windows as if in a trance.

Romilly wriggled impatiently. In a few moments they would break for a glass of milk and biscuits. If Madame went down to the kitchen to have coffee with Nanny Bea then

150

perhaps Romilly would be able to creep up to the attic.

The hallway clock began to strike the hour. It was echoed by a terrified scream from downstairs that made Madame sit bolt upright as if she had been shot between the shoulder blades. For a moment she froze and the colour seemed to drain from her face. There was such a look of shock and fear on her face that it made Romilly afraid.

Then Madame rose quickly from her desk and hurried from the room with Romilly close behind her. Madame raced through the nursery and down the stairs while Romilly lingered on the landing, peering anxiously over the banisters.

Down in the hallway Nanny Bea lay collapsed face downwards on the floor. Her woollen skirts had risen above her knees and the elastic garters that held up her baggy stockings were on show along with the faded pink of her winter drawers. Romilly put her hand across her mouth to stifle a rising giggle.

Madame Fernaud reached Nanny Bea, turned her gently over on to her back and pulled her clothes down to cover her embarrassment.

Nanny Bea blinked frantically and then opened her eyes wide. Madame helped her to a sitting position.

'What happened?'

Nanny Bea opened her mouth to speak and her false teeth slipped from her mouth and clacked together noisily.

Romilly giggled.

Madame looked up at Romilly and gave her a stern look.

Nanny Bea adjusted her teeth behind her hand and muttered, 'There was a man staring in through the kitchen windows as brazen as you like.'

'Who was he?' Madame asked, her voice rising with fear.

'The Killivray black man!'

Romilly drew in her breath with excitement, galloped down the stairs and stood behind Madame, peering down inquisitively at Nanny Bea.

'Can you stand, do you think?'

'I don't know. I feel so very weak. It gave me a real turn, just staring in at me with such a funny expression on his face like that.'

For a moment Madame looked troubled but then pulled herself up sharply and said, 'It was probably just a hawker or a tinker looking for a free meal. Romilly, run quickly and fetch a little brandy for Nanny Bea.'

Romilly hesitated. She didn't want to go; she was far too interested in listening to what Nanny Bea was saying. She'd heard Mama tell Miss Naylor the story about the black man. He blew out his brains with a shotgun and was supposed to roam around the grounds after midnight looking for his lost love. Nanny Bea had told her it was all just fiddlesticks and poppycock.

'Romilly, hurry!'

Romilly obeyed reluctantly. She went into the drawing room and poured a large amount of brandy into a tumbler and carried it carefully back to the hallway.

Madame had helped Nanny Bea on to the high-backed settle and sat alongside her stroking her hand.

'Thank you, Romilly,' Madame said, taking the glass from the child's hands and holding it up to the old woman's lips.

Nanny Bea drank thirstily and then handed the empty glass back to Romilly.

'A little rest for Nanny Bea would be good,' said Madame with a hint of a smile. 'I think perhaps you are a little overcome with all the hard work you've been doing, maybe a sleep will make you feel better.'

'So kind of you, but I have lunch to prepare and a thousand other jobs to be getting on with.'

'Nonsense, I will prepare you a little something to eat, a warm drink also and then I insist that you try to sleep. Don't you agree, Romilly?'

Romilly blinked with surprise. She wasn't used to being asked her opinion on anything.

She bit her lip and nodded.

'Romilly and I are quite able to prepare our own lunch and amuse ourselves for the afternoon, aren't we, *ma petite*?'

Romilly stared in mounting bewilderment at Madame and waited for Nanny Bea to protest. None of the other governesses had ever prepared lunch before; they'd hardly even been allowed to go into the kitchen without permission.

But to Romilly's astonishment Nanny Bea did not protest, she merely smiled weakly at Madame Fernaud, nodded her head in meek agreement and said, 'I think you are right, my dear, I am a little overwrought and tiredness can overwork the imagination.'

Madame helped Nanny Bea gently to her feet and up the stairs while Romilly hurried into the kitchen, pulled a chair to the window and climbed up on it.

There was no sign of the black man outside. How could there be? He was a ghost and ghosts only ever came out after midnight.

Then she saw the large footprints that led from the summerhouse and across the lawn towards the kitchen window. Ghosts didn't make footprints, everyone knew that. So someone really had looked in at Nanny Bea. Maybe it was the same man that Romilly had seen in the summerhouse? Except he wasn't black. Or was he? She couldn't be sure because his face had been in shadow. A frisson of fear jiggled between her shoulder blades; she wasn't sure if she were terrified or thrilled.

Sometime soon she must sneak out to the summerhouse and see if Archie Grimble had left her a note. Archie might know who the man was; maybe he lived in the Skallies?

★ ★ ★

Madame and Romilly lunched together in the kitchen on toasted muffins spread with butter, biscuits and sweet tea. They ate in an uneasy silence until at last Madame, clearing away the crockery, spoke.

'A walk, I think, would be very good for us

154

while Nanny Bea rests.'

Romilly stared at her. 'A walk?' she exclaimed. 'But it's snowing!'

'You don't like to walk in the snow?'

'I don't know. Yes, I think so, but I wouldn't be allowed.'

'Well, I am allowing you. Who is to stop us?'

'But if Papa finds out he will be very angry.'

'Who is going to tell your papa?'

Romilly fell silent.

'Would your mama be angry if she knew you went for a walk in the snow?'

Romilly put her head on one side and her eyes filled suddenly with tears.

Madame Fernaud watched Romilly with interest.

'No. Mama always wanted to go out even in the rain but Papa has forbidden it. We only walk on fine days and then only close to the house.'

'Well, today we shall walk together in the snow,' Madame said with a laugh.

Romilly chewed her lip nervously and brushed away her tears. Madame was a fool. She knew nothing of life in Killivray. The house had big ears. Someone always told Papa. Papa knew everything that went on in Killivray House even when he wasn't there.

'Well, Romilly, answer me. Who do you think will tell your papa?'

'Why, Nanny Bea, of course!' Romilly cried impatiently.

'But she will not know.'

'She knows everything.'

'I have given her a little powder that will make

her sleep and while she sleeps we shall walk in the snow together.'

Romilly felt her eyes widen involuntarily. Nanny Bea always told Papa everything that went on at Killivray but if Nanny Bea didn't know . . .

The possibility of walking outside in the snow was too wonderful but what if she were being tricked? What if Madame just wanted to see if she would disobey Papa's orders and then go running back and tell him?

Papa would be furious with her.

He was scary when he was angry. His eyes narrowed the way a cat's did when it caught a bird.

Once when Mama raised her voice he threw a decanter at her. It hit the dining room wall with a cracking thud and the air was sharp with shards of glass and the smell of whisky.

'Have you the galoshes and a warm coat? It will be very cold outside,' Madame said.

Romilly nodded eagerly and ran to the cloakroom to fetch them in case Madame had a change of heart.

Five minutes later they were hurrying across the lawns of Killivray and fresh snow was wiping away their footprints as if they had never walked that way.

★ ★ ★

Archie and Cissie Abelson stood together on Skilly Beach looking up at the old Boathouse in wonder. The snow had transformed it from its tumbledown state and it looked like something left behind from a fairy tale. Long icicles dripped from the guttering like chandeliers and shimmered in the late morning light. The windows were latticed with frost and sparkled like diamond dust. Drifts of snow had covered the broken roof and swaddled the crumbling chimney on top of which a robin was singing energetically.

A bewildered crab scuttled across the sand looking for the cover of rocks and a gull pecked discontentedly at the frosted skeleton of a fish.

Archie held Cissie Abelson's hand as they crossed the beach. Nan followed close behind them with a breathless Mrs Galvini in tow.

As they neared the Boathouse, Archie held more tightly to Cissie's hand. He looked warily up at the window and was startled to see mad Gwennie looking out at them curiously.

He pulled Cissie along impatiently, afraid that at any moment the door would open and mad Gwennie would appear brandishing a gun.

The faint strains of the Donkey Song filtered out into the cold air.

Cissie and Archie climbed the slippery steps that led around the side of the Boathouse and then waited for Nan and Mrs Galvini to catch up.

Archie looked back across the beach towards the wobbly chapel and felt for the keys in his pocket. One day soon he was going to get back in there and have another good snoop around, hopefully in daylight if he could do it without anyone seeing him. He wondered if he'd ever find out what the two other keys would unlock?

Nan and Mrs Galvini joined them and they walked on along the cliff path. Suddenly Cissie yanked Archie's hand and pointed. A short distance in front of them the curious Misses Arbuthnot were hurrying along, both wrapped from head to toe in ancient fur coats and hats. They wore faded galoshes that made a slopping sound as they walked and the smell of mothballs and lavender was strong in their twittering wake.

Archie thought about what Mr Galvini had said about the people in the Skallies. What could two old ladies be running away from? They were a strange pair, that was for sure, and out of place in the Skallies with their fancy music, bone china and butter knives. Mammy always said God help them, they were distressed gentility, down on their luck.

There was only a light fall of snow on the cliff path as it was sheltered by high bare hedges drizzled with ice that glinted in the strange pinkish light that swathed the path before them. Archie felt as though he were walking through a pleasant dream.

For a while he and Cissie pretended to smoke, sucking on imaginary cigarettes and blowing steam into the cold morning air.

Later, while Cissie sang her nonsense songs quietly to herself, Archie's head was teeming with thoughts. He wondered when he'd be able to go back to the summerhouse and leave a letter for Romilly Greswode. He didn't have that much to tell her but he really wanted to write to her, keep in contact, and see her again. He couldn't wait to go back to Killivray, he felt the pull of the house as if it were a giant magnet drawing him towards it.

Cissie jingled the pennies in her coat pocket as she skipped along happily beside Archie. Nan had emptied her penny pot and given them five shillings each to spend. Archie was thrilled; he had no money left after the fat porker had taken all his savings. He'd kept well out of his way ever since but when they did meet his father gave him strange sideways looks and always seemed to have a sly smile on his face as though he was plotting something.

Mammy had been quiet the last couple of days as though she had something on her mind, something heavy that was squashing out all her thoughts. She had new bruises on her arms too, ugly blue ones, joining up with older yellow ones.

If he could, Archie was going to use the money Nan had given him to buy something for his mammy, something nice that would stop her being so sad.

When they reached the point where the path divided, Archie and Cissie stopped and waited for Nan and Mrs Galvini. To their left a rabbit path led away down towards Skilly Point, straight on led around the coast to Nanskelly. While Cissie jumped up and down and clapped her hands to keep warm, Archie gazed out to sea and thought of poor Thomas Greswode and how he'd drowned in the deep cold waters off Skilly Point.

★　★　★

159

Nan had walked the cliff path many a time since she'd lived in the Skallies and sometimes she'd seen the girls from Nanskelly School out on a walk. They were a quaint-looking bunch in their old-fashioned uniforms and felt hats. Usually there were middle-aged schoolmistresses with them chivvying them along and pointing out the wonders of nature.

The school was in an isolated spot and the inhabitants had little contact with the outside world apart from trips to the station at St Werburgh's. All sorts of rumours abounded about the place; that the two old biddies who owned it were more than just friends, they were lady lovers. The girls were, it was said, mainly down-at-heel princesses from foreign countries who didn't have a pot to piss in.

Nan was enjoying being out in the fresh air and away from the Pilchard Inn. She and Mrs Galvini, red-faced and puffing, walked companionably together keeping an eye on Cissie and Archie.

Nan had seen the posters about the bazaar up in the shops in Rhoskilly and thought it might do them all good to have a long walk and a nose round Nanskelly. She smiled now at the sight of Archie and Cissie chattering excitedly together.

'He's a lovely boy, that Archie,' she said. 'He's good company for Cissie, he's always patient with her slow ways and never mocks her the way the other children do.'

'He very good boy, that Archie. If I ever has a son I like one like him.'

Nan looked sideways at Lena Galvini and smiled sadly.

It was a bloody shame that Lena hadn't had any children, she and Alfredo would make wonderful parents.

'I feel sorry for him having a father like that. He's a pig of a man,' Nan said with feeling.

'*Si*. I thinks the same. I not like him. He smell like a bad lot. Not a good husband. I not like to share my bed with him.'

'Not on your Nelly.' Nan grimaced and went on, 'It's strange, though, he's never done a day's work since he's been in the Skallies and yet they seem to manage for money.'

'You ask me, I thinks Martha Grimble come from good family, family with money,' Lena said, dropping her voice.

Nan looked at her quizzically. Martha Grimble looked as if she didn't have a penny to bless herself with.

'How do you mean, Lena?'

'You looks at her shoes, her handbag, very old but cost very much money, I thinks. And that watch she wear. Solid gold and worth, how you say, a boomb.'

'A bomb,' Nan said with a laugh. 'You'd make a good policeman, Lena.'

'Pah! Where I come from police no good. No difference between police and bad men.'

Nan would love to have asked her more about where she came from but there was a kind of unwritten rule in the Skallies that you didn't pry too much into other people's lives. You listened to what they wanted to tell you but didn't ask for more.

'I seen that Fleep the other day. He come

161

running up from the beach like there is a bear at the behind of him,' Mrs Galvini said.

'Did you? I wonder what was up? Sometimes he looks frightened to death,' Nan replied.

'He a nice-looking man if he scrub up a bit.' Lena gave Nan a wink.

Nan blushed. 'I haven't looked that closely.'

Lena chuckled and nudged Nan in the ribs. 'You need start looking. You still young, finds you a nice man for cuddling up, keep you feets warm.'

'Lena! If I want warm feet I'll use a warming pan. Men just bring trouble with them as far as I'm concerned.'

'My Alfredo never bring me no trouble.'

'Alfredo's a good man, Lena, there's not too many of them about.'

'He have a lot of bad dreams,' Lena said.

'Who? Alfredo?'

'No. No. This Fleep man I talking about. Sometimes I hears him in the nights crying like a *bambino*.'

'You do?' said Nan with interest.

'And other times he laughing like a bloody fool!'

'Do you think he's a lunatic?'

'No. Well, maybe a little. I thinks he's sad, like he needs a good woman!'

'Come on,' said Nan, 'let's catch up with Cissie and Archie.'

They hurried on as a cold wind blew in off the sea and whipped their faces to a healthy pink.

★ ★ ★

162

Fleep walked deeper into the woods until daylight barely penetrated them. He stopped when he came to a small clearing, sat down on a rotting log, took out his tobacco tin and rolled a cigarette.

He sat smoking and staring about him for a long time. In the canopy of trees above him rooks called out and a rabbit appeared from behind a tree, watched him for a moment and then skittered away.

The ground beneath his feet was soft and deep with pine needles. He had an overwhelming urge to lie down and never get up again. Maybe if he lay there long enough he would be covered in a blanket of pine needles and he would gradually sink down and melt back into the ground as if he'd never existed.

He remained seated, though, lost in his thoughts until suddenly he pricked up his ears. He could hear the sound of distant laughter, rising and falling on the air. He got stiffly to his feet and walked on through the woods. Eventually the trees thinned out and from the cover of a large tree he watched as a woman and a small child played together in the snow.

The child, a little girl of about nine or ten, was making a snowball, patting it excitedly into shape. She was a funny little thing to look at, all dressed up in very old-fashioned clothes as if she were a throwback from an earlier generation. She lifted the snowball behind her head and threw it clumsily at the woman.

The woman had her back to Fleep and as the snowball flew in her direction, she turned her face towards him. The snowball hit her on the back of her head and she gasped and then burst into a peal of laughter.

Fleep stared at her in wonder. Her face was flushed with exertion and rarely had he seen a look of such pleasure on another's face.

He watched as the woman threw a snowball back at the child. The child squealed as it struck her on the shoulder and then her laughter rang out in the icy afternoon air.

Such a simple scene to behold, yet there was such an innocence about it that cut him to the quick. He'd abandoned innocence a long time ago, allowed himself to be led willingly into a dissolute life. A life from which now there was no chance of return. He turned away quickly and made off back into the woods. He began to run, feet kicking up the pine needles, snow falling gently from the branches of the trees, the sound of laughter ricocheting inside his head.

* * *

Archie helped Cissie over the stile that led into the grounds of Nanskelly School and then waited while Nan helped Mrs Galvini over with much shrieking and wheezing.

Nanskelly must have been a beautiful house in its time but now the paintwork was peeling, the masonry crumbling and the roof was a patchwork of misshapen tiles. To the left of where they stood there was a run-down sports pavilion and in front of it a bumpy hockey pitch, criss-crossed with the prints of gulls.

The door of Nanskelly was ajar and Nan stepped briskly inside, beckoning the others to follow her.

It was drab and gloomy inside the house. The walls were the colour of congealed mustard and the tiles on the floor, though patterned, were worn and faded. A few colourful paintings hung on the walls but the velvet curtains at the windows were washed out and worn thin with age. There was a pervasive smell of old shoes and worn Wellingtons; of chalk dust and sugar paper; pencil sharpenings and cheap glue.

Suddenly a small girl poked her head round a door on the left and yelled, making them all jump, 'There's more customers, Miss Thomas! Loads of them!' before disappearing again. They followed her hesitantly into a large hall with a stage at one end and stalls set out around the outside.

A handful of girls stood excitedly behind the tables and several more were in charge of a table bearing an enormous tea urn and a mountain of cakes and biscuits.

'I'm parched. I could kill for a cup of tea,' Nan said. 'Come on, Lena, you and I'll have a drink, let these two have a look around first and spend their pennies.'

Archie and Cissie walked shyly around the room looking curiously at the assorted items for sale. Cissie picked up a well-worn teddy bear and clutched it to her chest while Archie sifted through a box full of assorted cars and cigarette cards.

Soon the room filled up as more and more

people arrived. Archie recognized Old Willy Spencer from Rhoskilly Village and the Payne brothers from the Peapods as well as the Misses Arbuthnot.

Cissie grew slowly in confidence and went from stall to stall handing over her pennies as if they were going out of fashion. Soon she was exhausted and went to sit with Nan and Mrs Galvini with an enormous pile of old toys lined up at her feet.

Archie spent his money more carefully. He bought a few trinkets that he thought his mammy would like, a few old detective books for himself and lastly a shiny red cricket ball.

When he next looked around, he saw that Nan, Mrs Galvini and Cissie had joined the queue for fortune-telling. They beckoned him over to join them but he shook his head shyly. He wasn't going to part with his money to be told a lot of old nonsense.

He bought himself a cup of tea and a slice of walnut cake from the two smiling girls and sat down near an old man who was eating an enormous slice of Victoria sponge cake.

'All right, lad?' the old boy called across.

'Yes thanks.'

'Ever been up here to Nanskelly before?'

'No.'

'I first used to come here when I was a nipper. Used to scrump apples from the orchard here. Used to eat too many and end up with a hell of a belly ache. I got a job here in the end. Can't eat the apples now, though, 'cos I haven't enough bloody teeth in my head.'

166

Archie grinned and moved a little closer.

'You like cricket?' the old man asked, nodding at the ball in Archie's lap.

'I don't know, I've never played it.'

'You never played cricket? That's a crying shame.'

'I've got a bad leg,' Archie said, nodding down at his calliper.

The old man looked down at Archie's leg and winced.

'That's damn bad luck. I'm the same,' he said. 'Lost this bugger in 1914.'

He tapped his right leg with his knuckles and Archie flinched at the sound of old bones on wood.

'Gangrene. Took it off at the knee and later the whole bloody thing. Anyhow, why'd you buy a ball if you can't play cricket?'

'I don't know. I liked the colour, I s'pose, and I liked the feel of it.'

'Great game, cricket,' the old man said. 'Used to be a big game of cricket here at Nanskelly every summer in the old days. Nanskelly School versus the village boys.'

'Did they play against the girls?'

'No. It were a boys' school in the old days. The Villagers was a team made up of young lads from Rhoskilly and the Skallies and they used to play the Nanskelly boys.'

'Did they ever win?' Archie asked.

'Couple of times. The Headmaster, Mr Fanthorpe, was a nice fellow, cricket mad he was.'

'Did you ever play?'

''Course I did. I had two good legs then. Bit

of a fast bowler in them days.'

Archie looked up at the old man with wonder; he couldn't imagine him ever being a boy, he was so ancient.

'Tell you what, son, finish your grub and we'll take a walk out to the pavilion, show you a bit of history.'

Archie ate his cake, swallowed down his tea and then followed the old man.

As they walked through the hallway the old man said, 'See, these floors here was all laid by Spanish craftsmen. Need restoring now but in the years gone by they reckon this were a real palace of a place.'

Archie looked down at the shabby tiles and shrugged. It didn't look much like a palace now.

The door to the sports pavilion was stiff and with much puffing and pushing the old man managed to open it.

'Wood expands in the damp weather, see, that's what makes the door stick. Come spring it'll free itself up. Bit like me, I stiffen up in the winter then come the spring it's like the Almighty has dripped a bit of oil in my old joints.'

They stepped inside the pavilion and stood together looking at the racks of worn hockey sticks and moth-eaten shoe bags dangling from rusty hooks. There was a sprinkling of snow on the floor beneath a hole in the roof.

'We used to change in here. Not that we had bugger all to change into. Us lot used to have the arses hanging out of our trousers and we went barefoot most of the time in the summer. The

Nanskelly boys were proper gents, had all the clobber, white shirts and flannels and proper boots.'

The old boy opened a door to the right and stepped into a large room sparsely furnished with a few rickety tables and chairs arranged as if it were a café.

'This is where they used to serve up the teas after the game. Lovely grub it were. Huge scones with great dollops of cream and jam. Cream puffs as big as a babby's head. Sandwiches, apricot tarts and all sorts. Used to think we was in heaven. We never had a penny to our names in those days.'

'Sounds lovely,' Archie said, his mouth watering.

'There you go, look, up there on the wall. That's me up there. Eighteen ninety-seven.'

He pointed to the far wall where a brown board hung precariously on a bent nail.

Archie screwed up his eyes and read the faded gold writing on the board, 'Nanskelly v Villagers 1897. Villagers won. Player of the Match: William Dally.'

'Was that you?'

''Course it were me. Told you I was a dab hand with a cricket ball.'

Archie read on down the list.

He stood transfixed when he came near to the bottom.

'Nanskelly v Villagers 1899. Nanskelly won. Player of the Match: Charles Lewis Lloyd Greswode.

'Was that Old Mr Greswode who used to live

at Killivray House?'

'That were he. Tidy cricketer he was. Spiteful little bastard though.'

Archie looked at the next entry, then stood spellbound, almost breathless with excitement.

'Nanskelly v Villagers 1900. Villagers won. Player of the Match: Thomas Gasparini Greswode.

'Thomas Greswode! Why did he play for the villagers?'

'He was asked, of course.'

'But the other one, Charles Greswode, he played for Nanskelly?'

'That's right. Both the boys were at school here. They used to be educated at Killivray but came here after the tutor at Killivray had a fall-out with Mr Greswode and left. Charles was Captain of sports or whatever they called them in those days. He got to pick the school team that played against the villagers.'

'I don't understand.'

'Good old-fashioned jealousy, son. Like I said, his cousin Thomas was at Nanskelly School too. Lovely lad he were, sunny temperament, no side to him. Charles Greswode didn't pick his cousin Thomas 'cos he were too good a player, would have taken the shine off himself.'

'But that's not fair.'

'Life ain't fair, lad, so don't ever go believing it is.'

Archie sighed. Benjamin always used to say the same thing.

'Well, Charles Greswode thought he'd got all his own way like he always did but then it all

170

backfired on him,' the old man said with a chuckle.

'How do you mean?'

'Well, Mr Fanthorpe, the Head, he was a fair-minded man. Said that if Thomas wasn't playing for Nanskelly he was entitled to play for the villagers seeing as he was a local boy.'

'Blimey.'

'A corker of a game Thomas Greswode had even though he were only young. Best left-handed bat I ever saw. Made eighty-nine with two sixes and a handful of fours.'

Archie's brow wrinkled in puzzlement. He didn't understand much about cricket.

'Even though it were donkey's years ago I can see his face now when Mr Fanthorpe presented him with the cup. Chuffed to bits he were. We carried him shoulder high all the way back to the Skallies, we were that proud of him.'

'He died not long after, didn't he?' Archie said suddenly.

William Dally nodded, 'Never got to make old bones sadly.'

'He drowned, didn't he?'

'He did and bloody tragic that were. Awful waste of a young life. He had a natural way about him, young Thomas, not like the rest of the bloody Greswodes.'

Archie saw a tear prick in the old man's eye as he took out his handkerchief and blew his nose.

'Mr Fanthorpe was real cut up about it, we all were. But he blamed himself for a long time after.'

'Why?' Archie asked.

171

'Apparently, Thomas came out to see him one day, must have been a few weeks after the match. The school had broken up for the holidays. Young Thomas was in a terrible state.'

'Why?'

'The Lord only knows. But Mr Fanthorpe wasn't here.'

'So why did Mr Fanthorpe think it was his fault?'

'Thought if he'd seen Thomas he'd have been able to talk to him. Maybe he wouldn't have gone back out in his boat.'

'And was that the day he drowned?' Archie asked.

'No. It were the following day. The old gardener came here to the pavilion. Found Thomas here where he'd slept the night.'

'What happened?'

'The gardener sent him packing. Told him to get home else his uncle Mr Greswode would be angry.'

'But he didn't go home?' Archie said sucking in his breath.

'No, he didn't. He never went back to Killivray. A couple of hours later he were gone for ever.'

'He drowned off Skilly Point, didn't he?'

'He did, poor devil; must have rowed out way past Skilly Point and the boat were found days after that. Eventually he were washed up on Skilly Beach 'bout three weeks later. It was Master Charles that found him. I never liked him but that must have been a hell of a shock.'

'Why do you think he didn't want to go back to Killivray?'

'No idea, son. Had a tiff, argument or suchlike, I spect. You know what kids are. No one ever knew for sure, it were just a terrible accident.'

'You don't think he meant to drown himself?' Archie asked.

'Good God no! He were always full of the joys of spring. Had his whole life ahead of him. Whatever makes you ask a daft question like that?'

'I don't know.'

'Anyhow, not long after, Mr Fanthorpe closed the school.'

'Because Thomas Greswode drowned?'

'No, lad. Mr Greswode, Charles Greswode's father, gave him notice to quit Nanskelly.'

'What does that mean?'

'The Greswodes owned Nanskelly back in them days. They fell out after Thomas died and that was that. He was a vindictive old bugger, Mr Greswode, like most of the family.'

'That's why there were no more matches then?' Archie said, looking up at the board.

'That's right. End of an era. Fair broke Mr Fanthorpe's heart having to close Nanskelly. Greswode sold the house and a family lived here for a good many years. Then, lo and behold, Miss Fanthorpe and Miss Thomas came back from abroad and started up the girls' school.'

'I see.'

'Miss Fanthorpe, she's Mr Fanthorpe's daughter, 'course he's long dead now, God rest his soul.'

Archie thought about the letter that Benjamin

had left for him. What was it he'd said? *There's a couple of old biddies over at Nanskelly School who would do you a good turn if you were in need.*

The old man interrupted his thoughts, 'Anyways, that's enough of all this maudlin talk. Come on, then, we'd best be getting back or your folks'll think you've gone missing.'

'They won't. They're queuing up for fortune-telling.'

'Good for them. That Miss Thomas has a way with her telling fortunes. She can see into the future, they reckon.'

They walked together back across the lawns in silence and stopped at the front door.

'If you're ever up this way again, call in for a chat. I'm mostly round and about, most probably find me over there near the potting shed.' He pointed away to the left.

'Thanks,' Archie said.

'I could tell you plenty of tales about the past. Not many lads like listening to old men talking, but you do, you're different. I could do with a bit of male company once in a while. I'm surrounded by bloody women most of the time.'

Archie watched William Dally walk stiffly away, whistling to himself as he went.

★ ★ ★

Romilly had never had so much fun in all the ten-and-a-half years she'd lived. Her face glowed with radiance and her eyes were bright, and she could not keep the smile off her face.

She and Madame had walked the length and breadth of the Killivray grounds and then they'd had the most marvellous game of snowballs. Romilly had never played snowballs before. It was such fun! They played until they were both covered in snow and their noses were pinched and blue with the cold.

Eventually when Romilly was completely exhausted she had sat herself down on a log. She clapped her hands together to knock the encrusted snow off her gloves and rubbed her eyes. She smiled up at Madame shyly and her teeth chattered noisily.

Madame turned away for a moment to wipe the steam from her spectacles and then turned and smiled back.

'That was fun, wasn't it, *ma petite*?'

Romilly nodded enthusiastically.

As they walked together towards Killivray House the snow began to fall again and dusk settled gently around them.

They slipped quietly into the dark and silent house like conspirators.

In the hallway Madame said, 'Hurry now and take off your wet things and I will put them to dry. While you put on some dry socks I shall check on Nanny Bea.'

Romilly took off her coat, hat and scarf and sat down to remove her galoshes. Then she went slowly upstairs. She grinned when she heard loud snoring coming from Nanny Bea's room. Madame was right. Nanny Bea would not be able to tell anyone about their wonderful walk in the snow.

She went into the nursery and fetched a dry pair of socks and sat on the bed to put them on.

She heard Madame come upstairs and go into Nanny Bea's room but there was no sound of any talking.

Madame poked her head round the nursery door. 'Nanny Bea still sleeps like the baby. I am going to prepare some supper. Do you want to help?'

Romilly shook her head and thought that Madame looked a little sad. 'I am so tired after our walk,' Romilly said, yawning.

'Then you must rest for a while. I will call you at seven o'clock.'

'Thank you,' Romilly said and she lay back on the bed and closed her eyes.

Madame left the room and made her way downstairs. Romilly waited until she knew that she was safely in the kitchen and then she took a candle from the bottom drawer of the tallboy, along with a box of matches, and made her way stealthily to the attic stairs.

★   ★   ★

Nan unlocked the door to Hogwash House and stepped nervously inside.

It was freezing in the house and already the smell of damp was strong in the air. She shivered, thinking that she wouldn't want to hang about long in here.

She climbed the steep stairs and stood for a moment on the landing, listening. The boards creaked beneath her feet and the house seemed to sigh around her.

She turned the handle of the door to Benjamin's bedroom and stepped inside.

The room was large and, though dusty, was clean. There were few signs of its last occupant.

The ceiling was sloping, ancient black beams stark against the white plaster. The floorboards were shiny with age and uneven, partly covered by a square of rush matting. There was a large rocking chair next to the fireplace, the grate was already filled with wood and just needed a match putting to it.

There were no ornaments in the room, no clocks or clutter on the mantelpiece. There were no pictures on the wall except for a framed sampler hanging above the bed.

Nan smiled as she read it.

Usually they said boring old things like GOD IS GOOD or BLESS THIS HOUSE. This one said, SHUT MOUTH NEVER CATCHES FLY.

That was typical of Benjamin.

There were a few clothes of his hanging in the wardrobe but not much else; it seemed as if he'd had a good clear-out before he'd died. No personal bits and pieces anywhere.

She walked down the stairs and went into the kitchen. There wasn't a lot to sort out in the way of possessions in here either, and yet she was sure that there'd been a very fine clock on the dresser, one that would have been worth a pretty penny. Benjamin had lived simply here in Hogwash House and hadn't accumulated a lot of clutter in his lifetime. She'd have to come back soon and pack up the rest of his things.

Suddenly she was quite sure that she was not alone in the house. She felt her body go rigid with fear as she smelled a faint but definite whiff of tobacco. Then she heard the click of the front door as it closed softly.

She hurried out into the porch and looked up and down Bloater Row. There was no one around, but then she heard the door of Bag End close. Walter Grimble! What the hell was he up to? Sniffing around where he wasn't wanted. She went back and locked the front door, pocketed the key and then left. She hurried along Bloater Row and let herself into the Pilchard Inn.

★   ★   ★

Up in his bedroom, by candlelight, Archie Grimble wrote to Romilly Greswode, dipping his pen into a pot containing his mixture of invisible ink and trying to keep his invisible handwriting neat.

He told her all the things that he'd found out about Thomas Greswode from William Dally up at Nanskelly and Mr Galvini's aunt from Santa Caterina but it didn't seem to add up to very much. Still, maybe she'd be able to tell him what she had found out and if they pieced their information together, then maybe they'd get to the truth like real detectives did.

Downstairs the wireless was playing and dance music drifted up the stairs. His mammy loved to listen to music.

Sometimes when she thought she was alone in

178

the house she danced backwards and forwards, round and round, holding a broom for a partner. When he was littler he used to stand on her feet and she whizzed him around too.

He heard the outside door open suddenly and the porker came into the house, puffing and panting as though he'd just run a mile.

Downstairs the music of the wireless was soon drowned out by the rumbling noise of arguing.

Archie knew that the porker would be wheedling for money so that he could go to the Pilchard and fill his fat belly with ale. He crept out onto the landing and listened.

'What do you expect a man to do? Sit here on my arse listening to music all bloody night with a wife who barely speaks?'

'You find fault with everything I say if I do speak.'

His mammy's voice, softer, tired sounding.

'Some great entertainment we have here. The boy barely talks to me, just sits staring at me like I'm some kind of halfwit.'

'You hardly speak to him, Walter, and if you do you've barely a kind word to say to him.'

'What are you doing putting your coat on?'

'I promised to go down to Periwinkle House and do some ironing and a few bits and pieces for the old dears.'

'Why can't they do their own ironing? Pair of stuck-up bitches!'

'They pay me well and I enjoy their company.'

'So I get to stay here and mind Archie while you're off gallivanting.'

'Hardly gallivanting, Walter.'

'Where is Archie?'

'Upstairs. I can take him with me so he's out from under your feet.'

Archie didn't fancy going to Periwinkle House; he found the two old women a bit scary. The older of the two was all right but the younger sometimes said strange things for an old lady. Once she had whispered a string of swear words in his ear that had made him blush the colour of rhubarb. Another time she told him that she had a body hidden in the cellar. It wasn't true of course, but it made him feel afraid all the same.

It wasn't much of a choice though; to go to Periwinkle House or stay here with the porker. Then he had an idea. He stepped back into his bedroom and went through his pockets. He hadn't spent all the money that Nan had given him. He still had three shillings left.

He tiptoed slowly across the landing and into the bedroom his parents shared. His mammy's purse was on the tallboy near the window where she always left it. He crept towards it and opened it as quietly as he could. There was nothing in there except a few pennies and halfpennies. He slipped the money inside and scurried back to his own room.

Moments later he heard his father wheezing his way up the stairs. Just as he thought he would, he heard the click of the purse opening and the clink of coins being removed.

Then his father was hurrying back down the stairs. The front door banged shut and Walter Grimble made his way down Bloater Row

180

whistling cheerfully as he went.

'Do you want to come with me to the Arbuth-nots', Archie?' his mammy called up the stairs.

'No thanks, Mammy, I'm real tired. I'm doing some writing and then I'm going to bed,' he called back.

'All right, love, I'll be back by ten, half past at the latest. If you need anything you know where I am.'

'Okay, Mammy, love you.'

'Love you too, Arch.'

He finished the letter to Romilly, folded it carefully in two and slipped it into his pocket. It was now or never. He'd been brave once before and he could do it again.

He had a couple of hours; all he had to do was make his way down to the beach, through the woods and into the summerhouse. He would leave the note in the stove and then run all the way back. Easy peasy. Lemon squeezy.

★ ★ ★

Romilly climbed the first few steps of the attic stairs and then stopped and listened.

Downstairs in the kitchen Madame was singing as she clattered about preparing the supper. Nanny Bea snored on.

Romilly was terrified; she had never been into the attic at night before. It was spooky in the daytime but at night it would be worse. But she had no choice. In a few days Papa would be home for Christmas and then she wouldn't be able to move.

181

She took another few steps and then hesitated again. All was quiet.

She climbed upwards, her heart beating fast, the steps creaking beneath her feet.

She slipped off her shoes at the top of the stairs and opened the door.

It was almost pitch black in the attic, just a sliver of watery moonlight showing the spooky outline of the gramophone and the bird cage. With shaking hands, she managed to strike a match and light the candle. She made her way carefully, holding the candle high, jumping with fright when the flame spluttered and almost died.

She sat down before the trunk belonging to Thomas and set the candle down on a nearby box. Slowly she raised the lid of the trunk and the familiar smell of camphor drifted up.

She lifted out the scrap book and then took out a pile of letters and put them in her lap. She turned them over one by one but soon grew irritated because all the writing was in a foreign language so she couldn't understand anything.

Next she lifted out the diary. She turned it over in her hands. It was heavy and bound in thick leather and there was a sturdy lock on the front.

She fiddled around with the lock but it refused to open. She knew that bad people could pick locks, thieves and burglars did it all the time, the only trouble was that she didn't know anyone who could help her.

A noise in the far corner of the attic startled her. A scratching sound like something trapped.

Mice or rats or maybe a bird come in under the eaves? She bit her thumb to stop herself from crying out in alarm.

The noise stopped, leaving just the sound of the wind sighing around the roof and the creak of the oak tree branches. She grabbed a few more things from the trunk and then carefully closed the lid and stood up with shaking legs. Lifting up her dress she slipped the diary and the photographs inside the front of her liberty bodice. She shivered because the leather was cold against her goose-pimpled skin. If she walked carefully and rested her hand on the diary she'd be able to sneak it downstairs.

She picked up the candle and tiptoed back across the attic, breathing fast with excitement. She wanted more than anything to run but she forced herself to walk slowly. Blowing out the candle, she wet her fingers with spit and doused the wick. Then she went quietly down the stairs, hurried along the corridor and into the nursery. She stuffed the diary behind the dolls' house. Later she'd try and sneak out to the summerhouse. Perhaps Archie would know someone who could pick locks; there were bound to be burglars living in a place like the Skallies.

★ ★ ★

Archie Grimble made his way cautiously through the Killivray woods. He did not turn on his torch until he was a good distance into the woods for fear of being seen. All around him the trees

183

loomed up like abandoned giants, twisted branches stark against the night sky, the ground dappled here and there with moonlight filtering through the leaves of the evergreens.

After an age he emerged from the woods on to the lower lawns of Killivray. He turned off his torch, paused to catch his breath and then hurried across the grass and on up the steps through the rose garden. There he stood and looked in wonder at Killivray House. In the dark it looked even more spectacular than in the daytime. Several of the windows were lit and smoke curled up from the enormous chimneys.

It was a beautiful and eerie-looking place. This ancient building could tell a lot of stories, he'd bet.

He thought of Thomas Greswode, imagined him sleeping there on the night of the cricket match. Probably too excited to sleep, going over in his mind all the happy memories of the day.

What had happened in the days after that? Probably Archie would never know. He wondered what Thomas Greswode was thinking the last night he'd ever spent in Killivray? What had made him run off and spend the night in the sports pavilion? Something had made him really unhappy, something he wanted to tell Mr Fanthorpe about. Thomas hadn't meant to die though, William Dally had been quite sure of that. He said he'd always been full of life.

It must have just been an accident. And yet Archie had the strangest niggling feeling that it hadn't been and that Killivray House held a lot of secrets.

He crossed the shadowy lawn, ducking low when an owl flew close above his head.

The door to the summerhouse creaked on its hinges and he hesitated. What if there was someone in there, someone watching him, ready to pounce as soon as he stepped inside? He'd come this far, though, so he couldn't go back. Benjamin had always told him not to be afraid of the dark.

He put his head cautiously round the door and peered anxiously into the darkness. The smell of mould and damp caught in his tightening throat.

It was still and sinisterly silent.

The boards creaked beneath his feet and he paused in mid step, one leg outstretched like someone walking in slow motion. Just a few more steps and he could put the letter into the stove and then he could get out of there and run off home.

He inched more closely to the stove. He was trembling as he opened the door and delighted when he felt something. He turned on the torch, cupped his palm around the beam to muffle the light and peered inside.

There was a book and a thick envelope. He could hardly contain himself as he lifted them out. He took from his pocket the letter that he'd written to Romilly, put it into the stove and closed the door carefully.

Shaking with excitement and fear, he couldn't wait to get home to read what she'd written in her letter. Straightening up he walked across to the window and looked out into the night. Then he noticed the light on in an upstairs window and someone looking out into the garden.

He stepped outside and watched the window. It was hard to tell whether it was a grown up or a child. He kept to the cover of the bushes that lined the path. Then he smiled. It was Romilly; he could see the outline of her plaits and the large ribbons.

He flicked the switch of the torch on and off and for a second the beam of light hit the window and Romilly jumped back. Then he heard the sound of the window opening.

He inched closer to the house until he was almost on the gravel path.

'Archie Grimble, is that you down there?'

Her voice was an excited whisper.

'Yes.'

'Aren't you afraid being out in the dark?'

'No,' he lied through chattering teeth.

'Did you get the things I left in the stove?'

'Yes. And I've left you a note. You need to warm it to read it, remember.'

'Thank you. Did you come through the dark woods?'

'Yep.'

'You're so brave.'

He puffed up with pride and hissed, 'I'll come again soon, write you another letter.'

Before Romilly could reply, Archie heard the noise. Suddenly headlights appeared round the corner of the drive and Archie was trapped in the glare of lights like a wide-eyed animal.

The window slammed shut and Romilly disappeared from sight. Archie froze. Then with a shriek he took off, haring across the lawns as fast as he could. He heard a car door slam shut, footsteps running across the gravel and an angry voice called out into the darkness, 'Whoever you are, if I get my hands on you, I'll break your bloody legs. This is private property!'

Archie didn't look back. He kept on running, skittering down the steps from the rose garden. What a fool he was; making out to Romilly that he wasn't afraid of anything. He was afraid now. He was bloody terrified. He shouldn't have got that close to the house.

Holy smoke! He couldn't run any faster and if the man was chasing him he'd be bound to be caught. Any minute now and he'd be a dead boy. He skedaddled across the lower lawn yelping with fear as he went, forcing the leg with the calliper to move faster than it had ever moved before.

He could hardly breathe; he felt his Adam's apple knocking against his rattling ribs, his head wobbling dangerously.

By the time he reached the edge of the woods he thought he would die of terror or exhaustion. He stopped when he could go no further, bent double to ease the stitch in his side. He looked back towards Killivray House fearfully.

Thank God, there was no one chasing him.

As he stood panting in the cover of the trees, he heard a car door slam and a woman laugh. The light went out in the room where Romilly had been. He'd just get his breath back and then he was out of there, back to the safety of the Skallies.

He looked up and let out a cry of terror. A man stood silently before him, watching him intently. He felt his heart flutter and then squeeze into a tight knot as he held on to the trunk of a nearby tree to stop his legs from buckling.

Fear pricked his skin like nettles. Sometimes when your brain got too hot you saw things. Fear could make you hallucinate.

Once when Mammy had a fever she said she saw tiny naked leprechauns dancing along the top of the wardrobe. He closed his eyes, opened them again quickly.

Holy Jesus and all the sacred saints of heaven. He was dreaming. It couldn't be true.

He was staring into the face of the black man of Killivray.

Then he fainted.

★　★　★

Whenever Madame Fernaud caught sight of herself in a mirror she almost did a double take at the stranger staring back at her. She looked so plain and quaint with the grey wig with the little bun! And those spectacles were positively grim. Without her usual make-up, mascara and rouge, she looked so unattractive, her eyes so small and uninteresting. The make-up she used now made her skin so much darker and aged her by many years.

Wearing the matronly clothes even made her carry herself differently. She walked with a purposeful stride and the youthful spring was gone from her step.

Still, so far things had gone well at Killivray House. Nanny Bea and Romilly had accepted her as the person she was supposed to be: Madame Clementine Fernaud! Dear God, if they only knew her real identity they would be hoRrified! All she had to do now was carry it off when Mr Greswode arrived. Thankfully there were a few days left before his arrival, time in which to practise her composure.

She turned away from the drawing room mirror and went back into the kitchen to check on her cooking.

In a while she would rouse Nanny Bea and Romilly and they would eat supper together in the kitchen. It was a long time since she'd cooked and yet she had enjoyed herself enormously. A *coq au vin* was bubbling away in the oven and soon she would pop in the latticed apple pie she had made for dessert.

She was crossing the hallway when she saw the lights of the car. She put her hand to her head in alarm. Who on earth could it be? The only callers at Killivray were the tradesmen and delivery people and they always arrived in daylight hours.

She panicked, was tempted to make a run for it; to grab her valise and run out through the back door, maybe run all the way to the station and get on the first train out of St Werburgh's. Maybe her secret was out.

She must keep calm. She heard a car door shut noisily and an angry shout.

Her heart slammed against her ribs and her body felt as though it was out of her control. She heard the sound of someone running across the gravel, and soon after a woman laughing.

Then came the sound of a key in the front door and Mr Jonathan Greswode stepped into the hallway with a smiling but haughty-faced young woman on his arm.

★ ★ ★

Romilly stared in horror at Archie Grimble. He stood like a small statue, spotlit in the headlights of Papa's car. She wanted to scream at him, make him run. It seemed for ever that he stood there like a fool just waiting to be caught.

She was willing him to move, to run as fast as he could. If Papa caught him he would be in such trouble.

Then suddenly Archie did run and she was filled with a mixture of fear and the desire to laugh out loud at the sight of him careering across the lawns like a boy followed by a grizzly bear.

Then suddenly he was eaten up by the darkness, and safe.

The lights of the car were turned off and she heard a woman laugh. Hooray! It was Mama! Papa had brought Mama home for Christmas!

Before she could race downstairs Nanny Bea came hurrying into the nursery.

'Romilly, just look at you, child, there is dust in your hair and your clothes are positively grubby. What have you been doing?'

'Nothing, Nanny Bea.'

'Your papa is here. Quickly, wash your face

this instant and put on a clean frock. He will be most angry to see you so untidy.'

When she finally escaped Nanny Bea's assault with a flannel she ran excitedly downstairs. Madame Fernaud was waiting for her at the bottom of the stairs.

'Your papa has arrived unexpectedly, Romilly, and requires you to eat with him in the dining room.'

Madame's voice was quieter than usual and Romilly saw that her hands were trembling.

'Don't be afraid, Madame,' she whispered, 'I won't tell about the walk.'

Madame looked down at the child and smiled sadly. She stood up straight, patted her hair and went into the kitchen.

Romilly winked at her and hurried to the dining room.

Then she stopped in her tracks and her stomach turned over so tumultuously that she almost stumbled against the sideboard.

Papa was sitting at the head of the table looking steadfastly into the eyes of a small, white-faced woman sitting on his right where Mama usually sat.

Jonathan Greswode looked up suddenly and saw Romilly.

'Come in, Romilly dear, and meet one of my oldest and dearest friends, Miss Dimont.'

Romilly stepped into the room and met the hard, shrewd gaze of Miss Dimont.

Romilly blushed and averted her eyes quickly.

She walked across to Papa and kissed his cheek solemnly.

'Nanny Bea and Madame Fernaud are taking supper in the kitchen. I thought it would be good for us to dine together, for you to meet Miss Dimont.'

'Yes, Papa.'

Romilly climbed into a chair opposite Miss Dimont and unfolded her napkin.

'Tell me, Romilly, how have your studies been going with the new governess?'

Romilly cleared her throat and spoke, 'Very well, Papa. Madame Fernaud is a very good teacher.'

Papa looked up in surprise. 'Better than Miss Naylor?'

'Oh, yes, Papa. She is much stricter than Miss Naylor and we get so much more work done.'

Papa winked at Miss Dimont who lowered her gaze and smiled. 'Then my new appointment has been a great success. Not only is she an excellent governess but a very good cook too.'

Romilly looked down at the table. She wondered what he would do if he knew that she and Madame had been out walking in the snow? Papa wasn't supposed to arrive until Christmas Eve so why had he come earlier? Imagine if he'd arrived this afternoon and seen them playing snowballs!

She was so flustered that she could hardly control her thinking. What if he had caught her red-handed, snooping about in the attic?

It was too awful to think about.

While Madame Fernaud had been busy in the kitchen she had sneaked out to the summer-house and put the diary into the stove for Archie

Grimble. Thank goodness that she had got back inside the house before Papa had arrived. She shook inwardly when she thought that it could so easily have been her shown up in the headlights of the car. She couldn't imagine what Papa would have said if he'd discovered her outside in the dark!

'You seem very preoccupied, Romilly.'

'Sorry, Papa. How is Mama?'

Papa put down his glass and looked at Romilly. His face was serious, his eyes cloudy with a mixture of annoyance and indifference.

'Your mama is not well at all, Romilly. But for tonight we will not discuss this. I will speak with you in the morning.'

Romilly looked down into her lap and then busied herself with her food, although she had lost her appetite.

From across the table, Miss Dimont took surreptitious glances at Romilly.

'Tell me,' she said at last, 'what are you hoping to get for Christmas?'

Romilly looked up in alarm. She hadn't even thought about what she wanted for Christmas.

'I don't know,' she said.

'How priceless,' Miss Dimont said. 'How endearing to find a child not completely obsessed with material things.'

'Romilly has been brought up in a very unspoiled way,' Papa said with pride. 'Tomorrow, though, we will drive to St Werburgh's and make some purchases, get ourselves into the festive mood.'

Romilly felt her face flush with anger.

How could he think that she could be cheerful with Mama away and at Christmas too? She didn't want to spend Christmas with Papa and this silly woman who had a face like a suffocating goldfish.

'You have a very high colour, Romilly, are you feeling well?'

'I'm fine, Papa. I was asleep for a while before you arrived, that's all.'

'And what have you been up to while I've been away?'

Romilly bit her lip and held back a rising nervous giggle. She would love to see the expression on Papa's face if she said, Oh, Madame and I have been playing snowballs and I have been hunting through the attic with a lighted candle. Instead she smiled sweetly and said, 'I have learned all my spellings, written an English composition and I'm learning about the geography of Italy.'

'Very good, I can see Madame has kept you busy. Madame was telling me that Nanny Bea was taken ill this afternoon.'

'Yes, Papa, she saw the ghost of the black man of Killivray staring through the kitchen window.'

Papa dropped his napkin and laughed loudly, startling Miss Dimont who then dropped her fork with a clatter.

'Whatever does she mean, Jonathan?' Miss Dimont said. 'I do hope Killivray House is not haunted.'

'Just local tales, stuff and nonsense! There is supposed to be a ghost who walks Killivray at night. One of the menservants who, er, came to an untimely end.'

'What sort of an untimely end?'

'Er, not the sort to be discussed whilst eating, my dear.'

'Great Grandpapa Greswode had tigers and bears here when he was a young man,' Romilly said. 'And black servants too, didn't he, Papa?'

'Good heavens!' Miss Dimont exclaimed.

'He was, er, a little eccentric in his youth,' Papa said.

'I do hope it's not hereditary!' Miss Dimont said with a giggle.

'I assure you I take more after my mother, who was a much more serious creature.'

'That's Papa's Mama,' said Romilly, pointing to a large portrait of a woman whose face reminded Romilly of an enormous pink ham.

Miss Dimont looked up at the portrait with interest.

'How long has your family been at Killivray?'

'Hundreds of years,' Jonathan Greswode said proudly.

'You were born here?'

'Of course.'

'And Romilly too?'

'Correct. And almost all the Greswodes before us.'

'Except for Thomas Greswode,' Romilly blurted out. 'He was born in Italy.'

Papa looked at her in surprise.

'Who was Thomas Greswode?' Miss Dimont asked.

Romilly bit her lip.

'Thomas Greswode was my father's cousin. And it is a very long time since his name has been mentioned in this house.'

His voice was cool, his gaze frosty as he looked at his daughter. 'How do you know of Thomas Greswode, Romilly?'

Suddenly Romilly's tongue felt too large for her mouth and her throat seemed to shrink.

Jonathan Greswode continued to stare at her.

Just at that moment Madame appeared in the doorway bringing in the dessert.

'Thank you, Madame Fernaud. We weren't expecting supper and yet you have done us proud in the circumstances.'

Madame Fernaud was aware of the frostiness in the air and looking across at Romilly realized the girl was petrified. She put down the apple tart and left the room, lingering outside.

'Romilly, Thomas Greswode is a name we do not mention in this house ever. Do you understand?'

'Yes, Papa.'

Romilly clasped her hands tightly in her lap and wondered whatever had poor Thomas Greswode done to upset the Greswodes so much.

She ate up her pudding in silence and was relieved when Papa summoned Nanny Bea to take her off to bed.

★ ★ ★

Madame Fernaud had cleared the kitchen and now she stood outside the door at the far end of the drawing room listening in to the conversation between Jonathan Greswode and Miss Dimont.

Jonathan Greswode poured two large brandies and handed one to Miss Dimont.

'Why were you so angry with the child for asking about Thomas Greswode, Jonathan?'

'It's a long and unsavoury story, Lydia.'

'But you know how interested I am in everything about you and your ancient family, so do, do tell me.'

'Very well, but it's not a pretty story.'

'I do so love stories.'

'My father had a cousin, this Thomas Greswode who was a few years younger than him. He grew up somewhere abroad, France or Italy I think. He came to live here when he was about eight.'

'Why did he come to live here, did he have no parents?'

'His father had made an unsuitable marriage and his wife, Thomas' mother, had died. He was in a bad way after her death and he remained abroad.'

'And Thomas came here?'

'He did. Thomas was sent back to England for his schooling and he went to a local prep school with my father, but it didn't work out well having him here.'

'What happened?'

'He tried to murder my father.'

'My God! A young boy of eight! How terrible.'

'It was a few years after he came here. He would have been about twelve. My father always told me that Thomas was a very jealous type of boy. Apparently, they had an argument, the way boys do and he took a gun from Grandpapa's

197

cabinet and took a shot at my father.'

'My God! What happened?'

'Fortunately he missed. You can still see the bullet hole in the old summerhouse roof.'

'What happened to him? Was he locked up?'

'My grandfather did not wish the police to be involved because of the Greswode good name. There was the most awful row and Grandpapa gave him a good beating and he ran away like the coward he was.'

'Did they find him?'

'The silly boy went off in his boat and got himself drowned.'

'What an awful story and how terrible for his father, to lose a wife and have a son die like that.'

'It was awful for him of course and sadly he died round about the same time.'

'So that whole side of the Greswode family was wiped out?'

'Yes. A form of evolution, I suppose.'

'Evolution? I don't understand.'

'There was an eccentric strain running through some of the Greswodes and I think that they were the masters of their own destinies. The weak die through their own short-comings and all that.'

'And the strong live to fight on? How romantic.'

Jonathan Greswode got up and refilled their glasses.

'My grandfather, you see, was the younger of two brothers. If Thomas had lived he would have inherited Killivray from his father, and stolen my birthright.'

'So your father wasn't the master of Killivray and if Thomas had lived, no doubt the other Greswode line would be here now?'

'My Great Uncle David, Thomas' father, had inherited Killivray as the oldest son, my grandfather merely acted as caretaker while he was abroad sowing his wild oats. My great-uncle had squandered a good deal of the estate. We used to own half the countryside around here at one time but he involved himself in all kinds of foreign business ventures and sold off a lot of the land.'

'Maybe it's just as well he didn't live to throw away Killivray as well.'

'Yes, thank God.'

'It must be enormously expensive to keep up a place like this.'

'Frightfully.'

'My darling, you've gone quite pale, what is it?'

'Well, I'm afraid that things were left in a financial mess when my father died. He'd had some difficulties in his last years and he'd sold the house. I am here now merely as a tenant.'

'Who owns the house now?'

'Some charitable organization in London but I am allowed to remain here for the rest of my life. After that it will leave the Greswode family.'

'But why did your father sell without telling you?'

'I don't know. He was very agitated about something before he died. I often wonder if he was being blackmailed.'

'How awful. Is there any way that you could

buy the house back and keep it for future Greswodes?'

'Not unless I inherit a great deal of money and the owners want to sell.'

'And are you likely to inherit money?'

'Not from my own family but my wife is a very wealthy woman in her own right.'

Madame Fernaud withdrew a little from her hiding place.

There was something in Jonathan Greswode's voice that chilled her to the marrow.

'It must have been so awful for you having to cope with a sick wife and a child all on your own.'

'It has been hard but soon my wife will be transferred to a mental institution for her own good and I will be more or less a free man.'

'So we will have to be discreet for now, but later?'

'But later, we will be free to have a very good time, a very good time indeed.'

Madame was aware that the couple were embracing and she could barely make out their muffled conversation.

She made to go but then Jonathan Greswode said, 'I have to visit the convent in the next few days to make plans for my wife's transfer. After that unpleasant business we shall endeavour to enjoy Christmas, my little savage.'

Miss Dimont giggled coquettishly.

Madame Fernaud was about to move away when she heard a movement close by. She stood absolutely still, ears pricked. She peered anxiously into the shadows. It was nothing, just the multitude of sounds old houses made at night.

She moved silently along the corridor and up the servants' stairs. She slipped into her room and locked the door. Moments later Romilly clambered out from her hideaway and followed her, trying desperately to hold back her sobs until she reached the nursery. She sat down and wrote a letter to Archie Grimble, her tears dropping down onto the paper as she wrote. When everyone was asleep she would creep back out and put it into the stove.

*　*　*

Fleep was sitting at the window looking out to sea when he heard the knock at his front door. He walked to the door and called out, 'Who's there?'

'Thrash the bastard!' called the parrot.

A voice, breathless with exertion, answered, 'Just open the door, man, for God's sake.'

It wasn't a voice that he recognized from the village.

Slowly he drew back the bolts and opened the door a fraction.

He looked out to see a large black man in his fifties, holding what looked like a dead child in his arms.

Fleep opened the door wider and indicated with a jerk of his head that the man enter.

He looked from the man to the child in bewilderment. 'What's happened? Is he alive?'

'He's alive all right. He's just had one hell of a shock.'

'Put him down on the bed, for God's sake, before you drop him.'

Thankfully, the man laid Archie Grimble down on the bed.

'He's only a whippersnapper, but goddamned heavy to carry any distance, all the same.'

'You want a drink?'

The man looked at Fleep gratefully. 'Sure thing.'

He was an American by the sound of him but what the hell was he doing in the Skallies at this time of night?

Fleep uncorked a bottle of wine, poured some into two mugs and handed one to the man.

From the bed the boy groaned softly.

'Does he need anything, a doctor maybe?'

'No, he'll be okay in a while. Do you know who the little fellow is?'

'He's called Archie Grimble. He lives just up the way. In Bag End.'

'Bag End?'

'The last house on the right.'

'Do you know his folks?'

'Not really. I'm a bit of a stranger here, only arrived a few weeks ago. His mother looks frightened out of her wits most of the time and the father's a drunk, nasty-looking man. He'll be over in the pub if you want me to fetch him.'

'No, let's just leave the little fellow to rest a while.'

Fleep took a slug of his wine, put down his mug and put out his hand. 'Philippe, but just call me Fleep, all the locals do. Pleased to meet you.'

'Dom Bradly,' the man replied, taking Fleep's

hand in a powerful grip.

'And you're wondering what the hell a fellow like me is doing in this place, huh?'

Fleep smiled, 'You're a long way from home by the sound of it.'

'I'm on a working holiday, searching for murder scenes.'

Fleep blanched. 'You a policeman?'

'Don't look so nervous, I'm in the movies and I'm checking out possible locations. The spooky house through the woods looks like the perfect spot.'

'Oh, I see.'

Fleep coughed and changed the subject. 'Are you staying around here?'

Dom Bradly laughed, 'No, I'm not staying round here. I got myself one of those camper van things. Didn't want to turn up in a small place like this and start tongues wagging. Thought I'd do a spot of investigating in the dark. People don't take too well to a black guy pitching up on their doorstep, you know how it is?'

Fleep blushed deeply. He was only too aware of the signs he'd seen in London lodging houses. NO BLACKS. NO IRISH. NO WELSH.

'I popped up to the Big House this morning. Had a peep through the windows and some old woman inside takes up screaming like a mad thing when she clapped eyes on me. Didn't think I'd get much of a welcome there.'

Fleep smiled, 'From what I've heard in passing the people up there are like hermits, they don't have any dealings with the locals.'

'Shoot the bastards,' yelled the parrot.

'That's a sweet-talking bird you got there,' Dom Bradly said.

'He's got a vile mouth on him, nothing to do with me. I kind of inherited him.'

Just then Archie Grimble stirred.

'Maybe best if you go to him,' Dom Bradly said. 'I don't suppose he's seen many black faces in this neck of the woods. I don't want to put him into another faint.'

Fleep drank the rest of his wine and moved towards the bed.

He placed his hand on Archie's feverish brow and Archie opened his eyes wide.

He looked up at Fleep in alarm, his one good eye bright with fear. 'Help me, Fleep,' he whimpered.

'It's okay, son, you're all right. You just had a nasty shock, that's all.'

'I saw the . . . '

'It's okay, hush now.'

'I saw the ghost in the woods. The Killivray black man. He was after me but I managed to fight him off and get away.'

'Arseholes,' screeched the parrot.

'Will I put a rug over that bird's cage and shut him up?'

Archie sat up suddenly and looked towards Dom Bradly.

'It's okay, fellah, you've nothing to be afraid of.'

'Y . . . y . . . you're not a ghost?' Archie said.

'Hell no, I ain't no ghost. So sorry that I gave you a scare.'

Archie couldn't take his eyes off the man.

He'd never seen a black man before, except in books.

'You feeling okay?'

Archie nodded weakly. Life was easier when he'd been a coward.

'Will you be okay to get him home?'

Fleep nodded.

'Is your mother home?' he asked Archie.

'What time is it?'

'Five and twenty past nine.'

'She'll still be at the Arbuthnots'.'

'Look, I really gotta be off. Sorry for the intrusion. I hope to meet you again some time. Good to meet you both.'

Dom Bradly held out his hand to Archie. The boy took it and marvelled as his own tiny hand was enveloped by the man's huge fingers.

'Take that for your trouble,' he said, peeling a note from his pocket and handing it to Archie.

'I'd be real grateful if neither of you mentioned seeing me, if that's okay?'

Archie nodded. He could keep secrets.

Dom Bradly shook Fleep's hand. 'If I don't get to see you before I go back, this is my card. If you're ever in the States then look me up. Same invitation goes for the little fellow.' He handed Fleep two business cards.

Archie watched him go, with wonder. Dom Bradly turned at the door, put on his hat and smiled and then he was gone.

'Eat shit and die,' cried the parrot.

★ ★ ★

205

Jonathan Greswode, Miss Dimont, Nanny Bea and Romilly set out from Killivray straight after breakfast on their way to St Werburgh's to do some Christmas shopping. Clementine, complaining of a headache, declined the invitation to accompany them. She offered to prepare dinner but Jonathan Greswode said he was planning to eat in a hotel on the other side of St Werburgh's.

Clementine watched the car disappear down the drive, with relief. She put through a call on the telephone and spent ten minutes talking rapidly. Then she dressed in her warmest clothes and made her way down through the grounds of Killivray, out through the gate and towards the Skallies.

It wasn't yet nine o'clock and Bloater Row was deserted. She hurried up to the door of the Pilchard Inn and tapped on it.

There was no answer but from inside she could hear the sound of laughter and chatter. She tapped on the door again and waited impatiently.

Nan Abelson opened the door and almost swallowed the mouthful of hairgrips that were clenched between her teeth. Her thick dark hair was loose and hung down way past her waist and she looked much younger, more fragile than Madame Fernaud remembered from their first meeting.

She spat the hairgrips into the palm of her hand and stared at Madame Fernaud.

'It's a little early for a glass of wine, but I can give you freshly made coffee.'

206

Madame Fernaud followed Nan into the Pilchard.

'Come through to the kitchen.'

Madame followed Nan behind the bar and through the curtained doorway into a warm and cosy kitchen that smelled of fresh baking and strong coffee.

'Just give me a moment while I do my Cissie's hair and then I'll be with you.'

Madame Fernaud smiled at a little girl sitting up on a stool.

The girl smiled back, a huge smile that split her round, pale face in two.

Nan brushed the girl's hair, then put two round pink hair slides on either side of her fringe and lifted her down from the stool.

'You're to go straight to Archie's, okay?' she said, cupping the child's chin in her hand.

The girl nodded with exaggerated seriousness.

'Mrs Grimble said you can play with Archie for an hour or two. Then I'll come for you.'

The girl nodded again, her eyes wide with trust.

'Ask if you need the lavatory, okay?'

'Ask if you need the lavatory, okay?' the girl repeated parrot fashion.

'Go on then.' Nan Abelson kissed the child who flung her arms around Nan's neck and showered her with kisses.

Then she skipped past Madame Fernaud and out of the kitchen.

Madame sat down at the table and watched as Nan expertly caught up her own hair and twisted it into a thick plait.

Then she poured coffee and busied herself at the oven, emerging red-faced with a tray of perfectly formed golden croissants.

'How wonderful they look,' Madame said.

'My speciality,' Nan said. 'Learned at my mother's knee.'

'Well, it's so good to be out of the house. You were right; it does get rather oppressive and lonely up there.'

Nan sat down opposite Madame. 'Whereabouts in France are you from?' she asked abruptly.

'Just outside of Bordeaux,' Madame replied.

Nan drank her coffee. Just outside of Bordeaux, my arse, and yet she speaks English with a Parisian accent.

'Do you speak French?' Madame enquired.

'No,' Nan lied. 'Apart from *bonjour, merci,* and the usual bits one remembers from school.'

'Where did you go to school?'

Nan bristled but covered her annoyance and replied, 'Just outside London. Essex.'

'And how old is your little girl?'

'Almost ten.'

Madame Fernaud thought that Nan didn't look old enough to have a child of Cissie's age.

'Have you lived here a long time?' Madame asked.

Nan felt her anger rising fast. This woman asked too many questions for her liking. It was more an interrogation than a conversation.

'I'm just going to check that Cissie has shut the door properly, I'll be right back.'

Madame Fernaud drank her coffee and

thought that this woman wasn't being quite straight. Anyone who could turn out a croissant like that had seen the sky above France. Despite her English accent she'd bet that Nan spoke fluent French. They had something in common, they were both hiding something.

Nan went through the bar and drew the bolts across the door. She stood for a moment, thinking fast. She was damned sure this woman wasn't who she said she was. She was too interested in Nan and Cissie's history.

She made her way silently back into the kitchen, poured more coffee, put a croissant on a plate and placed it before Madame Fernaud.

She made as if to sit down then suddenly she grabbed Madame Fernaud around the neck, pulled her roughly to her feet and spat out the words, 'I don't know who you are or what your game is but you try and harm a hair on our heads and I'll fucking kill you.'

Madame Fernaud opened her mouth to scream but Nan's hand came down hard across her mouth and the sound died in her throat. She struggled to get out of Nan's grip but Nan was too strong for her.

'Sit there and don't think of leaving,' Nan grated through clenched teeth, shoving Madame Fernaud roughly back down into the chair.

Madame Fernaud did as she was bid, rubbing her neck and struggling to catch her breath. Then she watched in horror as Nan picked up a sharp kitchen knife from the dresser and came towards her with a look of such fury on her face that it made Madame Fernaud more afraid than she'd ever been in her life.

'Who are you?' Nan spat out the words.

Madame Fernaud put her hand to her head and with a flourish she whipped off her grey wig.

Nan put her hand to her mouth and her eyes widened with astonishment.

'I think you know who I am. Listen, listen to me very carefully, I need your help.'

Outside in the backyard the wildcats growled and seagulls screeched above the roofs of the Skallies.

* * *

Archie Grimble had slept badly in the nights since he'd met Dom Bradly in the woods. When he did sleep he dreamed such vivid dreams that he began to wish he was awake.

He dreamed of tigers chasing him through the woods at Killivray. Of escaping into the summerhouse and hiding behind the busted sofa. Then suddenly relief turned to renewed terror as he saw the giant tiger heads looking in through the dusty windows, the squeak of their claws on the glass. Then the door creaking open and the pad of their paws on the wooden floor. Their rasping, foul-smelling breath and the stench of stale blood. Sunlight stirring the dust motes into a myriad of rainbows. The tiger's mouth opening . . .

Benjamin shouting to him, 'Put your hand down into their bellies and grab hold of the tail and pull them inside out!'

The glint of their teeth, sharp, silver teeth

ready to rip him limb from limb.

Then suddenly an army of toy soldiers smashing their way through the dirty glass of the cabinet, firing their pistols, charging with fixed bayonets . . .

He dreamed of Romilly waving at him excitedly from her window. The headlights of a car bright as a tiger's eyes. Someone shouting. He and Romilly running together across the lawns hand in hand . . . The smell of cinnamon and roses and fresh laundry making him feel light-headed.

Then Romilly standing beside him in the wobbly chapel looking up at the window of coloured glass. Kaleidoscope colours bathing them in a warm and syrupy light.

Then the gravestone on the floor moving, sliding quietly open . . .

Thomas Greswode climbing out of the hole in the ground, holding a brand new shiny cricket ball. An old, toothless nun following him, a silver fish clasped in her gnarled hand. The fish's mouth opening and spewing out tiny silver saints that tinkled as they fell to the floor.

Behind the nun a black man, with a parrot on his shoulder . . .

On the third morning after his fright in the woods he woke bathed in sticky sweat, his mouth dry and his whole body stiff and sore.

He lay without moving for a long while, glad of the daylight seeping through the thin curtains and happy to see the familiar things in his room. The curled-up virgin drinking up the daylight, the outline of the washstand and the mottled glass of the wardrobe that reflected his ashen face.

Hearing the sound of excited voices out in Bloater Row, he got unsteadily out of bed and staggered across to the window. He drew back the curtains and looked out.

Outside the Pilchard Inn a noisy crowd had gathered round a flustered-looking policeman.

Archie dressed hurriedly and went downstairs.

Mammy was in the kitchen, sitting at the table with a cup of tea welded to her hand and a worried look on her face.

'What's happening, Mammy?' he asked.

She looked up at him and he knew that she'd been crying.

'What is it, Mammy?'

'There's been terrible trouble up at Killivray House.'

'At Killivray House? What sort of trouble?' He could barely keep the panic out of his voice.

'The police are here in the Skallies asking questions.'

Archie swallowed hard. 'What sort of trouble, Mammy?'

She didn't answer for a moment. It was as if she hadn't heard his question.

'I mean it's not as though we knew any of them but it's still a terrible thing,' she said absently.

'What kind of trouble, Mammy?'

'The worst sort of trouble, Archie.'

Archie sat down heavily in a chair.

'Make sure that you keep away from the policemen, Archie. Don't be letting them ask you

212

any questions. And if they do ask, just tell them you've never been near the place and you don't know anything.'

'What's the worst sort of trouble, Mammy?' His voice sounded as though it was being filtered through his socks.

'Murder,' Martha Grimble said.

Part Three

Part Three

All over Christmas the snow fell incessantly and the air was filled with the distant ringing of police bells.

In the Skallies doors were slammed shut and curtains were drawn when the hard-heeled policemen came tramping along Bloater Row with their notebooks at the ready.

They were opened later when the foxy-faced reporters came creeping around in their soft-soled shoes, with their offers of free beer and fancy fags.

By the end of December the police were gone and the reporters lingered to drink the Pilchard dry. Then suddenly the thaw came. The icicles began to melt, dripping faster and faster, teetering dangerously and then crashing down onto the cobbles of Bloater Row.

Black slush filled the cracks and crevices of the cobbles and water dripped relentlessly from the broken guttering on the houses. The pipes burst in Periwinkle House and Mrs Galvini got sick and lost the baby she was carrying and gossip was rife that Mrs Kelly was expecting another.

Archie Grimble went down with a bad case of the chickenpox along with the Kelly boys.

In the backyard of the Pilchard Inn three of the wildcats died in one night.

★　★　★

It was quiet in Bag End. The porker had taken himself off to London on the pretence of looking for work at the first sniff of the police in the Skallies.

Up in his bedroom Archie languished in bed. His head ached and he was pickled in blisters and made to wear white cotton gloves so as not to scratch the scabs and scar himself for life.

In between sleeping and his mammy covering him from head to toe in calamine lotion, he read and reread his Christmas annuals and eked out the contents of his selection box.

All the while he was in a sweat of sickness and anxiety over what had happened at Killivray House. His mammy was tight-lipped about it and she kept the door firmly shut to keep out the nosy police.

After he had been a whole week in bed Cissie Abelson was allowed to visit and came every day bringing him sweets and fizzy lemonade. Archie was desperate to know what had happened up at Killivray House but he couldn't get an ounce of sense out of her other than her shouting Bang! Bang! then falling in a pretend swoon to the bedroom floor clutching her chest.

He persuaded her to smuggle him in some old newspapers carefully hidden inside piles of old comics.

Archie read them with mounting horror. Jonathan Greswode had been murdered, found dead by a woman guest called Miss Dimont, the daughter of a wealthy London banker. He had been shot through the head with one of his own guns by the new French governess.

And, worst of all, she had abducted ten-year-old Romilly Greswode!

Archie reached out for the battered old dictionary that Benjamin Tregantle had given him a few years ago.

'Abducted: To carry off by force, to kidnap.'

He sat open-mouthed, staring down at the paper in shock, a blur of tears making the newspaper print wobble.

Wiping his eyes on the sleeve of his pyjamas, he carried on reading.

The police and someone called Interpol were looking for the murdering governess and poor abducted Romilly.

The governess, the papers said, was a woman of many names; Clementine Fernaud alias Marianna Dupois alias Renee Armand were a few of the names she went under.

She was a conniving thief and con artiste who owed vast amounts of money to people in a trail from Monte Carlo to Bournemouth.

Stories and rumour abounded in the papers. She was once a small-time actress in Paris, a brassy dancer at the Moulin Rouge. She was a bigamist, a forger and an out-and-out wastrel as well as a cold-blooded murderess and kidnapper.

A week after the murder Miss Fanthorpe's car, which had been stolen from Nanskelly on the night of the murder, was found abandoned forty miles away. There was no sign of the governess or Romilly.

Every day Archie waited impatiently for Cissie to arrive with the latest newspapers. Each day they reported sightings of the wicked governess across Europe and beyond but they were false trails and she was not found. Neither was the child, Romilly Greswode.

There was much colourful speculation on why Clementine Fernaud had shot Jonathan Greswode.

Maybe, the papers pondered, he had discovered her true identity and challenged her? They hinted that she may have been his abandoned and jealous mistress. The one question was why had she taken an innocent child with her? Had she taken her as a hostage or worse?

Stories about Margot Greswode, Romilly's mother, came next.

She was the only daughter of wealthy parents, the late Mr and Mrs Edgar Lee. She had been educated abroad and had been an aspiring young actress, tipped by many for a great future. She had married Jonathan Greswode and soon after retired from the theatre due, it was said, to a debilitating nervous illness. She had lived quietly in the country with her husband and young daughter.

She was, the papers said, indisposed at present and being cared for in a nursing home. Sister Mary Campion told reporters that, understandably, Mrs Greswode was overwhelmed with distress both for her dead husband and her missing child and was not well enough to give an interview.

Archie read the papers over and over again. There was a photograph in one of them showing Romilly standing between her parents. It was faded and a little out of focus. Jonathan

Greswode was a tall, sniffy-nosed-looking man and Mrs Greswode had a pretty face and a sad smile. Romilly was looking at the camera curiously, her head on one side, one hand clasped in her mother's, the other firmly behind her back as though she didn't want to hold hands with her father.

Archie fretted for Romilly and prayed for her each night before he went to bed. He lit a special candle and placed it in front of the Virgin. He hoped that Romilly was safe and that the crazy woman wouldn't harm a hair on her head.

There was no point in him ever going up to Killivray House again now that Romilly was gone. He would never discover what had happened to Thomas Greswode without her help.

It had been a daft idea anyway. Him and his mysteries! How could two kids have ever found out about someone who died so long ago? And what was the point?

He just hoped that the police would find Romilly soon and bring her back safe and sound to Killivray. If she did come back then maybe they could start being friends all over again?

Suddenly he remembered the things that Romilly had left for him in the stove the last time he'd been up to Killivray. What with all the fright of the car arriving and seeing the black man in the woods he'd shoved it all away in his cupboard. And before he had a chance to look at them he had gone down with the chickenpox.

He slipped quietly out of bed. His legs felt as weak as a kitten's and he had to drag himself

221

slowly across the room. Catching sight of himself in the wardrobe mirror, he was shocked at his reflection. He'd got even skinnier since he'd been ill and had to hold up his pyjama trousers to stop them falling down round his ankles. He opened the cupboard door quietly, because if Mammy heard him up and about she'd play merry hell with him.

Grabbing the diary and the envelope from the back of the cupboard, he scuttled back to bed.

He tried for ages to open the lock on the diary but it would not budge. Then he had a thought. He got back out of bed and found the bunch of keys that Benjamin had left him. Painstakingly he tried the smallest of the three keys but he had no luck. It was a sturdy lock and rusted in parts and he'd need to get something like a hammer to belt it with. A bloody sledgehammer, even.

He turned then to the pile of letters. They smelled vaguely of pine and were thin and yellowed, curling up at the edges. The ink was badly faded and in parts they were almost unreadable.

At the top right-hand corner an address was written: Casa delle Stelle, Santa Caterina, Italia . . .

The letters were written to Thomas Greswode all right and signed by his papa but that was all he could make out. If only he could read Italian! Impatiently he folded them back up and put them under his pillow. Then he opened the envelope and looked inside.

There were three photographs inside the envelope. They were rough around the edges and looked as if they had been hastily ripped out of a photograph album. He took up the first one and examined it closely.

It was a peculiar photograph and it took him a while to realize which way was the right way up. There was a man hanging upside down on a trapeze and flying towards him was a woman with her hands outstretched. Archie felt giddy just looking at it. Seconds later the photographer would have seen their hands meet and the audience would have known that she was safe and clapped like billy-o! But you couldn't be sure, looking at the photograph, that he did catch her!

The second photograph was a sepia picture of a young boy. It took Archie some moments before he realized that the boy was standing outside the summerhouse in the gardens at Killivray. How different it looked in the olden days! The wood looked new and there were even curtains at the windows. The boy was smiling, a really happy smile. He was dressed in an old-fashioned sailor suit and he was holding a cricket bat. On the back someone had written in sloping handwriting, *Thomas at Killivray July 5th 1900*. He turned the photo back over quickly and knew that he was looking into the face of Thomas Gasparini Greswode. It felt really peculiar to be looking at someone who was dead and buried beneath the floor in the wobbly chapel.

He picked up the third photograph and looked at it. There was a white tear line running through the middle of it as if it had been ripped in half.

He looked at the back and saw that someone had glued tracing paper over the back in an attempt to mend it. It wasn't half as interesting as the other two. It was a photograph taken at a wedding; disappointingly there was nothing written on the back.

He lay the photographs down on the bed and compared them. Then suddenly he gasped.

The man in the wedding photograph was the spit of Thomas Greswode, just older looking. He stared at the photograph of the bride, a very pretty woman looking up at the bridegroom as if she could eat him up. She looked the way people were meant to look when they were in love. Yuk!

He looked again at the face of Thomas Greswode. He had a nice face, cheerful and honest-looking, the kind of boy you'd want to have as a friend.

With dismay he heard the clattering of crockery downstairs. Any minute now Mammy would be up the stairs bringing him beef broth or junket and other disgusting muck that was supposed to be good for him but tasted terrible. He shoved the diary and letters hastily underneath the bed, folded his hands across his chest and assumed an air of innocence.

★　★　★

One cold and dank morning in the middle of January the bells tolled in Rhoskilly Church for the funeral of Jonathan Greswode. Folk from the Skallies made their way along the sodden lane and together with the villagers of Rhoskilly they took their seats in the ancient church.

There were only a few family mourners sitting stiffbacked at the front of the church. There was a wizened old woman who sniffed incessantly. She was the old nanny from Killivray. There were a few well-dressed friends from London including a pale-faced, haughty young woman and a tall, stern-faced man they assumed was her father.

After the service the villagers stood at a discreet distance from the other mourners and then, when the final prayer was over and a handful of soil thrown onto the coffin of the late Jonathan Greswode, they moved slowly away.

Jonathan Greswode was laid quietly to rest with his father Charles beneath the towering stone angel.

Nan walked back to the Skallies with Freddie and Charlie Payne. They were silent until they were halfway back.

'Funny old funeral,' said Freddie Payne. 'Hardly any flowers. He couldn't have been a popular man by the amount of mourners there.'

'Who was that woman who was weeping her socks off?' Charlie asked.

'I think she was the one staying at the house when he was murdered,' Freddie replied.

'Perhaps it was her who murdered him; she was a hardfaced little bint by the look on her.'

'Nan! Don't be so wicked!'

'Well, I wouldn't be surprised if Miss Brazen Face was his fancy woman,' Nan said defiantly. 'She had that look about her.'

'Nan! Shame on you. You shouldn't speak ill of the dead.'

'Well, that's what it looked like to me.'

'His wife weren't there, though, were she? Funny thing that, a woman not turning up to her own husband's funeral.'

'Maybe they didn't get on,' Nan said with a shrug.

'Whether they got on or not it's a mark of respect to go to your husband's funeral.'

'It said in the paper she was in a bad way with her nerves. Not well enough to be let out,' Charlie remarked.

'Think she'd have made the effort though. Them nuns could have brought her,' Freddie grumbled.

'I don't suppose the poor devil's in a fit state what with the husband killed and the little girl missing,' Charlie added.

'They'll catch up with that governess woman sooner or later, you mark my words, and if she's hurt that child she'll swing.' Freddie Payne shook his head.

'That'll be the last of the Greswodes in Killivray House, mind. The child can't live there on her own even if she's found, which I very much doubt.'

'By law the wife should inherit, I suppose, but I can't see her coming back after all that's happened, can you?'

'Maybe she will, one day,' Nan said. 'Maybe she'll enjoy the place better without him.'

'You're a cold-hearted bugger, Nan Abelson,' Freddie said, looking at her in surprise.

'Well you never know what goes on between a husband and wife in a marriage; he could have been a cruel devil to her and the child for all we know,' Nan said angrily.

'Even so I don't expect she would have wished him to end up losing his life at the hand of a murderess,' Charlie said, shocked by Nan's outburst.

'Who knows?' Nan remarked coolly. 'I saw her once or twice in the village. She looked a gentle type, downtrodden if you ask me.'

Charlie and Freddie Payne looked at each other with raised eyebrows.

They'd always known that Nan had a downer on men at times. They put it down to a past bad experience for in all the time she'd been in the Skallies she'd never made a mention of Cissie's father or whether she'd been married or not. The fact was she was on her own and left with a young child to bring up. It couldn't be easy raising a child like Cissie who wasn't the full shilling.

'Well,' Nan said, brightening, 'it'll all come out in the wash, I dare say. Do either of you two fancy a pint? On the house of course.'

'Go on then, funerals always brings on a thirst in me,' Charlie replied enthusiastically.

'Have a drink while we still can, you're a long time dead after all,' Freddie mused.

★ ★ ★

Spring came with a rush to the Skallies. The sun rose earlier each morning, bringing with it a

227

weak yet welcome warmth. Fresh winds blew in from the sea, drying out the houses and whipping away the fusty damp smell that had plagued them all winter.

Spring cleaning began in earnest except at the Kellys'. Washing flapped on the makeshift lines strung up along the beach. Windows were cleaned with vinegar, front steps scoured with carbolic and brass buffed up until it gleamed. Rugs were battered mercilessly out of upstairs windows and curtain nets dipped in Reckits Blue.

In Killivray House cobwebs festooned the diamond-paned windows and dust blew under the doors and gathered in the corners of the abandoned rooms. Birds roosted in the towering chimneys and mice nibbled at the feet of the stuffed brown bear at the top of the stairs.

The hedgerows in the surrounding lanes grew thick and primroses and snowdrops flowered in profusion.

Bluebells and yellow poppies sprang up in the grass of the sand dunes and apple blossom drifted down from the gardens of Killivray House and speckled the beach with petals.

Three mewling kittens were born in the backyard of the Pilchard Inn and the Paynes brought in a catch of fish so large that it almost sank their boat.

And Archie thanked his lucky stars and winked at the Virgin on his wall because there was still no news from the porker.

In late April a boatload of trippers landed on Skilly Beach and invaded the Skallies, keen to hear the gruesome details of the Killivray murder and see the strange folk in the Skallies that the newspapers had talked about.

After that they came each fine weekend. Life in the Skallies began to change and there was a busyness and sense of purpose that hadn't been there before. Nan was run off her feet in the Pilchard and Cissie learned how to wash glasses and clear the tables.

The Payne brothers found a couple of battered tables and set them up outside the pub and the Arbuthnots surprised everyone by serving afternoon teas in their front parlour. Cissie sold bracelets made from shells and the Paynes smoked mackerel and set up a fish stall outside the Peapods.

★ ★ ★

In Cuckoo's Nest Mrs Kelly waited until the youngest children were taking their afternoon nap before she steamed open the letter that had arrived that morning.

It was addressed to her husband but he was out fishing with the older boys and wouldn't be back until dusk. She couldn't wait that long to find out who had written to him. The postman hadn't called at Cuckoo's Nest in years. Who in all the world would want to contact him after all this time?

She read slowly, struggling over the longer words and when she came to the end she slumped down onto a chair and fanned herself with the letter.

It must be some sort of a joke. It couldn't be right. This sort of good fortune didn't come the Kellys' way. They weren't the sort of family that fortune favoured, they were born unlucky. And yet, and yet this looked like an official letter from a solicitor in London. She replaced the letter in the envelope, stuck it back down and put it behind the broken clock on the mantelpiece.

Jesus, Mary and Joseph, if this were true then they had no more worries.

She felt the baby quicken in her stomach and made the sign of the cross.

★   ★   ★

Archie had no luck trying to pick the lock on the diary. He poked at it with a rusty compass and a bent hairgrip but nothing would make it budge. In the end he sneaked a saw from the cupboard under the stairs but it took him ages to saw through the leather band that attached the lock to the front of the diary.

He took himself down to the beach, settled himself behind a rock and opened the diary.

He skipped through the slippery pages until he came to an entry in June of 1900. He read avidly, enthralled as life in the past began to unfold.

June 2nd
Received a letter from Sizzie today. She is well but broke her wrist falling out of an olive tree! She doesn't say what she was doing up the tree

but she is quite wild! The fiesta is soon to be held and the flags are up in Santa Caterina. How I would love to be there. Everyone will eat and eat until they are stuffed and stay up half the night. Sizzie's mama has been looking after our house while Papa is away. He arrives back there tomorrow. Sizzie said a brother from the monastery drove his cart off the road and ended up on the roof of Signor Rabiotti's cantina. Sizzie's cousin has had a baby boy called Allesandro.

Sizzie is sad that she won't be able to wheel him around Santa Caterina . . . She used to wheel me out in the perambulator when I was little and race through the narrow streets like a mad thing. How I used to love it! I miss her. Uncle gone to London.

June 8th
Today the cricket list went up and I am not in the team! Not even a reserve. Willis Minor is in and although he is a good chap he can't catch for toffee. G says not to fret but Chas knows I am good enough for the team. G says Chas is a spoiled brat and she would give her eye teeth to give him a sock in the jaw! Bo and I walked in woods. He told me all about his home in Africa, about the enormous sunsets and the calling of elephants and lions at night. He still misses his family badly and I think he would like to go back one day. I can't say I blame him. I wouldn't want to work for Uncle.

Z upset cook with his bad language. She threatened to make him into a stew.

June 9th

Beaky F called me to his study after Latin . . . I am to play for the villagers' cricket team! Hip hip hooray! As G says, every cloud has a silver lining.

Beaky says best not to tell Chas — he will get a well-deserved shock on the day when I walk out to the wicket.

G has gone shopping to St Wers and wouldn't let me go with her. She is v secretive of late . . . Perhaps she has a young man there. She is very pretty and such good fun!

June 11th

Aunt talked all through dinner about cricket and how Chas has the makings of a first-class cricketer and could bring home the honours. Chas has head size of a soccer ball, he is so boastful. He has been bought spanking-new whites and a new bat for the game. Went for walk with G but she came back to house. She is not herself at all.

June 13th

The builders have finished the new summer-house — Papa wanted it built in honour of Mama. Have taken some toys and books down there — it is ace! Except for Chas who thinks he owns it. Met Benj in woods and went back to s/house. Chas was a pig. Says he won't have Skallies lads in his summerhouse! Said other frightful things about catching things off those sorts of people. Benj and I ignored him and went down to beach. Benj is twice the boy

Chas is. He may be poor but he is a true friend. The best chap you could meet.

Beaky F says if Benj took the exam he could get a scholarship place at Nanskelly. That would be terrific.

June 20th

Uncle is back and very bad-tempered. It must have been hot in London because he is very suntanned. The best day! Chas and all went to St Wer. G gave me a present — a spanking-new cricket bat. It's the tops. Bo bowled to me down on the bottom lawn for hours. G not feeling well. Probably the heat. It is boiling!

Cook and G made lemonade and parkin and we sat in shade. Fell asleep. When I awoke G was whispering to cook. I shouldn't have listened but I did. G said she was at her wits' end with his advances — she said he was like an octopus with St Vitus' Dance and she was afraid to be alone with him. She didn't say who he was but perhaps it's a chap from St Wers. I don't know why she sees him if she's afraid of him. Perhaps she is lovesick! Cook said he had always had a 'thing' about G and the best thing she could do was to find another position.

G said that Bo was looking to go home. Then cook said, I hope to God, Gwennie my girl, that you and he aren't dilly dallying . . . all that would come of that would be tears. They talked in riddles half the time so I learned nothing. I hope Gwennie does not leave or Bo either. That would be awful.

V excited about the match.

June 21st

Pipi was not well tonight. Her nose is dry and she even refused a bone from cook.

Uncle says she will get over it and would not call the vet. Bo and I sat with her for ages.

June 22nd

Pipi was a bit better this morning and ate a little bread and milk. Called for Benj but he was out in boat. He's a fine sailor and knows so much about the sea and fishing and things like that. Mrs Treg gave me tea and cake. She is nice. Hogwash House is a very friendly place and nothing like Killivray! I cannot wait for Papa to come back at Christmas! I wish he would write to me soon — it's an age since I last heard from him. I saw the little Payne twins outside the Peapods in pram. Can't tell them apart. They are as brown as berries. Saw G's father coming out of Pilchard. He was blotto.

July 5th

Benj and I out in boat at dawn. Caught five whopping fish. I took two for cook and she was very pleased. G has borrowed a box camera. Took photo of me outside s'house. Chas inside sulking because he wanted his photo taken first.

Pipi is v sick again. Slept in stables with her last night. Bo thinks that she may have eaten rat poison. Her heart is weak and she can hardly stand. Fed her with milk through a straw but she cannot swallow.

Bo came in just after midnight and brought me some bread and cheese.

Pipi passed away just after five o'clock. She was only young for a dog. Papa bought her for me as a leaving present when he left me here at Killivray with Z.

Bo and G going to help me bury her in woods. I was not brave at all and hooted like a girl. Bo was a great comfort, he understands how I feel. Aunt says what a fuss over a mere animal.

July 11th

Bo has made a small headstone and engraved Pipi's name on the stone. We buried her beneath a horse chestnut tree. G and I picked flowers for grave.

I am very sad tonight. I would give up my place in cricket team if only I could have Pipi back.

Chas said Pipi was just a mongrel. Pedigrees were best and didn't get sick. Chas is a mongrel and I wish he would get sick, very sick indeed in fact!

July 15th

G is helping to make teas at Nanskelly tomorrow so that she can see me play. Beaky F is going to teach Benj to score. I am so excited. Chas and rest still have no idea I am playing. Z escaped and was caught in kitchen eating a seed cake cook had just taken out of oven! Saw Bo on cliff path — he'd been out to Nanskelly. He asked me to post a letter for him in Rhoskilly. He was very excited and when he is he can't stop smiling.

July 16th
Hooray! Just the best day ever. Chas' face was a picture when I walked out to bat. He was livid. I scored 89 not out! And I made two sixes that nearly went over the cliff. Chas was bowled by Dally after only 3 balls! Dally took two magnificent catches. I won the cup. I won the cup! Never felt so proud in all my life. I shall write to Papa to tell him my news. Team carried me to Skallies — a wobbly ride I can tell you and I was half afraid they would drop me.

Bo was really pleased. Gwennie said she was that proud she could burst. She might one of these days as she is getting very fat. Mr D from Pilchard bought ginger beer all round and Mrs D made us magnificent pasties.

Dally got scratched by one of the wildcats that live in the backyard of the Pilchard.

Dally says there have always been wildcats in the Skallies and sometimes when the moon is full you can see the outline of a cat's paw on its surface — Wildcat Moon always means change is on its way . . . On way home I took cup to show Pipi. The flowers had all been taken off the grave, ripped up and thrown around. I picked more but I swear if Chas goes near her grave again I will beat him to a pulp.

Late for dinner so sent to room.
G sneaked me up a beef sandwich.

July 26th
My photograph of Mama and Papa was missing from my trunk. I found it in nursery cupboard ripped in half. I hit Chas as hard as I could and bloodied his fat nose. I know it was him. No one else would do such a thing. G has taken it to mend. I hate Chas and his parents even if they are my family. Uncle has stopped my pocket money for a month and made me apologize. I did but crossed my fingers behind my back so I don't mean it. Very glad there is a lock on this diary. It was a wizard idea of G's to hide it under floorboards in s/house. I wouldn't put it past Chas to sink low and read a chap's private diary.

August 1st
Saw Beaky on cliff path and talked to him for ages. He says that he is going to organize a painting trip to Rome in October. Told Chas but he said that he wouldn't go even if he was paid. He hates the Eyeties as he calls them. He is an ignoramus — I don't think the Italians would be charmed by him. Glad he doesn't want to go. I have put down my name and am writing to ask permission from Papa. How I should love to go home again. Sometimes I dream of home, I am in Santa Caterina again with the glorious smell of the sea and the strong whiff of the fish being landed in the harbour. Colourful washing is flapping on the

balconies of the houses and the sun is hot on my neck. I can smell the bread being baked and hot coffee on the boil.

All around me the loud happy chatter of the people. If I go on Beaky's trip Papa may be able to get to Rome to see me. How I should love that. I do hope that he writes soon, I haven't heard in ages and that is most unlike him.

August 5th
Went to early chapel. Benj not there — he cut his hand badly and has had to be stitched. Good job it's his left hand otherwise he won't be able to score . . . Chas passed me a note in hymnal and I cannot write what filthy things he said about Mama. I swear one day I would like to kill him . . .

Archie took off his spectacles and rubbed his eyes.

He could hardly bear to stop reading but his eyes were beginning to ache.

He looked up to see a boat approaching the beach with some speed. For a moment he thought it was the Payne brothers but realized as it got closer that it was the Kellys back from their fishing trip. He gathered up the diary and made his way swiftly up the beach and out of their way.

In Bag End Mammy was dozing in the kitchen so he crept upstairs and settled himself down on his bed to read on.

He wasn't surprised that Thomas Greswode wanted to kill Charles Greswode. Archie would

238

have liked to kill him himself — he was horrid. Fancy ripping up the photograph and taking the flowers off the grave!

He knew that the photograph must be the same one that Romilly had put in the envelope! He rushed to the cupboard and pulled it out. So this was the very photograph that Charles Greswode had stolen from the trunk and ripped up!

It must have been hateful living in Killivray. And why didn't Thomas' papa write to him? At least G and Bo were good to him.

And poor Pipi. Why hadn't Thomas' uncle called out the vet?

It was strange to read about life in Killivray in the olden days. He was sure that Benj must be Benjamin Tregantle and it was funny to think of Benjamin as a boy. And if he had taken the exam he would have ended up going to Nanskelly School. Archie knew that he never did get to go to Nanskelly, though, because the school had shut down soon after Thomas drowned.

He opened the diary and read on eagerly.

August 12th
Chas gone riding with Uncle. Benj and I played soldiers in s'house. Made tea on stove and toasted muffins. One night we are going to sneak out of our houses and sleep the night here and have an adventure. I have moved out of nursery and into long room — supposed to be a punishment for thumping Chas but it is bliss. I don't have to look at his insufferable smug face, hear his insults or listen to him

239

snoring half the night.

I have lost the silver bird necklace that Mama always wore — Papa gave it to me after she died. I have hunted high and low but cannot find it; it's too awful, the clasp must have broken. I have treasured it and it is the only reminder of her that I have.

August 14th
Walked out to Nanskelly but Beaky has gone away . . . My name is on the board in pavilion written in sparkling gold. It made me so proud to see it! Nanskelly is the only good thing about living here. It is a wizard school. No one gets beaten ever. Beaky is the tops as a headmaster.

Bo has gone to Bristol on errands for Uncle. G has been put to bed sick. I heard cook talking to G and she said that she was sure that G is hiding something and the sort of something she's hiding can't be hid for ever.

G was crying and begging cook not to tell. Cook said she knew it was on the cards and God help Gwennie if her father got to hear.

Women are very hard to understand, they seem to talk in a code that us chaps can't work out however hard we try . . . Why will G's father be angry that she is ill?

Looked everywhere for necklace but no luck.

August 15th
Benj brought a whole coconut cake in a tin and we ate all of it washed down with sweet

tea. Delish. Taught Z to say some new words! Polite ones. Next week Benj is going away for two days to visit his folks. I will miss him.

Bo back from Bristol. He does not seem himself at all. I saw him in the long room and he almost jumped out of his skin when he saw me. He asked me how long it was since I'd heard from Papa. After dinner I heard Uncle shouting at him in library — I heard him say that if Bo interferes in family matters he will be out on his ear. G is still in bed and looks very ill. I hope she doesn't die.

August 16th
Bo spoke to me today and he looked so sad. I wonder does Bo know that I am planning to escape? He asked me some strange questions about Santa Caterina, whether I knew anyone with a telephone there . . . He said that if he has to go away suddenly I must not fret. He will never leave me but there is something that he has to do. An honourable thing. He seemed happy and worried at the same time. If he does go he will write to me care of Nanskelly.

August 17th
I am in deepest trouble and no one except Bo and G, and I think cook, believes me. Chas has made up the most awful lies about me. He said that I took a gun from the cabinet and tried to shoot him. As God lives, he is a liar.

I was in s'house reading when he came in. I jumped to see him with the gun because Uncle has banned us from ever touching them.

241

Then he began to taunt me. He called my mama the most awful of names. He said she was a trollop and a whore and that my papa was forced to marry her. He is a liar. He said that everyone knew that I was a bastard.

He said the word over and over, spitting it into my face. He said that I should never be allowed to inherit Killivray because I was a bloody filthy Eyetie.

He pushed me down onto the sofa and pointed the gun into my face.

I have never been so terrified. He has eyes that are quite mad and he almost froths at the mouth like a rabid dog. I managed to get up and tried to get past him.

I truly feared for my life. He would not let me past and I had to wrestle with him. The gun went off and a bullet went straight through the roof.

There was the most awful scene. Uncle swearing and Aunt crying and begging him to call for the police. Chas screeching that I had tried to kill him. On God's life I never did. I couldn't even speak up I was so shaken. Then cook came and Bo.

Later the key to the gun cabinet was found hidden in my trunk and I swear on Mama's grave I do not know how it got there. I know now how much he truly hates me and I am fearful for my very life.

August 18th
Uncle did not call for the police because of the shame it would bring on the family. I wish that

he had and that they believed me — maybe they would lock Chas up. Uncle beat me so badly. I have weals on my back and legs and could barely stand. G brought me some ointment and cook sneaked up some soup and cheese but I cannot eat a thing. I am going to see Beaky F to ask for his help. I cannot endure it here a moment longer.

Benj has already gone away so I won't be able to say goodbye to my best friend in all the world. I shall write to him as soon as I get back to Italy. I shall miss G and Bo and I am sad that I will not be able to visit my faithful Pipi's grave but one day I will come back with Papa and throw Chas and his frightful family out of this house. I will take care of G and Bo because they have been so good to me.

Soon I will leave here and I swear that they will not stop me. Bo came in to say goodnight. I am sure that he knows what I am planning.

Archie put the diary down and walked over to the window. He looked across at the distant chimneys of Killivray House and imagined Thomas inside there afraid and still sore from his beating. He imagined how frightened he must have been when he was planning to run away. Archie wouldn't even know how to start out on a journey to Italy.

If he had managed to run away then things might have turned out differently. He might have come back and chucked Charles and his horrible family out of Killivray. He would have looked after Bo and G and let Mr Fanthorpe stay in

Nanskelly. And the world would have been a different place.

He felt as if he would burst with anger on Thomas' behalf. Charles Greswode was a monster, a spoiled, lying, pig of a boy. It wasn't fair. Life wasn't fair, though, was it? Just like Benjamin used to say and he was right.

He looked across at Hogwash House and imagined a young Benjamin coming back from the visit to his folks and finding out that his best friend was gone, not run away but dead.

Why hadn't Thomas just run off to Italy? Why did he go out to Nanskelly? And then in the boat out past Skilly Point? If he hadn't then surely he would have lived?

There were only a few pages of the diary left to read now and he sat down near the window devouring the last words that Thomas Greswode had ever written before he was lost to the sea.

August 19th

I have packed a few of my most precious things in my little suitcase and hidden it in the Boathouse. Tomorrow I am going to Nan-skelly. I know Beaky F will help me if he can. Benj has said I can use his boat while he is away. Maybe I will row much further round the coast. If I can only get to a station and then on a train to London I can get to France and can somehow make my way down to Italy. It will take an age but I have no choice. I will not stay here in this house. I have some money saved and I will get to Italy however hard it is. I desperately want to take Bo and G into my confidence but if they were caught helping me Uncle would go berserk and throw them out. It will break my heart not to say goodbye to them but it must be so.

Soon, soon, I shall be in my beloved Italy and away from here. I shall see my dear papa and tell him all that has happened. I am very tired and afraid but I shall be as brave as I can be.

Archie stayed at the window for a long time pondering over what he had read. Then he closed the diary sadly and put it back in its hiding place at the back of the cupboard.

★ ★ ★

In the Boathouse Gwennie wound up the gramophone and poured a drop of whisky into an old enamel mug.

She raised the mug and downed it in one go and then poured herself another.

She sat by the window and watched the darkness creep in off the sea, the shadows gradually eating up Skilly Beach. A thin crescent of a frail new moon was rising in the dark sky.

She'd known ever since the Wildcat Moon that things would start happening in the Skallies. And she'd been right too. And if she'd learned anything from the past she knew that the changes weren't over yet.

Another Greswode was buried in Rhoskilly graveyard. God forgive her but she wasn't sorry about that one little bit. His father had been a pig of a man and he'd only allowed her to live in the Boathouse because he was afraid that she knew too much . . .

She'd barely spoken to Jonathan Greswode but she knew from the look of him that he was a bully and worse. There was something about him that made her flesh creep, something about him not right at all. He was a chip off the old block, a nasty bastard.

She'd only seen the governess a few times. She'd watched her once, from the cover of the woods, walking with the child in the snow and another time hurrying in through the bottom gate.

She had to hand it to her, she was a clever bugger. There'd been something furtive and watchful about her. Oh, yes, Clementine Fernaud was a mystery of a woman all right. There'd be no bringing a wily minx like her to justice, that was for sure.

By God she'd been surprised at all that had gone on in the past weeks. Folks weren't what you thought they were at all . . .

She poured herself more whisky and laughed quietly to herself as the night darkened and the stars pricked the sky one by one.

She looked across at the wobbly chapel and shivered. She hadn't been inside there for years. Not since . . .

Maybe, just maybe she should go back in there one more time and face up to the horrors of the past.

★ ★ ★

246

One Saturday afternoon Archie walked out to Nanskelly in the hope of seeing William Dally again.

It was good to be alone on the cliff path and away from the Skallies. The breeze was fresh and out at sea the waves were topped with white flecks. Seagulls screamed in the wake of an incoming fishing boat and in the distance a steamer ploughed doggedly out towards the curve of the horizon.

Archie climbed the stile and gazed across at Nanskelly School. The windows were open wide and the sound of a piano reached his ears and the tinkling of cutlery from the kitchen.

Archie breathed in the smell of cooking. Suet pudding and beef with thick gravy. Sticky treacle tart and custard without skin.

His mouth watered and his belly rumbled like a sink emptying.

Inside the school someone began to sing . . .

'Early one mor-or-ning just as the sun was ri-i-sing, I heard a maiden si-ing in the va-a-lley below. Oh, never lea-ave me, oh don't decei-eive me. How-ow could you lea-ea-eave a por-or maiden so . . .'

The voice was young, high and pure with a tremble running through it the way the names of places ran through sticks of pink seaside rock.

It brought tears to his eyes and made his backbone weak with longing.

He found William Dally outside the potting shed.

'Well, I'll be buggered. I'd given up hope of seeing you again,' he said looking up from his weeding.

247

'I've had the chickenpox,' Archie said.

'Poor old you. Fancy a cup of tea?'

'Please,' Archie replied.

'Come on in the shed and plonk yourself down on that box and I'll fix us a brew.'

Archie sat down and looked around the potting shed. It was full of dusty flower pots of all shapes and sizes, shovels and forks, twine and old potato sacks. It smelled good in there, earthy, peaty and musty.

He'd have liked to work in a place like Nanskelly and have his very own private potting shed like William Dally.

'Had a right old time over there of late, haven't you, what with all the goings-on up at Killivray House?'

'I missed most of it. I was in bed pickled with spots.'

'A queer old business altogether that was. Strange how that governess woman upped and murdered the master. Mind you, knowing the Greswodes, it probably weren't all her fault.'

'But she murdered him! And she was a thief! It said so in the papers. And she stole Romilly Greswode!' Archie said with feeling.

''Appen she did but I don't think she'd have reason to harm the child, do you?'

'I don't know.'

'You'll probably find she'll leave the child somewhere safe once she's got far enough away.'

'But where? And what if it's so far away Romilly can't find her way back to Killivray?'

'She's got a tongue in her head. She'll have to ask. Look, I know it ain't right, the Lord only knows that, but you shouldn't be worrying your head about all this, son.'

'But she was my friend.'

William Dally looked up with interest. 'Who was?'

'Romilly Greswode.'

'First I heard she had any friends. It was all the talk she was kept in the house like an exotic plant.'

'She was but I met her a couple of times, kind of by accident.'

'Oh, right.'

'She stole the car from here, didn't she, that governess?'

William Dally looked thoughtful. 'She did, right enough.'

'Did the police come here asking questions?'

'They did indeed. Quite a stir there was, the girls getting all overexcited and acting proper daft.'

'What did the police say?'

'Just wanted to know where the car was when it was stolen and how she got hold of the keys.'

'And how did she?' Archie asked.

'Well, Miss Fanthorpe's usually most careful with her keys but she'd left them in the car that night. Mind you, like I said to the police, she does get very forgetful some days. Last week she went into assembly wearing odd shoes! One red one and one blue one.'

Archie giggled, and then looked up with a start to see a woman standing in the doorway.

Archie stood up quickly.

William Dally blushed deeply. 'Morning, Miss

Fanthorpe,' William muttered.

'Pray stay seated, young man, I only want a word with William,' she said to Archie.

'Let me introduce you to Master Archie Grimble.'

Miss Fanthorpe's eyes lit up and she held out her hand.

Archie shook it shyly.

'How pleased I am to meet you. I know a little about you already.'

'Do you?' Archie said with surprise.

'A mutual, er, friend of ours told me all about you.'

Archie didn't know what mutual meant so he stayed silent.

'Mr Benjamin Tregantle!' Miss Fanthorpe said with a twinkle in her eye.

Archie smiled back at her; it was a long time since he'd heard Benjamin's name spoken out loud.

'I knew Benjamin real well,' he said.

'You must miss him dreadfully, I know I do.'

Archie looked down at his feet; he could feel the tears rising.

'It's good to talk of the dead, however painful. It brings them to life, you see, means that they're not forgotten.'

'I s'pose,' Archie replied with a sniff.

'When you two have had a good old yarn, could you bring in some potatoes, William? Oh, and I've another letter for you to post. Bring Archie inside at the same time — cook's made some apple muffins and I'd like to get better acquainted with him. I've heard such good things about you, Archie.'

Archie felt the blood run to his face. There wasn't much good for anyone to hear about him.

Miss Fanthorpe left them alone, walking briskly across the lawns and into the school.

'She likes you, I can tell,' William Dally said. 'Here get that tea down your neck, douse the fire in your face, you're red as a bloody beetroot.'

'Did you know Benjamin Tregantle well?'

'In some ways I did and in others I didn't,' William Dally said.

'That's a funny answer.'

'He were a complicated character. Larger than life at times. Quiet at other times. He were twice the man, mind, of a lot of his contemporaries.'

Archie nodded. 'What was he like when he was a little boy?'

'He were quite shy as a boy, thoughtful like. Fancy all his travelling made him come out of himself.'

'Did he play cricket?' Archie asked.

'No. He were sickly when he were a child. Bad chest. He used to love the game, though, never missed a match if he could help it.'

Archie couldn't imagine Benjamin ever being sickly or quiet. He'd always looked so healthy.

'He were great friends with young Thomas Greswode we was talking about the other day.'

Archie's ears pricked up. 'I didn't know that,' he lied.

'Like Siamese twins they were, joined at the shoulder.'

'He must have been really sad when Thomas died.'

'Terrible cut up he was. Made himself quite ill over it at the time. He got over it in the end, though.'

Archie fell silent. It still made him feel funny thinking of Benjamin and Thomas being friends. Benjamin had never mentioned Thomas Greswode to him but perhaps it had still made him sad even after such a long time. Then he remembered that folk in the Skallies used to say that Benjamin would cross the road to avoid Old Mr Greswode.

'He didn't get on with Charles Greswode, Thomas' cousin, did he?'

'No. I fancy he didn't.'

'Why was that?'

'I s'pose he blamed the Greswodes for the loss of his friend and of course there was trouble at Thomas' funeral.'

'There was?'

'The Greswodes only invited family and friends. None of us locals were allowed in. As soon as they were all inside the old chapel the door was locked.'

'And Benjamin was angry?'

''Course he were angry. All the folks round here were, they wanted to pay their respects as was right and proper.'

Archie sat thoughtfully, trying to take all of this in as William Dally went on.

'That night, after the proper funeral, we got into the chapel in the dark and held our own little service for him. Devious little buggers we were and we weren't being told what to do by Old Greswode!'

Archie stared at William Dally open-mouthed.

'How did you get inside the chapel if it was kept locked?'

'Well, Gwennie's father who lived in the Grockles used to caretake the chapel. She pinched the key and let us in.'

'Blimey,' Archie said.

'Oh it got better. That Gwennie were a right girl and a half.'

Archie gulped, 'You don't mean mad Gwennie who lives in the Boathouse?'

'One and the same.'

'You knew her?'

''Course I did, grew up with her. She was a bit older than us and to tell the truth we was all a bit in love with her.'

Archie stared at William Dally in disgust. How could anyone be in love with mad Gwennie? She was ugly as guts and had no teeth.

'Don't be looking at me like that, lad, she were a cracker when she were a young girl.'

Archie blew out through his mouth and tried not to laugh.

'I don't want to hear all those soppy bits. Just tell me about getting into the chapel.'

'Like I said, Gwennie got the key and we had our own little funeral for Thomas. Damn, it's queer thinking about that night after all this time. You're a real touchstone for me, I can magic up the past like it was yesterday when you're around.'

'Tell me the rest . . . ' Archie urged impatiently.

'Well, we were only nippers really; Gwennie was that bit older, mind. We started to read out the funeral service from the prayer book as I remember but it was full of long words. So in the end we sang a couple of hymns and each said a few words.'

'How many of you were there?'

'Me, Benjamin Tregantle and Gwennie of course. There was a boy called Wilf Dennis whose father kept the Pilchard. Poor Wilf got killed in the war.'

'His mammy made wonderful pasties,' Archie mused.

'She did. How the hell do you know that?'

Archie bit his lip so as not to smile. 'What hymns did you sing?'

'Oh Lord, you're asking me now. It were bloody years ago. Let me see, 'Eternal Father Strong to Save'. That would have been my choice. And Benjamin would have picked . . . '

'I know!' Archie declared.

'You do?' said William Dally.

'He didn't like hymns much but he told me once there was one he'd liked since he was little . . . he was always humming it. It was about Father Christmas' cat.'

William Dally shook his head, 'No, it weren't that one. I never heard no hymns about Father Christmas' cat.'

Archie looked crestfallen.

'It was, oh, damn, it's on the tip of my tongue . . . 'All Things Bright and Beautiful', that were the one.'

254

He hummed a few bars of a tune for a few seconds and then burst into song, 'All things bright and boooteefull . . .'

Archie put his hands over his ears and chuckled. William Dally had a worse voice than Benjamin.

'Please stop singing and tell me what happened next.'

'Well, we put some flowers we'd picked on the altar and then we went. The odd bit, though, was this . . .'

'Go on!' Archie was desperate to hear the rest of the story.

'Well, when we'd finished, Gwennie asked us to lock her in the chapel, said she knew a trick like Houdini. She was trying to cheer us up, I think, 'cos we were all right down in the dumps.'

'I've heard of Houdini. He could escape from chains and things, couldn't he?'

'That's right. Well, we did what she asked. Wilf Dennis locked the door and snuck the key back into the porch at the Grockles.'

'Without her father knowing?'

'Yes. That was easy, he was always as drunk as a skunk.'

'And what next?'

'We climbed back down to the beach and the next thing up popped Gwennie from behind a rock and frightened us bloody witless! Funny, I'd forgotten all about that 'til we started talking.'

Archie could barely contain himself. He knew how she'd done it all right!

'She must have had another key, I reckon. Can't fathom out how else she could have done it,' William Dally mused, scratching his head.

Archie shivered with excitement. He was one of the few people then who knew about the secret way out of the wobbly chapel.

'You got any ideas on how she managed that?'

Archie shook his head solemnly and looked away.

'What happened next?'

'Next thing she was running back up through the dunes to Killivray House laughing her bloody head off!'

'Why was she going to Killivray House?' Archie asked.

'She worked there.'

'She did?'

'She were a maid for the Greswodes.'

Archie fell silent. Gwennie must have been the G that Thomas mentioned in his diary! And he'd said that she was pretty too. She was kind and bought him a cricket bat. He'd like to talk to Gwennie about Thomas Greswode but he never would because she wasn't right in the head and she was dangerous.

'She's a mad woman, isn't she?' Archie said.

'Maybe she is, maybe *she* isn't and we are. She just likes to keep her own company these days, that's all.'

'She fired a gun at us once,' Archie said. 'We could have been killed.'

'Did she now? She wouldn't have missed if she meant to hit you. She was a good shot, Gwennie. Her old man was a bit of a poacher round these parts, learned her art at his knee as it were.'

256

'Why did people stop using the wobbly chapel?'

'After the awful thing that happened in there. Haven't you heard about that?'

'No,' Archie answered truthfully.

'There used to be a fellow lived up at Killivray, a black man who Mr Greswode had brought back with him from Africa.'

'Go on,' Archie urged.

'It ain't a pretty story. He blew his brains out in the chapel one dark night.'

Archie folded his arms and flinched as a shiver shot up his backbone.

'Why did he do that?'

'He didn't stop to explain himself, he was just found the following day.'

'That's horrible.'

'It were. They used to say his ghost stalked Bloater Row.'

'They still do but I didn't know he'd killed himself in the chapel.'

'Anyway, Mrs Greswode flatly refused to set foot in the chapel ever again and not long after Mr Greswode had it locked up and no one has been inside up to this day, as far as I know.'

Archie was sorely tempted to say that he'd been in there, that he had the key in his pocket, but he changed the subject quickly.

'And Gwennie, did she stay at Killivray?'

'No. She was away visiting a cousin up the line when it happened. She came back but not long after she upped and left. Went and joined the circus, some said. Other folk reckoned she had a little secret that went with her.'

257

'How do you mean?'

'I don't know as it's right to be talking to a youngster like yourself about such things. She were up the duff.'

Archie shrugged. He didn't know what that meant.

'Benjamin Tregantle moved away too, didn't he?'

'He went away to war like a lot of us, only most of us came back.'

'And he didn't?' Archie asked.

'He didn't come back to the Skallies for years.'

'Where did he live?'

'Don't you ever stop askin' questions?'

For a moment Archie looked crestfallen.

'I'm only pulling your leg; it's good to ask questions. You keep on asking them, son. It's how we learn. Far as I know, Benjamin worked abroad and then about ten years ago he came back to Hogwash House to spend his retirement in the place he were born.'

'He was real kind to me,' Archie said.

''Course he were, you're a grand little fellow. He could see the potential in you.'

'What's potential?'

'It's something inside you, a bit like a dried-up old sea sponge. Dribble water on it and it gets bigger and bigger. Potential is like that. Feed a child who has potential with knowledge and there's no knowing how far they'll go in life.'

'Well, I think I understand. Is it a bit like the way plants grow?'

'Mayhap it is.'

'Like, you know, there's a tiny little seed, looks

258

like any other little seed and no one knows what it will become. But inside that seed there's a miracle.'

'Go on.'

'Some seeds grow into daffodils, potatoes, poppies or tomatoes. There's something inside them that can't be stopped as long as they get what they need. Sunlight and water and looking after.'

'Well, bugger me. You've a hell of a brain on you, boy. I fancy you're right.'

'Did Benjamin Tregantle come out here much?'

'Well, he used to walk out here a few evenings a week and have a drink with Miss Fanthorpe. Between me and you, I reckon she had a very soft spot for old Benjamin.' William Dally winked meaningfully.

Archie pulled a face.

'Anyhow, I'm just blathering on now. Come on, let's get you over to the school. I got another of Miss Fanthorpe's blooming letters to post and you don't want to miss those apple muffins now, do you!'

★ ★ ★

Miss Fanthorpe offered Archie a second apple muffin and watched in delight as he ate it hungrily.

He sat self-consciously in Miss Fanthorpe's study, balancing a plate on his knees and trying to eat daintily.

She noticed that he tried to tuck the leg with

259

the calliper away under the chair and hide it from her.

'Did you know Benjamin Tregantle for a long time?' he asked eventually.

'Only since I've been back here at Nanskelly,' She replied.

'I've known him since I was little,' Archie said proudly.

'My goodness, you knew him pretty well then,' Miss Fanthorpe said with a grin.

'He was very kind to me.'

'He spoke very highly of you, Archie. Said what a bright boy you were, a very bright boy indeed, and that's a great compliment from a man like Benjamin.'

'I don't know about that, Miss Fanthorpe.'

'You mustn't be so hard on yourself, young man. And stop hiding that leg away.'

Archie blushed with embarrassment.

'It's nothing to be ashamed of, Archie. Please don't hide it. Keep it on show, let the sun get to it.'

'I've never seen you in the Skallies, Miss Fanthorpe. How did you know Benjamin?'

Miss Fanthorpe stood up and wandered across to the window before she spoke.

'He used to walk out to Nanskelly occasionally, like you have today.'

She didn't look at Archie for a long time and there was something about her that made him think she was tearful.

When she turned back to face him, he knew he'd been right.

'He was quite a remarkable man in many ways

and a very kind man,' she said, but her voice was quiet, barely audible.

After a while, she spoke again, changing the subject.

'Do you like school, Archie?'

He looked down at his feet and said, 'No, Miss Fanthorpe, I hate it.'

'What do you hate?'

'Our teacher shouts all the time and I'm afraid to speak in case I get the answers wrong. And some of the boys beat me up.'

'How very sad. It's a shame you couldn't come here.'

'But it's all girls, Miss Fanthorpe, I'd feel a ninny.'

Miss Fanthorpe threw back her head and laughed, 'Why, so it is but it wasn't always.'

'I know,' Archie said. 'There used to be boys here in the old days. That was when your father was headmaster, wasn't it?'

'There were, Archie, and it quite broke my father's heart when the school was closed.'

'Why didn't he open another one?'

'It wasn't that easy, Archie. When Nanskelly was forced to shut it was a terrible time — he felt he'd let the boys down.'

'Couldn't they just go somewhere else; I mean they were all rich, weren't they?'

'A lot of them were but there were others here, scholarship boys, who had nowhere to go. That was the worst bit for my father.'

'Benjamin Tregantle nearly came here, didn't he?'

'Yes he did. He was a fine pupil, I believe.'

Archie scratched his head. 'I don't think he did, Miss Fanthorpe, because Nanskelly closed before he could take the examination.'

'How silly of me, of course it did. Do you know, my memory plays tricks on me these days.'

Archie suppressed a smile; William had said her memory was bad and that she'd worn odd shoes one day.

'What did your father do after he left Nanskelly?'

'He was a broken man, Archie. He went abroad for many years; he scraped a living teaching here and there. He was a very good artist and he made some money painting portraits. Then, luckily, he met my mother late in life and had me.'

'And when you grew up you wanted to be a teacher just like him?'

'I wanted to carry on the tradition like him of giving a good education to those who were in need, those without the means. I have been lucky, Archie, in carrying on for so long but soon I fear Nanskelly may close again.'

'Oh,' Archie said with surprise. 'Are there orphans here at Nanskelly now?'

'There are. Most of the girls are fee-paying and they help pay for the others who are not so fortunate.'

'Nanskelly closed because of Mr Greswode, didn't it?' Archie asked eagerly.

'How ever do you know that?'

'In my spare time I'm a detective,' he said innocently.

Miss Fanthorpe struggled to conceal her mirth.

'My father rented Nanskelly from Mr Greswode. After Thomas was drowned, my father and Mr Greswode had words, very angry words and Greswode took his revenge and made sure my father had to close the school.'

'That was a very spiteful thing to do.'

'According to my father, he was a very malicious man and his son took after him. You know, Archie, I never heard my father speak ill of anyone except the Greswodes and he hated them with a passion.'

'They don't sound very nice.'

'He used to say that they were powerful people round these parts. I remember he said that even the local doctor would give the Greswodes a death certificate if they needed one.'

'I don't understand.'

'Just that Old Greswode had a lot of people in his power. He could make people do him favours. My father always said that there were a lot of skeletons in the Greswode cupboard.'

Archie was puzzled. 'What does that mean?'

'Well, it's just a way of speaking. They didn't really have skeletons in the cupboard but they had secrets that they wouldn't have wanted anyone to know. I think, you know, my father knew more about the Greswodes than he ever let on.'

'I don't understand.'

'Never mind, have another apple muffin.'

★ ★ ★

Nan locked the door to the Pilchard and began to clear up. She was exhausted but she felt happier than she had in a very long time. The bar was littered with empty glasses and bowls that she had served the seafood in; cockles and whelks and shrimps that the Paynes had caught. If things went on at this rate she'd have to get in some extra help. The Pilchard was turning out to be a little gold mine. Maybe she'd ask Martha Grimble to give her a hand and earn herself a few bob, God knows she needed it. She could even pay Archie to do some odd jobs around the place.

She was worried about Archie Grimble; he'd looked so sad since the events up at Killivray, but it shouldn't have affected him too much because he'd never had any contact with the folk up there. And sure as eggs he wasn't missing that father of his. It was months now since Walter had taken off.

The postman had told her that there'd been no mail delivered at Bag End in weeks so he hadn't even bothered to contact Martha. Nan would bet her eye teeth that that was the last Martha would see of him unless he ran short of money.

Trade was brisk in the Pilchard since the trippers had started arriving at weekends and even though they were a brash nosy lot on the whole, they brought with them such a freshness she felt for the first time in ages that at last she was in touch with the rest of the world.

★ ★ ★

Killivray House looked forlorn. Archie walked across the lawns, which were covered in daisies and buttercups now. Standing despondently beneath the window where he had seen Romilly for the very last time, he sighed sadly and thought that he seemed to spend a lot of his life looking at windows and trying to conjure up the faces of people who had left.

He turned miserably away from the house and wandered over towards the summerhouse.

Inside it was silent and gloomy and a breeze stirred up the dust and made him sneeze. He imagined Charles Greswode in there sulking while outside Gwennie took a photograph of Thomas in his sailor suit.

He shivered, he didn't like the thought of being in the same room as Charles Greswode.

He wandered around disconsolately and peered into an old tea chest that was covered in cobwebs. Dislodging a cricket bat from where it lay between a broken ball and a toy cart, he wiped away the cobwebs and held it up. It was covered in mould and the wood was rotten. He wondered if this was the bat that Thomas had used in the match at Nanskelly. He held it awkwardly and played a few imaginary shots. Then he put it back into the chest. He perched on the edge of the sofa and imagined Thomas reading there quietly and the fright he must have got seeing his cousin come in with the gun. How terrified he must have been, looking into those mad eyes and that frothing mouth.

What had made Charles fetch the gun in the

first place? Then he had a thought.

The key to the gun cabinet had been put in Thomas' trunk so that the blame would be put on him when it was found.

Could it be possible that Charles Greswode had really meant to murder his cousin and not just frighten him?

It was possible. If Thomas hadn't wrestled with him and the gun hadn't gone off and brought people running it might have turned out differently. He could have shot Thomas and then made up the story about it being Thomas who had pointed the gun at him. His father would have believed him and probably nothing would have happened to Charles if they thought he was trying to protect himself.

Archie walked around the summerhouse squinting up at the roof.

There, in the far corner above the shelf with the broken crockery, was a small hole in the wood where the bullet had gone through.

It made him feel wobbly legged to see it.

Charles Greswode had won, though. He'd made sure that people thought Thomas was dangerous. And a few days later Thomas was dead and out of the way for ever.

The door to the stove where he had left his letter for Romilly was shut and wedged tight with a stick. It was curious because it hadn't been like that when he'd been here last. He took out the stick, opened the door and peeped inside.

His heart beat wildly, for inside the stove there was a rolled-up piece of cloth and a letter.

Romilly must have left them here some time before she was abducted! He snatched up the letter first and opened it eagerly.

Dear Archie,
Thank you for the letter. I read it without burning my hair off! I hope you have been able to find out more about Thomas. Have you been able to open the diary yet? I am dying to know what is in there. Tonight I heard Papa say that Thomas did drown so you were right and I was wrong! I think I just imagined seeing the boy in the summerhouse because I was lonely and wanted a friend so badly. And then of course that same day I found one. You. Papa was angry when I said Thomas' name. He said that his name has never been mentioned in Killivray House because he tried to murder my grandfather! That is what Papa says anyhow but I don't believe him. I hate it here at Killivray except for my governess who is very kind. Papa has brought a horrid, horrid woman with him — an ugly old fish! He kissed her and I saw and I hate hate hate her. I am going to run away to find my mama. Will you help me if you can? I will write to you soon.
Love from your friend,
Romillyxx

He reread the letter in mounting disbelief. Why had Romilly been planning to run away? She'd never said anything to him about that. She was mad! Kids couldn't just run away, they got caught real quick by the coppers and brought back and locked up if they kept on doing it! And why did she think the governess was nice? She couldn't be nice, look what she'd gone and done.

People said that bad folk had a way of getting around kids, being nice to them so you thought they were all right and then, when you least expected it, they pounced and did very nasty things to you! His mammy said sometimes grown-ups gave you sweets or offered to show you puppies and if you were daft enough to go with them that was your lot. They strangled you or put you in a hole in the ground or bricked you up behind walls!

And why was Romilly so sad about her papa kissing a woman? He'd be glad if his mammy kissed another man and married him instead of the porker.

It was strange to think that once a long time ago a boy who lived in Killivray House was planning to run away and years later Romilly was thinking about doing the same. It suddenly occurred to him that Romilly and Thomas Greswode were related. He tried to work out how but it was real complicated.

He knew that his mammy's dead sister was called Lissia and she was his aunt and if she'd ever had children they would have been his cousins. And Mammy and Lissia had the same mammy and daddy and they were his grandparents even though he had never met them.

Mammy said that he had met Lissia once before she died and he had a vague memory of looking through a gate into a garden full of washing. He could smell soap and starch and saw bubbles being whipped away on a fierce breeze. But he could never picture Aunt Lissia's face properly — except for two excited blue eyes peeping from behind billowing white sheets and a small white hand waving sadly at him.

So, if Thomas was a cousin to Charles Greswode that meant their fathers were brothers which meant they had the same grandparents. So that meant that Thomas and Romilly were what? It made his head ache trying to work it out. He must have been some kind of great-uncle maybe? Or cousins? That was it, some kind of cousins. Distant cousins.

Romilly hadn't run away like she said, she hadn't had the chance to because she'd been stolen away by that governess woman who had murdered her father.

Archie folded the letter and put it into his pocket and then picked up the cloth. He opened it out carefully. It was a lace handkerchief with the initials R M G in one corner. In the middle of the handkerchief lay a silver bird on a silver chain along with a slip of paper.

He lifted it up and the rays of sun that had wormed their way in through the dusty windows made it glint fiercely.

His hands shook and his mouth grew dry. This must be the necklace that Thomas had lost, the treasured gift from his dead mother. He shivered when he saw the writing on the paper.

Dear Archie, I found this stuffed down the back of a skirting board. Isn't it lovely? It's for you. Merry Christmas, Archie!

She'd sent him a Christmas present! The silver bird that Thomas was so sad at losing. He couldn't have lost it though; someone must have stolen it and hidden it. And Archie had a good idea who that someone was! He held the silver chain and the silver bird tightly in his fist for a long time.

Sitting down on the dusty sofa, he began to sob. He cried for Thomas Greswode who had such a sad, short life. For Benjamin Tregantle and Romilly Greswode and Aunt Lissia who he hadn't really known. He cried for his mammy who wasn't happy. For Cissie who wasn't right in the head and for Mrs Galvini who had lost her unborn baby. He cried for all the people that he loved and those he had loved but would never see again.

Then, when he was washed out with crying, he rose, closed the door to the summerhouse softly and walked away.

He was never coming back here again as long as he lived. Never. It was a sad, scary place that everyone wanted to escape from . . .

What was it Romilly had said about Killivray House? 'It's horrid and haunted and I hate it!'

He turned around and looked back at the house. He wondered if at night the tigers and bears came back to life and roamed around in the dark? Hugging himself, he turned away and climbed down the steps into the rose garden. The first roses were coming into bloom. He stood looking down at a clutch of small red roses with petals as delicate as silk, the red so bright it made his eyes water.

Then he made his way back through the woods.

★ ★ ★

Martha Grimble was busy in her kitchen in Bag End. The wireless was on and she hummed to herself as she kneaded dough on a floured table.

She had been very happy to take up Nan's offer of some work and was busy making bread ready for the following day when the trippers would turn up ravenous at the Pilchard. She was in dire need of money and she'd heard nothing from Walter since he'd gone. He'd taken her watch with him and the few pounds she'd had hidden in the biscuit barrel in the parlour.

She just hoped that he'd gone for good this time and that he wouldn't stir up trouble for her and Archie. She wouldn't put it past him to try a little blackmail if he was short of money. Still, she had little left to give him now. He'd robbed her clean these last ten years and she'd used up all her savings, pawned all her valuables. Yet if he did give her away out of spite and set people on her trail, she could end up losing Archie and that would be worse than death itself.

Maybe one day soon she'd need to think of leaving the Skallies. But where in God's name could she run to?

She kneaded the dough expertly the way cook had taught her when she was a little girl, and as she did she thought about Lissia and how they used to stand on chairs at the kitchen table side by side, wrapped in aprons that were far too big for them, playing with scraps of dough and shaping them into tiny loaves. She felt the tears slip down her cheeks and wiped her eyes on her pinafore.

Poor little Lissia with her sad, sweet smile. She would never have harmed a fly and yet look what a blow life had dealt her . . .

★　★　★

In the Pilchard Inn, Archie was filling the shelves with bottles. Cissie was helping as best she could but was slowing him down more than speeding things up.

Nan had told him to wipe the top of the bottles with a damp cloth when he took them out of the wooden crates because dogs cocked their legs over the crates and widdled over them. When he'd done that, he had to stack them neatly on the shelves with the labels facing out.

Nan was out in the kitchen making one of her delicious, thick soups and singing cheerfully as she worked.

Archie stacked the last sticky beer bottle, stood up and stretched. He'd have to go out into the yard to fetch another crate. All this lifting and carrying was making him much stronger. He had muscles in his arms; sure they were only the size of peas but they were muscles just the same. He wouldn't need to send off for the Charles Atlas kit any more.

He slipped through the curtained doorway into the kitchen just as Nan turned on the wireless. There was a crackling noise and then a

272

whistling sound as it warmed up.

He was just about to step out into the yard when the announcer's voice said, 'Today police began the search for Mrs Margot Greswode, widow of the late Jonathan Greswode of Killivray . . . '

Archie held his breath.

The voice continued, ' . . . who was murdered last December. Mrs Greswode had been under the care of the nuns at St Mary's Convent. It is believed that while left unattended for a matter of moments she escaped through an upstairs window. Her nightclothes and some personal belongings were found on the cliffs at nearby . . . '

Archie was transfixed.

' . . . Police think that Mrs Greswode has tragically taken her own life and there is little hope of finding her alive. In London today a man was arrested for stealing a parrot from a pet shop in Ealing . . . '

Suddenly Nan switched off the wireless and turned around. She was smiling broadly and had a look of such triumph on her face that it shocked Archie rigid.

Seeing Archie, she drew her hand rapidly across her mouth as if wiping away the smile.

'I didn't hear you come in, Archie. Terrible news,' she said. 'Just terrible.'

But she didn't fool him one little bit. She didn't look upset at all and Archie knew that she didn't mean what she said.

'That means that the little girl from Killivray is an orphan, doesn't it?' he said with a tremble in his voice.

'I suppose it does, Archie.'

'That's very sad,' he said, watching Nan carefully, but she turned quickly around and continued to dice potatoes without speaking again.

By the time he had finished stocking the shelves the tiny bar was filling up with customers.

Charlie and Freddie Payne came in first and busied themselves putting logs on the fire and drawing up a blaze. They were followed by a beaming Mr Kelly. The Paynes looked at him as though he were a ghost. Archie looked slyly at him from behind the bar. Mr Kelly was actually smiling, a proper smile that showed his buckled teeth. He had teeth the colour of marzipan.

Archie had never seen Mr Kelly smile before. He must have won the pools or had a big win on the gee-gees.

Then Nan came bustling out into the bar, removing her apron and greeting her customers.

'Why, Mr Kelly, to what do we owe this pleasure?'

Mr Kelly rested his arms on the counter. 'I'd like a jug of your best ale to take out, a bottle of ginger wine for the missus and a jar of pickled eggs.'

'Are you celebrating something, Mr Kelly?' asked Nan.

'No. No. The missus had a fancy for a little drink and I thought I'd join her.'

Nan busied herself with filling an enamel jug with frothy beer and then dusted off a bottle of ginger wine she had fetched from the cellar.

'Will that be on the slate, Mr Kelly, or are you paying cash?'

'On the slate, Nan, if that's all right with your good self.'

Nan took up a notepad and wrote quickly on it.

'Enjoy your drink, Mr Kelly,' she said watching him go with a surprised look on her face.

Mr Kelly went on his way whistling merrily.

'Well, I'll be buggered. In all the time he's lived here that's the first time he's ever been in here.'

'Do you think he's come into money?' Charlie Payne asked.

'He's won himself a smile, that's for sure,' Nan quipped. 'He usually has a face like a blocked drain.'

'Aren't you going to tell them the news about Mrs Greswode?' Archie piped up.

Nan looked enquiringly at Archie and flushed. He'd surprised her in the kitchen and she knew that he'd seen the look of delight on her face which she hadn't had time to cover up. Archie Grimble didn't miss much. He was a shrewd little monkey for all his quiet ways.

'What's the news?' Freddie Payne asked.

Nan lowered her voice, 'It's just been on the wireless. They think Mrs Greswode from Killivray has taken her own life.'

'Dear God, the poor woman,' Freddie exclaimed.

'All we've heard lately is bad news,' Charlie added.

'Are you off now, Archie?' Nan asked.

'Yes. Same time tomorrow, Nan?'

'That'll be grand. You can pick up your wages then.'

Archie waved to Cissie who was sitting near the fire drawing, and then he left.

'There's a hell of a change in that lad,' Charlie Payne remarked.

'In what way?' Nan enquired.

'He speaks up more now and he's starting to look livelier, not so fearful of everybody. You know he reminds me of Benjamin a bit.'

'In what way?' asked Nan again.

'Well, everyone always said he were a quiet lad as a nipper but come out of himself as he got older. I mean he weren't quiet when we knew him, was he?'

'No,' Nan said distractedly.

'Archie seems to have more to say for himself and gets out and about a bit more. There's a lot of things changing round here at present.'

'Let's hope it's all for the better,' Nan said.

★ ★ ★

The last of the trippers were leaving the Pilchard Inn. They wound their way along Bloater Row and down onto the beach to board the boat that would take them back to Plymouth.

Fleep stood in the window of the Grockles watching them go.

He was starting to feel well again and the last few nights he'd slept better than he had in months. His mind was growing calmer and clearer and he was beginning to remember snatches of the life he'd led before he'd come to the Skallies. Nothing that really made any sense at the moment but hopefully some day he'd be able to piece things together.

He remembered being thrown out of the room he'd been renting in Paris, walking out in the snow with no idea of where he was going. He'd met a man in a bar and out of the blue he'd told the man all his woes, unburdened himself to a complete stranger. And then later, later . . . it was no good he couldn't remember any more.

★ ★ ★

It was early when Nan came knocking at Bag End to tell Martha Grimble the news.

She followed Martha into the kitchen and sat herself down next to Archie at the kitchen table.

He eyed her warily; he hadn't forgotten the look on her face when the news about Mrs Greswode had come on the wireless. Why would she be glad that Mrs Greswode was dead?

But when she leant across and ruffled his hair, he smiled; he couldn't be cross with Nan for long.

'Nan, you look flustered, is everything all right?' Martha asked.

'You'll never believe what I'm going to tell you.'

'What is it?'

'Well, I couldn't sleep this morning so I got up early and went for a walk and guess what?'

'What?' Archie and Martha Grimble said together.

'The Kellys' front door was wide open and banging in the breeze. I stopped and listened and there wasn't a sound coming from inside the house.'

'Maybe they were all still asleep,' Archie said.

'No. The little ones are always awake early. They make such a racket that I can hear them in here,' Martha said.

'I had a feeling in my water that something was up. I went inside and . . . '

'And what?' asked Archie excitedly.

'Martha, I had to put a handkerchief over my face first. It stank to high heaven in there. Anyhow I called out but there was no answer.'

'Where were they?' Archie asked with interest.

'The kitchen was deserted, Martha. The fire was out and the table was piled high with dirty dishes and a baby's bottle lay on its side dribbling milk from a leaky teat.'

'Get to the point, Nan.'

'You'll never believe,' she said. 'The Kellys have done a moonlight flit.'

Martha Grimble put down her tea cup and stared at Nan.

'They never have!'

'What's a moonlight flit?' Archie asked but no one answered him.

'The place is empty. They've gone, I tell you. Upped and bloody gone without a word to any bugger.'

'What's a moonlight flit?' Archie asked again.

'It's when someone ups sticks and buggers off

in the dead of night,' Nan said helpfully.

'Well, who would have credited it?' Martha Grimble said.

'I heard nothing, Martha, and I live next door,' Nan exclaimed.

'Come to think of it, Nan, I woke in the night and was sure I heard a baby cry. But I thought it was probably the wildcats in your yard and went back to sleep.'

'Fancy not even saying goodbye, and where would they go? They hadn't a penny to bless themselves with,' Nan said.

'They were a funny family except for that one boy.'

'Peter,' Archie said. He'd always liked Peter but he'd never had a chance to make friends because of the other Kelly boys.

'She owed me fifteen pounds,' Nan said. 'She had a lend because she said she needed to buy some things for the new baby that was on the way.'

'You'll not see that again.'

'That's a fact. And Mr Kelly came in last night for beer and ginger wine. That was odd because he'd never been in before. Well, that's one slate that'll not be settled. Ah well, more fool me!'

'Have a cup of tea, Nan, and then you can take the bread over with you, it's due out of the oven any time now.'

'Oh, go on then, I will. Did you hear the sad news about Mrs Greswode?' Nan said avoiding Archie's gaze.

Martha winked at Nan and nodded towards

Archie. She didn't like to talk about bad things in front of him.

Archie took the hint, got up and went to fetch a comic from his bedroom. Then, when they were chatting away at full steam he slipped back into the kitchen and curled up in a high-backed chair in the corner near the door where they wouldn't notice him. It was called Earwigging.

'The poor woman must have been half out of her mind to do such a thing. You'd think she'd have wanted to live for when they find the child, wouldn't you?' Martha said.

'You would,' Nan replied.

'But I don't think there's much chance of that now after all this time, do you?' Martha said despondently.

'I don't suppose so,' Nan said glumly.

'Have they found Mrs Greswode's body?' Martha Grimble asked.

'No. I don't suppose they will or it'll be unrecognizable by the time it's washed up. A body was washed up down the coast a few weeks back and it had been half eaten by fish,' Nan said.

Archie felt sick at the thought. He wondered had that happened to Thomas and Benjamin? He hoped not.

'Have you seen Lena?' Martha asked.

'I called in yesterday. She's not looking the best. She's taken the loss of this baby really badly. She's getting on in years and time is running out for her.'

'God help her. The world can be a cruel place, Nan.'

'Alfredo looks real cut up about it. She hadn't realized she was in the way and was further gone than they thought. She had bad pains but before they could get the doctor she was already losing the child. She was in agony and there was blood all over the place by the time the doctor got here from Rhoskilly . . .'

Nan and Martha Grimble turned suddenly as Archie fainted clean away, slipped out of the chair and hit the floor with a sickening thud.

Later that night he lay on his bed looking up at the ceiling and thinking of what Mr Galvini had said to him: 'Maybe we all running away from something. Some of us knows it and some of us don't . . . Then one day maybe we go away as quickly as we come. No one knows what the future is holding for us.'

He wondered where the Kellys had come from and where they'd run away to? He wondered what would happen to him and his mammy in the future and if Romilly Greswode would even have a future.

He got up and lit the stub of candle and placed it in front of the Virgin. Then he knelt down and prayed as moonlight slipped into the room and glinted on the silver bird that hung around his neck.

Later he lay in bed thinking of all that Nan had said that morning. Over and over again he whispered the words: Moonlight Flit. Moonlight Flit. Moonlight Flit. The words had a kind of magic quality about them.

It sounded like something that fairies did.

It was late evening when Archie put the key in the lock of the chapel door and turned it. He stepped swiftly inside the wobbly chapel, closed the door and locked it.

The dying rays of the sinking sun lit the round window and a myriad of colours dappled across the altar.

He wiped away a layer of dust from one of the pews and sat down.

He tried to imagine William Dally and the other kids standing in here on the night of Thomas Greswode's funeral.

Stooping down, he picked up a dusty hymn book from the filthy floor. It was damp to the touch and the pages were melding together with age and mould. He prised the pages apart and looked down. Hymn number 15, 'Eternal Father Strong to Save' . . .

The hymn that William Dally said they'd sung!

He looked up at the hymn board.

Hymn number 15.

He turned the pages of the hymn book as quickly as he could.

Hymn number 176. 'All Things Bright and Beautiful' . . .

He felt a shiver whisper up his backbone. It was as if no time at all had passed since the night when William Dally and his friends had been right here in the wobbly chapel. They'd sung their favourite hymns and even put the numbers up on the hymn board.

Then Wilf had locked in Gwennie and she'd

frightened the life out of them popping up from behind a rock down on the beach. And not long after the black man had blown his brains out in here and the chapel had been locked up and abandoned.

He looked around warily; more fearful now that he knew someone had killed himself in here. He didn't like to think of funerals and people blowing their brains out.

Then he remembered what Benjamin had said in his letter, *'You're a scholar and a gentleman, the type of boy who could find out things like a proper detective if he put his mind to it and stopped being afraid of every bloody thing.'*

He stood up very straight and thrust out his chin.

He wasn't afraid. He wasn't afraid. He wasn't afraid of ghosts or any bloody thing! So there.

He had muscles now and he was growing stronger.

He wondered why on earth would anyone come in here to kill themselves?

And why did the black man want to kill himself? Was it because Thomas had died?

Or because of the row he'd had with Mr Greswode? He didn't know and he'd never know.

He wandered around and paused close to the door. There was a stone receptacle for holy water but it was dry as a bone. Next to it, set into the wall, was a metal-fronted collecting box and he wondered who had last emptied it before the chapel was closed down? There was a rusted-up keyhole on the box and some words written in Latin on the front.

He made his way over to the font and walked around it.

The top was covered with a thick round wooden lid, shaped like a millstone. He tried to lift it but it was stuck fast. He noticed, though, that there was a small hole in the middle of the lid.

With enormous effort he clambered up on top of the font and sat there looking around him at the ruined chapel.

He couldn't for the life of him fathom out what Benjamin had wanted him to find in here. Unless, unless he'd just wanted him to do something brave for once in his life. Maybe talking about there being mysteries to solve was just to get Archie interested!

There was nothing to be found here. The best thing he could do was to lock the place up, throw the key away and leave well alone.

One day soon the winter storms would bring the chapel to the ground, it would be blown away into the sea and nothing would be left.

He was about to climb down from the font when he turned his attention to the hole in the middle of the wooden lid. He wondered if there was still any water in the font and who the last child to be christened was.

The hole was small but his hands were little. Mammy often asked him to help get things out of small places.

He rolled up the sleeves of his jumper and squeezed his hand down into the hole. It was a long way down and he had to lie across the font. His hand made contact with the stone basin but it was dry as a bone; the water must have dried up years ago. He pulled out his hand clutching a ball of mouldy feathers, before thrusting his arm in again and scrabbling around until his fingers touched against something hard. He got it between his fingers and lifted it out. He turned it over and realized that it was an old button. There was a loop on the back where it would have been sewn onto a garment. Maybe it had fallen off the priest's arm when he was baptizing a baby. He spat on the button and rubbed it on his jumper. He spat again and rubbed harder. There was some sort of pattern on the front of the button. He took out his penknife, flicked it open and began to scrape away the grime. It took him ages but as it got cleaner he could see that it was an ivory button on which someone had carved an elephant.

It was unusual and lovely.

He put it down on the font and put his arm back down into the hole.

His arm began to ache and his ribs grew stiff. Then just as he was about to give up, his fingers touched against something else. He managed to get a hold on it but then dropped it. He tried again and moments later he pulled something up out of the hole.

In the palm of his hand lay a small, ornate crucifix on a broken chain. It was covered in dust and mouse droppings and he shook it to remove the worst of them. He spat on it and rubbed it on his jumper. As he held it up, it shone dully in the dying light.

Suddenly, he heard a noise behind him and

spun around, lost his grip and fell off the font. He landed with a thump, scrabbled to his feet, rubbed his bruised knees and tried to stop the scream that was growing in the pit of his belly.

Jesus! There was someone here in the chapel.

There was a clunk. The sound of wheezing, and a slow deep groaning.

Any minute now he was going to pee himself with fright.

Bugger Benjamin Tregantle telling him not to be afraid of anything.

Help me, Mammy!

The door to the cupboard next to the altar creaked open and he stood rooted to the spot, looking into eyes as fearful as his own.

★　★　★

Gwennie blinked and stared at the small boy peeping over the top of the font.

It was the boy they called Archie Grimble who lived in Bag End. The one she'd tried to save from those bloody Kelly boys. The boy looked back at her aghast, his mouth wide open and the sun glinting off his spectacles.

Gwennie spoke first.

'What in God's name are you doing in here?'

'I . . . I . . . I'm allowed. I have a key,' he stammered.

'You do?'

'I know how you got in though. I found out the secret way by accident.'

'Did you now? What are you snooping about in here for?'

'Nothing,' he said and blushed crimson.

'You're not a very good liar!'

Archie looked down at his feet.

'Well, this place could tell a few stories if only the walls could speak.'

'It's a shame they can't,' he muttered.

'I haven't been in here since . . . '

There was a long and awkward silence until Archie said, 'You had a funeral in here for Thomas Greswode, didn't you?'

She looked at him quizzically. 'How do you know about that?'

'I'm a detective in my spare time.'

She threw back her head and laughed a toothless laugh.

Archie stiffened and took a step backwards.

She grew quiet and watched him with shrewd, lively eyes.

'Don't worry, son, I'll not hurt you. I went to two funerals for Thomas Greswode. I mourned him twice over.'

He took another step away from her.

'I'm not doing any harm here,' he said. 'I'm just looking for clues.'

'You're trying to solve some sort of mystery?'

He nodded.

'And what's the mystery?'

'I don't know.'

'How can you solve a mystery if you don't know what it is?'

Archie looked down at his feet again.

She smiled a gummy smile. 'I came here to bury the past and yet I find a young whippersnapper in here ferreting about. I don't know what mystery you're trying to solve but I'll bet the wobbly chapel has plenty of secrets. It dates back hundreds of years. See the altar there, that was part of an old ship.'

'Was it?'

'It sank off Skilly Point. Everyone on board except two perished and one of them was the fellow who built the first house here on Bloater Row.'

'That was Hogwash House, wasn't it?'

She nodded.

'He was a Spaniard. He's buried over here, look, along with his missus.'

Archie looked at the memorial tablet set into the floor.

'Angeles Gabriel. Only the locals couldn't get their tongues round a mouthful of a name like that so they called him the Angel of Espagne. Gradually it got changed to Spayne and no doubt after that to Payne . . . '

'Like the Paynes in the Peapods?'

'That's right. You've only got to look at the colouring of that pair to know their ancestors are not English.'

'So they'd be related to the first settler?'

'I reckon it's likely. Angeles Spain made a fortune and built Killivray House and then he lost it all again. A bit of a gambler, it was said. If he hadn't lost his fortune then there would probably be Paynes in Killivray House today.'

'So when did the Greswodes get Killivray House?'

'The story is that one of the Greswodes had a bet with Angeles. The Greswode family used to live at Nanskelly. The Spaniard lost and the Greswodes got Killivray. And a sad day for Killivray it was when they moved in.'

'You don't like the Greswodes?'

'Like them? I wouldn't piss on them if their arses was burning.'

Archie looked at her with wide eyes.

'Why do you think the black man killed himself?'

'The black man had a name,' she said. 'He was called Bo, well that's what we called him. His full name was Boreo Orore.'

'Oh,' said Archie and he remembered the Bo mentioned in the diary who had been so kind to Thomas.

'I think that he killed himself because he was a coward when it came to it, in the end.'

Archie wrinkled his brow. 'He couldn't have been a coward to blow his own brains out.'

Gwennie winced and clasped her hands together tightly. 'It might have seemed like a brave act to him but he left me to face the music alone. And yet all along he'd promised me he would take the three of us back to Africa . . . '

'To see the enormous sunsets and hear the calling of elephants and lions at night?'

'How do you know that?'

'I told you, I'm a detective,' he said with a shy grin.

For a moment the wrinkles seemed to fade and her face looked almost young.

'What were you doing up on top of the font? Trying to christen yourself?'

'No. I was just investigating. You see there's a

hole in the top. I wondered if there was anything in there.'

'A mountain of muck, I shouldn't wonder.'

'I found these.'

He held out his hand and showed her the button and the crucifix.

She looked down at them in silence and Archie watched in consternation as her lip began to tremble and tears slipped from her eyes, gathering in the wrinkles of her face, making tributaries down her cheeks.

He fumbled in the pocket of his shorts for his handkerchief and held it out to her. She took it and wiped her eyes and face.

'Can I touch them?'

'Yes.' He held them out to her and she took them with a shaking hand.

'These belonged to Bo,' she whispered in a voice cracked with emotion.

Archie wrinkled up his forehead in puzzlement. 'How do you know?'

'I knew everything about him.'

'Why do you think someone put them in the font?'

Gwennie looked up and there was a light in her eyes that alarmed him.

'He would never have taken this off,' she said, holding up the crucifix. 'It was a parting gift from his mother before he left Africa for England.'

'He wanted to go back to Africa, didn't he?'

Gwennie looked at Archie steadfastly. 'He never wanted to leave in the first place. He came on the promise of being able to go back one day, to make some money and help his family.'

'Why didn't he go back?'

'Greswode always kept him poor. Worked him to death and made sure there was no chance of him ever returning.'

All the while she spoke she didn't take her eyes off the crucifix and the button.

'He would never have taken the crucifix off,' she said again. 'And if he did why would he have put it in the font?'

Archie thought hard. 'To hide it?'

'No. I know he would never have taken it off willingly.'

'You mean someone might have taken it off him? Or it got broken in a struggle maybe?' Archie mused.

Gwennie stood quite still.

'Ay, that's what must have happened. And the button, the elephant button is from a shirt of his . . . a beautiful blue shirt that he used to wear for best.'

Archie listened with bated breath, afraid to speak in case she stopped.

'He used to look so handsome in that shirt, the blue showed off his black skin a treat. I sewed those buttons on myself and they wouldn't have fallen off easily, it must have come off in a struggle.'

'And if that's what happened then maybe the person he struggled with hid them in the font, but why would anyone do that?'

'Perhaps whoever did it panicked, had to hide them to cover things up. I remember thinking that his blue shirt wasn't among his belongings when they packed them up after his death.'

'So do you think he wore his best shirt here but someone changed him after, after they . . . ?'

'Killed him,' said Gwennie coldly. 'I don't think my Bo killed himself, and all this time I've blamed him . . . '

'If he struggled and the shirt was ripped then maybe the police would have known that he hadn't done it himself.'

'You are a very clever boy,' she said absently. 'I should have trusted him; I should have known he wouldn't leave me.'

'You weren't to know, though, were you?'

'I see now that it was all so nicely covered up. I was away when it happened . . . '

Archie tried to make sense of it but her thoughts were too fast for him to keep up.

He chewed his lips nervously and listened.

'You see, I made cook tell me everything when I found out. She said that when they found him he was wearing his working clothes . . . they had to burn them because they were covered in . . . '

'Covered in what?'

'It doesn't matter . . . you see he wouldn't have worn that shirt to work in . . . maybe he had come to the Skallies to see my father. And all these years I doubted him . . . '

Archie was confused. Why would the black man have come to see Gwennie's father?

Then a thought struck him. 'How would Bo have got in here?'

Gwennie smiled sadly, 'I'd shown him the secret way. We used to meet in here sometimes.'

'Maybe he came in that way and there was

someone already here.'

'Someone who'd arranged to meet him?'

Gwennie put her hand to her head as if trying to catch hold of a thought.

'I remember afterwards, Wilf from the Pilchard said that the last time he'd seen Bo he was coming down through the sand dunes. He said he was whistling and seemed excited about something.'

'He wouldn't have been excited about blowing his brains out, would he? I mean no one would.'

'I think,' she said, making the sign of the cross, 'that my Bo was definitely murdered.'

'Why do you think someone would murder him?' Archie said breathlessly.

'I don't know but there was something bothering Bo in the weeks before he died. He said that there was something not right and that someone wasn't telling the truth and he didn't like the way the master was with me. Neither did I.'

'How was he with you?'

'It's of no consequence. He had wandering hands.'

'Maybe Bo found out something and then he had to be killed to shut him up.'

'I'll never know for sure but I'll bet that the Greswodes had a hand in it. Maybe he'd worked out that I was with child . . . that Bo and I were going to go away together. He was a very jealous man.'

She became silent then and shuffled across to a pew and sat down looking ahead of her. Archie sat down beside her.

The sunlight played across her face and the crucifix in her hand glowed brightly.

'You can keep the crucifix and the button if you like,' Archie said. 'To remind you of Bo.'

She looked up at him and her eyes were extraordinarily blue and full of tears.

'Thank you,' she said and she closed her hand around them tightly.

'I think that I need some time alone now.'

Archie nodded and got to his feet.

'I'd like it if you didn't mention this to anyone, Archie. There's no point raking up the past now, there's no one left to be punished for what they did. You've done me a very great favour.'

'Have I?'

'Oh, yes. I'm sure, Archie, that coming here today you've worked out what did happen to Bo. And I know now that he wasn't meaning to leave me. It makes it almost bearable.'

The sun died behind the window and darkness seeped into the chapel like smoke.

Afterwards he would never forget the look on her face as she watched him go but it would be a long time before he heard the end of her story.

He let himself out of the chapel and pocketed the keys.

'Bang! Bang! You're dead!' squawked the parrot from the Grockles.

'Ah, bugger off!' whispered Archie Grimble and he walked slowly back along Bloater Row.

* * *

294

Archie and Cissie were sitting out on the step of the Pilchard counting marbles when the postman came along Bloater Row. He smiled at Archie and Cissie, posted a letter through the letter box of Skibbereen and then went whistling back the way he'd come.

Archie was putting the last glass marble into the drawstring bag when the noise started.

Inside Skibbereen someone shrieked piercingly. This first shriek was followed by hollering and yelping and the sound of someone banging on saucepans.

Archie and Cissie leapt to their feet in alarm and ran inside to fetch Nan. The three of them stood together listening to the racket.

Then the door to Skibbereen was flung open and out stepped Mrs Galvini.

It was the first time Archie had seen her in ages and she looked thinner, paler than usual but she was beaming from ear to ear and pulling Alfredo along behind her.

'Lena, what's happened? You were making such a racket, they could hear you in Rhoskilly.'

'Mother of God! Nan, we just had letter. Letter with very good news. Oh, such good news I think I having an attack of the heart. My heart going boom bomb boom.'

Archie and Cissie began to giggle.

'What's the news, Lena?'

'Is such happy, happy news and I say to my Alfredo pinch me and he did. See, I have bruise here on my bum bum. I can't believe this happen to us. One minute and I gonna wake up and find I dream it all!'

'Lena! What has happened?' Nan urged but there was not any sense to be had from her.

'I so happy I want to dance. Hey, Archie, you dance with Lena, eh?'

Archie escaped into the doorway of the Pilchard Inn, leaving Cissie to be Mrs Galvini's dancing partner. He watched in mortification as Mrs Galvini took Cissie's hands and they danced up and down Bloater Row.

Nan, with her hands on her hips shook her head and looked at Alfredo in despair.

'Alfredo, it's a good job that one of you two has some sense. Will you tell me what's happened? I can't stand the excitement.'

'We have letter to say we have inherit house in Italia. Big house, lots of rooms. We going back, Nan, even after all this long time we go back.'

'Alfredo, that's wonderful! But I'll miss you both.'

'*Si*. Nan, we miss you lots but now we maybe have business again. You can all come stay and have holiday in Italia. Now, maybe my Lena stop worrying a little, take her mind off all the bad things.'

'Lena, stop spinning Cissie around so fast or she'll be sick!' Nan yelled.

Archie slipped inside the Pilchard to avoid having to congratulate the Galvinis.

He felt the tears rising and he blinked to try and clear them. He didn't want the Galvinis to leave. It was different with the porker and the Kellys, he hadn't minded them going, his life had been better without them. First Benjamin, then Romilly and now the Galvinis. To lose the

Galvinis would be a terrible thing.

He couldn't imagine Skibbereen without them. He loved that house to bits, loved the laughter, and the everlasting smell of cooking. The tinkle of the music boxes and the wonderful colours of the tiny glass animals.

Mr and Mrs Galvini had always cheered him up when he felt miserable, fed him when he was hungry. What was happening to everyone in the Skallies?

One by one they were all disappearing.

'You must come into the Pilchard, the both of you. We must have a drink to celebrate. Run and fetch your mammy, Archie, and tell the Paynes and the Misses Arbuthnots,' Nan called out.

Soon the Pilchard Inn was full. The Paynes appeared and even the Misses Arbuthnots came shyly in. Martha Grimble arrived flushed from baking bread. Soon the small bar was filled with laughter and animated chatter. After two drinks Nan grew bold and went and knocked on the Grockles. Even the stranger Fleep got out of bed to join in the celebration.

Archie sat with Cissie near the fire and sipped his ginger beer. He smiled whenever he caught the eye of Lena and Alfredo Galvini but the lump in his throat was almost choking him.

★　★　★

At Nanskelly Eloise Fanthorpe sat in a wicker chair near the sports pavilion, looking out to sea. A book lay open in her lap but she had abandoned it because she could not concentrate.

297

She was thinking about Archie Grimble when, as if summoned up by magic, he appeared, clambering over the stile.

She watched him as he walked, unaware of her presence, towards the school and then stopped quite still.

He looked quite different to the last time she'd seen him. He'd put on a bit of weight, looked a little more confident, perhaps? He had more colour in his cheeks and he wasn't dragging his leg as badly. Benjamin Tregantle would have been pleased to see him looking so well.

She called out to him and he turned around, smiled and made his way over towards her.

'Hello, Miss Fanthorpe. Is it all right for me to find William?'

'It's all right by me if you come here whenever you like but I'm afraid that William is away for the day.'

'Oh.' He sounded disappointed.

'Why don't you sit yourself down? You must be hot after your long walk, I'll bring us a cool drink. It's peaceful here this afternoon as the girls are out on a nature ramble and won't be back for a while.'

Archie sat down on the grass and watched Miss Fanthorpe hurrying towards the school.

What was it Benjamin had said? That Miss Fanthorpe would do him a good turn if he ever needed it. Yet Benjamin had never mentioned Miss Fanthorpe to Archie when he was alive.

Miss Fanthorpe returned with a jug of orangeade and a plate of butterfly cakes and sat down.

'How is my favourite detective doing?' she said as she filled a tumbler with orangeade.

'Well, I think I may have solved a mystery from a long time ago.'

'You have? My goodness, that was quick. You must tell me!'

'Well, it's a bit of a secret but Benjamin said you could be trusted.'

'I swear not to tell a living soul,' she said seriously, laying her hand across her chest.

'I found out, by accident really, what happened to Boreo Orore, the black man from Killivray.'

Miss Fanthorpe looked nonplussed, as though she had expected him to say something entirely different.

'That's the poor man who er . . . .'

'Blew his brains out?' Archie said.

'That's right. I've heard lots of stories about Boreo from my dear father. He used to walk out here like you do; he spent a long time talking to Father.'

Archie smiled.

'It was really sad that he died. My father said he was a fine, handsome fellow, wise and honourable. He used to talk to my father about going back to Africa one day.'

'I know he wanted to go back and it's really sad that he never did.'

'I remember Father saying that he was brought back to England by Old Mr Greswode. I expect that you've heard about all the animals that used to be kept at Killivray?'

'Yes. But he got rid of them, didn't he, when he got married?'

'He did. He was a rich young man and was fooling around with things he didn't understand. It was quite horribly cruel to bring exotic creatures like that over here on a whim and then abandon them.'

'What happened to them?'

'Some were shot and stuffed and kept at Killivray. I believe the tiger cubs were given to the circus. I used to cry when I was a little girl, thinking about the poor things being taken away from their mother. Papa said it broke Boreo's heart.'

'Your father must have missed him after he died,' Archie said.

'It's curious, Archie. You see just before my father left Nanskelly he had lent Boreo some money to help him get back to Africa. He was in some kind of trouble but Father had left Nanskelly before he killed himself. I know he often wondered what happened to him and was surprised that he never heard from him again. I only heard about his death when I came back to Nanskelly and that explained why he never contacted my father.'

'What sort of trouble was he in?'

'That I don't really know. I think it was something delicate and my father was very old-fashioned in some ways. He wouldn't discuss certain things in front of children and women.'

'The thing is, though, Miss Fanthorpe, I don't think Boreo did kill himself. In fact I am sure that he didn't.'

Miss Fanthorpe looked at him aghast.

'But everyone knows that he went into the

chapel and shot himself. I gather that the police were involved and it caused a great scandal round these parts. Come now, Archie, you must tell me everything you know.'

He recounted the story of how he had met Gwennie in the wobbly chapel and found the crucifix and the elephant button belonging to Boreo Orore.

Miss Fanthorpe listened attentively.

'Have you told anyone else about this?'

'No. Gwennie said she didn't want to rake up the past. She was glad to know the truth. You see, Boreo had promised that he'd take the three of them back to Africa.'

'Who were the three of them?'

'I don't know, that's just what she said. Maybe it was Thomas Greswode, or the cook from Killivray?'

'Maybe,' said Miss Fanthorpe, smiling down at Archie and thinking that her father must have known the delicate nature of Boreo's trouble and tried to help but someone else had taken matters into their own hands.

So, her father had been right, there were plenty of skeletons in the Greswode cupboard.

'How is life in the Skallies?' she said, changing the subject.

'Not too good.'

'Why is that?'

'Everyone's moving away and soon there'll be no one left. My friends Mr and Mrs Galvini are going to Italy in a few days' time and I don't want them to go.'

'And where in Italy are they going?'

'Someone has left them a house in a place called Santa Caterina and they want to open a restaurant. Mrs Galvini is a very good cook.'

Miss Fanthorpe smiled. 'How lovely,' she said.

'Have you ever been to Santa Caterina, Miss Fanthorpe?'

'Oh, no,' she replied and she looked away quickly.

'Why look, the girls are back. I really must go. I have a Latin lesson with the third form. Goodbye, Archie Grimble.'

'Goodbye, Miss Fanthorpe.'

'Well done with your detective work. You've unlocked one secret. I wonder how many more you will unlock?' and she looked at him with a very funny expression on her face.

He climbed the stile and walked back along the cliff path thinking of everything that had happened since he'd first gone into the wobbly chapel.

He had the feeling that the mystery of Boreo Orore wasn't the mystery that Benjamin had meant him to solve. If Benjamin had known that those things were hidden in the font he'd have told someone years ago, wouldn't he? No, there was something else that Benjamin had wanted him to discover but he hadn't been clever enough. He'd been on the wrong track with Thomas Greswode; there was no mystery about Thomas Greswode's death; it had been sad and unnecessary but just an accident.

He looked out across the sea, sparkling away to the horizon, a calm, blue, summer sea, the sort of sea that Thomas had sailed into on the last day of his sad life.

He kicked out at a rock on the path and realized that he'd kicked out with his bad leg. It was getting stronger. Maybe one day he'd be able to get rid of this hateful calliper.

He pulled a blade of grass from the hedgerow and chewed on it as he walked back to the Skallies.

★　★　★

The sun was high and a light warm breeze rippled the surface of the rock pools where the blennies and shrimps were dozing. It riffled through the long grass of the sand dunes and stirred the washing on the makeshift lines strung along the beach.

The windows of the houses in Bloater Row were opened wide and the sound of Cissie's laughter drifted out from the Pilchard Inn and mingled with the chiming of the church clock in Rhoskilly Village.

Lena Galvini looked round the bare kitchen of Skibbereen sadly. The stove was unlit for the first time in years and there were no smells of cooking filling the air. The kitchen dresser was bare of jars and crockery and the scullery was empty. The hams and smoked sausages she had already given out to the folk in the Skallies.

Their prized possessions were packed up in two trunks and had already been taken to the end of Bloater Row where soon the car would arrive to take them to St Werburgh's and the start of their long journey home.

In the parlour she took down the last two musical boxes from the mantelpiece.

Alfredo came into the house and found her there, tears streaming down her wide face.

He held her tightly to him and rocked her gently.

'Don't cry, Lena. We been happy here, eh? We was lucky to be brought here when times was bad but now is time to go home, eh? Feel the warm sun on your skin . . . drink a little good wine . . . '

'And we can open our *ristorante*? Maybe one day we have children to leave it to?'

'Maybe,' he said, 'maybe we do, maybe we don't. I have you, Lena, and you got me. That's all that matters.'

She kissed him and clung to him for a long time.

'It's time to go,' he said softly.

Everyone was out in the Skallies to see them off. The Misses Arbuthnot, like two windswept birds were waving from the doorway of Periwinkle House.

The Payne brothers, damp around the eyes and smiling bravely.

Nan and Cissie on the steps of the Pilchard were crying one minute and smiling the next. Archie Grimble with a long face was standing with his mammy outside Bag End.

There was much hugging and kissing and Archie did not escape the strong arms of Lena Galvini.

'I gonna miss you lots, Archie Grimble.'

He nodded but couldn't find any words to say.

She handed him a music box and he stood looking at it through his welling tears.

'Thank you,' he croaked.

It was a small round silver box with a silver lady standing on the top.

He turned the music box over and wound the key. It whirred and clonked at first and then the music began, light and tinkling in the breezy air.

Da da da da da da dad a dad a doh . . .

It was a tune that he didn't know the name of and yet it was strangely familiar.

He watched the Galvinis walk slowly down Bloater Row, hand in hand. The Skallies folk followed behind to wave them off.

The doors to the waiting car opened and everyone called out their farewells noisily.

Archie turned and handed the music box to his mammy and then he pushed his way past Nan and Cissie and flung his arms around Lena Galvini.

'I'm going to miss you loads and loads, Mrs Galvini, but I'll write every week.'

'And I write back,' Lena said through her tears.

Then Alfredo hugged Archie close and kissed him once on each cheek and then the car doors slammed shut and he watched the Galvinis' faces looking out through the back window of the car as it bumped along the rough track that led away from the Skallies.

The car disappeared around the bend in a cloud of dust and Archie turned away.

As the dust cleared the postman came into sight, whistling cheerfully. 'A letter for you, Mrs

Grimble,' he called out.

Martha Grimble looked up, 'But no one ever writes to me.'

'Well, someone from Ireland has. The postmark is from County Cork,' he said.

Martha Grimble's face grew ashen and beads of sweat erupted on her top lip. She took the letter with a trembling hand, hurried inside Bag End and shut the door.

Archie watched her go fearfully. Behind the door of Bag End Martha Grimble, with her heart thumping painfully, opened the letter that was to change their lives.

Part Four

It was still hot when the boat docked in the port even though it was late in the afternoon. The sun burned ferociously in a sky the colour of the Virgin's robes and a warm breeze blew the last wisps of clouds aimlessly towards the horizon.

The port was a terrifying madhouse of a place. The air was filled with dust and noise, clattering and banging, shrieking and wild laughter. Steam engines whistled shrilly and sirens blasted as though in competition with one another. Crane drivers dropped crates into the gaping holds of ships and the air crackled with the sound of splintering wood.

A sad-faced mule clopped over the cobbles pulling a cart full of melons, and an old man with a tray of old shoes hung around his scraggy neck hobbled along calling out to those around him.

A caged bird piped a warbly song and someone nearby sang the snatch of a catchy tune. Sailors whistled and shouted and a group of brown-legged, barefoot urchins danced nimbly among the fishing nets.

An old woman dressed all in black stood behind a fish stall, her skin dark as Christmas Brazil nuts, her eyes like cut-outs from the sea.

Archie Grimble stood alone, his legs still wobbly from being on the boat for so long. Every now and then a wave of nausea snatched at his belly and the ground beneath him lurched and made him feel giddy.

He blinked in the bright light and wiped the sweat from his brow with a crumpled handkerchief. His bad leg grew hot and uncomfortable behind the calliper, the knapsack he was carrying on his back was heavy and he could feel rivulets of sweat dribbling between his shoulder blades. He had no hat and his hair was as stiff as straw baked by the sun.

He had never known such a fierce heat as this and his skin pricked and tightened uncomfortably. A fly perched on the lens of his spectacles and he swatted it away irritably.

A beggar limped towards him, paused, stared curiously up into his face and let fly a mouthful of strange words.

Archie was sure that at any moment he would faint.

Then, with delight, he saw Alfredo Galvini elbowing his way through a group of loud-voiced sailors, striding towards him across the cobbles, his arms outstretched and a smile as wide as a whale's.

'Archie! Oh, my little Archie!'

'Mr Galvini!' he shouted.

Archie looked at his old neighbour from the Skallies in delight. He looked different beneath an Italian sky, browner, healthier, more at home in his skin.

'Come, Archie. Is so hot! I have my boat a little way from here. I take you to see my Lena. She been so happy you coming.'

'Is she waiting in the boat, Alfredo?'

'No, she at home. I don't bring her because she so excited and jumping about so much I afraid she tip up the boat and we all get a soaking, eh?' Alfredo laughed.

Archie giggled. It was so good to see Alfredo again.

'Is Santa Caterina a long way away?' he asked excitedly.

'Is quite a way. For some people many hours by boat but I a good rower and gets you there more quick. Lena been cooking all day, so when we get there you eat like a prince.'

'That'll be good, I'm starving.'

Alfredo took Archie's heavy knapsack and slung it over his shoulder as if it were a bag of feathers, then he handed him a cap to keep the fierce sunlight out of his eyes.

Archie walked beside Alfredo, holding tightly to his hand as they passed through noisy throngs of people.

'How is life going on in the Skallies, Archie?'

'It's all right. The Pilchard is really busy and Fleep works for Nan now. He's a real good cook and at weekends they serve proper meals and some people come from miles away.'

'That's good. And how is those Arbuthnot women, the funny little ones?'

'Oh, they're fine. The younger one, well she's not young but you know what I mean, she gives piano lessons now to some of the kids from Nanskelly School. And they still run a tea shop at weekends. The cakes they make are gorgeous. Giant cream puffs and chocolate éclairs.'

'They do? That's very good, eh? Make them

311

happy. And the Paynes?'

'They're just the same as ever. Either out fishing or in the Pilchard drinking beer.'

'No news from your father?' Alfredo ventured.

'Nope.' Archie was unable to disguise his pleasure.

'You gonna stay with us for whole six weeks?'

'Yes, while my mammy is away.'

'She say in letter that she gone to Ireland?'

'Yes, but I don't know why, she wouldn't tell me,' he said sadly.

'Don't look so worried. You have good time here, time pass very quick and then soon you mammy be back and you no worry any more.'

Alfredo helped Archie down the steep, slippery steps and into the bobbing boat.

Archie sat in the front of the boat and looked around him in wonder as Alfredo rowed them expertly away from the bustling port and further on round the bay.

Gradually the port grew smaller then disappeared from view and the sounds from the land died away.

The sun beat down and the movement of the boat threatened to rock Archie to sleep, but he fought to keep his eyes open so that he didn't miss anything.

All around him fish jumped and plopped in water the colour of a peacock's tail.

The oars skimmed through the waves and Archie dangled his arm over the side, letting the cool water splash over his hot skin.

As they turned a craggy headland the sun began to slip lazily towards the sea.

It was a special feeling sitting there alone with Alfredo in the little boat. It was peaceful and comforting, like they were the only two people in the world.

'Santa Caterina,' Alfredo said nodding towards the land. 'I think you going to like it here.'

Archie looked with awe at the small, higgledy-piggledy village rising above the shore. It looked quite magical, drizzled red and gold by the sunset.

He yawned and shivered; it felt cold now that night was falling. On the coast lights began to twinkle brightly and the sound of an accordion being played drifted across the darkening waters.

Alfredo smiled and thought how good it was to see this little fellow again.

He and Lena had been surprised to receive the letter from Martha Grimble. She had written to ask if they could have Archie to stay with them for the summer holidays. There was some problem with her family in Ireland and she wanted Archie well away from the Skallies in case he was in any danger. She didn't say what sort of danger he might be in but they had agreed straight away and written back. Alfredo would keep him safe in Santa Caterina, nobody would harm one hair of his precious head as long as Alfredo Galvini had breath in his body.

'We nearly there now. I can see Lena at the window holding an oil lamp,' Alfredo said.

But in the front of the boat Archie Grimble was soundly asleep.

★ ★ ★

313

The rain stopped and steam rose from the cobbles of Bloater Row. A rainbow arched above the chimneys of Killivray House. Nan Abelson opened the door of the Pilchard Inn and stepped outside. The morning air was fresh and sweet after the downpour and piano music drifted out from Periwinkle House and mingled with the shrieking of gulls above the Boathouse.

She looked across at the misted-up windows of Skibbereen and sighed. She missed Lena and Alfredo sorely. Still, it was wonderful for them to be able to realize their dream and return to their homeland. Sometimes she ached to return to the place of her birth and yet . . . and yet she wasn't ready to face up to the past, maybe she never would be.

Skibbereen looked cold and unloved; the little glass shrine set into the wall was streaked with grime and the candle stub long since snuffed out. She missed seeing the light of the candle in the night time; she'd liked the way it had made a small oasis of light in the darkness of Bloater Row.

As she passed Bag End she wondered how little Archie was doing; she hoped he'd arrived safely in Italy and wasn't too homesick. She couldn't get over Martha Grimble packing him off like that for the whole six weeks! Sure, she'd said that the shipping company had agreed for someone to keep an eye on him during the voyage but even so he was only ten years of age! He was far too young to be making a journey like that on his own.

She remembered the fear that she'd felt when

she'd set sail for England. She'd been only a few years older than Archie was now. She'd lain in the bunk in the dingy cabin, drowning in tears, her body limp with exhaustion. And with every roll of the boat she had felt her past sucked away from her, everything she'd known drowned by a hungry sea that was shunting her relentlessly towards a strange new land.

Martha Grimble had told Nan that she had urgent family business to attend to but Nan hadn't believed one word of her story. Nan had a bloody good idea that she'd gone to London looking for Walter Grimble. Some women never learned, they'd stick with a man however badly he treated them. She'd never leave Cissie for any man, that was for sure!

She walked along the track that led up to Rhoskilly and in through the churchyard gates.

In the distance the smokeless chimneys of Killivray rose above the canopies of the trees and rooks circled in the sky above.

Nan was worried about the little girl from Killivray. It was months now since the woman had visited her at the Pilchard and asked Nan for her help. She'd been plausible, said that it was a matter of life and death that she got the child away, but afterwards Nan hadn't been so sure. She'd promised to make contact with Nan and let her know that everything had gone to plan and that the child was all right. When Nan agreed to help she hadn't banked on there being a murder involved. That had shaken her up all right when the police had arrived in the Skallies. She'd kept her composure, though, and said that

315

she'd never come into contact with anyone from Killivray House.

Now she made her way between the gravestones until she came to Benjamin Tregantle's grave and then stooped and placed a small bundle of herbs on the grave, rosemary for rememberance.

She wiped a tear from her eye and thought of the last time she'd seen Benjamin. Two nights before he'd died he'd come into the Pilchard earlier than usual for a drink. He'd looked exhausted and worried and was wheezing and coughing as though he'd had the flu. She'd offered to get him some medicine but he'd said he was past the stage of medicine. He'd laughed then and said that every bugger died of shortness of breath in the end.

He'd told her that he'd been busy of late, had a lot of sorting out to do before he went on his travels. She'd asked him where he was going and he'd said, 'Just here and there, Nan, business mainly, a few loose ends to tie up before I go on to a better place.'

Hell, she missed him! He'd been so good to her when she'd first arrived here in the Skallies. She'd picked up the keys to the Pilchard from an address in St Werburgh's and walked all the way to the Skallies carrying Cissie in her arms. When she'd arrived, exhausted, she'd been horrified to find that the place she was renting had once been a pub. She'd just assumed that it was a house of some sorts but the rent had been cheap and that's all that mattered at the time, that she and Cissie had somewhere safe to stay.

Benjamin had been her first visitor, bringing her a basket of fresh food and a bunch of spring flowers to cheer the place up. He'd suggested that they could do with a pub in the Skallies again and that she might as well open it up seeing as everything was there. Benjamin had helped her to scrub the place out from top to bottom. He'd brought kindling and logs and lit a fire to chase away the gloom, and in the following days he'd lent her money to order stock, shown her how to sort the beer barrels out, clean the cellar and keep everything shipshape.

And that was it, almost overnight she'd become the landlady of the Pilchard Inn. Not that she'd made much of a living from the meagre trade from the Skallies folk and a few locals who braved the stigma of drinking down in the place where the odd people lived. Still, she and Cissie hadn't asked for much, they'd been happy in this little backwater. They'd had a roof over their heads and food in their bellies.

Of late, though, trade had been brisk and the takings were more than she'd thought possible.

'You were a good man, Benjamin Tregantle,' she said sadly, 'and there aren't many of your sort left, more's the pity.'

She looked down at the grave and smiled. Benjamin would have laughed to see her standing there talking to herself. Death had never worried Benjamin. He'd always said that death was the only thing we could be certain of in life. She blew a kiss towards the grave and then she walked slowly back down towards the Skallies.

★　★　★

Dawn was breaking over Santa Caterina. The dark sea took on a purple hue and the pink wash of the sun seared the lightening sky.

Sister Isabella looked down from her window in the Convent of Santa Caterina perched high above the village and watched as the houses emerged from the shadows of the night.

She saw the first fishing boat making its way in towards the small harbour.

The shutters began to open in the houses and the old cockerel crowed down in the garden of the Casa delle Stelle.

The shutters were still closed there but someone was up; she could see a thin wreath of cigarette smoke rising into the air. One of their guests having an early morning smoke out in the secluded garden. Soon it would be time to move them on, away from the safety of Santa Caterina to a new life elsewhere. *Il Camaleonte* would be in contact soon telling them when the move was to be made.

She watched the blue shutters opening in the tallest house down near the harbour in the Via Porto. Lena Galvini was up bright and early. It was so good to have Alfredo and Lena here in Santa Caterina, just knowing they were there made her feel happy. She hoped that one day soon Lena Galvini would be blessed with a pregnancy that didn't come to grief. What joy it would be to know that she would have descendants living here in the village, someone to carry on the Galvini name.

Then she took up her binoculars and trained them on Lena. Sister Isabella watched her as she hung out her washing on a line strung out across the balcony. She was pegging out a small pair of shorts and a shirt . . .

Sister Isabella put down the binoculars. Why would Lena be washing children's clothes? Unless she had visitors and now wasn't a good time for visitors in Santa Caterina.

She must find out who was staying there; they didn't want outsiders setting the cat among the pigeons and ruining their plans.

A monk on a bicycle appeared on the steep track below the convent, his robes billowing around him and the pate of his head pink with the sunrise.

Sister Isabella put her fingers in her mouth and whistled, a piercing shriek of a whistle. The monk braked, swerved dangerously, came to rest in a cloud of dust.

He looked up with a grin.

'Sister Isabella, you be the death of me one of these days!'

She leant out of the window. 'There is someone staying at Lena and Alfredo's. Be a good man and find out who it is.'

'Of course! I call in on my way back. Be sure to have breakfast for me. The food in the monastery is vile.'

Down in the convent the first bells began to ring and Sister Isabella knelt down in front of the stark crucifix on the bare white wall of her cell, clasped her hands together and prayed. Then she rose and made her way through the winding corridors and down the stairs to the ancient church.

★   ★   ★

Miss Noni Arbuthnot was polishing the tables in the parlour of Periwinkle House. She loved the smell of beeswax and when she'd finished polishing she looked down at her reflection in the burnished wood; a small, prim face looked back at her with a smile.

Across the hallway in the dining room her sister Agnes was playing the piano. Noni put down her duster and moved over to the doorway, careful not to make a noise and distract her sister while she played. She watched as Agnes, head bowed, stroked the keys with her long slender fingers; oblivious to everything except her music. The black and white of the piano keys reminded Noni of the way Agnes was. Black and white. That was the way Agnes saw the world, there were no shades of grey. Good and evil. Right and wrong. She'd always seen things that way ever since she'd been a small child. She'd been different to other children, lonely and with-drawn, unable to join in their games of make believe. Unable to tell a lie, and that had almost been her undoing in the end. Yet when she'd found music she had blossomed. Black notes on a white page. Black and white piano keys. The rules of music were easy for her to follow: play the right notes and you made a wonderful sound. And with her piano playing she had been able to lose herself and subsequently find herself in a world that responded to her touch.

It was so good to hear her play again and despite all the years in the Skallies when she had refused to open the lid of the piano, she had not lost any of her formidable talent.

It had happened the night it had started to snow; she had wandered over to the piano and lifted the lid.

Noni had waited with bated breath and then suddenly Agnes had put her fingers to the keys.

It was a miracle.

Noni looked up and saw Nan Abelson passing the window. Nan looked so much better these days and she'd wager it had something to do with that Fleep fellow from the Grockles. Good for her! She could do with a little romance in her life, put some colour in her cheeks.

The Skallies folk called the fellow Fleep but his real name was supposed to be Philippe Martin. Well, it wasn't the name he was given at birth! He wouldn't know who she and Agnes were, of that she was sure, but she remembered him well enough. She'd attended his christening at St Mark's Church in Chelsea. The last time she'd seen him he'd been about twelve years of age, a bored boy yawning his way through the recitals in the drawing room at the Sefton Brynes' house in Bloomsbury. She'd remembered thinking at the time how very like his father he was to look at.

Years later she'd seen the engagement notice

in *The Times*. 'Mr and Mrs So and So announce the engagement of their daughter . . . to James Peter Etherington, only son etc.'

And later, there'd been some kind of scandal only she couldn't remember what it was all about, it was at the same time as Agnes's trial, those dark dismal days she'd rather forget.

★ ★ ★

Archie awoke with a start at the sound of loud talking and laughter beneath his bedroom window.

He sat for some time in the half dark of the strange bedroom. He remembered arriving in the boat last night and Lena almost smothering him with her hugs and kisses. Then he had eaten an enormous supper and Lena had shown him up to this room and he had fallen asleep before she'd finished tucking him in.

He clambered out of bed and crossed to the window. He fumbled with the catches on the shutters and opened them wide.

Sunlight caught him like a backhanded slap in the face and he stepped away from its fierce glare.

It took him several minutes to get his eyes accustomed to the brightness of the light and then he stepped towards the window again and looked out.

High up, he looked down on a group of old men talking and laughing as they sat on the harbour wall below. How lovely it was here in Santa Caterina! He could understand why Lena

322

and Alfredo had wanted to live here. And no wonder Thomas Greswode had wanted to escape back here from the gloom of Killivray House.

It was just as Thomas had described it in his diary! The sun was hot and on the balconies washing of every colour was flapping in the sea breeze. Archie sniffed up the morning smells; just like Thomas, he too could smell baking bread and hot coffee on the go. And down below his window the loud, happy chatter of the people.

He dressed quickly, pulled on the calliper and made his way carefully down the steep stairs that led into the kitchen.

There was no one around but through a curtained archway that led off the kitchen he could hear the sound of someone singing joyfully.

He pulled back the curtain and looked into a large bare room where Alfredo was perched precariously on a dilapidated cart painting the walls bright yellow with an enormous paint brush.

'Archie! You sleep your head off! You feel good?'

Archie nodded.

'See here I am making this room ready for when we open our *ristorante*.'

Archie smiled, 'It'll be grand, Alfredo.'

'Ah, now I have little rest from painting, give you some food.'

'Where's Lena?'

'She gone to market and she be there chattering for many hours. She got a bell on every tooth, that wife of mine! You and I eat and then I going to teach you to swim before it gets too hot.'

'Alfredo, I can't swim.'

'Everyone can learn to swim!'

'But I have this thing on my leg!'

'Ah, so we take it off when you in water. You swim a little and then after you puts it back on.'

Archie shook his head and bit his trembling lip.

He was far too embarrassed to take off the calliper and let everyone see his withered leg.

'I know what you thinking. You no want anyone to see you leg. I understand this so we go to little place where there is no one to see. Just me and you in my little boat.'

Archie nodded nervously and without enthusiasm.

In the kitchen Alfredo made him coffee and gave him some peculiar bread that was rubbed with tomato and something strong that made his eyes water. It tasted good, though, and he hadn't realized how hungry he was even though Lena had served him up a feast last night.

Later, with Alfredo holding his hand they stepped out of the house on to the cobbled path. Archie looked around him in awe, eager to feast his eyes on his new surroundings in the daylight.

The houses strung out along the small harbour were tall and narrow and gracefully shabby. They were painted in pastel colours, pinks and lemons and palest turquoise, colours bleached by the hot sun, the paint bubbling and peeling in parts. The balconies groaned under the weight of earthenware plant pots that were filled with bright flowers.

Outside most of the houses were small, glass-fronted shrines built into the walls, and behind the glass stood the statues of small, faded saints, with the stubs of burned-out candles at their feet.

Alfredo seeing his interest in the shrines explained, 'Many years ago in Naples, there only a few shrines. But there were many robbers there who waits till the dark and then jumps on you and takes all you money. So people have idea to make many shrines with candles, make the night lighter, chase the dark away and stop them robbers.'

'Are there many robbers in Santa Caterina?' Archie asked looking up at Alfredo anxiously.

'No! Santa Caterina very peaceful place. See, most of the saints here in the shrines here is Santa Caterina. She our saint and people here loves her and think she holy.'

'Who was she?'

'Long time ago she nun up at the convent and she help many children who don't have no parents. She can do miracles.'

'What kind of miracles?' Archie asked eagerly.

'She make sad people happy, weak people strong and scared people brave!'

'Oh.'

'You see, Archie, this only little place but makes many people with great courage. Santa Caterina, and the man they called *Il Camaleonte*.'

'Who's he?'

'You never hear of him! *Il Camaleonte* is very famous in Italia. He very brave man and in the war he help many children escape from Germans. He work with peoples here in Italy and France to save the children. He very good man but have many enemies.'

'Why'

'The Germans don't like him but also the bad men in Naples don't like him and want to kill him if they finds him.'

'Is he here now?'

'No, no one ever see him. He old now. Maybe even dead.'

'What's his real name?'

'He don't have real name, he have many names, many disguises.'

'And Santa Caterina, is she dead too?'

Alfredo laughed and patted Archie on the back.

'What's so funny?'

'Oh, she dead for many hundreds of years.'

'What happened to her?'

'Ah, there big mystery about Santa Caterina. She go out fishing one day and she don't come back. Some peoples say she drown and others say the pirates takes her.'

'Blimey,' said Archie, 'but no one really knows the truth?'

'No, no one ever know now, there all kind of stories. Sometimes they digs up old houses and finds skeleton and say, Ah! We have found bones of Santa Caterina, but it never true.'

'Why would anyone want to find her bones?'

'Because she holy. People of Santa Caterina

like to have her bones buried here.'

'Oh,' Archie said. 'How would they know if it was her bones? I mean, I expect that all skeletons look the same.'

'Ah, but she different! She have six fingers on one hand and only one leg.'

'Crikey!' Archie said. 'She'd be easy to recognize then, as a skeleton. Why did she only have one leg?'

'She sick when she little girl and they have to take off her leg with saw and they say she never even cry out, she have much courage.'

'Don't tell me any more, Alfredo, I feel sick.'

Alfredo looked down at him. The boy was as pale as mozzarella cheese and sweat was pricking his forehead.

They walked together hand in hand and Alfredo called out a greeting to a couple of bent-backed old men who were mending nets on the quayside.

The old men looked up with interest, waved and called out to them.

'I don't speak any Italian, Alfredo, what will I say to people if they talk to me?' said Archie in a panic.

'You just smiles you lovely smile and say *buon giorno*! Is good morning. Very soon you will learn many words. By end of summer you speak like an Italian.'

They walked together through the narrow streets of Santa Caterina, past opened doors that led into dim and intriguing interiors. Archie sniffed up the multitude of smells eagerly: oil and tomatoes; freshly baked bread and marzipan; apples and lemons; ham and herbs; coffee and soap suds; the heady scent of freshly watered flowers in terracotta pots.

Alfredo and Archie crossed a tiny piazza where an ancient dog with a triangular scarf knotted around his neck chased the shadows of pigeons across the sun-baked ground. A fountain in the centre of the piazza bubbled and splashed and old women leant from precarious iron balconies and called out to them as they passed. Children ran out of some of the houses and the metal curtains tinkled tunes at their passing.

They stared at Archie with wide brown eyes then ran back inside calling out excitedly.

'They happy, they have new friend to play with in Santa Caterina.'

Archie sighed. He didn't make friends easily and he didn't want to come up against the Italian version of the Kelly brothers.

Alfredo noted his troubled expression and said, 'Don't be afraid, Archie. While you here I look after you. If you find friend you like then you go play. If you don't want play I no make you, eh? Then next year when you come again maybe you ready to make friends!'

Archie brightened up.

A small dog ran out of a house and sniffed Archie's legs and then ran off piddling as it went.

Alfredo pulled a hat from his pocket, gave it to Archie and helped him into the little boat. He put in a bulging knapsack and soon the boat was nosing through the clear waters. They made their way out to sea, followed the curve of the coast and after some time they headed in towards a small deserted beach.

'Today is market day so people is busy. You can only get to this place by the sea so nobody be here today.'

Archie undressed and took off his calliper. He looked across at Alfredo shyly. Alfredo smiled; he was such a frail little boy, like a skinned rabbit with his pale flesh and skinny legs. A few weeks here in Santa Caterina would soon put a bit of meat on his bones, some colour in his face.

When Alfredo coaxed a terrified Archie into the water, he was surprised to find it warm and not like it was in the Skallies.

Tiny silver fish darted beneath the surface and tickled his legs. Alfredo splashed him and he splashed back timidly, turning his head away so as not to get his face wet.

After they had played for a while, Alfredo carried him in a little deeper.

Archie clung to him, trying to climb higher up Alfredo's body.

He put him firmly down and Archie stood, petrified, up to his neck in warm water. He shivered with fright as he watched Alfredo untie a strip of cloth from around his wrist and told Archie to slip it between his teeth.

'See that way you can't shout! I pulls you along and you make swimming actions like this.'

Archie bit his lip and held back his tears.

'Come, it's fun and I no let you drown. This way is how my papa teach me and his papa before him.'

'But I don't want to be able to swim, Alfredo.'

'Here in Santa Caterina you have to be able to

329

swim. We go in boat and if we tips up and in you go, you needs to swim!'

Archie swallowed hard and took the cloth between his teeth. He flailed around with his arms and Alfredo walked away keeping the cloth taut and the terrified boy afloat as he thrashed his limbs like a landed octopus.

Archie wanted to scream and make Alfredo stop, to get his feet safely back on the ground but if he opened his mouth to shout he knew he would sink.

They carried on for a long time and slowly Archie relaxed and moved his arms and legs the way Alfredo had shown him. He felt the water buoying him up, the sun making the waves sparkle around his face. It wasn't as bad as he had imagined, but he held on to the cloth for grim life, half afraid that his teeth would come out.

Finally, Alfredo gathered an exhausted Archie up in his strong arms.

'Okay, you done well, you must rest now.'

'I think I could do a little more, you know!'

'One more go, eh, and then we rest? We do a little every day. We build up them muscles in you bad leg. Soon you swims like a silver fish!'

They stayed in the water a while longer as the sun rose higher into the sky.

'We stop now, else you skin burn and shrivel. Sun gets too hot. Come, we have a little lunch.'

Alfredo laid out towels on the sand, fetched an enormous umbrella from the boat and started to put it up.

'Do you think it's going to rain, Alfredo?'

Alfredo threw back his head and laughed. 'Maybe but not until September! This for keeping the sun off us while we eat.'

They sat beneath the shade of the giant umbrella eating slices of spicy sausage and chewy bread washed down with a lemon drink that was so sharp it made Archie screw up his face and smack his lips together.

Alfredo yawned and said, 'Now is time for siesta.'

'What's a siesta?' Archie asked.

'A time to sleep and dream while the sun is too hot. Here in Santa Caterina we have two days instead of one.'

'I don't understand.'

'We gets up early while it still cool. We work and play and then we eats and then we sleeps. Then we gets up again and does some more work and play and eats again, then we stay up very late and talks while it's cooler.'

'That sounds good,' Archie said with a yawn.

'Take you a little time to get used to the heat. You feel tired at first.'

'Oh, no, I'm fine. I'm not tired at all,' he said with another wide yawn and moments later he was fast asleep.

Alfredo covered him with towels and sat for a long time looking down at the peaceful, sun-pinked face of Archie Grimble.

★　★　★

It was a warm, clear evening when Eloise Fanthorpe and William Dally set out in the car and drove through the winding lanes towards the Skallies. They kept the car windows down and the soft air was filled with the smell of wild thyme, lavender and honeysuckle and the drone of weary bees.

It was quiet when they stepped inside the Pilchard Inn. Eloise sat down at a table near the porthole window, while William went up to the bar.

Eloise looked around her with interest. It was an ancient place with low-beamed ceilings and walls ingrained with years of tobacco smoke and decorated with washed-out pictures of long dead Skallies folk holding up giant fish and fat-faced babies.

A young woman appeared suddenly from behind a curtain that separated the bar from a back room and Eloise was reminded of an actress making an entrance. She was a good-looking woman, with an intelligent, strong-boned face, olive skin and thick dark hair tied in a plait. She looked like a no-nonsense sort of woman and yet there was a vulnerability about her too, a well-disguised nervousness.

'How can I help?' she said to William Dally.

'We come over from Nanskelly to try out your grub that everyone's harping on about.'

'I don't think you'll be disappointed. Our Fleep's a damned good cook. What did you fancy?'

'What you got?'

Nan handed him two menus and he made his way across the bar to Eloise.

'There you go, Miss Fanthorpe. Don't know

332

about you but I could eat a scabby donkey.'

'Let's hope you don't have to,' she said absently.

Eloise Fanthorpe gathered her wits and looked at the proffered menu. It had been carefully written out in a childish hand and decorated around the edges with small drawings. She looked at it with growing interest. There were drawings of a variety of animals: miniature elephants and wizen-faced monkeys; coiled pythons and dancing bears; there was even a circus caravan and a Big Top.

After a while she swapped menus with William Dally and smiled with delight. On this one there were pictures of a house, or possibly a pub, and a very small child sitting outside in a pram. Above the pub the sky was peppered with stars and a huge moon. She looked closely at the moon and saw that there was the imprint of a cat's paw on its surface. In another corner there was a picture of a girl running towards a tall grey house with many windows and in each window there was a smiling face, faces looking out into a bright sunlit day.

Along the top of the menu was a long train, the carriages rattling along at speed, and in the window a woman held a baby in a shawl, both looking out with startled eyes. They were truly remarkable drawings. How she wished that her father was still alive to see the raw talent of this artist.

As Eloise looked up from the menu, a small girl stepped out from behind the bar and came towards their table hesitantly, carefully carrying knives and forks and linen napkins.

Eloise Fanthorpe smiled at her and the girl smiled back.

'Do you know who drew these?' she asked pointing at the menu.

The girl nodded. 'Cissie Abelson drew them,' she said.

'Is she here?'

The girl nodded slowly.

'Do you think I could speak with her?'

'She don't speak much,' the girl said. 'And she's not allowed to speak to strangers ever.'

Miss Fanthorpe smiled and said, 'Could you fetch her?'

'It's me,' the girl said. 'I'm Cissie Abelson.'

Eloise looked nonplussed. The child standing awkwardly in front of her with her mouth hanging open was obviously not a bright child, not in the accepted sense, but anyone who could draw like this was exceptionally gifted.

'These drawings, Cissie Abelson, are very good, very good indeed. Who taught you to draw like this?'

The girl's face grew blank and she shrugged her shoulders, looking troubled.

'When did you go to the circus?'

The girl looked dumbfounded and scratched her nose. Eloise looked up suddenly to see the woman behind the bar eyeing her with displeasure.

Eloise coughed, handed the menu back to the little girl hurriedly, took a slug of her drink and then winced.

'She was giving me a filthy look for talking to

the child,' Eloise hissed at William, nodding towards Nan who was wiping down the bar.

'Funny folks round here, on the secretive side, always have been. Best not to ask too many questions in the Skallies, if you ask me.'

'I was only being friendly. Anyway, the child's drawings are quite wonderful.'

' 'Ave you picked what you want to eat yet?'

'I'll have the sea bass,' she said with a smile. 'And you?'

'Fish and prawn pie. My old mother used to make that. It were a ceiling floater of a dish.'

The woman came out from behind the bar and took their order, before whisking the menus away.

Soon the smell of fresh fish cooking filled the air and out at the back of the pub someone was singing cheerfully.

Two dinner plates emerged through the curtains followed by a man's head. He stopped in his tracks, blushed deeply, handed the plates quickly to the woman and disappeared but not quickly enough. Eloise Fanthorpe recognized him immediately but looked down at the table diplomatically.

William Dally ate his meal with enthusiasm. The pie was cooked to perfection, the pastry crust golden and moist, the prawns and fish mouth wateringly scrumptious. He hadn't been in the Pilchard for years; the last time he'd eaten food here was when the Dennis family had kept the place. After they went, it had gone to the dogs. But damn, this young woman was doing well here now and whoever had done the cooking knew what they were doing. It was a bloody grand place and served a damn fine drop of ale too.

As Nan Abelson cleared away the empty plates, William Dally said, 'Don't suppose you know if Archie Grimble is anywhere around?'

Nan looked at him suspiciously.

'He's not here at the moment. He's away with his family.' As she spoke she was aware of Eloise Fanthorpe scrutinizing her face as if she were looking for something concealed there.

Nan turned away as William Dally said, 'Gone anywhere interesting, has he?'

'Abroad,' Nan said and walked away.

'Well, I'll be buggered,' William Dally said with a shake of his head.

Eloise Fanthorpe had gone very pale and was looking ahead of her as if in a stupor.

★ ★ ★

The bread shop in Santa Caterina was called Il Panettiere and it was halfway up a very steep hill overlooked by the towering and ancient convent.

The first time they went to fetch bread, Alfredo showed Archie the way through the narrow streets and taught him how to ask for bread in Italian.

Each day after, it was his job to climb the hill and fetch the early morning bread.

Every day as soon as he woke he dressed and slipped out through the jangling curtains of the Galvinis' house and made his way there.

In those first few days he hurried past the

groups of local men smoking and gossiping along the harbour wall and avoided the old women who seemed always to be out sweeping the cobbles in front of their houses. But day by day his confidence grew and he began to return their calls of *buon giorno.*

He knew now that when they called out *Come sta?* they were asking him how he was and now he replied, '*Molto bene, grazie.*' Very well, thank you. And he was delighted when they smiled and laughed and waved at him. And he did feel well, he felt better than he'd ever felt!

When first he had climbed the steep hill to the bread shop his bad leg had ached and the calliper had chafed his skin raw. But since he'd been having his daily swimming lessons with Alfredo his leg was growing stronger.

After he had been in Santa Caterina for almost a week he set out as usual on his daily errand for bread. Climbing slowly up the steep, cobbled hill, he managed for once not to have a rest halfway up. He arrived at the *panettiere* hot and dusty but pleased with himself.

He bought two loaves of bread and exchanged a smile and a *come sta?* with the young woman behind the counter and then left. Coming back down the hill he paused and looked along a narrow alleyway that led off to the left. It was dim and dark and halfway along an old woman in a black dress and headscarf slept on a low chair outside a house. Up until now he had always taken the route that Alfredo had shown him but he was sure that if he went down the alley and then turned right he should come back to the harbour only further along.

He stepped timidly into the alleyway and made his way along it, tiptoeing so as not to wake the old woman. As he came level with her she grunted, looked up at him with lively brown eyes and held out her wrinkled hand.

Hesitantly he inched his hand towards her.

She took hold of his hand, so pale against the deep weathered brown of her own skin. She held his hand for some moments and then looked into his eyes.

She let go of his hand reluctantly. Archie smiled at her and moved on quickly, conscious of her eyes boring into his back. Turning right into a wider street, he made his way towards a café in front of which chairs and tables were set out on the cobbles.

He peeped inside the café. It was empty except for two old men who stood at the counter smoking.

They turned and looked at him inquisitively and called out to someone.

A small man, barely big enough to see over the counter popped up and stared at Archie. He had bright, twinkling eyes and an enormous moustache that curled upwards towards his eyebrows. Archie blushed and made to walk away but the tiny man called out to him.

'*Buon giorno!*'

Archie muttered a reply and walked on.

The small man called out again but he spoke fast and Archie could not understand what he was saying.

He grew flustered and quickened his step.

'*Inglese. Non capisco!*' one of the old men said.

The small man hurried out from the café and came towards Archie, grabbed his arm and pulled him inside. He took the loaves of bread from him and laid them down on the counter, and then he lifted Archie up onto a high stool in front of the bar. Then he hastened behind the counter, poured a glass of lemonade and pushed it towards Archie with a smile.

'*Grazie,*' Archie murmured from his perch on the stool, his legs dangling down and his calliper in full view of the watching men.

After a while they ignored him and continued their talking. There were ten or so tables that had seen better days and set around them were rush-backed chairs with wobbly legs. The stone floor was littered with cigarette ends, screwed-up pieces of paper and toothpicks. On the rough-hewn walls there were pictures of dead popes and a flyblown poster advertising a circus. Beneath the poster there was a blurry photograph of a woman and across the bottom of the photograph someone had scrawled their name illegibly in a whorl of faded black ink.

Beneath the photograph, on a narrow shelf, there was a jar of fresh flowers and in front of the flowers a candle burned in a small red glass. It was a shrine of some sort.

One of the old men saw Archie looking and Archie pointed at the photo and said shyly, 'Santa Caterina?'

The old man clapped his hands against his leg, threw back his head and laughed loudly.

'Santa Caterina! *Non!* *L'ucello d'argento!*'

Archie shook his head in embarrassment.

The small man behind the counter translated for him, 'She no Santa Caterina. Santa Caterina very good woman but very ugly. This one very beautiful. In English she called the silver bird. In Italia we say *l'ucello d'argento.*'

Archie grinned foolishly and sipped his lemonade.

He sat for a while longer, finished his drink and clambered down awkwardly from the high stool.

Arrivederci!

Arrivederci!

The three men turned and watched him go, with interest, and then they turned back to the bar and continued their conversation.

Archie arrived back at the house to find Lena sitting out on the front step shelling peas into a large metal bowl.

'You been a long time today.'

'A tiny little man, about the size of a dwarf, gave me a glass of lemonade in a café round the corner from the baker's.'

Lena looked up. 'Ah, I know, the Silver Bird Café.'

Archie nodded. 'Is it called after the girl?'

Lena put down the bowl of peas and patted the step for Archie to sit down beside her.

'That's right. Here in Santa Caterina once was a little girl. She orphan at Santa Caterina. Very beautiful, very mischief full, always running and jumping like a boy and making the nuns shake their heads and pray to Santa Caterina to make her quieter. When she fifteen she falls in love and runs away with the circus and she gone many years. When they hear of her again in Santa Caterina she very famous, she how you say, she fly through the air in circus.'

'A trapeze artist?'

'*Si*, that's the words, trapeze artist.'

'Did she ever come back to Santa Caterina?'

'*Si*. She make her peace with the nuns. She have a child. For many months she travel with circus all over Italy and France but for some months she come back here to Santa Caterina. But later come the terrible tragedy for our little silver bird.'

Archie looked up at Lena and held his breath.

'One day, the circus come to village near Santa Caterina and she, the one they call the silver bird, have very bad accident.'

'What happened?'

'She do the trick high in air and let go, but the man she do trick with doesn't catch her. Was terrible. She fall like a little bird from the nest and breaks her neck.'

Lena shook her head sadly and crossed herself.

Archie sucked in his breath through his teeth with a whistling sound.

Just then Alfredo came walking along the path carrying a bucket full of fresh fish.

'Archie have a drink in Luca's café this morning and I telling him the story of the woman they call the silver bird,' Lena said.

'Ah, that was tragedy! You know, my mama was there in circus tent with her sister when it happen. For long time she not speak of it because it was too terrible. Give her bad night dreams for many years,' Alfredo remembered.

'That's a real sad story.'

'Ah, *si*, and the poor husband and child was there when it happened.'

Archie blinked back his tears. 'The silver bird wasn't her real name, though, was it?'

'No. She called Rosa Gasparini.'

Archie looked down at his skinny knees, they were shaking uncontrollably and his mouth was as dry as a burnt twig.

Rosa Gasparini!

Thomas Gasparini Greswode. Rosa Gasparini. He tried to conjure up the face of the woman in the photograph that Romilly Greswode had given to him. Rosa Gasparini, the silver bird who had fallen to her death was the mother of Thomas from Killivray.

She was the pretty bride in the photograph looking up at her husband outside the tiny church.

He felt for the silver bird necklace around his neck.

'You all right, Archie?' Alfredo asked with concern.

'Yes, I'll just put the bread away and then I'm going to have a lie-down. I think it's the heat making me feel faint.'

He made his way shakily into the cool of the house and climbed unsteadily up the stairs.

When he had gone Alfredo said to Lena, 'You know, he very sensitive little boy. Don't be telling him too many sad stories.'

'I understand. Maybe, you know, I think Archie got a sad story of his own that he don't know nothing about. Is funny Martha sending him to us.'

'How you mean, Lena?'

'Well, all time we know him she don't let him out of her sight much. Then she send him all this way to us on boat. I very glad he come but I worry what she hiding.'

'I worries too. Is odd how the father go and don't come back and then she hurry off like that. If I had a son like Archie I never leave him.'

Upstairs in the cool of his bedroom Archie lay down on his bed and watched the slivers of sunlight slip through the slats of the shutters, watched the sunbeams playing across the bare wooden floor. He closed his eyes and imagined Thomas Greswode sitting proudly in the circus Big Top, hearing the gasp of the audience as they watched his brave mama high on the trapeze.

Then, looking up at her and holding his breath as she flew through the air . . .

He knew that in a split second she would be safely in the hands of the man on the trapeze hanging upside down waiting to catch her. And then the audience would clap and shriek with delight.

But then it had all gone horribly wrong.

Their hands had never met and she had crashed to the sawdust floor.

After she had died Thomas had been sent back to England. He had left behind sunny Santa Caterina here in Italy to live in gloomy Killivray House, the house his father had inherited. And he would die young and never return here.

Archie felt for the silver bird necklace around his neck and held it tightly.

★ ★ ★

Nan poured two cups of tea and passed one across the kitchen table to Fleep.

'Well, it was quiet tonight except for that peculiar couple and the Paynes at last knockings,' Fleep said, lighting a cigarette with trembling fingers.

'It'll be busy tomorrow, mind, the forecast is good. We'll be rushed off our feet.'

Fleep didn't answer and Nan looked across at him curiously.

'Fleep, you seem on edge. What's wrong? Was it something to do with that woman? I didn't like her either; it was like she was here just to snoop on us.'

He looked up suddenly and said, 'Seems like she rattled you too, Nan. Why?'

'It was just the way she was looking at the menus that Cissie had made and then asking her questions about her drawing.'

'There's nothing wrong with that, is there? Cissie draws beautifully. You should be glad that people recognize her talent.'

'I am in a way but I hate people nosing around. I've noticed that in her drawings Cissie describes her past life. It's quite weird because she draws things that happened when she was quite small, things you wouldn't think that she even remembered.'

'Is that a bad thing?'

'Oh, it's just me being testy. I'm too protective over her, I know that. Anyway, why did she make you feel so awkward? You went crimson when you saw her.'

'It was a while back. When I first arrived I did something rather foolish and she saw me.'

'What did you do?'

He blew smoke rings towards the ceiling and then said, 'I was going to put an end to things. I'd had enough, you see.'

Nan sat with the cup halfway up to her lips. 'You don't mean . . . not seriously . . . '

He nodded and the colour drained from Nan's face.

'But why?'

'I'd been so depressed, made a real mess of my life. My parents were old when I was born and they died quite close together. I frittered away my inheritance; blew thousands on drugs and drink, mixing with the wrong sort. I had a broken romance, then ran off abroad to lick my wounds.'

'And how did you end up here?'

'That's the strange bit, Nan. I'd been making my way up through France. I'd been thrown out of the place I was staying when I couldn't pay the rent. I was penniless, on my uppers. I'd spent my last cents on a bottle of cheap brandy and was drunk as a lord. It was snowing and I'd passed out in an alleyway somewhere near the Rue Popincourt. I was woken up by a parrot screeching in my ear. It was really weird, Nan, there I was all alone with a monumental hang-over staring at a foul-mouthed parrot, and tied to the cage was an envelope and inside a key with the address of the Grockles.'

'And so you just pitched up here?'

'I did. Well, I was half out of my mind on drink and drugs, I thought it was some sort of joke. But when I got here and the key fitted the door to the Grockles I could hardly believe it. How did you come to live in the Skallies, Nan?'

Nan was silent for a moment.

'It's a long story and I'm not sure I'm ready to tell it yet.'

Fleep patted her hand.

'Anyway, Fleep, tell me what has the woman who was here tonight got to do with you trying to end it all?'

'I'd made my decision, decided there was nothing left in this life for me. I went around the coast, there's a small beach there and I had a lot to drink. I'd planned to walk out into the water, keep on walking, then swim out to sea and drown myself.'

'You don't still feel like that?' she asked anxiously.

He shook his head and smiled. 'Not any more. The worst bit was that all of a sudden that woman and her friend appeared with hundreds of schoolgirls and I was . . . '

'You were what?'

'God, this is so embarrassing. You see, I was standing there absolutely naked.'

Nan put her hand over her mouth. 'You're joking!' she squealed with laughter.

Fleep nodded and blushed. 'There didn't

seem much point walking out into the sea with clothes on.'

'Oh, my God, and they all saw you, all those schoolgirls?'

He nodded again and covered his face with his hands.

'Nan, I still have nightmares about it. It was awful.'

But Nan couldn't answer she was laughing so much.

'I hope she didn't recognize me tonight,' Fleep said.

'She wouldn't with your clothes on!' Nan shrieked.

'Pack it in, Nan, it wasn't funny. There was another woman with her who was screaming for her to call the police. I could have been locked up.'

She tried to stem her mirth but every time she looked at Fleep's horrified face it set her off again. She laughed until her sides ached and she felt weak all over. Soon Fleep was laughing too and the Pilchard echoed to the sound of their laughter. Outside, the wildcats slept on the outhouse roof under a soft and silver moon.

★ ★ ★

From her eyrie in the convent Sister Isabella watched the small English boy who was staying with Alfredo and Lena climb the hill to the baker's each day. At first he climbed slowly, dragging his feet, looking over his shoulder as though he were afraid that someone was

347

following him. With each day, though, he seemed to grow stronger, and his withered leg grew a little more sturdy.

Taking up her binoculars, she focused on his face and saw that the hue of his skin had grown steadily darker and the blue of his eyes more vivid, the front of his hair bleached fairer.

The day he had stood nervously, looking into the alleyway just below the *panettiere*, she had watched him with fascination. He was curious but afraid, finding his way round hesitantly. Little by little he was getting braver and ever more curious about life in Santa Caterina. He was just a child, though; he wouldn't get in the way.

She turned away from the window and made her way down the steep stairs and out into the enclosed courtyard.

It was hot and the courtyard was deserted. Most of the sisters were inside busy with their chores. Now she was so old she had little work allotted to her and so she was free to do whatever took her fancy. Most days she went to the library to write up her memoirs of life here in the convent but of late she grew tired more easily and spent more time outside in the courtyard in the shade of the old lemon tree.

She sat down stiffly, dipped her hand into the cool waters of the fountain and drifted off into her memories of the past.

When she'd first entered the convent she'd come under false pretences. She'd had no vocation to be a nun; she'd just been trying to run away from the pain of unrequited love. Life as a nun had been an escape from a world too painful to contemplate. She'd imagined a life of meditation and serenity, of prayer and praise and long periods of silence. How wrong she'd been!

She looked up then as the children came out of the door on the far side of the courtyard. A crocodile of chattering boys and girls on their way to breakfast under the watchful eye of Sister Benedicta. Their voices filled the courtyard and she smiled to see their faces. A small girl who was holding the hand of a tiny boy caught her eye. Sister Isabella waved to her and the girl waved back. She had arrived as a silent, frightened little girl and now she was in the middle of every sort of mischief. A spirited soul saved from a life without hope, with the whole world ahead of her now. The children's voices died away as they went through the door into the refectory for their breakfast.

She closed her eyes and prayed that the convent would always be a place of sanctuary for the lost and dispossessed. She opened them to look up at the clear blue sky above the convent. A bird soared to a great height and then swooped, singing joyously. A fat lemon fell from the tree and landed with a thud, sending up a small cloud of dust from the parched soil.

★ ★ ★

In the kitchen of Killivray House the tap dripped with a monotonous regularity into the sink. A film of dust covered the stone floor and cobwebs dangled from the light bulb. On the dresser flour spilled from a broken bag and a trail of mouse droppings led across the kitchen table.

The clock in the hallway had stopped and the stag's head looked down forlornly from the wall. The air was thick with silence and a pall of mustiness hung over the whole house.

Mice had built their nest in the foot of the brown bear at the top of the stairs and in the nursery the draught from a broken window made the rocking horse creak. The one-eared teddy bear was gone from the window seat, and the front of the dolls' house was opened and the tiny dolls lay scattered on the floor as though someone had hurriedly tried to scoop them up.

In Margot Greswode's room a bottle of perfume was overturned and had stained the walnut dressing table. The smell of *Midnight in Paris* hung faintly on the air. The wardrobes were still full of her clothes and her shoes were lined up tidily in a rack.

Gwennie walked stealthily from room to room. At the end of the corridor, past the long room, was the governess's room. It was damp and airless and a spider dangled from a broken gas mantle. No doubt the police had gone over it with a toothcomb after the murder.

On the dressing table there was an empty spectacles case and next to it a pile of hairpins and a hair net. She opened the cupboard but it was bare, just the smell of moth balls and mildewing newspapers lingered.

She remembered with a smile how once Thomas had hidden in this cupboard and frightened the life out of her. The cupboard was back to back with the one next door in the long room and between the back panels of the cupboards there was a hidden space. The little monkey had hidden there and while she was going about her jobs he had made eerie noises. She'd looked under the bed, in the wardrobe and the cupboard but found nothing. Then when she'd moved on to clean the long room the same thing had happened. His giggling had been his undoing in the end.

He'd clambered out from his hiding place and shown her how you could lift up the wood and get inside. He'd said it was a big secret that only a few people knew of. His papa used to hide there when they played hide and seek when he was little and he'd never been caught once.

Sometimes, when she'd been unable to snatch a few moments with Bo, she'd left notes for him in here. If only she could close her eyes and make time turn backwards. Thomas would still be hidden here in the cupboard, trying to stifle his giggles. The baby would be growing inside her and soon she and Bo would be gone from Killivray House forever . . .

Gwennie tried to get a grip on the wood and push it upwards and to her surprise it lifted easily. There was a large space between the two cupboards and someone had stuffed a brown paper bag in there. She fished it out and opened it. Pulling out the contents, she looked at them in astonishment. A grey wig and a pair of spectacles.

Then things began to fall into place. The

description that the police had put out for Clementine Fernaud had described her as grey-haired and wearing spectacles. It wouldn't be very helpful in finding her though. All those dubious sightings of a grey-haired woman hadn't been Clementine Fernaud at all; she'd left the spectacles and the grey wig here at Killivray just before she'd fled. No one even knew what she looked like so there was little chance of her being caught.

Gwennie stuffed the wig and spectacles back into the bag and shoved them back into their hiding place and then she saw a drawstring pouch in the far corner, shrouded with cobwebs. She got down on her hands and knees and pulled it out. She slipped the wood back into place and sat down on the bed.

The string threaded through the top of the leather disintegrated at her touch. She slipped her fingers into the mildewed pouch and pulled out a roll of oilcloth. Opening it, she looked at a roll of once crisp bank notes. They must have been hidden here in the cupboard for years. Who on earth would have put them here? She slipped her hand back into the pouch and fished out three small cards. Then she stood up unsteadily, walked back out onto the landing and walked slowly down the stairs.

She sat down heavily at the kitchen table and thought about the dreadful day when she'd returned to Killivray and cook had told her the terrible news about Bo. She recalled the baby moving suddenly inside her and the wave of nausea spreading through her whole body. She'd sat without moving, her mind unable to take it all in.

And cook had said, 'Gwennie, it's not safe for you here. There's gossip about you, all the talk is that Bo shot himself because of the baby.'

She sat now as still as she had that day, unable to move, unable to sort out the thoughts in her head.

She was sure now that Bo had been murdered, but why? Old Greswode had been a nasty piece of goods but he wouldn't have murdered a man because of jealousy over her. He'd had wandering hands where any woman was concerned. His motive must have been stronger than that. Now she wouldn't have put anything past Charles Greswode but he was only a child, he could never have overpowered Bo. Bo must have known something, something that the Greswodes wanted keeping quiet — but what?

Cook had been right. If she'd gone there and then maybe things would have worked out. But she hadn't because she'd been paralysed with grief. And soon after Greswode had sent for her father and they'd taken her away from Killivray screaming and kicking, howling like a dog for all that she'd already lost and was about to lose.

She put the cards down on the table. They were faded and spotted with mildew and she could barely read the writing on them. She squinted, screwed up her eyes. Dear God! Three one-way tickets on the SS *Northern Horizon* sailing from Bristol to Africa. Bo had bought tickets for the three of them. He was planning on taking her to Africa. And then he'd been killed!

He must have bought the tickets before Thomas had disappeared and was meaning to take him too. But that didn't make any sense, did it? Bo would have known that Thomas would have wanted to go back to his father in Italy so why buy him a ticket?

And then she realized that Bo had known something important and Greswode must have panicked and taken it upon himself to get Bo out of the way.

Standing up slowly, she made her way towards the back door. She closed it softly behind her and wandered down over the overgrown lawns where once the peacocks had proudly strutted on those far-off sultry afternoons of her youth.

★ ★ ★

The cemetery at Santa Caterina was on the left-hand side of the twisting road that led up towards the towering convent.

Once a month Alfredo and Lena made the long walk there to visit the graves of Alfredo's family.

One Sunday Alfredo suggested that the three of them go together and then afterwards have a picnic in a pretty spot he knew below the convent.

The graveyard was a peculiar place. It was full of white tombs that reminded Archie of iced wedding cakes. There were huge ornamental angels, shiny crucifixes and photographs set into the headstones.

'Is the woman they called the silver bird

buried in here?' he asked nonchalantly.

'*Si*. Over in shady corner near the wall.'

While Alfredo and Lena tidied the graves of long-dead family, Archie sauntered among the graves whistling to himself.

He stopped suddenly. He was quite sure that someone was watching him. He looked around the cemetery but there was no one there except Lena and Alfredo who were busy arranging flowers in glass pots and taking no notice of him.

Turning around slowly, he looked up at the convent towering above him. There, at a high window, a nun stood looking down at him. He knew that she was watching him and it made him shudder.

He turned away and wandered on, looking for the grave belonging to Rosa Gasparini.

Finally he saw it. A dainty white angel with frilly wings and standing on one leg guarded the grave, poised as if to fly off at any moment.

He read the inscription. 'Rosa Gasparini Greswode *e Morto Agosto* 4th 1895'.

Beneath her name another name was written: 'David Thomas Greswode *e Morto Giugno* 10th 1900'.

So Thomas would have been about seven when his mother had fallen to her death and twelve when his father had died.

It was sad that the mother and father were buried together but poor Thomas was buried all alone in the dark and spooky chapel back in the Skallies.

He looked down at the grave in puzzlement.

355

Something didn't make sense.

He reread the words on the grave.

David Thomas Greswode died June 10th 1900. That wasn't possible. He couldn't have died two months before Thomas had drowned. He remembered Thomas saying in his diary that he had written to his father and he wouldn't have written to him if he knew he was dead, would he? Someone would have told him if his father had died, you didn't keep important things like that a secret. Archie racked his brains. Thomas had said in his diary that he hadn't had a letter from his father in a long time. Dead men can't write letters. But surely when his father had died someone here in Santa Caterina would have written to the Greswodes at Killivray House.

It didn't make any sense.

If only he could find out how Thomas' father had died and why no one had told Thomas! But how was he to do that?

He so wished that he could talk to Romilly again. It wasn't half so much fun trying to solve a mystery on your own.

He walked on and paused before a simple cross that bore no name. He walked around it slowly, so lost in his thoughts that he didn't hear Alfredo and Lena approach him and he jumped in alarm when Lena rested her hand gently on his shoulder.

'Archie! Why you so frightened? What's the matter?'

'It's just graveyards, Lena, that's all, they make me jumpy.'

'You don't need to be scared of the dead.

Dead is nothing to worry about,' Alfredo said, ruffling his hair.

Alfredo's words reminded him of Benjamin, 'Death's nothing to be afraid of, Archie. You're alive now and before you were born you must have been dead, stands to reason.'

And he remembered saying to Benjamin, 'But I can't remember before I was born' and Benjamin had laughed and replied, 'You'd remember, though, if it were bad, wouldn't you, you silly young bugger!'

And for the first time for ages as he looked up at Alfredo's smiling face he was able to conjure up Benjamin's face in his mind, recall the sound of his voice. He felt very close to the old man then, closer than he had in a long time. It was almost as if Benjamin hadn't died but rented a room in Archie's head.

'Alfredo, why is there no name on this grave?'

'I thinks is someone killed in the war and no one know the name; the unknown soldier.'

'That's sad,' Archie said.

'Come on, then, enough of the cemetery, we go for picnic now,' Alfredo said and took Archie's hand in his.

When they reached the cemetery gates Alfredo stopped and waved up at the convent.

'Who are you waving to?' Archie asked.

'Sister Isabella, see she up in the window, look.'

Archie looked up to see the nun who he was sure had been spying on him.

'Is she your relation, Alfredo, the one Lena told me about when we were in the Skallies?'

'That's right,' Lena said.

'She is my mother's older sister,' Alfredo said. 'Look, she waving at you, Archie.'

'Is she locked up in there?' he asked hopefully.

'In a way but we allowed to visit. One Sunday soon we go to mass at the convent and we meet with her. You like her, I think.'

Archie wasn't so sure. He was afraid of nuns. He didn't like the way their faces peeped out menacingly from their wimples, or the smell of incense, strong soap and stiffening starch that clung to their clothes.

Once, in St Werburgh's a nun with a collecting box had stopped to talk to his mammy and he'd been terrified and hidden his face in her skirts and howled like a baby.

★   ★   ★

Freddie and Charlie Payne were minding the pub for Nan who had gone out for a walk to Nanskelly with Fleep. There were no customers and they sat sipping from their pint pots and playing dominoes. Cissie was perched on a stool at the bar busy decorating a letter that she was sending to Archie. She looked up as the door opened. Her eyes widened with surprise and her pencil and pad slipped into the hearth with a clatter. She got up and hurried behind the bar.

Freddie Payne looked up at the visitor and spat a stream of beer down over his stubbly chin. Charlie Payne stared, mouth opening and closing like a beached cod, his pint perched halfway to his quivering lips.

358

A man stood in the doorway, the dying rays of the sun outlining his body in gold and pink. Freddie and Charlie Payne sat silently gawping. Cissie peered over the top of the bar.

'I'm looking for a woman called Gwennie,' the man said.

Cissie could not take her eyes off him. He was beautiful, the most beautiful man she had ever seen. Her eyes soaked up his appearance greedily and her fingers itched to draw him. She took in the colours of his skin, skin as dark as raisins, an indigo tinge around the cheek bones and eye sockets; the soft tight curls on his head around which the light played tantalizingly. His eyes were dark as a mermaid's purse, his lips soft and dusky as velvet. She marvelled at the deep slow tones of his voice.

At first she'd thought he was the Killivray ghost but he wasn't a ghost. He was real. He was blood and bone and breath and heartbeats . . . She could see the pulse in his neck moving like an anemone in a dark rock pool. She knew who he was . . . He was the river man, the old man river who just kept rolling along . . .

She loved that song. They had it on a record upstairs and sometimes she played it over and over again. It rattled her bones and filled her eyes up with tears. He must have heard them playing it and come to visit them to say hello. She wasn't afraid any more. He was a good man, she could tell good men, she could always tell. Cissie looked across at Charlie and Freddie Payne and giggled. They looked funny with their eyes as round as marbles, their bushy eyebrows arched

359

like old railway bridges.

'Do any of you know where I could find a woman called Gwennie?' the man asked again.

He had a voice like warm treacle sliding over the back of a spoon.

'She moved away from here years ago,' Charlie said in a quiet voice.

'Ay, that she did. And then she died,' Freddie said looking down into his pint pot.

The man turned around slowly. His shoulders were wide and she could see the movement of his muscles through the cloth of his shirt. The door banged shut and bottles rattled on the shelves.

Cissie ran upstairs, two steps at a time and watched him walk back along Bloater Row towards Rhoskilly Village.

★   ★   ★

The days in Santa Caterina passed quickly, built up into weeks and still there was no word from Martha Grimble. Sometimes Archie felt sad and his belly ached with the wanting of her. At those times he took himself off to his bedroom and Lena and Alfredo let him be because they knew he was missing his mammy, fretting in case she had abandoned him.

Most of the time, though, he was blissfully happy living with the Galvinis. He went swimming most days with Alfredo and some-times with Lena who shrieked and screamed all the while and made Archie weak from laughing.

Soon he was swimming on his own and they

had to coax him out of the water.

Alfredo had promised him that once he was a good swimmer he would take him out fishing in the boat.

That day had finally come. Lena packed them off with a bundle containing their supper and Alfredo rowed out through the clear green waters.

They sat together in silence as the sun set, dappling the water around them in gold and crimson. Alfredo showed Archie how to let the nets down into the water.

Then they rowed back slowly as night began to fall. Archie thought it was the most magical experience of his life.

He loved it here in Santa Caterina, couldn't think of a better place in the world. He sat entranced in the front of the boat, watching as they slid towards the harbour.

The convent loomed above the houses of Santa Caterina, moonlight silhouetting it against an indigo sky. Oil lamps were lit in the houses and the candles in the small shrines glittered in the darkness.

Later, as they wound their way home through the narrow streets he asked Alfredo about the man *Il Camaleonte.*

'How did he help the children, Alfredo?'

'Well, in times of war, many people were taken away and maybe killed and they very desperate to save their children. *Il Camaleonte* works to get these children to places where they be safe.'

'Was he brave?'

'He very brave man and risk his life many times.'

'Did any of the children come here to Santa Caterina?'

'Can you keep secrets, Archie?'

'Oh, yes, cross my heart and hope to die, stick a needle in my eye and all that,' he said with shining eyes.

'In war very many children brought here to Santa Caterina. Very important that no one know. There lots of brave men and women who working with *Il Camaleonte* to bring them here and hide them. Many of these people lose their lives trying to bring the Jewish children here from all over Italy and France and Germany too. The children in great danger, you see.'

'And they gave up their lives just to save the children?' Archie said in awe.

'*Si*. Because they know what is right. They could have ignore children and nobody say they bad for doing this. But right is right and wrong is wrong. They know difference.'

Archie nodded. 'It's called conscience, isn't it, Alfredo?'

'*Si*, conscience. And do you believe in this conscience, Archie?'

'I do. Sometimes I know right from wrong from what my mammy has told me, but other times when I don't know I stay very still and quiet and after a while I just know. Only sometimes it's difficult because you need to be brave too.'

Alfredo smiled. 'Is not easy to be brave, Archie, when we afraid. Probably *Il Camaleonte* not always brave ... Brave is like a muscle — you needs to work it to make it strong.'

'What would have happened to the Jewish children if they hadn't been helped?'

'They would have been killed.'

Archie stared at him in horror.

'Alfredo, where were the children hidden?'

'In the convent.'

'With the nuns?'

'*Si*. The children was brought to Santa Caterina at night and on the nights when they arrive the good people of Santa Caterina puts out the candles in the shrines, closes their shutters and then frightened little children is brought up through the dark streets and into the convent.'

'Did they ever see their parents again, Alfredo?'

'Most of them didn't. They have to make new lives in new places.'

Archie imagined how afraid they must have been. To have left their families and not know where they were going. He shuddered at the thought of not seeing his mammy again. He loved her to bits.

'While they here in Santa Caterina the nuns keep them safe. The local people all keeps secret of *Il Camaleonte*. Many of them who lives here has been helped by him.'

Archie looked up at Alfredo with sparkling eyes. 'Alfredo, was it *Il Camaleonte* who helped you against the bad men from Naples?'

'*Si*.'

'What's he like?'

363

Alfredo laughed. 'I don't know, I never see him, nobody except a special few ever sees him.'

'What did the children do in the convent?'

'They looked after by the nuns, dressed the same as other orphans, they go to lessons and even to mass but they don't take the sacrament because they Jewish.'

'How long did they stay there?'

'Sometimes for short time, sometimes for long. When time is right they was moved on, try to get them to safe places. Many goes to England and America.'

'So the nuns were brave too?'

'Oh, very brave! Santa Caterina nuns the bravest in whole of Italia.'

'Was Sister Isabella brave?'

'*Si*. And Sister Angelica is best forger in the whole of Italy, whole of Europe even. Her father was a bad man, a gangster in Naples, good forger too. Sister Angelica no like him but she learn a lot from him. She can make you passport, give you new name, new identity just like that,' he said with a snap of his fingers.

Archie looked at Alfredo with eyes full of admiration and astonishment.

'A lot of people think they just silly women shut up away from the world but they not afraid to get their hands dirty, as long as they keep their souls clean.'

'But isn't making false passports against the law?'

'Of course! But it's God's laws they obey, they have to break the rules of men sometimes.'

'Do they still help people escape?'

Alfredo nodded. 'Not so much now, but *Dio grazie* there still brave people that carries on the good work of *Il Camaleonte*. Let's hope there always will be, Archie.'

At dawn, after their fishing trips Alfredo would creep into Archie's room and wake him gently. They made their way through the sleeping town to the boat and rowed out to empty the nets.

Alfredo showed him how to sort the fish and taught him the names of all that they caught: stingrays and squid; sole and mullet; sea crickets and cod.

And they took them all home in buckets to a delighted Lena. Alfredo explained that when they opened the restaurant it would be Archie and Alfredo's job to fish most days and then Lena would make lovely dishes to sell.

Each day Archie made the journey to Il Panettiere to fetch the bread and sometimes on the way back he stopped in the Silver Bird Café and practised his Italian on the old men.

He helped Alfredo finish painting the inside of the restaurant and climbed the rickety ladder to hang the coloured flags above the doors and windows ready for the opening night.

Painstakingly he wrote out the menus in his best handwriting and wished that Cissie was here to decorate them. He went with Alfredo in a borrowed three-wheeled van to a distant village to collect furniture from a restaurant that had closed down. They spent days rubbing down the wood with sandpaper and then painted them a cheerful blue. While they painted, Lena, nimble with a needle, sewed pink-and-white-check table cloths and napkins to match.

★   ★   ★

Eloise Fanthorpe sat in her study looking out to sea, an untouched gin and vermouth by her side. She glanced up at the photograph on the wall, and thought about a day in France a long time ago.

The day the photograph had been taken . . .

She had been out for a walk with Hermione. They'd been down to the market and passed the German soldiers in the square. There'd been a lot of activity going on, soldiers scurrying hither and thither, shouting out commands. There was an air of heightened nervousness, a tension that was born of fear.

Suddenly Hermione had grabbed her arm as a truck had pulled up outside the German Headquarters. Four people were bundled out and marched inside. Two men and two women. They walked with pride, heads held high, eyes trying to maintain a look of bravery. Both the women, though, were looking anxiously over their shoulders towards the direction in which they'd come.

Eloise remembered the younger woman's dress, a grey dress made of a soft material, stained across the chest. Eloise had put her hand to her mouth. This woman was a nursing mother, a mother whose milk was ready, her baby left behind God knew where.

Sweet Jesus! This war was barbaric.

It was strange as you got older, she mused, that events from the past could be so wondrously vivid in one's memory.

She and Hermione had made the long, hot walk back through the village in silence. The circus had arrived the day before and the Big Top had been set up on a piece of scrubby ground just outside the village. All the local children had been running around excitedly, pointing and squealing at the sight of the animals in the cages.

She recalled the pungent smell of the lions and tigers, elephants and camels. The soft, sweet aroma of wood smoke curling up from the chimneys of the painted caravans, of sawdust and toffee apples.

A man on stilts with a beatific smile had passed them and doffed his hat while a stocky woman turned cartwheels over and over on the scrubland.

On the steps of a caravan a bearded lady had smoked a clay pipe. Eloise had seen the face of a beautiful child looking out from the window of a caravan; a dark-eyed, dark-haired child with the most haunted expression on her face that Eloise had ever seen. Above the child's left eyebrow there was an angry red scar and the fear in her eyes was electrifying.

They'd passed the circus and then made their way back up the lonely track that led to the house.

They'd been surprised to find that her father had company. A nun and a tiny man with an enormous moustache were at the house; the tiny man gently crooning to a feverish baby in his arms.

The baby was the son of a local couple who had been arrested that afternoon and taken off. His sister had been found safe but terrified, hiding in the woodshed. She was being taken to a place of safety but the baby was too sick to be moved. They were still looking for another child whose parents had been arrested but despite the efforts to find her there was no sighting of her.

And so it came that she and Hermione had become mothers to the baby for a few weeks and had cared for the poor little mite until he had died . . .

Her mind went back to the beautiful child she'd seen looking out from the window of the circus caravan.

And last night in the Pilchard Inn she'd seen that same child again! She was a woman now, of course, but she still had the same dark hair and eyes and the scar, although faded by the years, was still visible when she had pushed back her hair from her face.

★　★　★

One Sunday in the middle of August Alfredo, Lena and Archie made their way slowly up the steep road to the convent and joined a crowd of people making their way in through the enormous doors of the convent church.

They emerged from the dark church an hour later. Archie was sleepy and giddy with incense

368

and his ears were ringing with the sound of the singing. As they left the church through a side door and stepped into the inner courtyard of the convent the enormous bells began to ring out and Archie covered his ears with his hands.

He followed Lena and Alfredo reluctantly across the sundrenched courtyard towards the door that led into the convent. As if by magic the door opened with a rasping sound and a nun's face peeped round it inquisitively.

They were led through the dark corridors to a dim cave-like room that smelled strongly of camphor and candles, of roses and a fleeting whiff of marzipan.

Sister Isabella was waiting for them there. She was old and gaunt and dressed in a severe black habit. She wore spectacles with thick lenses that magnified her beady eyes. She reminded Archie of a crow dipped in starch. She struggled to her feet with difficulty and her face creased up with pleasure. Alfredo hurried to her, embraced her warmly, and kissed her affectionately on both sunken cheeks. Then it was Lena's turn. Archie squirmed with embarrassment, trying to hold his fears in check.

His body began to shake and his breath caught in the back of his throat. He balled his fists and struggled to batten down a scream of terror that was gathering behind his ribs.

Sister Isabella turned to him, saw the look of fear in his eyes and was wise enough not to hug him but held him by the arms and looked him up and down with interest.

369

'This our friend, Archie Grimble,' Alfredo said proudly.

'I am very pleased to meet with you,' Sister Isabella beamed at Archie.

Archie looked up at her in surprise and she threw back her head and laughed.

'See, I still remembers some English from when I sent to convent in London, England! Sit down and I get Sister Angelica to bring us some drink.'

She pulled a worn red rope that dangled from the flaking ceiling. An eerie jangling started up somewhere in the convent and very soon a buck-toothed nun appeared bringing a tray with a plate of biscuits and a pitcher of wine.

Archie stared at Sister Angelica with wide eyes; he could hardly believe that she was a forger, the daughter of a gangster. She smiled sweetly at Archie and then left the room.

Archie sipped his wine and nibbled at the tiny biscuits that tasted deliciously of almonds. He grew bored at the adult conversation as they jabbered on nineteen to the dozen in Italian until Lena said suddenly, '*Dio mio!* Look at the time. We must get back, Alfredo, I still has much work to do.'

'Archie can stay with me a little while, I show him around the convent,' said Sister Isabella.

Archie was too polite to protest but he followed Lena and Alfredo to the door and watched them leave with a sinking heart.

He sat uncomfortably with old Sister Isabella beneath a tree in the courtyard, the warm sunlight flickering through the leaves, the smell of lemons making his nose tingle.

'I think you afraid of me, Archie Grimble. You don't need to be afraid, I won't do you no harm.'

Archie blushed and stammered, 'I . . . I'm not afraid,' he lied. 'It's just, I don't know, I used to have bad dreams about nuns.'

'What kind of dreams?'

'That one was trying to steal me away from my mammy. It used to make me afraid, but I'm not afraid any more, I'm a big boy now and I know it was only a dream.'

He still had the dream sometimes and whenever he did he woke up howling, clenching his fists and dripping with sweat.

'The nuns of Santa Caterina likes children, maybe you gets to like nuns while you here. You like living here in Santa Caterina, Archie?'

'Oh, I love it and I don't really want to go home, except for seeing my mammy. I would like to live my whole life here.'

The old nun smiled at him.

'You miss your mama?'

'Yes I do, loads.'

'You have explore Santa Caterina and starts to find you way around?'

'Yes,' he said.

'You find anything interesting here?'

There was something in her voice that made him wary. She was trying too hard to be friendly and was watching him as if he were something unusual on a microscope slide.

'What sort of things do you mean?' he asked innocently.

'Ah, little boys is always looking for things, for

adventures, for mysteries to solve.'

He looked at her anxiously; he felt as though she could see right through his forehead and read his thoughts.

The wine had loosened his tongue and he blurted out, 'Well, I am interested in mysteries. Can I ask you some questions?'

'*Si*, I no mind but you speak more slowly, eh? I rusty with English now.'

'Did you ever know a boy called Thomas Greswode?'

For a moment she looked flustered but then she sat up very straight, clapped her hands together and smiled with glee. '*Si*. I know Thomas but it very long time ago.'

'You used to take him for walks in his pram, run really fast and bump him up and down.'

'How you know this?' she said in surprise.

'Well, it's a secret really but if you promise not to tell, I'll tell you.'

'I promise,' she said gravely.

'Well, I met someone, a girl who lived in Killivray House, that's the house Thomas lived in when he was sent back to England after his mammy died.'

Sister Isabella nodded and fiddled with the beads of her rosary. 'I know, I write him letters to this place.'

'Well, this girl, Romilly her name is, she gave me a diary that belonged to Thomas and I read it.'

'Is funny name, Romilly. She is your friend?'

Archie nodded and his eyes began to water.

372

He took off his glasses and wiped his eyes hurriedly.

'It make you sad to talk of her?'

'Yes, because she disappeared. She was stolen away by her governess who was a very bad woman and she might even be dead,' he said through quivering lips.

'Why you think she is dead?'

'Because the governess took her as a hostage and she'd already killed Romilly's father. Once she'd got away she wouldn't want to keep Romilly, would she, because people might recognize them?'

'Did you ever see this governess woman, Archie?' she asked.

'No.'

'So you don't know what she looks like?'

'No, but if I did and I saw her then I would call for the police and get her put in prison,' he said angrily.

'But you'd know Romilly if you saw her?'

'Of course I would. She was very pretty and kind and she didn't make fun of my calliper or my wonky eye.'

Sister Isabella leant across and patted Archie's hand.

'She sounds like very nice girl.'

'She was and she was a bit like me too.'

'How was she like you?'

'She was lonely and she wasn't used to speaking to other children or playing with them. We were going to be friends, proper friends and now I'll never see her again.'

Sister Isabella bit her lip and looked hard at

the little English boy. He had the face of an angel and the unspoiled innocence in him was a joy to behold. It renewed your faith in humankind just to look at him.

She wished she could take his pain away but she couldn't.

'Anyhow, that's enough of that. In his diary Thomas said that someone called Sizzie had written to him. I've worked out that that's you, isn't it?'

She nodded. 'He can't say Sister Isabella when he little boy, so he just call me Sizzie. He was very lovely little boy. Like you, Archie Grimble, he clever and funny and good to be with. I miss him very much when he leave Santa Caterina and go live in England.'

'The thing that's puzzling me is that I saw his father's grave, down in the cemetery, and it says he died in June 1900.'

'You right. June 10th 1900.'

'Blimey, you have a good memory,' he said with admiration.

'I never forget that day.'

'Why do you remember it so well?'

'When you in love with someone and they dies, you never forgets.'

Archie blushed and looked away hurriedly; nuns weren't supposed to talk about love and things like that. It was against the rules.

'I see you shy for me to talk about love this way. Oh, when I young girl I in love for a long time with David Greswode. It is the truth so I must say it. The truth is very important. He so handsome man, very funny and kind. But he

374

choose somebody else and she my best friend so I must be happy for them but inside I very sad.'

'You were best friends with Rosa Gasparini?'

'*Si*. We was always together when we girls, both a bit mad, eh? She fall in love, she run away with David, go off together with circus. After she gone I joins the sisters here. Rosa get very famous and I very proud of my friend. Then she have Thomas and when she not with circus she come back here.'

'And then she died?'

Sister Isabella looked down and fiddled with the crucifix around her neck. Archie watched her and it looked as if a rain cloud had thrown its shadow across her bony old face. Her eyes misted over and her chin quivered like a baby who has had their bottle taken away.

'Terrible day the day she die. I don't like to think about it.'

'Sorry. Don't let's talk about it then. One thing that's puzzling me, though, is that David Greswode died on June 10th 1900.'

'That's right.'

'But you see Thomas didn't know that his father had died.'

'So, how do you know this?'

'Because he didn't mention it in his diary and he would have done. He loved his father, you could tell that from the way he spoke about him. And he was planning to run away from Killivray and come back here. And I can't work out why they hadn't told him that his father was dead. Why do you think they didn't tell him?'

'I don't know answer to these questions. You

have very lively mind, Archie, you like to find out things?'

'I do. How did his father die?'

'After shock of his wife dying he get, oh, how you say, problem with heart. And he take too many powders and he die.'

'Do you think he did it deliberately?'

'No!'

Archie was shocked by the fury in her voice, a sudden fury that soon dissolved and was replaced by a terrible sadness in her eyes.

'David Greswode was a man who love life very much. He sad, very ill after Rosa die but he love his son. He tell me that he decide he going to sell this Killivray House and give half of money to his brother. Then he bring Thomas back to Santa Caterina at the end of the summer and live here. He have big plans, he going to give money to us to help with orphans . . . '

'Where did he die?'

'Here in Santa Caterina. His brother find him and call for doctor, they try to save him but it not possible.'

'His brother!'

'*Si*, his younger brother, he was here staying with David.'

Archie scratched his head and pondered on what she'd just said. This was really curious. If Mr Greswode had been here in Santa Caterina when David Greswode had died then why hadn't he told Thomas about his father's death when he got back to Killivray House?

Archie clenched his fists, sat on his hands. His whole body fizzed with excitement. Unless David

Greswode hadn't died naturally. Maybe Old Greswode had killed him and then if he could get rid of Thomas, Killivray House would be his! He would inherit and after he died everything would go to Charles Greswode. Then Archie remembered that in the diary Bo had asked Thomas how long it was since he'd heard from his father! And later old Greswode told Bo that if he interfered in family affairs he would be out on his ear!

Maybe Bo had found out that David Greswode was dead. He knew too much and had to be got out of the way!

Maybe that's why Charles had taken the gun into the summerhouse — to kill Thomas and pretend it was an accident . . . Both father and son would be dead and Killivray would be theirs!

But then Thomas had run away and drowned.

'Anything else you want to know?' Sister Isabella interrupted his thoughts.

'Yes, do you know where the Casa delle Stelle is?'

She hesitated for a moment then said, 'You won't find the Casa delle Stelle because it burn down many years ago.'

'Oh,' Archie couldn't keep the disappointment from his voice.

'Why you want to know about the Casa delle Stelle?'

There was a note of mild irritation in her voice as though she were tired of all his questions.

'Well, I know it's where Thomas lived because the address was written on the top of letters that his father had sent. I sometimes think that you get a feeling about places; if you wander round them you can pick up clues.'

'Thomas Greswode been dead a long time. Perhaps there nothing else to find, Archie.'

'Maybe.'

'Sometimes is best to leave the past alone and concentrate on today.'

A group of nuns came walking across the courtyard and nodded at Sister Isabella. Archie lowered his eyes. As they passed he breathed in their smell. Freshly cut flowers, incense, garlic and a faint but definite whiff of tobacco. And something else that he'd smelled on his mammy. Perm lotion!

They must be a funny bunch of nuns here, talking about falling in love and smoking! And making their hair curly; proper nuns were supposed to be bald!

'And now I must go to Benediction. God bless you, Archie Grimble.'

Archie watched as Sister Isabella hobbled away across the courtyard towards the church where the huge bells rolled and clanged and startled birds flew up from the turrets into the blue sky above Santa Caterina.

★ ★ ★

Dom Bradly stood at the end of Bloater Row and lit a cigarette. Tomorrow he was off back to the States. He'd come to a dead end in his investigations. Having been round the local libraries and dug up some old press reports, he'd found out that his father had worked at Killivray

378

House as a manservant but that he had taken his own life. He hadn't been able to find out anything about his mother other than her name.

He sighed deeply. He'd been chasing a dream and that wasn't always a wise thing to do. He'd go back to his wife and kids, pick up the threads where he'd left off and abandon this lunacy once and for all. The truth was, and God knows he'd been warned enough, that adopted children didn't find princes and princesses waiting in the wings; they found rejection and shame and silence.

He'd uncovered as much as he could and he'd have to make do with that. His father had come over from Africa and worked at Killivray House for a guy called Greswode. Then, for Crissakes, he'd gone and shot himself, blown his bloody brains out! Jesus! And he'd had a child on the way, some poor local woman whom he'd left in the lurch. It must have been bad enough to be pregnant outside of marriage in those days but to be expecting the child of a black man! Christ, the world was a bloody mess! He'd always wondered whether his mother had handed him to the adoption agencies with relief, glad to see the back of her shame. He'd never know now.

He stubbed out the cigarette angrily and walked away towards Rhoskilly. He'd had enough of this queer little place. Suddenly he heard the sound of a soft footfall behind him. He stopped and swivelled around, he was sure that someone was following him. The lane was dark and empty, there was no one there. He walked on slowly, his footsteps loud in the night. Then he heard the voice, a sweet, faltering childish voice that sent shivers skittering up his backbone.

'Ol' Man River, That Ol' Man River, He must know sumpin' But don't say nuthin'. He jus' keeps rollin', He keeps on rollin' along . . . '

Dom Bradly stiffened, fear whispered up his spine, the hairs on his head tightened, tingled. He turned around slowly and saw her. The little girl from the Pilchard Inn, standing in a puddle of moonlight, singing like a siren.

He walked tentatively towards her as she sang, knelt down and looked into her face. She finished the song and looked at him. In her pale face her eyes were huge and pin-pricked with shimmering stars.

She took his hand in hers and led him back along Bloater Row, down through the hole in the rocks and onto the deserted beach. The moon was huge and mapped with blue veins. The waves broke onto the jagged rocks below the wobbly chapel and sent spray high into the air.

The wind riffled through the stiff grass of the sand dunes with the sound of whispered secrets.

She pointed across the beach to the Boathouse, a rundown shack of a place where a candle burned fitfully behind the salt-caked glass of a misshapen window.

An owl called out from behind the high walls that guarded Killivray House. Cissie nudged Dom Bradly and pointed towards the big house.

'Bang! Bang!' she said.

He felt the hairs on his neck prickle. The last

time he'd been here he'd sneaked inside the grounds and had a mosey around. He'd stood inside the funny little summerhouse and thought what a great setting for a murder the place would be. He'd written in the dust of the window, Murder Scene.

And then weeks later, he'd read the news about the death of the master at Killivray . . .

He felt his whole body quiver with foreboding as he saw the bent-backed silhouette of a woman crossing the window of the Boathouse.

'Mad Gwennie,' Cissie said.

Dom Bradly drew in his breath.

'Why do you call her mad Gwennie?'

'Everyone does. But she's not really mad, she swears a lot though. She's just sad and lonely, that's all.'

He looked down at the child and squeezed her hand.

'Thank you,' he said.

She looked up at him then and saw the tears gathering in his eyes. He looked down at her and knew that he would never forget the look in her lovely wide eyes, the precious innocence and strange intelligence set into the bones of her pale face.

'Go home now.'

He watched her clamber back up to the odd little place perched up on the rocks. She turned and waved. Dom Bradly waved back. And then she was gone, vanished into the darkness like a sprite. Bracing himself, he walked purposefully away across the beach towards the Boathouse.

Martha Grimble could hardly contain her excitement as she saw Archie coming down the steep hill towards her. He was walking slowly, head down as if he was deep in thought. She couldn't believe how much he'd grown since she'd seen him last. And the colour on him! He was suntanned and his hair had grown, bleached almost white at the front. Dear God in heaven, the Galvinis had worked miracles with him while he'd been here in Santa Caterina.

Suddenly he looked up and saw her. His face broke into a wide smile and he half ran, half walked into her outstretched arms.

'Oh, Archie, I've missed you, son. My, look at you, you're the picture of health.'

'Mammy, Mammy, I'm so pleased to see you. Guess what I can do?'

'Tell me!'

'Mammy, I can swim! Alfredo taught me.'

'Never to God, Archie, that's wonderful.'

'And I've caught loads of fish and I can make pasta and pizza. I can make you some if you want. Oh, Mammy, I've missed you.'

'I've missed you too but haven't you just had the best time in the world?'

'Why didn't you say you were coming, Mammy?'

'I didn't know if I was going to make it and I didn't want to disappoint you. Come on, though, Lena is making dinner and there's someone back at the house waiting to see you.'

Archie's heart sank. It was the porker! He just knew it.

Holding the beaded curtain open for his mammy to pass through into the house, he followed her reluctantly.

In the kitchen Lena was busy at the stove and Alfredo was filling an earthenware jug with wine.

A small-boned, pale-faced woman, more like a ghost than a real live woman, was sitting at the table, chewing hungrily on the cuffs of her shrunken grey cardigan. When she saw Archie she giggled her head off like someone who wasn't quite right.

'Archie, this is my sister Lissia. Lissia, this is your nephew, Archie.'

Archie swallowed hard and looked at his mother for an explanation. This couldn't be Lissia! Lissia was dead. 'Mammy, I don't understand. I thought that Lissia was . . . '

'There was a misunderstanding. She's very much alive, Archie, and we'll be looking after her from now on.'

'Come, sit down and eat,' Alfredo said quickly. 'Lena has cooked you mussels and to follow a lasagne.'

Lissia giggled again and dribbled down the front of her grey pinafore dress.

Archie sat up next to his mammy and watched Lissia warily out of the corner of his eye all through dinner. Why had his mammy told lies about her? You were either dead or alive. You couldn't make a mistake about that.

★ ★ ★

Alfredo had finished painting the walls and the paint on the tables and chairs had dried to a glossy finish. Candles were set in niches in the walls and Alfredo had found old-fashioned photographs of Santa Caterina and hung them around the room. Lena had made all the table cloths and napkins and they were neatly ironed and ready to be laid. The room was beginning to look like a real restaurant and to Archie's delight Alfredo had painted a name on the outside wall of the house in large curly blue letters, *Ristorante Skilly*. In memory, he told Archie, of their time in the Skallies.

In a few days' time they would open and Lena was so excited she hardly kept still for a moment.

Alfredo was teaching Archie how to take orders from imaginary customers and wait at table and his mammy was having Italian cooking lessons with Lena. Lissia got under everyone's feet and so Archie often took her with him on his travels round Santa Caterina.

One hot afternoon while the grown-ups took a siesta Archie took Lissia with him for a walk. He was getting used to her now, with her peculiar ways and her daft talk. She was a bit like Cissie Abelson only much dopier. She didn't act like a grown-up woman at all. She was nosy and tried to peep inside people's houses the way a toddler might. She was always picking things up off the floor, bottle tops, foil paper, shells and dried seaweed. Sometimes her pockets got so heavy that she jangled when she walked.

He had to watch her like a hawk when they went to the market because if he took his eyes off her for a minute she got herself into mischief; one day she had picked a rabbit from a cage and was walking off with it. Another time a beggar showed her a trick, pretending that he'd pulled a baby crab out of her ear and she laughed so much she peed herself and he had to take her home for his mammy to change her.

They were walking up past the bread shop when Lissia saw the cat. She squealed with delight and stooped to pick it up but the cat took fright and bolted. Before Archie could stop her she was off in hot pursuit. Archie called out to her but she was like an elephant after buns when she saw something she wanted and she went deaf if she didn't want to hear what you were saying.

He hurried after her, lost her in a dark side street then caught sight of her turning into an alleyway to the right, close to the convent walls. He'd seen the alleyway before but he'd never been up there because a faded sign on the wall said PRIVATO! Lissia never took notice of signs at all; he wasn't even sure if she could read.

At the end of the alley, there was a rough path that climbed steeply between high stone walls. Lissia was way ahead of him now and he caught a glimpse of her disappearing through an archway overgrown with geraniums. He followed her through the archway and into a garden that was dense with straggly, drooping sunflowers.

'Lissia,' he hissed, 'come away from there, this is someone's private garden!'

She turned and smiled at him but ignored him.

He lost sight of her again and had to follow the hissing noises she made as she stalked the cat.

Eventually, he found her sitting on a broken bench in front of a whitewashed house, the cat now purring happily in her lap.

He was about to scold her and drag her away when his heart skipped a beat. On the wall of the house, written in faded blue paint, were the words, Casa delle Stelle.

House of the Stars.

He stood staring at the words in disbelief. Sister Isabella had told him it had burned down. Why had she lied to him? Nuns weren't supposed to lie! It was against the rules.

Why would she want to stop him from finding the Casa delle Stelle?

'Lissia, put the cat down and come away this minute or Mammy will be mad we're away so long!'

He had to be stern with Lissia sometimes, for her own good.

She stuck out her lower lip and her eyes filled with tears. He hated it when she did that.

'It has a fat belly and is going to have kittens,' Lissia said, pointing excitedly at the cat.

'Come on, put the cat down now.'

She smiled suddenly, reluctantly let the cat go and allowed him to take her hand and lead her back through the garden.

He looked back at the house longingly; how he'd love to have a nosy around but he couldn't take Lissia inside the house, there was no knowing what she'd get up to. One day soon he'd come back here alone and have a good scout around.

★ ★ ★

The front door of Casa delle Stelle was locked and the faded blue shutters on the downstairs windows were closed fast. Archie skirted around the outside furtively and found a small window at the back that was warped with age and not shut properly. He tried to open it with his fingers but it was stuck fast. He found a rusty skewer on a window ledge and with much huffing and puffing he managed to prise the window open. The gap wasn't very large and it would take some doing but if he breathed in and twisted like a rubber man he should be able to get in. He'd have to take his calliper off first though.

He looked around the garden for something to stand on, found an old bucket and set it down below the window. He took off his calliper, tested the bucket with his weight and then climbed tentatively onto it. Taking a deep breath, he heaved himself up onto the windowsill. He'd have to get through head first which would make it difficult . . .

He was breathless by the time he'd wriggled in through the window and landed in a heap on the floor inside the house.

He lay puffing with exertion, his laboured breathing loud in the quiet of the house.

He was in a cupboard that smelled of garlic

387

and onions, cinnamon and tomatoes. He shuffled over to the door, lifted the latch and stepped out into a large room and looked nervously around him. It was dark and hard to make out anything except the outline of furniture. He inched towards the windows, fumbled around and opened one of the shutters.

Light flooded greedily into the house. He moved slowly around the room, taking in everything. Someone still lived here by the looks of it; maybe they'd just popped out on an errand and might come back in at any moment.

There was a large table on which stood a half-empty bottle of wine and a bowl of fruit.

There was a bookcase crammed full of books in different languages. There were lots in Italian, some in French and English. There were dictionaries and rail timetables and an A to Z of London.

There was an enormous sideboard with a glass front that contained glasses of all shapes and sizes, cups and plates and oil lamps. There was a bottle of whisky and a half-full bottle of gin. There were paintings on the walls that looked as though they had been done by children. He opened the door at the far end of the room and stepped into the kitchen. It was a normal sort of kitchen with a large stone sink and wooden shelves filled with jars of bottled fruits and vegetables. There was a stove filled with wood ready for lighting and a basket of logs next to it. There were strings of purple onions and hams hanging from hooks in the ceiling. On the table there were two places laid ready for a meal.

He wondered who lived here now and what they would do if they came back and found him snooping around in their house.

He thought sadly that this was the house that Thomas Greswode had wanted to come home to and never did. This was the place he had dreamed about in his miserable days at Killivray House. If he had managed to get back here, though, he would have had a terrible shock to find his father dead and buried.

Archie found the stairs and climbed them cautiously, feeling like Goldilocks in the house of the three bears.

It was lighter upstairs because the windows were unshuttered although outside the daylight was fading fast. He stood nervously on a small landing area keeping his ears peeled for the sound of anyone returning home. Opening a door to his right, he stepped into a small bedroom. There were two narrow beds with gaudy knitted blankets thrown over them. Near the window there was a small writing desk with a few dusty books on the top. He went across to the wardrobe and opened the door. It smelled vaguely of flowery soap and freshly washed clothes. It was empty except for a few coat hangers that jangled and made him feel nervous.

He closed the wardrobe door and stepped up to the desk. There was a sheaf of yellowing papers on the desktop. He lifted them up and looked through them. There was nothing written on them. No clues there. He put the papers back down on the desk, slid open the drawer and looked inside. There was a chewed-up pencil, a pen and a bottle of dried-up ink, a mildewed lemon and a sheet of pink blotting paper.

He knelt down by the bed and looked underneath it. There was nothing except a thin layer of dust and a scallop shell full of dried-up dog ends with crimson lipstick stains.

He left the room and closed the door quietly. The next bedroom was larger, there was a big double bed and a large wardrobe and a blanket box. The blanket box was full of starched sheets and pillowcases but nothing interesting. Underneath the bed there was just an old pair of cracked black ballet pumps.

He turned the key in the lock and the door to the wardrobe grated open. The strong smell of mothballs caught in his throat and made him sneeze.

There, hanging up, were a variety of costumes. Faded red satin, moth-eaten silver and gold, sequins and spangles . . .

He drew in his breath sharply. These must have belonged to the silver bird: Rosa Gasparini. He closed the door and struggled to steady his breathing.

Outside a lone star pricked the sky above the Convent of Santa Caterina.

There were two more rooms left for him to see. He crept stealthily along the corridor, lifted the latch and walked into a large room. There was an ancient roll-top desk and nailed to the whitewashed wall was a gigantic map. He stepped up to the map and studied it. There were small flags stuck into it here and there as though someone had been on a long journey and wanted to remember all the places where they'd been.

On the other walls there were a few uninteresting oil paintings and circus posters.

Slowly, he lifted the lid on the roll-top desk and peered inside. There was a thick wadge of bills stuck on a spike. They were stamped PAID with red ink. A pen was stuck in a dried-up inkpot on the left-hand side. There were balls of string and sticks of red sealing wax. He picked up a sheaf of papers that had pictures of houses on them. He flicked through them. Le Petit Bijou, Almond Cottage, Dos Casitas, The Kilpenny. He put them down and picked up a red leather-bound book. He glanced at the first page.

Adler. Jacob and Ruben
Abrahams. Rudi and Ruth
Blomstein. Miriam
Goldberg. Benjamin
Solomons. Daniel

It was some sort of address book. Closing the book, he opened a small drawer at the back of the desk and peered in; he drew back when he saw the shiny black gun, the sort that gangsters had in books.

He cocked his ears. He was sure that he'd heard a noise somewhere in the house, the sound of a key turning in a lock.

He stepped back out into the corridor and listened. He was probably just imagining it; he did that when he was afraid. He crept back along the corridor and tried the door of the last room. It was locked. He bent down and put his eye to the keyhole. The door was locked from the inside, he could see the key. He stood stock-still, suddenly conscious that someone was inside the room, someone on the other side of the door who was as afraid as he was, someone in there hardly daring to breathe.

He felt the fear weaken his legs, his heart squeeze up into a double knot. Why would you lock a door from the inside? The shadows around him grew deeper and downstairs a clock chimed the hour. Holy mackerel! If the clock chimed then that meant that someone wound it up regularly. A floorboard creaked and outside a bird squawked as it flew away over the rooftops.

He was absolutely sure now that there was somebody in the house, every muscle and sinew in his body told him so.

It was important not to panic! But Holy shit! Whoever lived here had a gun. He tiptoed back along the landing and into the first room he'd gone into and crossed to the window. He peeped down into the garden. The lemons on the tree had turned to black and the sunflower heads bobbed like people hiding. A palm tree waved, making shadows that looked like arms.

He looked up at the spooky convent towering above the house. In a lighted window he was sure that he could see the outline of a nun. Sister Isabella, looking down at where he stood quaking by the window.

That was fanciful and daft. She couldn't possibly know he was in here. As he watched, though, the light was extinguished, then lit again.

He was sure that she was watching the house; spying on him. There was something creepy about Sister Isabella. He wasn't sure if he could trust her.

Outside a cat growled a warning. Jesus, he'd had enough. He was off. Out of here. Fear clutched at his heart as he clattered noisily down the stairs. He raced back into the cupboard, heaved himself into the gap and wriggled through the window. He landed head first in the grass, terrifying the cat who shot off through the waving sunflowers with a wail.

He hurtled back through the narrow streets startling old people who were sitting outside their doors taking in the cooler night air. Bats arced above his head and a dog barked at his passing. He arrived back at the house just as they were sitting down for supper.

His mammy looked up as he came in. 'Where've you been, Archie? I was worried sick when it got dark and you didn't come back.'

'Oh, I was just out and about and lost track of the time,' he gasped.

'You been running, Archie, you face all pink and you breathing hard,' Alfredo said.

'Where's your calliper, Archie?' Martha Grimble asked.

He looked down at his naked leg. He'd run all the way back without it and hadn't even realized it was missing.

Martha Grimble looked at him in wonder and made the sign of the cross.

'It's a bloody miracle, that's what it is,' she said.

'A bloody miracle!' yelled Lissia and laughed like a drain.

In the kitchen the oil lamp burned dimly and shadows danced along the whitewashed walls. Alfredo, Lena and Martha sat around the kitchen table talking.

'What did Archie mean when he say he think Lissia dead?' Alfredo asked, pouring wine for everyone.

'Alfredo, it's a long old story. Have you got half the night?'

'*Si*. I enjoying myself with all my favourite people round me. I good listener too.'

'I made a big mistake in telling him she was dead. It seemed the easiest thing at the time. The truth is that Lissia has been in a convent in Ireland for years.'

'She was a nun?' Alfredo said in disbelief.

'No, she wasn't a nun but she was looked after by the nuns.'

'I see, because she not able to look after herself?'

'She's never been able to look after herself; she has the mind of a child.'

'Was she always this way?' Lena asked.

Martha took a long drink of wine and put down her glass before she spoke again.

'She seemed normal when she was a little girl but as she got older it was more and more obvious that things weren't quite right.'

'And so she was sent to the nuns?'

'No, not exactly.'

Martha paused and wiped her mouth with the back of her hand.

Alfredo refilled her glass.

'When she was fifteen she got herself into trouble. God help her she wouldn't have even known what the fellow was up to . . . '

'My God! You don't mean she have a . . . '

'Yes, she had a baby,' Martha said. 'I had moved away from home after my mother died and was working in Dublin. My father and I didn't get on; when he found out Lissia was expecting he went berserk. He beat her to try and get her to tell who the father was but the poor girl hadn't a clue. Some unscrupulous bastard took advantage of her being simple.'

'God help the poor child,' said Lena.

'My father was a hard, unfeeling man and he put Lissia with the nuns, working in a laundry, and she was there until I fetched her a few weeks back.'

'Why did you wait for so long?' Alfredo asked.

'My father would never have agreed to her leaving the place. But he died recently and now I'm her next of kin and I agreed to take her away. Oh, Alfredo, not a day went past when I didn't think of her. It broke my heart to think of her shut up in there.'

'What happened to the child?'

'The child was put up for adoption to a good Catholic family. The Connollys from Wexford were going to take the baby on and bring it up as their own.'

'I hope to God these Connollys peoples was good peoples?'

Martha finished her wine and put down the glass.

Alfredo refilled it along with his own.

Martha Grimble's face was flushed and her eyes bright with recklessness.

'The thing was, the Connollys from Wexford were bogus.'

'What is this bogus?' Lena asked.

'They were only pretending to be the Connollys from Wexford. When the real Connollys turned up, they were too late. The child had been stolen.'

'Stolen! Who would steal a little baby?' Lena said.

'Did they find the child?' Alfredo asked.

'No. There was a massive police search but they never found the baby.'

'That's terrible. I wonder where the poor child is now.'

Martha Grimble took a large swig of wine and banged down her glass.

'Upstairs asleep in bed,' said Martha Grimble.

Lena Galvini choked on her wine and Alfredo stared at Martha Grimble, eyes wide with fear.

'You see,' said Martha, 'Walter Grimble and I were the bogus Connollys who stole him.'

Outside an owl called, bats squeaked and the bells of the ancient convent tolled the midnight hour.

★　★　★

Cissie had finished the letter that she was writing to Archie Grimble and was painstakingly writing

396

the address on the envelope. Next she was going to do him some drawings.

She smiled as she worked. She was so full of being happy that she thought she might burst.

Fleep and Nan had taken her out to meet the lady who had liked her drawings and soon, soon she was going to start school with all the other little girls. She was going to have brand new clothes to wear. A uniform. And at the school there was a big room full of things to paint and draw with. Easels and big sheets of paper. Fat brushes and thin ones. Smudgy charcoal and waxy crayons . . .

And if she liked it she was going to sleep there and Nan and Fleep were going on holiday.

Cissie liked Fleep. He smiled a lot and he cooked the best food ever. And he'd kissed Nan. Twice in the kitchen and once on the lips!

That meant they had to marry and then she'd have a daddy all of her own.

She finished addressing the envelope, then got up and moved her chair closer to the parrot who sat on his perch looking around him inquisitively.

Cissie approached the cage apprehensively, cooing and lisping.

The parrot looked at Cissie and squawked. Cissie giggled.

'Good morning,' Cissie said.

The parrot chewed a sunflower seed and stared at Cissie.

'Good morning,' she said again.

The parrot put his head on one side and eyed Cissie quizzically but stayed sullenly silent.

'Who's a pretty boy?'

'Arseholes,' screeched the parrot.

Cissie put her hand to her mouth to stop herself laughing.

She picked up her pad and began to draw the bird, tongue poking out between her teeth, totally immersed in her drawing.

Nan and Fleep came out from the kitchen. Nan pulled a pint for Fleep and poured herself a small nip of brandy.

'Well, you could have knocked me down with a bloody feather when Gwennie came in here and told me the news,' she said.

'What happened exactly?' Fleep said.

'Well, first of all the Paynes said a fellow came in here the other night asking after Gwennie. They had no idea who he was, just knew that she didn't take kindly to visitors so they told him she was dead.'

'So how did he find her?'

'I don't know. But find her he did. She came in here first thing this morning. Told me that her son had turned up and she was off to live in America with him.'

'Why did she come here?'

'She said she'd got a message for Archie Grimble. I didn't think she even knew Archie Grimble.'

'What was the message?'

'To tell him he was looking in the wrong place. That he should look in the collecting box.'

'What did she mean by that?' Fleep asked.

'God knows. I asked her that and she tapped her nose and said Archie would know what she meant.'

'Well, what a turn up for the books.'

'None of us knew she had a son, even. What a dark horse she turned out to be! Anyhow, she said her son was adopted and he grew up in America, does some sort of work in films, a producer or some such thing. Apparently she had him years ago by the black fellow who worked up at Killivray. He came to a sad end and her father made her give the baby up.'

'What an ending.' Fleep said.

'Imagine living in a dump of a place like the Boathouse and then being whisked off somewhere glamorous like America. Los Angeles, I think she said he lived. Mind, she deserves a bit of comfort after the life she's had.'

Cissie finished her drawings of the parrot and crept closer to the bird, holding her head on one side the way he did.

'What's your name?'

'Zucca. Who's a silly Zucca.'

Nan looked up from the bar. 'I hope he's not saying what I think he's saying,' she said, 'or he'll end up in a stew.'

'*Dio mio*! Gwennie's in a stew!' the parrot yelled.

'You're a silly young bugger!'

'He's a very rude bird,' Cissie said. 'But I like him.'

★　★　★

Archie barely had a moment to himself once the Ristorante Skilly was opened. Lena and Alfredo, Martha, Archie and Lissia were run off their feet. The inquisitive villagers of Santa Caterina

399

trooped down to taste Lena Galvini's cooking and pronounced it good. In the following days old men came early in the morning and took up residence at the outside tables, drinking wine and coffee, playing cards and smoking. Soon it was as if the Ristorante Skilly had always been a part of Santa Caterina. Tiny birds came on the search for scraps and a three-legged dog adopted the doorstep. A few tourists found their way to the restaurant and soon word spread and the place was full most evenings. As Lena worked tirelessly in the kitchen, she glowed with happiness and Alfredo watched her with pride.

Martha Grimble worked alongside Lena and learned how to make pizza, pasta, risotto and many other things. For the first time in years she was happy, although sometimes she caught Lena looking at her as though she hadn't quite fathomed her out.

Lissia washed up like a trouper, never tiring of the piles of plates and dishes that came relentlessly in from the restaurant. In quieter moments she blew bubbles between her thumb and finger and all the while Martha watched over her solicitously.

Archie, resplendent in his first ever pair of long black trousers, became the apprentice waiter to Alfredo, who watched him proudly as he handed out the menus to the customers and took the orders. Sometimes he looked from Lissia to Archie and wondered how the boy would take it if he ever found out she was his mother, and it made him afraid. Secrets of this sort weren't good for anyone, they could only bring sorrow.

★ ★ ★

The letter from the porker came out of the blue at the end of the first full week of the restaurant being opened. It had been sent to Bag End but the postman had taken it to the Pilchard and Nan had sent it on. Archie watched his Mammy with trepidation as she read it.

He was dreading the day when they had to leave Santa Caterina. He didn't want to imagine living under the same roof as the porker ever again. And what about Lissia? She would hate him and he would be unkind to her.

'What does it say, Mammy?' he asked. 'Is he coming to fetch us?'

Martha Grimble put down the letter and wiped her eyes. Lena paused in her kneading of dough. Alfredo eyed Martha warily over his coffee cup. Archie held his breath while Lissia yawned and sucked the ends of her hair.

'No, Archie, he's not coming for us.'

Archie let go of his breath and uncrossed his fingers. That was the best news he'd heard in ages.

'He's never coming for us,' she said mysteriously and put the letter into the stove where the flames snatched at it greedily and reduced it to ash.

Archie, hardly able to keep the smile off his face, slipped quietly out of the kitchen.

Alfredo poured a small brandy for Martha and

sat beside her at the kitchen table.

'You feel okay, Martha?'

She looked up at him with tear-filled eyes.

'What does he say in this letter?'

'Alfredo, I was so frightened that he would blackmail me, he was always threatening to tell the authorities what I did, what we both did. I always bought him off until the money ran out. But you see I couldn't let them take Lissia's baby. I couldn't let him go, not my own nephew.'

'I understand. Is not really stealing to take your own family,' Alfredo soothed.

'The authorities wouldn't see it like that. My father wanted nothing to do with the child, he wanted him adopted, forgotten about. It was all my idea to steal him, I persuaded Walter to go along with me, to pose as Mr Connolly from Wexford. Anyhow he's written me to say that he's sorry that he ran off so quickly but that just before he left the Skallies he'd been threatened. Someone had followed him back from the phone box one night and had told him to stay away from me and Archie.'

'Who would threaten him?' Alfredo said.

'He's probably made that up to get himself off the hook. The man is a born liar. He's fallen on his feet, got himself a little business of some sorts, met someone in London and says that he has feelings for her.'

'My goodness, I don't know what to say.'

'Hah, he's never had feelings for anyone in his life! The selfish bastard! He wants a divorce so that he can remarry.'

'I very sorry, Martha.'

'Oh don't be sorry, Alfredo. I have never felt better. Now, where are those sardines you wanted me to stuff with breadcrumbs and Parmesan cheese?'

Alfredo and Lena looked at Martha Grimble and couldn't quite believe what they saw. She was a different woman to the quiet, downtrodden Martha Grimble they remembered from Bag End.

★ ★ ★

Archie finished clearing the tables after lunch, then went upstairs and took off his waiting clothes. Everyone else was taking a siesta. Leaving the house, he made his way up through the silent shuttered streets. He walked quickly, past sleeping cats and panting dogs too exhausted by the heat to bark at his passing.

The garden of the Casa delle Stelle was deserted except for a beady-eyed cockerel who watched Archie from the top of a high wall. It was a lovely garden and it was a shame that no one tended it. William Dally would love it here: there was a vegetable patch badly in need of digging; tomato bushes weighed down with bulbous fruit; and a small dry fountain that was choked with weeds. Whoever owned the Casa delle Stelle now didn't take much pride in the place.

He stood among the sunflowers, looking at the house. A lizard skittered across the wall and disappeared into the trailing purple flowers that grew down from the roof. The cat that Lissia had chased was stretched out on the broken bench, asleep.

No sounds came from the house and the front door was shut. Everyone in Santa Caterina kept their front doors open when they were at home. He looked up at the convent and heaved a sigh of relief; the shutters were firmly closed against the heat and there was no sign of nosy old sister Isabella spying on him.

He made his way furtively round to the back of the house and climbed in through the window. It was cool inside and he opened a shutter so that he could see his way. The fruit bowl on the table was empty and the wine had been drunk so someone must be living here. Creeping quietly up the stairs, he went straight to the locked room and with bated breath tried the handle. To his surprise the door swung open.

He had been right! Someone must have been hiding in there the last time he'd been here. It stood to reason; someone had to be in a room to lock it from the inside. He peeped round the door anxiously but the room was empty.

There was a large bed that had been hastily made, a chest of drawers and a rush-backed chair over which a towel was draped. He picked it up. It was still damp.

On top of the chest of drawers there was a small powder compact, the sort that women used to take the shine off their noses. The room smelled faintly of rose-scented soap, of cigarettes and pine.

He made his way back to the room next door, opened the roll-top desk and looked through it again. There were piles of unused envelopes and writing paper, a packet of sunflower seeds but nothing much of any interest. He was wasting his time. Sister Isabella had been right, sometimes it is best to leave the past alone and concentrate on today.

He stepped up to the window and looked out. The garden was quiet, the sun bright in the afternoon sky . . .

Suddenly his heart lurched painfully. Down in the garden someone was singing softly. A face bobbed above the sunflowers. It was Sister Angelica, the nun who had brought them drinks the day he'd been in the convent. The one who could forge passports and whose father had been a gangster.

What was she doing here? What should he do? He went back into the first room where the single beds were and glanced around, shivering with fright. He wanted to be out of the cool house now, to feel the sun on his face.

He wondered if he had time to get back out through the window but already he heard the key rasping in the lock . . .

He scrabbled under the nearest bed and lay there listening. Downstairs Sister Angelica hummed to herself as she clattered about. He heard the sweep of a stiff brush as she cleaned and the sound of a tap running. She was humming loudly; it was a tune that he knew vaguely, the one played by the music box that Lena had given him . . .

Da da da da da da dad a dad a doh . . .

He wanted to hum along. He couldn't for the life of him remember where he first knew that tune from but he'd heard it even before Lena had given him the music box.

He prayed that Sister Angelica wouldn't come upstairs. He imagined her kneeling down, her face looking in at him as he cowered under the bed. He wondered who would be more afraid and he knew the answer.

He heard her climb the stairs and bit his fist in an effort to stem the rising screech that was building up in the back of his throat. He heard the pad of her soft-soled shoes go along the corridor and into the room where the desk was. He heard the drawer in the roll-top desk open and then the click as the gun was cocked.

He felt the hairs rise on the nape of his neck; goose pimples erupted like mini volcanoes on his arms and legs.

He listened as her footsteps approached. She stopped. The door to the room where he was hiding creaked as it opened. He bit the inside of his mouth to keep quiet. With relief he heard her go back downstairs.

He must have been under the bed for ages and he was aching all over. Finally, he heard the key turn in the lock and Sister Angelica singing as she made her way back through the garden.

Archie slipped out from under the bed and as he did his foot caught against something; there was an old shoe box tucked up against the wall.

He slid it out from under the bed, opened the lid and looked inside.

His eyes grew wide, his mouth dry. He slumped down onto the bedroom floor with the box in his lap. He sat motionless in a pool of dying light. He knew now what had happened to Thomas Greswode.

★ ★ ★

Sister Angelica poured a glass of wine for Sister Isabella and together they sat watching the moon rise above the convent.

'Was the boy in the house when you got there?' Sister Isabella asked.

'Oh, yes, he was hiding under the bed. I could hear his breathing from the corridor!'

Sister Isabella grinned.

'He's a persistent little fellow, isn't he? How did he get in?'

'Through the little window at the back. It was lucky you saw him snooping about and we had time to change our plans. Is everything organized, Sister Isabella?'

'Yes. We make our move tonight. A boat will arrive close to midnight to take our people out. From here they go to Ischia, they will remain there for several weeks and then move on to France. Are their papers all in order?'

'Yes. And from France where do they go next?'

'After that no one knows. *Il Camaleonte* prefers it that way.'

'Have they the gun in case of any trouble?'

'Yes. But I don't think they'll need it. After

tonight we will have no more worries for a while. And when they have gone our brave friend Miriam must make herself scarce.'

'Has she a new passport?'

'No, she has many already. She is as slippery as an eel, that one.'

'And soon our special guest arrives?'

'God willing that he's strong enough to make it here,' Sister Isabella said and made the sign of the cross.

★   ★   ★

Archie could not sleep. He crept out of bed, opened the shutters and looked out into the starry night. The moon was huge and dripped a silvered pathway across the gently heaving sea.

The candles in the shrines outside the houses lining the harbour flickered in the warm breeze and the smell of rosemary and lemons was strong in the air. Out at sea the lights on a fishing boat twinkled and then died.

He sat down on the side of his bed and began to reread the letter that Benjamin Tregantle had left for him.

. . . People aren't always what they seem — usually they're a lot better, but not always.

He thought of the nuns at the convent. They weren't what they seemed at all. He'd never heard anything like it. Nuns with guns and perms. Passport forgers!

He read on:

Take yourself down to the wobbly chapel
... you might be lucky, find yourself a
proper mystery to solve there, a real piece of
detective work.

And he had. He'd found out what had most
likely happened to Boreo Orore. Yet he was sure
that Benjamin hadn't known what Archie would
find hidden inside the font. If he'd known a
secret like that, he'd have told, brought the
murderers to justice, wouldn't he? And Benjamin
couldn't have known that he'd meet Romilly and
that his interest would be kindled in the life of
Thomas Greswode. This wasn't the mystery that
Benjamin had meant him to find, he'd just
stumbled into this by accident.

... you're the type of boy who could find
out things ... if you put your mind to it and
stopped being afraid of every bloody thing.

And he had put his mind to it and he had
stopped being afraid of every bloody thing but it
was luck that set him out on the trail. It was luck
that Gwennie had fired the gun and he'd run
into the woods. It was coincidence that Romilly
had been in the summerhouse and had asked
him if he was Thomas Greswode. Benjamin
couldn't have known that all those things would
happen to him.
Or that Romilly would give him the diary
she'd found in the summerhouse. He'd give
anything right now to talk to Romilly, to tell her
all that had happened to him since the last time

he'd seen her. He imagined the look on her face when he told her what he had discovered here in Santa Caterina.

He put the letter away and took the photograph out of his knapsack. He looked at the young, hopeful face of Thomas Greswode standing outside the summerhouse at Killivray.

He knew now what had happened to him but there were still some things that he was desperate to know and he was sure that there was only one person in Santa Caterina who could tell him the truth. And as soon as he could, he was going to pay her a visit.

'There are no secrets locked away in this world that the curious can't find a key to open up,' Benjamin had said.

As he stood at the window and looked out, he realized that something was different. The walkway beneath his window was darker than usual. He leant out and looked down. He saw that the candle had gone out in the shrine. Moments later the one on the house next door was extinguished too. He leant out of the window and watched.

A figure moved furtively amongst the shadows . . .

One by one the candles were stubbed out and apart from the moonlight the darkness was almost complete.

What was it that Alfredo had said? When the nuns wanted to move people in and out of the convent, the good people of Santa Caterina put out the candles and closed the shutters on their houses to give them cover of darkness.

A boat approached the harbour and the motor was suddenly cut. He heard the sound of oars moving almost silently through the water. There were muffled voices in the darkness below. Archie watched as two men climbed up the steps and their heads appeared over the harbour wall. He stepped back from the window in fright, the men's faces were covered in black masks and they looked eerie and threatening. Archie edged closer to the window again. One of the men looked up suddenly and saw him. His eyes glinted fiercely in the moonlight and he signalled to Archie to close the shutters. With shaking hands he obeyed and then sat down on the bed, quaking with fear.

He imagined the dark-clad figures making their way through the narrow streets of Santa Caterina towards the towering convent. He was sure that right now out there in the dark night the nuns would be opening the side gate to let people in or let them out.

Time passed slowly but as the church clock chimed one o'clock he was aware of muffled noises outside, the sound of a motor starting up and the stifled giggling of a child. He waited a moment, then he opened the shutters a crack and looked down. The boat was gone. The candles burned again in the shrines, small oases of light in the quiet darkness.

★   ★   ★

Archie woke just as the sun began to rise, streaking the sky with crimson and amber weals.

He got up, took off his nightclothes and looked at himself in the wardrobe mirror. Benjamin would have a real shock if he could see him now. He had grown at least two inches and his ribs didn't stick out like they did last winter. His face was fatter and he had lost that pinched and peaky look. His eyes looked very blue against his tanned skin. His legs had muscles and the thin one was beefing up a bit. He didn't wear the calliper all the time now that the leg was getting stronger. He smiled at his reflection, pleased with what he saw.

He dressed hurriedly, crept silently down the stairs and out of the house. Passing the bread shop, he waved to the sleepy-eyed young girl who was opening the shutters. She looked him up and down and giggled.

Breathless by the time he reached the convent, he yanked the bell. Deep inside, the bell rang out.

A small, wary-eyed nun who he had never seen before pulled back the grille in the door and peered out at Archie enquiringly.

'It's a bit early for callers,' she said sharply. 'The sisters are having their breakfast.'

'I need to talk to Sister Isabella. It's very urgent.'

She closed the grille, opened the door and let him in, glancing curiously at this funny little boy with his wide blue eyes and peculiar clothes.

Leading him along the cool corridor past candles flickering in red-glass pots at the feet of silent saints, the nun showed him into the same

412

dim parlour he'd been in the last time he'd been here.

He sat down in a chair and folded his arms. The nun glanced back at him, suppressing a chuckle, and then she was gone, the sound of her crêpe-soled shoes squeaking away into the distance.

It was cool in the room and Archie shivered. He waited impatiently. Soon he heard the approach of footsteps along the corridor. His heart beat wildly as the door opened and he got to his feet quickly.

Sister Isabella stepped into the room and peered at him.

'Who is it?' she asked but he didn't answer.

Impatiently she took out her spectacles from a pocket in her black habit and put them on.

A small scream escaped from her mouth and she made the sign of the cross, jabbing at her chest with a gnarled old finger. Then she slumped down into a chair, her hand pressed against her heart.

'Mother of God, you want to give me heart attack! For a moment I thought . . . '

Archie stood before her dressed in the old-fashioned sailor suit that he had found carefully folded in the shoe box at the Casa delle Stelle.

'For a moment you couldn't believe your eyes, could you? It was like someone had turned the clock back over fifty years, wasn't it?'

She nodded silently and stared at Archie Grimble in amazement. He was an incredible child. No wonder Lena and Alfredo had taken such a shine to him. How could such a little boy find out all these things?

'You thought that I was Thomas Gasparini Greswode?' he said.

She nodded again, unable to take her eyes off him.

'The first time he came back to Santa Caterina he was wearing these clothes, wasn't he?'

'He was.'

The bells began to toll slowly in Santa Caterina and sunlight edged in through the high slit of a window casting a luminous glow over the ancient walls.

'Someone once said to me that there are no secrets locked away in this world that the curious can't find a key to open up,' he said. 'And they were right.'

The old nun nodded and smiled weakly.

'Why didn't you tell me that Thomas hadn't died but had got back here?' he said.

'Like I say, maybe it is safer for everyone if the past is buried.'

He fell silent then and remembered Benjamin's words:

The tide washes over some secrets and covers them up but it throws up others, like flotsam and jetsam.

The truth is always the best option, I believe, however painful. So be sure to search for it and know what it is when you find it.

'Come,' Sister Isabella said, 'we go sit outside, I needs some air after the fright you gave me, some sun to warm my old bones.'

Archie and Sister Isabella sat together in the convent courtyard in the shade of the lemon trees. A weary-looking Sister Angelica brought Archie a bowl of steaming coffee, some freshly baked bread and honey, and while he ate Sister Isabella spoke.

'I couldn't believe it when I seen him that day. We thought he was dead, you see. The uncle had written to Father Benneto the priest to tell us here in Santa Caterina of his death. I was still mourning for David and the news of Thomas' death was such a shock. I loved him you see, like a little brother. He was the child of my best friend, Rosa, and of the man I loved.'

'Where were you when you saw him?'

'I had gone down to the Casa delle Stelle. There's a path that leads from the convent down into the garden. I used to go there a lot, I find it peaceful there.'

'And he turned up just like that?'

'It was in the October. I was sitting there quietly when suddenly I hear the swearing.'

'Swearing?' Archie exclaimed.

'Oh yes, he had a dirty mouth on him. Every word was a filthy one with that, what you call him, how you say in English? Pumpkin.'

Archie tilted his head on one side. 'Sister Isabella, what does a pumpkin have to do with anything?'

She laughed, 'Pumpkin was the bird. The talking bird. How you say in English?'

'A parrot. He had a parrot with him?'

'*Si*, he arrive here with parrot. First thing I

415

hear is parrot, then I see Thomas coming up the path. I think at first he was a ghost like I think when I see you today. He filthy and half-starved and very sick.'

'So, he didn't drown after all? He must have left Killivray in the August like he'd planned and it took him almost three months to get back here?'

'Si, and he have very bad time on his journey. He very afraid all the time and get sick. And when he get here he don't know nothing about his father's death. Like you said, nobody had told him and it break my heart to have to tell him this news. I take him to the grave because he get hysterical and he don't believe me.'

'But why didn't they tell him?'

'Like you, I think Thomas thinks that maybe his uncle responsible for his father's death. I think maybe he right but there no proof. And Thomas tell me later, his cousin try to kill him.'

'He did,' Archie said, 'I read all that in his diary. What happened to him then?'

'I bring him back here to the convent and we look after him, we keep him here for nearly a year while he get strong again. We can't understand why the Greswodes had told us he was dead.'

'Because they thought he was dead! They had a funeral for him and his grave is in the wobbly chapel with his name on ... but Thomas wouldn't have known that, would he? He would have thought that the Greswodes thought he'd run away and would be looking for him and that when they found him they would kill him!'

416

'He very surprised when I tell him that the Greswodes had written to say he was dead,' Sister Isabella said.

'Where did he go when he left here?'

'One day the circus come to San Donato. We tell them that Thomas is here with us and they come visit him. And then he go away with them.'

'He went off with the circus!' Archie said incredulously.

'*Si*, like his mama done before him. They like a family to him from days he live with them when his mama is alive.'

'Of course!'

'Then for many years I don't see him much but he write me many times from many different places. He clever boy, he get rich and have houses here and in Paris and London. Then after the war he stop writing and I not seen him since.'

'So you don't know what happened to him?'

She shook her head and looked down at her hands clasped firmly around her rosary.

'And the family back in Killivray, did anyone ever tell them that Thomas was alive?'

'No! He happy that they think him dead. He have a new passport from Sister Angelica, many passports, so he have many names. He don't want nothing to do with his family in England.'

'And Thomas never ever went back to Killivray?'

'Ah! I don't think Thomas go back to Killivray but I knows that he write to friend of his to tell him that he alive.'

'Who was that?'

417

'Just a boy who he like very much.'

'Benjamin Tregantle!'

Sister Isabella looked quizzically at Archie.

'You know him?'

'I did but he died a few months ago.'

'I see.'

'He's buried back at Rhoskilly. Did Benjamin write back?'

'*Si*. And boy get awful shock because he been to Thomas' funeral. And in war he come here once to Santa Caterina.'

Archie smiled, he'd bet that Benjamin had loved it here.

'Did he ever come again?'

'No, just the once. But many years later Thomas did see his cousin Charles in London and give the man a big fright.'

Archie squealed with delight.

'Because he thought he was dead and they'd buried him. That must have been a real shock!'

'*Si*.'

Archie would have loved to have seen the look on Charles Greswode's face. Imagine that he thought that their luck was in and then up pops Thomas! He must have almost had a heart attack when he bumped into someone he thought was dead and buried.

'I wonder who's buried in the grave in the Skallies that has Thomas Greswode's name on it.' Archie said.

'I don't know. Maybe no one ever know. But is strange because they would have known if the body wasn't Thomas,' Sister Isabella said.

'The thing is, sometimes when a body has

been in the sea a long time it gets eaten by fish and might not be recognized. And you see they would have wanted the body to be Thomas! And, and it was Charles Greswode who found the body washed up on the beach.'

'So?'

'I remember Miss Fanthorpe saying that the Greswodes were powerful people, that they could make the doctor give them a death certificate if they wanted one!'

Sister Isabella shook her head, she was finding it hard to keep up with this little English boy.

'I have something of Thomas Greswode's,' Archie said, pulling out the silver bird necklace to show Sister Isabella.

'That's the necklace that I give to Rosa Gasparini and when she die it given to Thomas. The silver bird I buy from man in Naples,' she uttered, looking at the silver bird in astonishment.

'Where you get this from?'

'Thomas had lost it and he was really upset about it. Well, I think that his horrid cousin had stolen it because Romilly found it hidden behind the skirting boards at Killivray House.'

'Mother of God! He used to talk about losing this — it was precious to him, the only memento of his mother.'

'Why did you lie to me and tell me that the Casa delle Stelle had burned down?' Archie asked.

Sister Isabella sighed and said, 'Because we use the casa sometimes for people we helping to stay in. Is very secluded there and easy to hide them. I don't want you involve in any trouble.'

'The other night, when the candles were all put out, I saw some men arrive in a boat . . . '

Sister Isabella threw back her head and laughed and Archie stared at her.

'You don't see any men, Archie Grimble!' she said.

He bristled indignantly and his face grew red with anger. 'I know what I saw and I'm not stupid! I saw two men climbing out of a boat!'

'Those not two men! The two you see is two sisters from the convent of Santa Maria in Naples.'

'And why would two nuns be dressed up like burglars and creeping about in the dark?'

'They come to pick up people who was staying here in Santa Caterina, people we move here when you starts being nosy parker.'

'So I was right. There were people staying there. Once when I was there the door to a room was locked but I knew there was someone in there, someone as afraid as me.'

'Oh, yes, that's why I watching you. Why we move them out.'

'So I messed it up a bit for you?'

'It was okay. We bring them here and they get away safely. I don't want you involved in anything dangerous.'

'I see,' he said, thinking of the gun in the desk.

'Anyway now you have solve mystery you must be very happy boy?'

'I am but I feel funny now that I know the

truth, that my mystery is solved. I'm really glad that I know that Thomas Greswode didn't die, that he got back here to Santa Caterina and I'm glad that he had a good life but I'm sad because there's somebody I'd love to tell and I know that I'll never be able to.'

'Who is it you want to tell?'

'It's the girl, Romilly, the one who gave me the necklace. We were trying to find out everything we could about Thomas together. I said he was dead and she said he wasn't. We were both right and both wrong in a way. It's sad that she'll never know the truth.'

'Maybe one day you meets again and you can tell her your story,' Sister Isabella said kindly.

'I doubt it,' he said sadly.

'No one knows what future holds.'

'Who owns the Casa delle Stelle now?' Archie asked.

She coughed. 'So many questions. Don't you ever stop! It still belongs to Thomas Greswode,' she said with a smile. 'But soon new owners will be moving in.'

'They're dead lucky, it's a lovely house,' he said wistfully.

Sister Isabella straightened up and said matter-of-factly, 'Well, I must go now, there much work to do.'

'Are you forging passports today or curling your hair?'

'Curling my hair? I have no hair! Today I have to peel onions and skin tomatoes.'

'Oh.' Archie blushed.

Suddenly he thought back to when he was

standing in the Casa delle Stelle looking at the map on the wall. Every flag pinpointing a journey. And the names in the address book . . .

Adler, Abrahams, Goldberg. They were the names of some of the children who had been saved in the war . . .

'Sister Isabella. There's something that you're not telling me.'

The nun looked flustered, played absently with her crucifix.

'I tell you too many things already.'

'I can keep a secret,' he said. 'Thomas Greswode was *Il Camaleonte*, wasn't he?'

She shook her head and Archie could not conceal his disappointment. He looked down at his shoes.

Sister Isabella saw how hugely disappointed he was. If there was a child who deserved to know the truth it was this one.

'Thomas Greswode *wasn't Il Camaleonte*. He is *Il Camaleonte*.'

Archie looked up at her suddenly, his blue eyes wide with incredulity.

'He's alive?' he whispered.

The old nun nodded and put out her hand and brushed a tear from his cheek.

★ ★ ★

The summer tipped slowly towards autumn and cooler winds skirted Santa Caterina, blowing a few stray leaves from the trees in the tiny piazza.

White-capped waves hurried towards the

beach and rattled the pebbles impatiently. The metal curtains over the doors clinked playfully and the wind ruffled the fur of baleful-eyed cats who scurried for cover.

It made the habits of the monks billow as they toiled in the fields and snatched at the veils of the nuns as they crossed the courtyard in the convent. The coloured flags that hung above the Ristorante Skilly danced wildly and the shutters on the windows clattered noisily at night.

Alfredo brought the tables inside and the old men took up their seats closer to the stove along with the three-legged dog who had taken up permanent residence.

In a few days' time Archie, Martha and Lissia were leaving for England. They were going back to Bag End and he would be sent back to school and all the misery that meant. The teasing and hair pulling, stone throwing and kicking. His mammy was very quiet and he'd heard her tell Lena that she was worried about how they would manage for money, especially as now she had Lissia to look after and she needed watching all the time.

A letter came from Cissie Abelson that made him want to laugh and cry. She told him how a man had come for Gwennie and she had gone off with him because he was her son and she'd gone all the way to America. She'd drawn a picture of Skilly Beach with a giant silver moon in the sky and in the window of the Boathouse two figures, one black, one white, were hugging.

Archie felt the tears fill his eyes. So Gwennie

had had a son. Bo's son. And he'd bet that Dom Bradly, the man who'd frightened the life out of him that night in the woods, was her son! He was so pleased for Gwennie. And how pleased Thomas Greswode would have been to know this news!

Cissie told him that she was going to go to Nanskelly School and do loads of painting and other nice things. He was happy for her but it meant that he'd have to walk to the school in Rhoskilly on his own each day. He'd be even lonelier than before.

He looked down at the other pictures that she'd drawn. She was a good drawer all right. There was a picture of Fleep's parrot perched on the grandfather chair near the fire in the bar of the Pilchard. A speech bubble came out of his beak. In it was written, 'Eat shit and die!' Archie smiled, then his eyes moved down to the PS written at the bottom of the letter. Nan had written something that made Archie sit up with a jolt.

'PS Gwennie said to tell you to look in the collecting box for your mystery!'

Archie clenched his fists. What a fool he'd been! He closed his eyes and tried to picture the inside of the wobbly chapel. He could recall the stone receptacle for holy water and next to it, set into the wall, was a metal-fronted collection box with a rusted-up keyhole and some Latin words on the front.

Tell him to look in the collecting box! Of course. He still had the bunch of keys that Benjamin had left him.

You'll find a bunch of keys in the porch of my house, on the third hook along from the door; take them and keep them safe. After I'm gone they'll belong to you. And anything they open, Arch, will be yours.

One key had opened the door of the wobbly chapel and one must be meant to open the collecting box!

When he got back he'd get in there and open it up. It was the only thing he had to look forward to in the Skallies.

Folding up Cissie's letter, he put it in his pocket and went out for a walk around Santa Caterina.

★　★　★

There was a buzz about the village, a frisson of whispered excitement in the air. The old men on the harbour spoke conspiratorially as they mended their fishing nets and blew smoke like question marks into the air. In the piazza the dog with the scarf around its neck ran round and round in ever diminishing circles.

A group of chattering monks trailed up the steep hill towards the convent, their heads bowed, sandals slapping against the cobbles, crucifixes jingling gaily.

In the Silver Bird Café the candle beneath the photograph of Rosa Gasparini glowed brightly and the tiny man with the enormous moustache sang to himself as he worked. Old women swept the cobbles in front of their houses and threw buckets of water to damp the dust. The streets and alleyways were fragrant with the perfume of freshly watered flowers.

Archie stopped and listened. In the garden of the Casa delle Stelle the cockerel crowed triumphantly and the sound of nuns singing drifted down from the convent.

It was that damned song again.

An old woman called down to him from where she sat knitting on a balcony. 'He is coming soon,' she hissed. 'On a boat from Naples.'

'Who is?' Archie asked.

'They have asked Signor Rabiotti to bring the car down to the harbour because he is so frail. They say he is coming back here to Santa Caterina to die.'

'Who is?' Archie asked impatiently.

But she shook her head and began to croon softly to herself.

Archie wandered home to find Lissia skipping outside the Ristorante Skilly.

She grabbed hold of his arm and kissed him on both cheeks.

'Why are you so happy?'

'Because my friend *Il Camaleonte* is coming to Santa Caterina.'

Archie stared at her and shook his head in disbelief.

'And because,' she whispered, 'I am going to have a kitten all of my own.'

'You can't, Lissia, because we're going home soon.'

'This is Lissia's home now,' she said. 'I'd like

to be a mammy cat and have little kittens.'

'You can't have kittens, Lissia, because you're a woman and women have babies.'

'I know where you get babies from,' she said.

'So do I. You get them from under cabbage bushes or sometimes rhubarb,' he said, though he didn't believe it any more.

Lissia giggled, 'I had one once but it came out of my tummy.'

'You know what Mammy has told you about telling lies — you'll get blisters on your tongue!'

★ ★ ★

The candles were lit in the shrines and a soft wind blew in off the sea. A full moon rose over Santa Caterina and bathed the convent in a silvery light.

As if on cue the villagers filed out silently from their houses and lined the harbour and the narrow streets.

Archie stood outside the Ristorante Skilly with Alfredo and Lena and watched as the boat made its way slowly towards the harbour and moored. They were bringing *Il Camaleonte* home to die.

A group of men came slowly up the steps half carrying an old man dressed in a white suit that was several sizes too large. He wore a large Panama hat that was too big for his head. The men helped him carefully into a black car, the engine spluttered to life and the car pulled away, moving slowly through the narrow streets.

Archie watched and saw that as the car drew alongside the waiting people they looked up, made the sign of the cross and then lowered their heads again.

Luca, from the Silver Bird Café had made his way through the crowd and stood next to Archie, his hand on the boy's shoulder. As the car approached, Archie saw that Luca's eyes had filled with tears and the hand that rested on Archie's shoulder was trembling.

Archie looked up and saw *Il Camaleonte* slumped in the back of the car between two stiff-backed nuns. For a moment he caught a glimpse of the sunken old eyes and his body felt weak. The old man raised his left hand feebly and waved to the silent people.

Archie swallowed hard. He'd never thought for a moment that he would find out what had happened to Thomas Greswode. He'd never dreamed that he would see him in the flesh, however briefly.

The little boy who Archie had thought was buried beneath the floor of the wobbly chapel had grown up to be one of the bravest men ever. And yet he'd chosen for people not to know who he really was. He'd wanted to work in secret.

Archie copied Luca and made the sign of the cross, shaking his head in wonder. Alfredo had been right. Santa Caterina did have its fair share of heroes for a little place.

Then as the car began to climb the steep hill the bells of the convent rang out joyfully to welcome home *Il Camaleonte*.

★　★　★

428

Miriam Blomstein had watched the headlights of the car as it made its way up through the winding streets and in through the gates of the convent. In a short while she would meet *Il Camaleonte* again. She remembered their first meeting in London, how a quirk of fate had brought them together.

She had been sitting in a misty-windowed café just off the Edgware Road trying to eke out a cold cup of tea. It was past midnight when the man had sat down opposite her and said quite simply, 'You are looking to escape, Madame?'

She'd been about to jump up and make a run for it but he'd put his hand firmly on her arm and looked into her eyes with such tenderness that she'd known immediately that she could trust him.

He had passed her the following morning's newspaper, an early copy of *The Times* with her photograph on the front and the headline: WANTED. JEWEL THIEF. Then he had turned to another page and shown her the advertisement. 'Wanted. Governess to teach ten-year-old girl . . . '

He had ordered fresh tea and a plate of toast and as she'd eaten hungrily she had listened in disbelief as he had carefully unveiled his plan to her. If she wanted the opportunity to escape the police, who he said were, as they spoke, searching her flat a few streets away, all she had to do was agree to help him. She was to visit a theatrical outfitter, buy a selection of wigs and spectacles, built-up shoes and several outfits. Then when her appearance was sufficiently changed, she must contact a Miss Vera Truscott and apply for the post of governess at Killivray House. In the meantime he would see that she had somewhere safe to stay in London.

The following day, he met her at a discreet distance from the agency and supplied her with forged papers in the name of Clementine Fernaud. She was to take a train from Paddington to Reading and stay overnight in an hotel. Then she was to await further instructions. She was to be well paid for a job that could be difficult and dangerous and then she was guaranteed safe passage abroad.

★ ★ ★

Il Camaleonte sat hunched in a chair wrapped in a woollen rug but still he shivered. Sister Isabella put a match to the fire and the kindling crackled and sparks were drawn up inside the enormous chimney. Then she sat down opposite him.

'Sizzie,' he said, 'it's so good to see you again. It's been too many years.'

His voice was barely audible, his breathing spasmodic. She watched him with eyes brimming with tears, leant across and took his hand in her own. His flesh was papery now and the pulse in his wrist feeble.

'I haven't long left now, Sizzie.'

'Hush, Thomas, with some rest you may get well.'

'Sizzie, you know the truth as well as I do. That's wishful thinking. I am tired now, it is my time. I've spent many months preparing for the end, so many loose ends to tie up. But everything

430

is taken care of . . . I have left money for the nuns here at Santa Caterina so that you can carry on your good work. My other properties have been left to other worthy causes . . . '

His body was suddenly racked by a coughing fit and Sister Isabella hastily fetched him a glass of water, holding it to his pale lips.

'Loosen my shirt, Sizzie, I feel as though I am choking.'

She undid his tie and opened his collar and saw the small star-shaped birthmark, the same one that Rosa Gasparini had.

'You are thinking of her? Aren't you?'

'I am. I often think of your mother.'

'And my father too?'

'Him too.'

'How I miss them both, Sizzie. If I believed in the afterlife I would think that in a short time I will see them both again.'

'But you don't believe?'

He shook his head.

'Everything has turned out well with our visitors?'

'*Si*, the mother and child have already gone off to Ischia. There were no problems and they are staying with the Gabbatini family. In a few weeks they will be taken to France. Where will they go next?'

'It's best that I don't say. No one will be looking for her now that they think she took her own life. Sister Angelica tells me she looks very fetching with the hair dyed black and permed.'

'Oh, quite a transformation!'

'Is Miriam here?' he asked.

431

Sister Isabella nodded. 'Shall I bring her to you?'

★   ★   ★

Il Camaleonte looked up as Miriam Blomstein came into the room. She was a striking woman, with dark, lively eyes and a beguiling smile.

'Well done, Miriam, you were wonderful! Now you must drink some wine and tell me all that has happened since we met last in London.'

She stooped and kissed him on both cheeks, sat down opposite him and poured herself a glass of wine.

'While I was at the hotel in Reading I got your instructions and I must say I was relieved not to be playing the role of governess! I'm not really the type at all! Anyhow, on the following day the woman was waiting for me at the railway station. As instructed I helped her to get into her disguise.'

'How was Margot?'

'Extremely anxious but once she was dressed up in the wig and spectacles the transformation was unbelievable! Of course it helped that she was a good actress so she took to the part incredibly well. She even had the French accent down to a fine tee. It must have been good because even her own daughter didn't recognize her!'

'Go on.'

'Well, then we swapped train tickets and papers. I took the train she was meant to take.

And Margot went back to Killivray as Clementine Fernaud.'

'And how was your time with the nuns?'

'Well, luckily they'd never seen Margot Greswode before so they didn't know they were being tricked. I just had to remain there and act a little deranged until someone made contact.'

'And did that come easily to you?' he said, with a hint of a smile.

Miriam laughed and took a drink of wine. 'Of course it nearly all went awry when Jonathan Greswode came back early to Killivray. Margot rang me in an absolute state because he said he was coming to visit St Mary's to arrange for me to be transferred to an asylum. If he'd turned up and seen me then that would have stopped our pretty plans!'

'What happened at Killivray?'

'Well, as you know the plan was for me to bide my time at the convent. When the time was right Margot and Romilly would make their escape in the car which you would be sending. But then things went horribly wrong. Jonathan Greswode turned up early, which put Margot into an absolute panic. He'd brought a woman down to Killivray with him and Margot overheard his plans to shut her up in an asylum. It was all getting too much for her and then . . . '

'Then what?'

'She found out what he'd been doing to the child . . . '

Il Camaleonte looked across at Miriam and saw the pain in her face.

'She'd gone up to her room and been woken by the child crying. The old nanny was asleep and stinking of brandy so she'd stayed with Romilly all night. Poor Romilly had no idea that Madame Fernaud was her own mother. And Romilly confided to her that Jonathan Greswode had . . . had . . . '

'You don't need to say more.'

'The next morning Margot went out to the Skallies and met with a woman there who ran the pub, to ask her if there was anyone local who had a car.'

'So the woman from the Pilchard helped her?'

'In the end, but Margot said she was a feisty devil and had ideas that Margot was spying on her and her child. Quite a character, from what I can gather.'

Il Camaleonte smiled and signalled that she continue.

'That's where it all took a turn for the worse. Margot took the key to the gun cabinet and took out a gun. Then she sat in his study and waited for him. She knew his habits, knew he was a bad sleeper and that he usually came down to his study in the early hours of the morning for a cigar . . . And when he did she was waiting for him.'

'Did she mean to shoot him?'

'I don't honestly know, she won't speak of it but I think so. She and the child had endured a terrible time at his hands. I think that she wanted to know that that was the end of him once and for all.'

'He was a bully like his father, Charles. Tell

434

me, how did you manage to escape from the good Sisters of St Mary's?'

'Well, the original plan was that Margot would contact me and let me know when they were leaving Killivray and then I would make my escape from St Mary's. Of course, as soon as the murder was discovered I had to take a gamble. If I ran away from St Mary's then suspicions would be awakened. Far better that the police thought the governess had done it and abducted the child.'

'You must have nerves of steel, Miriam.'

'I had good practice during the war,' she said. 'When the police came to tell me the news I gave them the theatrical works! Ranted and raged. The police realized they'd never get any sense out of me and left me to the nuns.'

'You are a genius, Miriam,' *Il Camaleonte* said with a smile.

'Well, I knew that the nuns feared for my mental state . . . thought me a likely suicide risk. I was in a room on the third floor and they watched me like hawks but one of the windows had been left open in the upstairs lavatory. I'd escaped from harder places than that and in the wink of an eye I was out . . . '

'Miriam, there is something that I must tell you,' he said softly, reaching out for her hand.

'What is it?'

'The woman at the Pilchard Inn is an old friend of yours.'

Miriam looked at *Il Camaleonte* in surprise.

'A friend of mine? I haven't had any friends in years, I've been on the move all the time.'

'Hannah Abelson,' he said and watched her face with interest.

'My God! She is alive?'

'Apparently very much so. One day soon you shall both meet, of that I have no doubt.'

'But I thought that she had perished along with the others from Bizier. How was she saved?'

'She was found in the woodshed at Le Petit Bijou after her parents had been taken. She had been out walking her baby brother when the Germans came for her parents.'

'I can't believe this. My friend Hannah is alive! And Solomon? Is he alive too?'

'No. Sadly, Solomon died.'

'What happened to the Abelsons?'

'They were sent to their deaths,' he said with a weary voice.

'Like my own parents.'

There was a long silence before *Il Camaleonte* spoke again.

'We scoured Bizier for you, Miriam, to try and get you out but we couldn't find you. I thought of you often in the years since that day, wondering how you had fared, whether you had made it.'

'I knew that I had to run away. I'd seen them take the Abelsons and I'd run home but by the time I got there I was too late . . .'

There was silence for a while and then she said in a barely audible voice, 'It was the day after we'd been on an outing to the beach . . . such a day we'd had, the last truly happy day that I can remember. The weather had been gloriously hot and Hannah and I had swum in the sea for hours and then played together on the sand. Mr Abelson took a photograph of us. Of course I've never seen it. I still have a shell that I picked up that I've kept all this time . . . '

'Where did you go, Miriam?'

'I knew it wasn't safe for me to stay in Bizier. I made my way down to Narbonne to some friends of my parents but they too had been rounded up. There was a beach hut I knew of on Narbonne Plage and I knew where the owners hid the key. I stayed there for many weeks, then I made my way up through France, stealing, hiding out until the war was over . . . '

'And since then?'

'I haven't led a very good life, I'm ashamed to say. I've got by — by foul means rather than fair. Tell me, though, how did you find me and come to be sitting in the café in London?'

'I'd been trying to track you down for many years. I picked up your trail and put out my feelers. I have many connections,' he said, tapping the side of his nose. 'And I was so pleased to be told that you were there in London. I needed someone very brave and you were the right person. Indeed when I am gone there will be much work for people such as yourself. If you don't feel up to that then I have left a little something for you as a thank you. Now I am tired and must sleep.'

Miriam got slowly to her feet and looked down at the old man. She'd heard the stories of many of the children he'd saved, but she'd never dreamed that she would meet him. His eyes were closed now and there was a hint of a smile about his mouth. She bent down and kissed him gently on his cheek and then she left the room, closing the door quietly behind her.

★　★　★

Sister Angelica lit the candles in the room to drive away the gloom but *Il Camaleonte* had asked for the windows to be left open. He wanted to hear the sound of the sea, the call of the owls down in the garden of the Casa delle Stelle. He knew now that by the time the old cockerel crowed again he would be safely out of this world, for good this time.

He would be buried with his mother and father in the hilltop cemetery amongst old friends. They would write: Thomas Greswode born in Santa Caterina died August 1960. It was amazing how many names one man could assume in a lifetime, how many times one man could be buried.

Down in the church the nuns were praying; if he listened really hard he could make out the low murmur of their voices, the clink of their rosary beads.

He closed his eyes and listened to all the night sounds down in Santa Caterina. The music of the metal curtains as the breeze caught at them. The tinkle of a music box as a child was stilled into sleep. The far-off laughter from the Ristorante Skilly; the smell of tobacco smoke mingling with the scent of lemon trees.

★　★　★

Archie could not sleep. He lay awake looking up at the ceiling. He heard a clock chime midnight. His rucksack was packed and soon he would be saying his goodbyes to the people of Santa Caterina. He stifled a sob and bit his fist. He'd been happy here, happier than he'd ever known that a boy could be.

Suddenly he sat up. Someone was moving around stealthily in the bedroom next door. Then he heard footsteps going down the stairs and the key turn in the front door. He got out of bed and crossed to the window, opened the shutter a fraction and looked down.

Holy Mary and all the blessed saints of heaven! What was she up to now? She'd be the death of him with all her antics!

Lissia, barefoot and still in her nightgown, was walking along the Via Porto as fast as she could go. He dressed as quickly as he could, made his way down the stairs and hurried after her.

★ ★ ★

Il Camaleonte was unaware of the door opening and the sound of soft footsteps approaching the bed.

A shadow moved across the white sheets. At the feel of the kiss on his cheek he opened his eyes with a start. No, it couldn't be . . .

A line of children had crept silently into the room and were standing around his bed watching him.

Louis Abner. A tiny bespectacled boy that

439

they'd brought out from Paris after his parents had been taken . . .

Next to him Douglas Abernethie. A foul-mouthed, cheerful little devil from an orphanage in Glasgow.

And there too was Rudi Abrahams and his little sister Ruth . . .

Dear God, he was hallucinating now.

He tried to raise himself up on his elbows but he was too weak.

He'd been reading through the red book earlier and reading all those names was playing tricks with his brain.

There was no one there . . .

He was all alone . . .

He closed his eyes.

Opened them again suddenly.

Sweet Jesus, is this what the end is like?

A bright-eyed ghost of a woman stood looking down at him, her white clothes billowing in the draught from the window . . . No. It couldn't be . . .

What the bloody hell was she doing here in Santa Caterina?

Alicia Murphy. The Convent of the Blessed Saints, Dungonally. The poor little girl who had given birth to the baby that he'd helped get out of Ireland.

He was hallucinating again. He blinked, and the woman was gone but he could feel the imprint of her kiss on his cheek.

Somewhere a floorboard creaked and a candle flickered, grew dim then bright again.

There was a brown-faced, wide-eyed angel

looking down at him now.

Angels don't wear spectacles with sticking plaster over them. Or open and close their mouth like a landed fish.

A lemon fell with a thud outside in the courtyard.

The nuns' voices grew louder, 'Santa Caterina, Santa Caterina, Santa Caterina daughter of the brave . . .'

Il Camaleonte looked up at Archie Grimble then passed his hands over his eyes as if he were seeing things that weren't there.

Archie Grimble looked down in incredulity at the emaciated face of Thomas Greswode. It was a long time before he could gain control of his mouth and speak.

'Bo didn't kill himself,' he said. 'He was murdered because he knew too much.'

The old man looked at him, stretching out his trembling hand towards the boy.

Moonlight swept into the room and they were both dappled in a shimmering, silvery light.

'Gwennie's son came back for her.'

The old man smiled and his eyes brimmed with tears. Archie shook his head. Everything was falling into place.

Parrots could live to over a hundred years of age. The word for pumpkin in Italian was *zucca*.

Down in the convent the nuns were singing, Santa Caterina, Santa Caterina . . .

The song that Benjamin used to sing. Archie had thought it was about Santa's cat.

He'd been surprised when William Dally had said that Benjamin's favourite hymn was 'All Things Bright and Beautiful'.

441

Archie Grimble looked down on *Il Camale-onte*, Thomas Greswode, the man of many names, and tried his very best to be brave.

'I am truly honoured to have you here at this time, Archie,' he whispered, pulling the boy towards him. And Archie Grimble buried his head in the old man's chest and felt the trembling hands on his back. He felt the tears fall onto his face and he knew what love meant and that it came from many places and that people weren't always what they seemed, they were usually better.

He stayed that way for a long time. Then when he felt the old man weaken he took the silver bird from around his neck and put it into his left hand and closed the gnarled old fingers around it.

Thomas Greswode was the best left-hand bat that William Dally had ever seen. The real Benjamin Tregantle had been right-handed.

The old man's eyes flickered.

'You found yourself a proper mystery in the end?'

Archie nodded.

' 'Night, Arch.'

'To sleep, perchance to dream; aye there's the rub,' Archie said and watched as a smile crept fleetingly across the lips of Thomas Greswode, the man that Archie had known as Benjamin Tregantle.

Archie bit his lip, brushed a tear from his eye and walked slowly towards the door.

'Now be off home, you silly young bugger, and be sure to check where that last key fits.'

Part Five

June 1971

The cockerel crowed exultantly in the garden of the Casa delle Stelle and up in the convent the bells began to clang noisily. Martha Grimble awoke, got out of bed and opened the window shutters, letting in the early morning light.

She made her way downstairs and unlocked the front door with the same key that Archie had mysteriously brought out of his pocket all those years ago.

Fancy that, *Il Camaleonte* had been so taken with Archie that he'd left him the Casa delle Stelle. It was odd really because they'd only met for a few minutes when Lissia had gone racing up to the convent in the dead of night. Mind you, life was strange when you thought about it. She would never forget the man in Dublin who had approached her in a run-down café. She'd been quite desperate at the time to get Archie out of Ireland and evade capture and then this man, a perfect stranger, had ended up getting them new passports and sent them to an address in St Werburgh's where they'd been given the keys to Bag End.

Archie's getting the Casa delle Stelle was truly a miracle though; she'd been worried sick about how they would have survived if they'd gone back to the Skallies. She'd known that Archie was dreading going back. And just as well they hadn't because there'd been the most awful storms there a few years later and half the place had been washed into the sea.

It had all worked out well in the end. Walter had sent a letter to the Pilchard saying he'd made a mistake and was leaving the woman he'd married; which probably meant that she'd run out of money or patience. Could you believe it! He'd wanted to come back. Huh! Not a hope in hell of that. And Nan, God bless her, had returned all his mail after that saying, 'Whereabouts unknown but last heard of in Western Australia.' That was the last she'd heard of him.

Martha still helped Lena with the cooking in the Ristorante Skilly and Lissia washed up and spent most of her wages on ice cream! William Dally had been out to stay several times and had taught Archie an enormous amount about growing things. Archie had worked hard and they grew enough fruit and vegetables in the garden to keep them going. God, she loved it here in Santa Caterina: it was paradise.

Lissia woke and stretched. She got up and picked up the cat from the bottom of her bed. Then she opened the shutters and peeped down through the purple flowers into the garden.

Martha was down there already, filling an earthenware bowl with peaches that they'd eat for breakfast. The fountain was gurgling and splashing and the cockerel was strutting among the sunflowers.

When she was washed and dressed it was Lissia's job to go and collect the eggs from the henhouse and then she would boil water to make the coffee.

Only two cups today because Archie was gone away.

She felt sad that Archie wasn't at the Casa delle Stelle but soon he was going to write a letter and Martha would read it to her.

Martha said that when Archie came back he was going to a place called a University in Rome. But he wasn't, because she knew a really big secret that no one else did . . .

She'd been hiding under the table up in the convent kitchen and she'd heard Sister Isabella whisper to Sister Angelica that now he was twenty-one Archie had come of age and that he was a fine man to step into the shoes of *Il Camaleonte* . . .

It was a big secret and she mustn't tell, ever. She was good with secrets though; she'd never told any one that the man who used to visit her at the Convent of the Blessed Saints was *Il Camaleonte* and she never would.

She listened. She could hear someone whistling, someone coming along the alleyway that led to the house and she'd bet she knew who it was. Luca from the café, with the funny moustaches. He came nearly every day now, bringing croisants and pastries for her and Martha.

Soon, when her jobs were done, the three of

447

them would sit together at the table near the fountain and she'd pretend that she couldn't see him holding Martha's hand beneath the table cloth . . .

★   ★   ★

Down in the Ristorante Skilly Lena drank her coffee and picked up her wicker basket. She loved the walk down to the market in the mornings. Tonight the restaurant was fully booked and she needed to buy peppers and tomatoes, courgettes and artichokes and maybe some nectarines; she had a real craving for nectarines at the moment and that meant only one thing.

★   ★   ★

Alfredo and Paulo were emptying the fishing nets. Alfredo looked down at his small son with delight. He had the same silky dark hair and cheerful smile as his mother, the same enthusiasm for life.

Paulo was bursting with pride because it was the first time he had been allowed to go out fishing with Papa. Archie had taught him to swim before he'd gone away and now Papa was teaching him the names of all the fish just the way he'd done with Archie.

Stingrays and squid; sole and mullet; sea crickets and cod.

★   ★   ★

448

Lucia Galvini climbed the hill to Il Panettiere and bought the bread. On her way back she called into the café. She was allowed to change the candle and light a new one in the little red glass that burned beneath the woman they called the silver bird. One day she might run away with the circus. But not today; she was only five and what she really wanted right now was an enormous strawberry gelato. Then she was going to call for Lissia who had promised to take her to see some kittens that had just been born up at the convent.

★ ★ ★

It was siesta time in Le Petit Bijou. The shutters were closed against the hot afternoon sun and upstairs the baby Marthe slept soundly in a wicker cradle in the cool bedroom.

In a downstairs room sunlight filtered through the shutters and bathed seven-year-old Pierre in a moving watery light. He was awake but his face was rosy from recent sleep and a smile played across his mouth as he thought of the dreams he had had: dreams of pirate ships and Vikings.

Next to him on the bed lay the elephant book end and he picked it up and carefully opened it, the way Cissie had taught him to, the way he would teach Marthe when she was bigger. He tipped out the treasures that he'd found this morning. A dead spider he had found beneath the fig tree and three dirty shells that were hidden in the soil near the workshop where Aunt Cissie did her paintings. Not that she worked all the time like she pretended to. He was tall enough to peep through the window now, if he stood on tiptoe. Sometimes when she said she was not to be disturbed she was in there kissing Henri from the village. Yuk!

Out in the garden a man lay in a hammock watching the sunlight filter through the olive trees. Soon, soon he would stir himself and saunter down to the village to fetch the bread and then he would wake Nan and together they would prepare the evening meal, something a little special tonight in honour of their visitor who was probably speeding along the roads right now like a bat out of hell.

Cissie closed the door to her workshop and hid the key under a bush. Later she would creep down here and Henri would be waiting for her. After dinner they were going to break the news . . .

She wound her way back up the path, through the olive trees. In the kitchen she washed the paint from her hands and face in the stone sink and looked at her face in the mirror. Sometimes people said she looked a bit like Nan but that was just to be kind. Nan was pretty, she wasn't. And anyway why would she look like Nan?

Cissie smiled; sometimes people thought that she was dafter than she was, even Nan.

She could remember the day quite clearly, even though she'd been ever so little . . .

It was dark and she'd been sitting in her pram, crying because it was cold and she was wet and hungry. She'd always been hungry, she was always left sitting outside while the woman who pushed her pram went inside and didn't come out for hours.

Once someone had walked past the pram and said, 'People like that didn't deserve to have children . . .'

And they didn't.

She remembered Nan's arms reaching down into the pram and lifting her, lifting her up towards the stars and then running and running. Nan had saved her.

★ ★ ★

Pierre wandered out into the garden. Soon it would be time for dinner, but maybe he could sneak off now while no one was looking and escape into the woods. After all playing was so much more fun than eating. Eating was boring. Yesterday, he and his friend Bernard had made a den and he'd found some tools down in the workshop that used to belong to his grandpapa. He was going to have another go at carving something from wood, the way Mama said Grandpapa had done. He'd already made Marthe a carved dog which he was going to give her for her first birthday; it wasn't half bad either for a beginner.

Then he remembered that Mama's old friend Miriam was arriving this evening. Maybe he'd leave the woodcarving until tomorrow. Miriam was such fun! She told such stories about her past and Mama always laughed and told her to stop telling such lies and filling his head with daft ideas. For a nun she was something else!

In Nanskelly Agnes Arbuthnot sat at the piano in the drawing room and played. Although she was old and frail her hands skimmed the keys and she was completely immersed in her music.

'She never makes a mistake, you know,' old Mrs Smythe said loudly to her neighbour.

'I know, dear. She was tipped to be a concert pianist when she was a young woman,' Mrs Jacobson said.

'They say there was some kind of scandal,' Mrs Smythe whispered. 'All to do with a young man, I expect. You know what young girls are.'

Mrs Jacobson tried to keep a straight face and winked surreptitiously at Noni Arbuthnot who was sitting across from them pretending to read.

Mrs Jacobson had known the Arbuthnots when she was young. She'd never thought that she'd see them again until her husband Solly had met a man outside the synagogue in Willesden Green who'd taken him for a salt beef sandwich in the café there. She stifled a tear thinking of Solly. He'd been heartbroken when his business had hit the rocks. He'd managed to pay off all his debts but there was the question of his pride. And then, out of the blue, he'd been offered the job of running Nanskelly. He'd been in his element here . . .

Her mind went back to the Arbuthnot girls then. A striking pair of girls they'd been although there was always something a little different about Agnes. She lived in a world of her own. Not quite able to function in the real world, but

452

there wasn't anything odd in that really. What was it Solly had said? There's room for all sorts in this peculiar universe and who are we to judge? We need to accept more and judge less.

Noni had always been the life and soul of any event if she got half a chance. Then of course that terrible thing had happened.

She looked across at Agnes now, head bent over the piano. She wouldn't say boo to a goose when she was a girl but in the end, like the worm, she'd turned. It was all quite ghastly really, a father getting that drunk and terrorizing his own daughters.

She caught Noni's eyes and smiled. Of course, Agnes had been the sort of child who told the truth, the absolute truth however painful, and she kept to her word . . .

In court she'd told the truth too, said that she'd told her father that if he laid a finger on Noni again she'd hit him with the poker. And of course she had!

If it hadn't been for someone employing a top lawyer, she would certainly have been convicted.

She was woken from her reverie by Mr Payne, holding out his hand to her for a dance.

He was always one for a bit of fun. She got up and followed him onto the dance floor.

Noni Arbuthnot watched them with pleasure. It was good to see him enjoying himself again, he'd been real down in the dumps after his brother had passed away. He wasn't a bad little dancer for his age, quite nimble on his feet.

Noni was feeling quite peckish and she was glad that soon it would be time for their afternoon snack. There was nothing like a stiff gin and tonic and a bowl of toasted almonds in the late afternoon. And my goodness, couldn't some of the residents here knock back a drink. Those two little Italian nuns who had come over for a short holiday could drink like fish and the elder of the two must be pushing a hundred at least!

★　★　★

A cool wind came in off the sea and whipped leaves along the pavement. The door of the telephone box swung open and creaked on its broken hinges. The few shops on the village main street were closed and the front doors shut fast against the worrisome wind.

A sign pointed the way down to the Skallies and the rough track that once led from Rhoskilly Village was tarmacked now.

His first sight of the place made him catch his breath and he had to steady himself against a lamppost.

Little remained of the Skallies now, many of the ramshackle houses he remembered so well were gone, washed away in the Great Storms at the end of the sixties.

He stood where Bag End had been; only the sea-facing wall remained and the arched window where he'd looked out the night of the first full moon after Benjamin Tregantle's death.

Opposite the ruin of his old home, Hogwash House still stood firm against the elements. The windows were brightly painted in a deep blue;

there was a shiny brass knocker on the door and colourful curtains hung at the windows. A lone gull still graced the chimney pot and a sign advertised Chameleon Trust: School Visitor Centre.

He looked around him in awe. The Peapods, Cuckoo's Nest and the Grockles were reduced to rubble but Skibbereen had survived and the shrine in the wall was now a rusted grotto full of empty milk bottles.

The wobbly chapel still stood, silhouetted against a restless sky. The roof was a skeleton of rotten beams and a DANGER KEEP OUT sign was nailed to the wall.

The Pilchard Inn looked as it always had and through the glass of the porthole windows a light burned brightly and a radio blurted out the shipping news.

He reached out and took hold of the door handle.

★ ★ ★

The landlord of the Pilchard Inn looked up at the handsome young man with the rucksack who had just come in.

'What will you have, sir?'

'A pint of Best,' he said, 'and a room for the night if you have one.'

'No trouble. We've only one other guest staying at the moment, and they're up at the school most of the time. You planning on staying long?'

'A couple of nights.'

455

'On holiday, sir?'

'Kind of. I came into a small inheritance when I was twenty-one, wanted to see a bit of the world.'

'You're not from round these parts then?'

'No, I've been most of my life in Italy. But I was here for a while as a kid. I lived in the house they called Bag End. And yourself?'

The man smiled. 'Bit of a halfway house for me, mate. Strange story really, I was down on my uppers and met a chap who asked if I fancied running this place until I got on my feet.'

'Did you meet him round here?'

'No, in a funny little all-night café off the Edgware Road.'

Archie Grimble smiled and took a sip of his pint.

'Does much go on round here?' he asked.

'It's very quiet in the winter but we get a lot of kids down staying at Hogwash House throughout the year. And quite a few of the staff from Killivray House come up for a drink evening times when they're off duty.'

'From Killivray?'

'Big place up through the woods. It used to be privately owned, by posh folk. It's a school now.'

'A school?'

'It's a great place, sort of international school, run by the Chameleon Trust, same people as own Hogwash and most of what's left of the Skallies. The kids come from all over the place. Bit like the United Nations, Chinese, Indian, French. They've a reunion on at the moment . . . '

Archie marvelled that Thomas Greswode's legacy stretched far and wide; even after his death there was a network of people still working, still helping people down on their luck. He still had an awful lot to learn about Thomas Greswode.

'You wouldn't know the name of the head teacher there?'

'Miss Fanthorpe; she used to be head of Nanskelly and came to Killivray when the school transferred. She was a regular here every Friday night, her and Miss Thomas. One fish and prawn pie, one sea bass and three or four large gin and vermouths.'

'You said was, is she not there any more?'

'Just retired. There's a new woman there now but I can't remember her name. Miss Fanthorpe's gone abroad to live.'

Archie looked disappointed. 'So, Nanskelly's not a school any more?'

'No, it's an old folk's home now, but the noise from that place makes you wonder what goes on half the time. A wild bunch of old codgers they are up there. Will you be wanting any food tonight?'

'I would, if that's all right.'

'Wife'll knock you up something. Fish and prawn pie, maybe? She makes a good pasty too; she found an old recipe book behind the dresser in the kitchen, belonging to a Mrs something or other.'

'Mrs Dennis,' Archie said.

'That's right. How'd you know that?'

'I'm a student of history and I've been a bit of

457

a detective in my time,' he said with a laugh but noticed the look of worry cross the man's face.

'I'm not a policeman,' Archie said quickly.

The landlord relaxed. 'Well, if it's history you like we've unearthed all sorts of junk in this place, I can tell you. We found a box of old photographs that was salvaged after the Great Storms. We had them cleaned up and reframed, see,' he pointed at the walls.

Archie put down his drink and stepped up to a large photograph that hung to the left of the fireplace. His breathing quickened.

'Apparently it's a photo of the family that used to live at Killivray House. Taken about the turn of the century, we reckon. Snooty lot of buggers some of them look.'

The picture was taken outside the front of Killivray House. A man and woman stood at the centre, stiff-lipped and unsmiling. A haughty-looking Mr Greswode and his sour-faced wife. On their right was a boy of about fourteen, stocky, buck-toothed and bullish-looking. Charles Greswode. On their left a young Thomas Greswode with a small dog at his feet, a dog looking up lovingly at his young master.

On the far right a smiling woman who looked like a cook stood next to a pretty, grinning parlour maid who was glancing surreptitiously along the line to where a tall, handsome black man stood, straight-backed and smiling shyly at the camera, his hand resting lovingly on Thomas' shoulder.

Archie moved on to the next photograph. It

was of a group of laughing boys outside the Pilchard Inn, holding a smaller boy aloft. A boy with one hand clinging on to a silver cup and the other to a cricket bat.

Archie held back a tear as he looked at Thomas Greswode in his moment of triumph.

Then his eyes rested on another boy who was looking up at Thomas, a boy with a large bandage around his left hand.

Thomas had said in his diary, 'Benj wasn't in chapel . . . because he'd cut his hand badly and had to have it stitched . . . '

Archie looked at the proud face of Benjamin Tregantle, a man he'd never met. Sister Isabella had told Archie that Benjamin had worked with *Il Camaleonte* and had lost his life trying to get children out of France. He was wounded near Bizier but they'd managed to get him back to Santa Caterina where he was buried in the unmarked grave; a grave that bore his name now.

Thomas Greswode had returned to the Skallies as Benjamin Tregantle. There he had met Margot Greswode and learned of her miserable existence in Killivray House and he had planned her escape . . . and his own death . . .

Archie made his way over to the last photograph.

The barman looked up.

'That one wasn't taken around here. If you look up close you'll see a name over the gates . . . Convent of the Blessed Saints, Dungonally. Somewhere in Ireland, I reckon.'

Archie stepped closer. It was a black and white

photograph taken looking through some wrought-iron gates. Beyond the gates was a garden almost entirely full of lines of washing.

It was a queer sort of photograph to take of a load of washing.

He put his hand to his head and closed his eyes . . .

He was being lifted up and his mammy was pointing in through the gates and whispering to him. The touch of the iron was cold on his small fingers and afterwards his fists tasted of tears and rust.

There was a strong smell of soapsuds and bleach; starch and scorched cotton . . .

He'd watched in fascination as rainbow-streaked bubbles drifted high into the air.

'Wave to Mammy, Archie, wave now, my darling boy, it'll be a long time until she'll set eyes on you again . . .'

He remembered a young girl peeping out from behind a billowing sheet . . .

He blinked, rubbed his eyes and looked back at the photograph . . .

There, peeping out from a sheet that looked as if it was about to take off, was a young girl, no older than about sixteen, a girl waving sadly.

'Are you all right, sir?' the barman enquired.

'Yes, fine.'

'My wife is from Ireland, not far from Cork. She thinks it was one of them laundry places where they used to put the poor little girls who had babies before they were married. Cruel bloody way to treat people, if you ask me.'

Archie stood very still, his hand to his mouth . . .

The tide washes over some secrets and covers them up but it throws up others, like flotsam and jetsam.

The truth is always the best option, I believe, however painful.

Maybe one day soon he'd make his way to Dungonally and make some enquiries. On the other hand he might not. Life hadn't dealt him such a bad hand.

'I'll have another pint and one for yourself,' he said. 'And I think I'll go for the pasty, for old times' sake.'

★ ★ ★

Winston Clark lay on the bottom bunk bed and looked across at the framed sampler that hung on the whitewashed wall. It wasn't like the ones they had at home in his house in Willesden. The ones that most grown-ups liked to put on the wall said GOD IS GOOD and BLESS THIS HOUSE. This one said SHUT MOUTH NEVER CATCH FLY.

He didn't think that was from the Bible.

What did it mean though? Who would want to keep their mouth open and catch a fly in it?

That was mad. He'd have to think about that one.

He'd done a lot of thinking since he'd been here in the Skallies. He liked it here in this

461

Hogwash House place. At first he hadn't wanted to come, he'd rather have hung round with his mates all summer but he'd liked the bloke that came and gave the talk at school; PeeJay was great.

Every year his school brought a group of kids to stay, kids who'd had a bad time of it, like he had losing his dad. It was free too, paid for by some toffee-nosed charity people or other. Just as well, though, otherwise there was no way he could've come, not with being one of seven and his mum working all hours just to put some food on the table and all that.

When he was older he was going to get a job here like PeeJay. That was a great job being out of doors most of the time, telling the kids all about the history and that and taking them down to the rock pools and showing them things. Blennies and shrimps; anemones and cuttle fish; things he'd never heard of back in London. He'd been swimming every day and climbed the rocks and his asthma hadn't given him no gyp at all.

And tomorrow they were going to help PeeJay clean out that dirty old Boathouse down on the beach. It was dead spooky, that place. Once a mad woman had lived there and sometimes they said you could hear music playing in the middle of the night. Ghost music . . .

PeeJay said there was all kinds of things in there that needed to be sorted out. Old-fashioned gramophones and the records they called seventy-eights that broke real easy. He couldn't wait.

He sat up and took the little capsule from his

462

pocket. He'd found it buried deep in the sand down below the place they called the wobbly chapel. You could unscrew the capsule and inside there was a tiny silver saint. It was magic.

He stood up and fetched his jumper; it got cold down on the beach in the evening. It was getting dark now and soon PeeJay would be lighting the bonfire and there was going to be hot dogs and beef burgers. He opened his door and called out to Clive. He was another boy who'd had bad luck: both his folks got killed in a car crash on the North Circular.

'Come on, Clive, is time for the bonfire.'

'I'm in the shower. Go down without me and I'll catch you up in a bit.'

'Nah, is okay, I'll wait.'

He wasn't going to walk down Bloater Row on his own, man, there was supposed to be ghosts that walked there after dark. One of the girls said she'd seen one, it was naked and it had no head and chains around its ankles.

There was a Spanish pirate too, with one eye and hooks where his hands should have been.

But the worst one of all was the Killivray ghost. Some Rastafarian guy who came wandering around moaning and sobbing and wringing his hands.

'Hurry up, Clive, you going to miss the food.'

'You afraid to go down on your own or somethink?'

'No way! I ain't afraid of nuthin'.'

He sighed, ran down the stairs, and stood for a moment in the porch. He sniffed; he could smell tobacco, the kind of old-fashioned stuff that his grandpa used to stuff down into a pipe. It had a rude name: Old Shag.

He peeped out of the porch and looked warily up and down Bloater Row.

The wind rocked the dilapidated upside-down boat that lay to the left of the house as if someone was under there and trying to get out.

He put the little silver saint in his pocket. For good luck. Then he pegged it down to Skilly Beach without stopping once.

★   ★   ★

Archie Grimble woke at first light. It was raining and a rough wind rattled the windows. In the room next door a radio was playing quietly and he heard the sound of a window opening.

He rubbed a clear patch in the misted window and looked out into Bloater Row. The rain was hammering down and he watched as it bounced off the cobbles, and listened to the splash as the gutters of Skibbereen overflowed. The door to the pub opened and he heard a squeal as someone stepped out into Bloater Row. He looked down and saw a young woman, head down, umbrella pointed like a shield at the wind. She hurried along Bloater Row, rain splashing up and spattering the back of her legs, her coat \billowing out like a sail. He could hear her laughter as she battled her way along and then she disappeared down onto the beach.

He made his way down to the bar for breakfast. There was a lingering hint of perfume in the air and a half-drunk cup of coffee and a hurriedly nibbled piece of toast left on the table.

'Thought you might have had company but the lady wanted to be up at the school early,' explained the landlord. 'Shame you won't meet her, she's off today, back to London.'

Archie was relieved to eat alone. He didn't want company at the moment.

The rain had stopped and the cobbles of Bloater Row steamed. Above the chimneys of Killivray House a rainbow melted away. He walked slowly down to Skilly Beach where he stood among the sand dunes listening to the breeze as it whispered through the long spiky grass. Smoke spiralled up from the chimneys of Killivray House and the sound of children at play drifted over the tree tops. He turned and looked across at the Boathouse. The door was opened and the sound of cracked gramophone music reached him.

There's a song in the air
But the fair señorita
Doesn't seem to care for the song in the air . . .
Señorita donkeysita, not so fleet as a mosquito,
But so sweet like my Chiquita,
You're the one for me.
Olé!

Hell, he'd been terrified of the Boathouse when he was a kid. The very sight of a candle flickering behind the salt-caked windows had been enough to turn his legs to jelly.

All the tales people used to tell about

Gwennie; that when she was hungry she went on the hunt for hens like a fox, bit off their heads and squeezed out their blood and drank it down in one gurgling gulp.

He'd believed all that nonsense too. God, he used to be afraid of his own shadow.

He sat down on a rock and watched in fascination as a man about his own age came out onto the steps of the Boathouse. He put down a box full of old newspapers, looked across at Archie and said, 'God, it's like Miss Havisham's junk room in there.'

Four lads came out laughing and gasping, carrying what looked like the figurehead from an ancient boat. They carried it unsteadily down to the beach and put it down on the sand.

'PeeJay, that is disgustin', all her thingies are on show, that's porn, that is.'

'Well, it's sixteenth-century porn by the look of it and that makes it history. Hell, when the museum folk pitch up they'll be doing cartwheels. Now get your backsides back up here.'

A red-headed girl came out next, wrinkling her freckled nose up in disgust, carrying a broken lobster pot; another girl behind her with what looked like the bleached ribs of a giant whale.

Then a black boy came running out excitedly. 'This looks like one of them hand grenade things from the war . . . '

Archie turned and looked at the thing in his hand.

He ran towards the boy.

'Stand still! Don't touch the pin. It'll blow you to buggery!'

He snatched at the grenade, knocking the surprised child off his feet, and lobbed it as far as he could. There was an enormous explosion and a shower of sand rained down upon them.

'To buggery and back again!' Archie said spitting out a mouthful of sand.

He looked across at the boy who was spread-eagled in the sand, eyes enormous with shock.

The needle on the gramophone was stuck and grated and screeched.

PeeJay appeared in the doorway, white with fear, the rest of the teenagers behind him.

'You okay, Winston?'

The boy nodded silently.

'I wouldn't touch anything else in there, if I were you,' Archie said, getting unsteadily to his feet.

'Jesus! What was it?' PeeJay said, racing down the steps.

'Hand grenade. Live!'

'He saved my life.' Winston Clark suddenly realized the close shave he'd had. 'And there's a whole box of them in the cupboard,' the boy said, scrabbling to his knees.

'Thank you so much,' PeeJay said. 'Do I know you from somewhere?' he added, peering at Archie.

The record jumped, the music started up again.

Señorita donkeysita, not so fleet as a mosquito,

But so sweet like my Chiquita,
You're the one for me.
Olé!

'You're Archie Grimble from Bag End!'

Archie looked up, batting sand from his hair.

'PeeJay Kelly. Peter. I used to live in Cuckoo's Nest. My brothers used to be bastards to you. My God, they wouldn't now, though, look at the size on you.'

Archie Grimble put out his hand and shook Peter Kelly's.

'What in the name of God are you doing back here, Peter?'

'Well, we left, as you know, rather suddenly as I remember.'

'I know, Nan came to tell us. We didn't have a clue where you'd gone.'

'To a pub in Ireland. The Kilpenny Arms. My folks inherited it from some distant relative they'd never heard of. They loved the pub life, did well enough for themselves, but I hated it. I had a stroke of luck, though, and got a letter about a scholarship to a school near Dublin and then when I left I came here to work. I love it. And where've you been?'

'Italy.'

'Well fancy that! Do you know, we had bugger all when we were here as kids and yet we haven't done bad, have we? Well, I'd better go and make sure that this lot don't blow up what's left of the Skallies. Are you staying here?'

'At the Pilchard.'

'I'll catch you sometime for a pint?'

'That would be great.'

'Tomorrow, they're opening up the wobbly chapel, if you're interested. God knows what they'll find in there!'

Archie watched PeeJay climb back up the steps and lock the door to the Boathouse.

'Come on, you lot, we'll go back to Hogwash and you can have a drink, while I call in the explosives people.'

'Do you know what?' Winston Clark said.

'What?' Archie replied, watching Peter Kelly walking away up the beach.

'I reckon that the saint saved me.'

'Which saint would that be?'

'I don't know her name, but look.'

He scrabbled in his pocket, pulled out the tiny silver capsule and opened it, tipping out the little silver saint into the palm of his hand.

Archie looked down in wonder. He lifted it from the boy's hand and turned it over. He hadn't seen that since the night he'd got into the wobbly chapel and nearly drowned himself.

'Her name,' Archie said, 'is Santa Caterina.'

'Can she do miracles?' the boy asked.

'Oh, yes.'

'What sort?'

'She can make sad people happy, weak people strong and scared people brave!' Archie said, remembering Alfredo's words to him all that time ago.

'Wo!' the boy exclaimed. 'She can do something else too,' he added, lowering his voice.

'What's that?'

'Can you keep a secret?'

'Honest injun and all that.'

'I've stopped pissing the bed since I found her.'

'That's fantastic. Where *did* you find her?' he asked but the boy was already gone, hurtling up the beach after PeeJay.

★ ★ ★

Archie walked up through the sand dunes. The door that led into the grounds of Killivray was unlocked so he went quickly inside. He wandered slowly up through the woods. A conker fell with a thud and something moved close by. He turned. A hare stood absolutely still eyeing Archie with interest. Then it bounded away into the undergrowth.

He followed in its path but it was long gone. He found himself standing in a clearing of small headstones, a miniature graveyard. He pulled the weeds away from the bottom of one of the graves and rubbed away the moss with his fingernails. The stone was engraved with a single name, Rajah.

On another, Pipi.

He looked around, picked a few wild flowers and laid them on the grave.

Then he got to his feet and saw the small wooden cross.

The ground around the cross was well tended and a bunch of red roses stood in a silver pot and attached to them was a card wrapped in cellophane with the name of a florist shop in St Werburgh's. He turned it over and read the writing.

'For Pop, love Dom x'

Archie put down the card and got unsteadily to his feet and then he walked on.

★ ★ ★

They found the secret way into the wobbly chapel quite by accident. Winston had been down on the beach with Rosita. They'd been climbing on the rocks when the tide was out and she'd dared him to see who could climb the highest. He didn't like heights much but he couldn't lose face in front of a girl . . .

Rosita wasn't afraid of anything, though, and soon she was high above him, then disappearing into a hole above his head . . .

She was dead brave for a girl, he had to admit. In the end he'd begged her to come down, but she'd called out excitedly, 'There's steps up here. Come and look.'

And he'd gritted his teeth and followed her.

He climbed warily up the slippery steps behind her, calling to her to wait for him but there was no stopping Rosita once she'd set her mind on something.

'Bloody hell!' she called down. 'I'm in some sort of cupboard inside the wobbly chapel. Come on, Winston! You afraid or what?'

'C . . . Course I ain't afraid,' he stammered.

They emerged from the cupboard into the chapel. It was gloomy, almost dark. Above their heads through the broken rafters the sky was full of stars.

'It's scary in here,' Winston said as they looked around.

'It's brilliant,' Rosita said, tiptoeing between bags of cement and shovels.

Winston stayed close behind her.

It smelled awful and he was sure that he could hear mice scratching or maybe even rats.

Rosita stopped and pointed at the wall.

'It's one of those things they fill up with holy water,' Winston said.

'I know that. We've got them in the church at school. Look at that though.'

There was a collection box set into the wall.

'What does it say on the front?'

'It's Latin, I think.'

'You know any Latin?'

''Course I do, I go to a convent.'

'What's it say, then?'

'I don't know, we haven't got to that bit yet.'

'We can't open it, we haven't got a key.'

'We could pick the lock.'

'Can you pick locks?'

''Course I can. Like I said, I go to a convent.'

She slid a hair clip from her hair and then busied herself poking at the lock.

'Hurry up, Rosita, I don't like it in here. There's graves and stuff.'

After an age the door opened and Rosita stepped back.

'What's in there?' Winston gasped.

'Some kind of a box.'

She took it out, blew the cobwebs off it and eased off the lid.

'What's in there?'

'It looks like a map with directions.'

'Is it in old-fashioned writing?'

'No. Just ordinary.'

'What's it say?'

'Give me a chance. Here we go:

Take a walk out west of Skilly. Pause, then
climb the wooden stile . . .
See a house that's very old,
Be not afraid, be very bold.
Ten yards left, five north . . . be sure to
measure,
. . . closer and closer to the Pirate's
treasure . . .'

'Bloody hell!' Winston said.

'Treasure!' Rosita cried. 'I've always wanted to solve a mystery. Come on.'

And she was off, back through the cupboard and down the steps with Winston Clark hot on her heels.

* * *

The late evening air was soft, heady with the scent of honeysuckle and herbs. Beyond the window of the summerhouse the sky was streaked with crimson weals.

On a shelf yellow poppies drooped in a jam jar and dust motes fizzed in the dying light. A wasp was busy in a box of windfall apples.

The match flared and soon candlelight flickered and the shadows of tin soldiers loomed on the walls.

The kindling in the stove crackled. A moth flapped wildly at the window and an owl called out timidly from the woods. The record on the gramophone turned slowly . . .

* * *

Archie walked quickly over the lower lawns where abandoned tennis racquets and toys lay in the grass. He climbed the steps and walked through the rose garden.

Before him the lights of Killivray glittered behind the diamond panes of glass. The sound of children laughing drifted down from an open window.

* * *

The door to the summerhouse opened with a sighing noise. Archie Grimble stood framed in the doorway, a pale moon rising behind his head like a halo.

Archie stood quite still, looking into eyes as startled as his own.

She no longer wore the old-fashioned clothes, and the plaits with ribbons were gone. Her hair hung down over her slender shoulders.

Her eyes sparkled in the flickering light as he walked towards her.

The air was filled with the smell of cinnamon and roses and freshly washed cotton. It was a smell that he'd never quite forgotten. He put his arms around Romilly Greswode and held her for a long time.

Through the window he saw the huge moon,

474

bursting at the seams, hovering in the peat-black sky.

A wildcat moon.

★   ★   ★

In the wobbly chapel the dawn light shone through the window and dappled the altar with a host of moving colours.

Two workmen came in through the door.

'You know what we're s'posed to be doing, Harry?'

'Moving the bones,' Harry answered. 'The floor is all rotten so we've to dig up the bones and then when we've sorted out the floor we're to rebury them.'

'Bloody load of old nonsense, if you ask me.'

'Ah, well, lad, apparently they're going to restore this place to its former glory!'

'Bloody daft,' the lad said.

'Come on, let's get on with it.'

The picked up their picks and began to prise up one of the flagstones from the chapel floor.

'Let's be having you, Thomas Greswode.'

They struggled to lift the stone and rested it against a wall. Then they stood together looking down into the deep hole.

'Look at that, the coffin's all rotted away but you can see the skeleton. How old did you say the boy was?'

The lad walked across to the stone, leant it towards him and looked at the back.

'Says, born in 1888 and died in 1900, that'd make him twelve.'

'They must have been big buggers back then, look at the length of his legs; he must have been well over six and a half foot tall if not more. That's some height for a bloody twelve-year-old.'

'That's tall for a man, that is. I remember my old grandmother saying that there was a fisherman went missing, oh, I'm going back years now, before the first world war — went overboard further round the coast. Big Ed they used to call him. My gran used to say that he was always chewing toffee and had lost every tooth in his head by the time he were eighteen except two at the front.'

He looked down at the skull and shivered. 'Bit like this fellow then, look there.'

They both looked down at the grinning skull with the two yellowed teeth . . .

'Well, they ain't the bones of a twelve-year-old, that's for bloody sure!'

'Had we best get on the phone and tell the governor?'

'No, it'll only cause complications.'

'It's peculiar if you ask me! Mind, this is a queer neck of the woods. When the bad storms came at the end of the sixties a tree came down on one of the graves in the cemetery and they reckon there was nothing in the coffin at all. It were completely empty. There was talk of grave robbers. Burke and Hare and all that sort of stuff.'

'Come on, let's hurry up and get the other one up. It's giving me the bloody creeps in here,' the lad urged.

'What sort of a name is that?' the workman

476

said, looking down at the flagstone.

'Spanish, I reckon, you can hardly read it though. Somebody or other, wife of Angeles. I can't read it properly, hang on, born in Italy . . . '

The flagstone came up like a rotten tooth and the air was filled with the stench of ancient dust and mould.

'No bloody coffin at all in this one, just a small skeleton.'

'Christ, look, this one only had one leg.'

'And there's six fingers on the one hand.'

We do hope that you have enjoyed reading this large print book.

Did you know that all of our titles are available for purchase?

We publish a wide range of high quality large print books including:
Romances, Mysteries, Classics
General Fiction
Non Fiction and Westerns

Special interest titles available in large print are:
The Little Oxford Dictionary
Music Book
Song Book
Hymn Book
Service Book

Also available from us courtesy of Oxford University Press:
Young Readers' Dictionary
(large print edition)
Young Readers' Thesaurus
(large print edition)

For further information or a free brochure, please contact us at:
Ulverscroft Large Print Books Ltd.,
The Green, Bradgate Road, Anstey,
Leicester, LE7 7FU, England.
Tel: (00 44) 0116 236 4325
Fax: (00 44) 0116 234 0205

Other titles published by
The House of Ulverscroft:

RECIPES FOR CHERUBS

Babs Horton

It's the summer of 1960, and to Kizzy Grieve it's imperative that she gets to Naples by 15 July — but not with her daughter in tow. So thirteen-year-old Catrin is despatched by her feckless mother to stay with her great aunt Ella at Shrimp's Hotel, in the sleepy village of Kilvenny on the Welsh coast. After all, Aunt Alice had always had a wonderful way with children . . . Aunt Ella on the other hand could be a bit of a tartar, but she was all right in her own way. It was a perfect idea, an enormous cheek maybe, but a lot of water had passed under the bridge since that last summer at Shrimp's . . .

DANDELION SOUP

Babs Horton

In the remote Irish village of Ballygurry,
middle-aged Solly Benjamin is roused at
midnight to find a child on his doorstep, a
length of cord tied loosely around her neck.
The attached tag bears his own name and
address. Who is she? And why would a
complete stranger send her to him? As Solly
attempts to find the answers, other Ballygurry
inhabitants are drawn into the mystery. Their
enquiries lead to the secluded monastery of
Santa Eulalia on the medieval trail to
Santiago de Compostela. As the Ballygurry
pilgrims begin to thaw in the Spanish
sunshine, a number of interwoven mysteries
from the past gradually unfurl to rekindle old
hatreds — and restore old passions.

A JARFUL OF ANGELS

Babs Horton

The remote town in the Welsh valleys was a wonderful, magical — but sometimes dangerous — place in which to grow up. It was there that Iffy, Bessie, Fatty and Billy experienced a plague of frogs one summer, stumbled upon a garden full of dancing statues, found a skull with its front teeth missing — and discovered just what it was that mad Carty Annie was collecting so secretly in those jars of hers. But at the end of that long, hot summer of 1963, one of the four children disappeared . . . Over thirty years later, retired detective Will Sloane, never able to forget the unsolved case, returns to Wales to resume his search for the truth . . .

DIVING INTO LIGHT

Natasha Farrant

Every summer throughout her childhood, Florence would return to her family home on the west coast of France. There, joined by her exotic, glamorous cousins, life as she knew it would begin under the benevolent eye of her grandmother Mimi. It was a heady existence of illicit drinking, stolen kisses and the bittersweet pains of first love. But now Florence is living completely alone with her new baby. Haunted by nightmares, she cannot open the letters from her grandmother accumulating on her mantelpiece. What devastating truth do these letters hold? Why has Florence turned her back on her past? And will she and Mimi ever be able to escape the guilt that is tearing them apart and has shaken their family to its very core?